THE PEARLS OF LUTRA

A Tale of Redwall

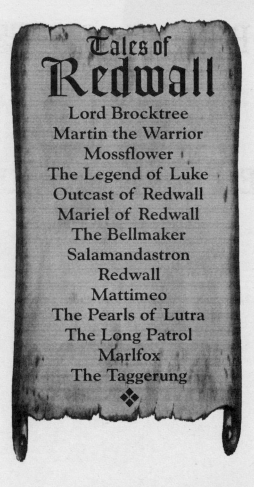

Click onto the Redwall website – and
discover more about the legendary world of
Redwall and it's creator, Brian Jacques!
http://www.redwall.org

BRIAN JACQUES

❖

THE PEARLS OF LUTRA
A Tale of Redwall

Illustrated by Allan Curless

RED
FOX

PEARLS OF LUTRA
1 86 230328 2

First published in Great Britain by Hutchinson,
an imprint of Random House Children's Books

Hutchinson edition published 1996
Red Fox edition published 1997

Papers used by Random House Children's Books are natural,
recyclable products made from wood grown in sustainable forests.
The manufacturing processes conform to the
environmental regulations of the country of origin.

Red Fox Books are published by Random House Children's Books,
61–63 Uxbridge Road, London W5 5SA,
a division of The Random House Group Ltd,
in Australia by Random House Australia (Pty) Ltd,
20 Alfred Street, Milsons Point, Sydney, NSW 2061, Australia,
in New Zealand by Random House New Zealand Ltd,
18 Poland Road, Glenfield, Auckland 10, New Zealand,
and in South Africa by Random House (Pty) Ltd,
Isle of Houghton, Corner of Boundary Road & Carse O'Gowrie,
Houghton 2198, South Africa

THE RANDOM HOUSE GROUP Limited Reg. No. 954009
www.kidsatrandomhouse.co.uk

A CIP catalogue record for this book is available from the British Library.

Printed and bound in Great Britain by
Bookmarque Ltd, Croydon, Surrey

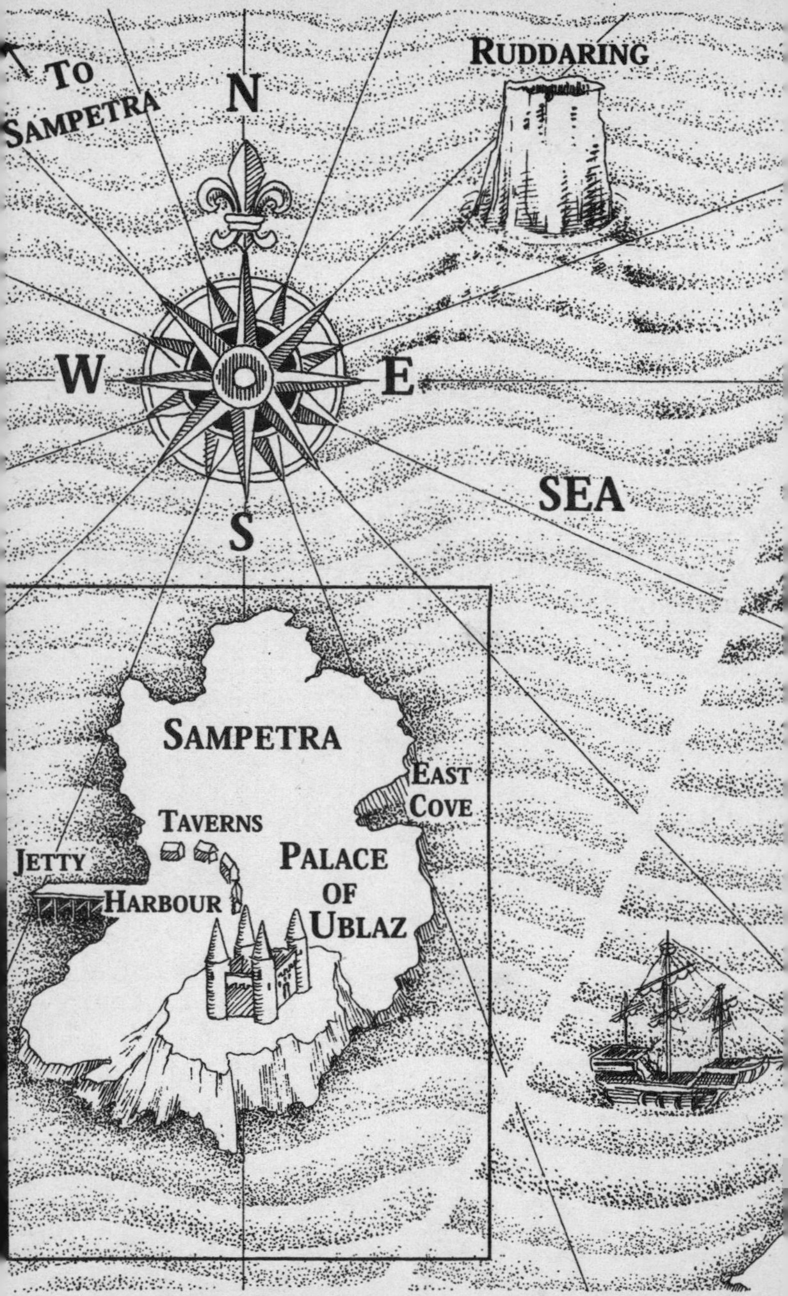

RUDDARING

TO
SAMPETRA

N

W   E

S

SEA

SAMPETRA

EAST
COVE

TAVERNS

PALACE
OF
UBLAZ

JETTY

HARBOUR

SEA

HOLT LUTRA *

ICEBERGS

SHORE

MOSSFLOWER

TO SAMPETRA

SHORE

SKELETON ROCKS

REDWALL ABBEY

NINIAN'S

O curse the name Mad Eyes
Say woe to the day,
When he tried to steal
Tears of all Oceans away.
All corsairs and searats
Whose messmates lie dead,
Saw blood and hot flame
Turn the seas flowing red.
Though northcoast lies far
And the ocean is wide,
Run from the green arrows
Of vengeance, and hide.
For the price of six tears
Through the dreams of us all,
Walks the fear of a Warrior
From the place called Redwall.
Now the life of our Brethren
Who followed the sea,
Will ne'er be the same
For such rovers as we.
'Twas the greed of a tyrant
That brought us to shame,
Six tears for a crown –
Curse the Emperor's name!

Verses taken from an old corsair ballad

BOOK ONE

Six Tears for
an Abbot

1

Though Tansy was still only a young hedgehog, she was known to be a veritable rock of good sense by the elders of Redwall Abbey. Because of this, she was one of the few youngsters allowed outside the Abbey walls, mainly to gather materials for Sister Cicely's remedies. Fine spring sunshine, tinged light green from the semi-transparent new leaves, filtered down through the high canopy of Mossflower Wood, and somewhere off deeper in the woodlands a cuckoo sang its repetitive aria to the growing season. Tansy put her basket down upon a mossy knoll and began setting out food: a little chunk of yellow cheese, small farls of soft nutbread, a few candied chestnuts and a flagon of elderberry cordial. Fussily she dusted out the insides of two wooden beakers on her apron, then she peered about at the surrounding tree trunks.

'I know you're there, Arven, now come out this instant, or I'll eat all this lunch an' you won't get a crumb!' she called.

The tiny squirrel leapt from a nearby elm, landing neatly in a sitting position right next to her. Tansy stifled her surprise at his sudden appearance, and busied herself unfolding two clean serviettes as she lectured her charge severely.

'What've you been told about wandering off? D'you know I'm responsible for you? Just look at those mucky paws, wipe them off on the moss before you touch a single thing, you maggot!'

Arven scrubbed his little paws on the clean linen smock he wore, leaving two muddy patches across it. He smiled winningly and grabbed a candied chestnut. 'Am never wandled oft, no need t'be asponsible f'r Arven, not gett'n lost, ho no, too starven t'be losted!'

Tansy tried to hide a smile, but found herself unable to. Chuckling, she poured out a beaker of cordial for her friend. 'You're a little maggot! What are you?'

'Me a lickle starven maggit, heeheehee! But Arven eat all lunch, then me be big maggit an' go hohoho!'

The little squirrel was never still. As he ate and drank he hopped around the knoll chanting, 'Miggity Maggity hohoho! Tanzee panzee toogle doo!'

'I'll Tansy pansy you if you make yourself sick jumping round while you're eating,' Tansy muttered, more to herself than Arven, as she checked over the plants she had collected. 'Hmm, old hogweed stalks, young angelica shoots, let's see, what else did Sister Cicely want . . . Wintergreen, there may be some by the rocks.'

She glanced up at the sky. It had been gradually clouding over as they ate, and now a few tell-tale drops on her face caused the young hedgehog to tut with annoyance. 'Tch tch! Rain! There was no sign of it earlier, sky was clear as a bell. Come on, Arven, help me to pack this lot back into the basket. You can finish your lunch while I search among the rocks, there's good shelter there.'

Swiftly the two friends repacked their basket and set off east, deeper into the woodlands. A chill wind sprang up, buffeting the treetops, whipping the increasing downpour until rain found its way through and began thrumming against the loamy earth. Tansy shielded Arven with her cape as he railed against the unpredictable mid-spring weather.

'Firsta sunny thena rainywet, it'sa maggit!'

The rocks were dark red sandstone ledges, tilted at a crazy angle in a small scrubby clearing. They pushed up out of the ground, piled against each other like a row of books gone askew on a bookshelf. Gaps caused by erosion formed many small shallow caves, and Tansy and Arven huddled under the nearest one as the wind chased the rain.

Arven went into a little dance, shaking himself vigorously. Tansy shielded her face by holding up the basket.

'Be still, you rogue. I'm quite wet enough without you splashing rain all over me. Oh look, wintergreen!'

Reaching out into the rain, she plucked a tiny plant with pale green, spear-shaped leaves.

Arven was more interested in warmth. 'Lighta fire, Tansy, make Arven dry'n'warm,' he whimpered.

Tansy studied the strong-smelling seedling, which had been crushed underpaw by them as they entered the cave, explaining to the little squirrel as she did, 'I don't have flints or tinder with me. Besides, old Rollo the Recorder says that only grown and experienced beasts are allowed to light fires in the woodlands. Fire is a very dangerous thing if it gets out of control.'

Arven was not impressed by old Rollo's words. 'Huh! Fire very dangerful, kuffwarh!' he said as he hopped out into the rain. 'Any'ow, Arven wet now, can't get more wetted, me gonna play.'

He bounded off out of view, with Tansy calling after him, 'Stay close to the rocks, d'you hear me? Don't go wandering off, and keep that new smock in one piece, or Mother Auma will tan your tail good an' proper!'

When Arven was out of sight, Tansy sat miserably, watching the rain pattering off the rocks and staring at the ground in search of other wintergreen shoots. The day out that she had planned for herself and Arven in Mossflower woodlands had been ruined by rain. It wasn't fair, especially after she had begged and pleaded with Auma to be allowed to take Arven with her. The morning had started off bright and sunny; she had made up the lunch and packed it herself, listened carefully to Sister Cicely's instructions, then set off holding Arven with one paw and the basket in the other, feeling very grown up and responsible. Wullger the otter was on gate duty, and he had winked and tipped his tail to Tansy as he let her out of the main wallgate.

She smiled to herself, remembering how Viola bankvole had been watching from the rampart steps. That snippy Viola! Mincing about and giving herself all kinds of airs and graces, always making smart remarks. But Viola was too flibberty-gibbet to be allowed out alone. The young hedgehog had made a special point of waving at her and calling aloud, 'Just popping out to Mossflower, see you later, Viola dear!'

The prissy bankvole had turned nearly purple with envy. Hah! that'd show her!

'Tanzeeeeee!'

Arven's scream brought Tansy back to the present like lightning. Tossing aside the basket, she hitched up her smock and went dashing out into the rain, scrambling up the rocks as she charged forward to the sounds of the screeching babe.

'Tanzeeee! 'urreeeeee!'

Hurtling along the uneven top of the sloping sandstone mass, Tansy yelled into the wind and rain, 'Arven, where are you? Keep shouting, keep shouting!'

'Fell downer 'oooooole! 'elp, Tanzeeeeeee!'

Speeding to the spot where the sound came from, Tansy threw herself on all fours, reaching her paws down into a broad crack in the rocks. She felt Arven's tiny damp paws latch onto hers and breathed a swift sigh of relief.

'Hold tight, I'll have you out o' there in a tick!'

Before she could start lifting him, the nimble little

fellow had scrambled up over her paws, stepped on her nose and onto the back of her neck, and leapt clear, shouting, 'Lookalooka! Down there! Eeeeeeee!'

Lying face down, Tansy gazed into the rift. With a gasp of horror she found herself staring into the eyeless sockets of a skull. Gap-toothed and grinning, with rain pattering on it to produce the most dreadful hollow sound, it stared back at her. Bleached bones and the ragged remnants of clothing clinging to them comprised the remainder of the skeleton, trapped in the jaws of the narrow rift. Thunder rumbled as a vivid flash of lightning lit up the stark scene. A scream of terror tore itself from the hedgehog maid's throat.

Forgetting plants, basket and picnic lunch, heedless of pelting rain and wind, Tansy grabbed Arven's tiny paw. Together they leapt from the sandstone rocks, rolling, stumbling and bounding down onto the wet grass. Both creatures sped off as if the skeleton had risen from the rift to pursue them. Blindly they rushed through the storm-lashed woodland, footpaws slapping the ground, hearts racing madly, as they sought the path back to the warmth, peace and safety of their home, Redwall Abbey.

2

Far across the heaving deeps of restless ocean, some say even beyond the place where the sun sinks in the west, there lies the Isle of Sampetra. At first sight, it's a lush tropical jewel, set in turquoise waters where seasons never change from eternal summer. But a closer look would reveal that Sampetra is rotten as a flyblown fish carcass. It is a crossroads of evil, haven to the flotsam of the high seas. Corsairs, searats and all manner of vermin wavescum make their berth at Sampetra, the domain of a pine marten, the mighty Emperor Ublaz!

He is also known as Mad Eyes, though none ever called him that to his face and lived. He dwells in a palace built on a flat-topped escarpment at the island's southwesterly tip. Any ship entering the harbour must pay tribute to Ublaz, and captains who do not choose to anchor at Sampetra are considered to be foes of the Emperor. It is his decree that their ships and even their lives are forfeit; they are fair game to his followers.

Mad Eyes is cunning, all-powerful. Like a spider at the centre of a great web, he rules Sampetra. No trees grow upon the island, but Ublaz has a vast timber stock in his courtyard. Wood for ship repairs is given only to those who pay him heavy tribute. The island is a good place for vermin from the seas to rest and roister: there are taverns dotted about the harbour area. Ublaz is served by a regiment of rats who carry long tridents as a mark of their rank; his Trident-rats patrol the harbour night and day. However, the most fearsome of his creatures are great flesh-eating lizards known as the Monitors, who have inhabited Sampetra for as long as anybeast can remember. Only the mad-eyed Emperor can control the dreadful reptiles, with the power of his hypnotic stare.

Conva the corsair captain was not a happy stoat as he watched his steersrat bring their craft, the vessel *Waveworm*, into the bay of Sampetra. On the jetty Conva could see lizards and Trident-rats waiting, and he knew what they were there for – to take him before the Emperor. Had the corsair known any pleas or prayers to the fates, he would have said them right then, hoping that Mad Eyes might have forgotten the treasure called 'Tears of all Oceans'. But then he recalled his meeting with Ublaz before the voyage, and the eyes, the strange mad eyes that had compelled him to return.

Sounds of singing, fighting and feasting drifted up from the taverns by the jetty as *Waveworm* hove alongside. Conva was relieved of his curved scimitar and marched off between two Monitors and two Trident-rats. The remainder of the guards boarded the ship, to make sure the crew stayed in their quarters until they received permission to come ashore.

As he was ushered into the throne room of the Emperor, Conva glanced around. It was the peak of barbaric splendour. There were silks, marble, rich velvet cushions and satin hangings, and the air was heavy with the scent of strange aromatic herbs smouldering in wall braziers. The Emperor was seated on a great carved cedar throne.

Though Conva feared Ublaz, he could not help but admire him. A big creature, this pine marten: strong, handsome and sleek, with fine brown fur from head to bushy tail, complemented by a creamy yellow throat and ears. He was clad in a green silk robe with a gold border; blue sapphires twinkled from the handle of a slim silver-bladed dagger, thrust into a belt of shark's skin. The face of Ublaz was immobile. Savage white teeth showed slightly through a thin, almost lipless mouth, and above the curled perfumed whiskers and light brown nosetip, two jet-black almond-shaped eyes stared at the corsair captain.

All was silence. Conva stood riveted by the eyes; they pierced him to the core. Silent and mysterious Ublaz sat, transfixing the corsair with his gaze until words began flowing from the hypnotized captain.

'Mighty One who knows all, your commands were carried out. We raided the den of Lutra the otter on the far north shores. They were taken by ambush and slain, every one of them, and all that they possessed was loaded aboard my ship.'

For the first time Ublaz spoke, his voice scarce above a whisper. 'Tell me what you took, everything.'

The corsair repeated a list of spoils. 'Beakers set with coloured stones, platters also, carved bone tail- and pawrings, one gold neckband, a box of small purple pearls and another box made from a hinged scallop shell. This shell contained six large, rose-coloured pearls.'

The Emperor drew in his breath sharply. 'The Tears of all Oceans, you have them!'

Conva began to shiver visibly. He collapsed to the marble floor, his voice trembling with fear. 'Mighty One, they were stolen!'

Ublaz sighed deeply, slumping back on his throne as if the bad news came as no surprise to him. 'Tell me how this thing happened.'

Two Monitors entered the throne room bearing a litter containing the booty from Conva's ship *Waveworm*. At a nod from Ublaz they set it down in front of him.

The corsair continued his narrative in broken tones.

'Two moons after we slew the tribe of Lutra I charted a course following the coast south. I knew a stream of freshwater runs out across the beach near an area named Mossflower. We dropped anchor there and took on fresh water. When *Waveworm* was ready to get under sail again, two of my crew, both weasels, Flairnose and Graylunk, were discovered missing. So were the rose pearls in the scallop shell – they'd stolen them and jumped ship. I gave chase, tracked them, leaving behind only three to guard the ship. We found Flairnose wounded sore three days later. They had quarrelled over the pearls, and Graylunk had stabbed him. We searched Flairnose – he had no pearls, though before he died he told us that he'd given Graylunk a bad skull wound when they fought.

'Two days on, following Graylunk's trail, we came upon a big building called Redwall Abbey. I had my crew scout around it in a wide circle, but the only track of Graylunk we could find went straight to the main door. This Redwall is a large, well-fortified place, with many creatures living there. We did not let them see us; their numbers were tenscore more than ours.

'Graylunk is inside Redwall with the pearls, or if he has died from his wound then the pearls are still within the walls of that Abbey. I could do no more, Mighty One, not with the numbers I had. I made it back to my ship with all speed and hastened here to bring you the news.'

Ublaz moved smoothly around the booty on the litter, sifting through it with his silver-bladed dagger. 'Dented beakers, bone tailrings, gold neckband, huh, more like brass,' he said to himself. 'Small purple pearls, worthless musselseeds. Except for the rose pearls, the tribe of Lutra had nothing of value – they were poor as beggars!'

He ceased his examination and stood over the quaking corsair. 'And you, bold Conva, what shall I do with you?' The Emperor's fearsome eyes bored into Conva's mind.

His spirit completely broken with terror, the corsair grovelled shamelessly at the Emperor's footpaws. 'Mighty One, Great Emperor, spare me. I will gather more crew and the help of other captains. Give me a chance and I will go to Redwall and bring back the Tears of all Oceans.'

Ublaz stepped hard on the back of Conva's neck, trapping his head against the floor. 'Scum of the sea, fool who cannot control his own crew!' the pine marten said, his voice dripping with contempt. 'Do you think I would let an idiot like you travel half round the world to fight a war against Redwall Abbey? I have heard of that place. The bones of warlords moulder at its gates; more than one has tried to breach those red walls and died miserably. If I am to retrieve the Tears of all Oceans it needs cunning strategy.' Ublaz pointed his dagger at a Trident-rat guard. 'You, go and fetch my Monitor General!'

Leaning down, the pine marten nicked Conva's ear with his dagger. 'You I will let live, until I know the truth of your story. Take him away and billet him in the Monitor barracks.'

Conva knew it was pointless to beg for mercy. He had escaped instant death, but how long would he survive unarmed in the barracks of the strange, flesh-eating lizards? He was led off stunned, almost speechless with terror.

Lask Frildur the Monitor General stood before the Emperor, flat reptilian eyes unblinking, scales making a dry rustle as his heavy spiked tail swished lazily against the marble floor. Ublaz nodded approvingly. The Monitor General had never let him down; everybeast on Sampetra knew and feared the reputation of Lask Frildur.

'Does all go well with you, my strong right claw?' Ublaz said, as he poured wine for them both.

The Emperor turned his head from Lask's foul breath

as the lizard answered, 'Yarr, Mightinezz. Lazk Frildur awaitz your orderz!'

The mad-eyed marten took a sip of wine and wiped his mouth fastidiously on a silk kerchief. 'Good! I want you to take the ship of Conva and carry out an important mission for me.'

The Monitor General's eyes flickered momentarily. 'I will go the endz of oceanz if Ublaz commandz!'

He accepted the goblet of wine that was pushed towards him, holding it at throat height. Lask never let his eyes stray from those of Ublaz; his head did not dip to the goblet, instead a long tongue snaked out and lapped at the wine as the Emperor gave his instructions.

'It is a long voyage to where the sun rises in the east, a place called the land of Mossflower. Take the *Waveworm* and her crew, with Romsca the ferret as captain, and a score of your Monitors. Here is what you must do . . .'

Outside the surf boomed on the sunwarmed rocks of the escarpment, and ships bobbed at anchor in the harbour. Sampetra shimmered under the midday sun, a once beautiful jewel of the oceans, now tainted by the evil of its ruler.

3

Sagitar Sawfang was bigger than most searats, lean and sinewy with a mean disposition. She was second only to Lask Frildur the Monitor General. Sagitar had fought her way up through the ranks of the Emperor's Trident-rats, until she held the undisputed title of Chief Trident-rat. Whilst the rats under her command patrolled Sampetra's harbour and taverns, keeping order among the sea vermin, Sagitar leaned on a jetty stanchion, watching *Waveworm* grow small on the eastern horizon, bound for Mossflower. Grasping her trident haft resolutely, she allowed herself a grim smile of satisfaction. Now she alone was the strong right paw of Ublaz, solely responsible for discipline among the wavescum who anchored at Sampetra.

Fate however is a cruel trickster. Turning her face west, Sagitar saw her happiness would be short-lived. The Chief Trident-rat knew the identity of the barque sailing in from the western ocean. No other vessel flew streaming red pennants from three mastheads – it had to be the *Freebooter*. She rapped the three-pronged metal head of her trident against the jetty timbers until a Trident-rat came running to her summons.

'Tell the full squad to muster on this jetty immediately!'

Lifting his trident smartly in salute, the rat hurried off.

Few ships that sailed into Sampetra had a master with a reputation for danger like Barranca, captain of the *Freebooter*. Scorning pawholds, he balanced perfectly, high on the heaving prow, reckless and daring. Barranca was every inch a real swashbuckler, clad in flame-red silks, with a long sabre thrust into his broad, black, garnet-studded belt. Loose ends of the corsair stoat's headband fluttered in the breeze as he pointed shoreward, calling out to his steersrat, 'Haharr, see, Guja, 'tis ole sourpuss Sagitar an' a welcomin' committee awaitin' us, let's not disappoint 'em!'

Swinging nimbly to the deck, Barranca whipped out his sabre and began roaring orders to *Freebooter*'s crew. 'All paws on deck, an' arm yerselves to the teeth, mates!'

The vessel's crew were a villainous and motley collection, mainly searats but with a scattering of ferrets, stoats and weasels. They fairly bristled with an array of cutlasses, daggers and axes.

Barranca drew his weasel mate Blowfly to one side. 'Don't stand any ole nonsense off'n Mad Eyes' creatures, y'hear?'

Blowfly produced a broad curved knife. Showing his blackened teeth, he licked the blade meaningfully, and said, 'Aye aye, Cap'n, we'll show 'em they cain't push *Freebooter*'s buckoes round, just you give the word!'

'Dangerous, matey, we're dangerous!' The corsair tossed his sabre high in the air, catching it skilfully as the blade flashed downwards. 'Haharr, you watch me tweak Sagitar's tail. I've never liked the cut o' that pompous rat's jib an' she don't like me, so there ain't no love lost atwixt us!'

Twoscore Trident-rats stood to rigid attention on the jetty. Grim-faced, Sagitar watched *Freebooter* heave starboard side on to the pier and make fast to it. Barranca's loud insulting challenge hailed her.

'Ahoy, miseryguts, where's Frildur an' his lizards today?'

Sagitar pointed her trident menacingly at the grinning corsair. 'Lask Frildur is the least of your worries. I'm the one who'll be dealing with you and your rabble if there's any trouble!'

Barranca leapt up, straddling the jetty and ship's rail. 'Yer don't say? Where's our ole mate the Monitor General then? Done us all a favour an' died, I 'ope. Haharrharr!'

Sagitar allowed herself a thin malicious smile. 'Not at all. Lask is still very much alive, sailing for the Mossflower coast on *Waveworm* at this very moment.'

Barranca turned and winked at Blowfly. 'Hoho, is he? I'll wager me brother Conva ain't too pleased about that, eh, mate, 'avin' that scaly ole reptile aboard as a passenger.'

Sagitar did not attempt to conceal the pleasure in her voice. 'Your brother Conva is no longer captain of the *Waveworm*. He is now a prisoner of Emperor Ublaz and is kept in the Monitor barracks. I'll give him your best regards when I see him. Right, let's see what you've got on board in the way of tribute.'

Barranca blocked the Chief Trident-rat's path aboard, his eyes fierce with challenge. 'Put one paw aboard o' my ship, rat, an' I'll gut ye! Crew, stand by to repel boarders!'

Freebooter's crew crowded the starboard rail, weapons ready for use against the Trident-rats. Barranca's gleaming sabretip hovered close to Sagitar's throat.

She gulped visibly. 'I warn you, this is the command of Emperor Ublaz you are defying!'

The corsair did not back down a fraction. 'No it ain't, this is one of yore fancy ideas. The tribute fer Ublaz will be unloaded onto this jetty by my crew – you can come back tomorrow an' collect it. Now shift yerself, rat!'

Sagitar knew she had lost the argument. Drawing back,

she marshalled her command, calling aloud to Barranca as they marched off, 'I'll report this to the Emperor. He will hear of your defiance!'

The derisive reply stung her as she left the jetty. 'Report wot yer like, ratnose! Ublaz knows my ship always brings the best booty to 'im, an' he trusts me to unload it!'

Word of Barranca's arrival ran like wildfire around the harbour. He was popular and well liked by all the pirates on Sampetra. Grog was broken out for all searat and corsair captains, who met with Barranca aboard his ship.

Having heard from them of his brother's arrest and imprisonment, he addressed them fiercely. 'Who does Mad Eyes think 'e is to lord it over us, mates? That pine marten was only a corsair like ourselves who chanced t' find this island first. Now 'e takes the best of our plunder, makes us live by some fancy set o' rules he invented, an' kills or imprisons who 'e likes. It ain't right, I tell yer!'

A grizzled searat captain called Slashback answered, 'Aye, messmate, but Ublaz has Trident-rats an' Monitors to do 'is biddin'. They enforce the laws round 'ere.'

Barranca whacked the flat of his sabre blade down on the table. 'I remember when seabeasts were free an' the only rules we 'ad were our own. Now look at us! Wot 'ave we come to, mates?'

A tall sombre weasel captain called Bilgetail shrugged. 'No one can stand against Mad Eyes an' his army.'

Barranca looked around the assembly. 'You, Slashback, an' you, Rocpaw, Bloodsnout, Rippdog, Flaney, yore all cap'ns, you command crews. By my reckonin' we must outnumber lizards an' Trident-rats two to one, think of that! An' 'ere's another thing: Lask Frildur ain't 'ere no more. Who knows if'n 'e'll ever make it back? Aye, an' a score o' Monitors gone with 'im too! If ever there was a right time fer us to take over this island it's now!'

There was a moment's silence, then Rippdog the weasel stood alongside Barranca and voiced her opinion.

'I'm with you, mate! Our lives ain't our own since we been dockin' at Sampetra. That pine marten even 'as us attackin' each other if'n we don't drop anchor 'ere an' pay 'alf a cargo to 'im!'

Bloodsnout, another female corsair, joined her companion. 'Rippdog an' Barranca are right, Ublaz is too greedy! He's got all the shipbuildin' an' repairin' wood piled up back of 'is palace. There ain't any good trees growin' on the island no more. Last trip my vessel run afoul o' rocks, ripped part of the stern away, Sagitar an' Lask took *all* my cargo in payment fer timber to fix 'er up again. We should get wood free, whenever we needs it!'

Bilgetail nodded, moving decisively to Barranca's side. 'I'll join ye. Mad Eyes is growin' too powerful, 'e executed two of my crew for arguin' with those Monitors over booty. Just 'ad 'em dragged off an' slain – you all remember it.'

Heads nodded around the table. Barranca stove in the top of a cask with his sabre handle. 'Dip yore beakers into this 'ere seaweed grog an' drink if yore with me, mates. Anybeast that don't dip a beaker is against us!'

The pact for rebellion was sealed as every beaker dipped into the cask.

Ublaz stood watching the ship *Freebooter* from the high window slit of an antechamber. Sagitar waited apprehensively at the pine marten's side. After a while, the Emperor turned to his Chief Trident-rat.

'Slashback, Flaney, Rocpaw – all the captains are aboard Barranca's ship. What would you say they are doing, Sagitar?'

The Trident-rat chose her words carefully. 'Mightiness, who knows what is in the minds of wave vermin?'

The silver dagger blade tapped gently against Sagitar's tunic. 'I do. Ublaz knows all, that is why I am Emperor. They are plotting against me, they think I am weak without Lask Frildur. But we will show them, won't we, my strong right paw?'

The Trident-rat bobbed her head respectfully. 'As you say, Excellency. I am yours to command!'

The pine marten tapped the dagger blade against his sharp white teeth a moment, before giving further orders. 'Take all your Trident-rats fully armed, quickly now, and block off the end of the jetty. Do not attack, but don't let any of the captains pass. Keep them aboard the ship, and await my command.'

Sagitar went swiftly off to carry out orders. Ublaz motioned to a Monitor guard. 'Assemble all my Monitors in the courtyard and bring the prisoner Conva here to me.'

Grath Longfletch, a daughter of Holt Lutra, should have been dead two seasons ago. She had been found three nights after Conva's attack on her family home, crawling through the mud of a half-dried stream with horrific injuries. Glinc the watervole and his wife Sitch dragged Grath between them to an overhang in a mossy bank, close to their den. As best they could, the voles tended the otter, but there was little the pair could do, save give her some hot soup and cover her with dry bracken.

Grath lay all season long, at the very entrance to death's door, some hidden inner flame keeping her alive – reliving in nightmares with loud cries the horrors she had survived. Gradually she recovered and spent her days eating and sleeping, growing slowly in strength and agility. At her request, Glinc brought a long sturdy yew branch to Grath. With a flint shard the otter scraped and fashioned it, wetting and steaming the wood over a fire. She strung it with flaxen threads, twined and greased by beeswax. Then one by one she made her arrows of ashwood, each as straight as a die, feathered with the green plumage of a lapwing Sitch had found dead upon the shore.

Then, early one spring morn, Grath rose wordlessly and strode off along the stream shallows. Glinc and Sitch followed the silent otter, watching her intently. They had never spoken to Grath, nor she to them, since the night they had found her. Glinc and his wife seldom spoke to one another; some bankvoles are like that.

Near the northern shore both voles sat on a streambank, where it broadened to meet the estuary. On the opposite bank, Grath was a long time out of sight, inside the holt of her father Lutra.

Emerging stone-faced and still silent, Grath set aside her weapons and went to work. Gathering twigs, root branches and stones she piled them up over the holt entrance. She carried mud from the riverbank and plastered it over the doorway, mixing it with grass and leaves. It took her a full day and most of the night to seal up the humble cavern, making it a tomb for her massacred family.

Afterwards, Grath washed herself in the stream. Silvery scar traces showed through her wet fur. Then, standing motionless in the water, she watched the gentle spring dawn spread its light across the skies, blinking as she shed tears for her kin.

Gathering her great bow and the quiverful of green-feathered shafts, Grath Longfletch waded to the far bank and took hold of the two bankvoles' paws.

'Friends, I know not yore names, but I thank ye both, for takin' care o' me an' savin' my life. I won't be back this way, so fortune care for y'both. Farewell!'

Grath shouldered her quiver and bow, then turning west she set off at an easy lope towards the dunes along the shore. Both watervoles stared at the back of the long figure until it was lost to view. Then Glinc spoke to his wife.

'I would not like to be one of the beasts that slew her kin. That creature carries death in her paws!'

4

Extract from the journal of Rollo bankvole, Recorder of Redwall Abbey in Mossflower country.

Spring weather can change suddenly as the mind of an old mousewife choosing mushrooms. Dearie me, how it can make the most carefully laid plans go astray!

This very morning the weather was so soft and fair that Abbot Durral decided to hold our first spring season feast out of doors. Poor Durral, he spent most of the night in the kitchens, cooking and baking with his friend Higgle Stump. Strange, is it not: Higgle was one of the winecellar-keepers of the family Stump, yet he wound up as Redwall's Kitchen Friar, and Durral was once a lowly kitchenmouse, but now he is Father Abbot of all Redwall. He is such a humble old fellow, his love of the kitchens never left him.

Ah me! Seasons roll upon seasons and yet our Abbey remains the same, a loving old place, filled with happiness and peace, even though our old friends are but memories to us now. We who were once young are now greyed with age. Orlando the Axe, our great badger Lord, roamed off long ago, as male badgers will, to end his seasons at Salamandastron, mountain stronghold of great badger warriors. I do not know if he still lives. Auma, his daughter, is now the Abbey Mother; badgers are indeed noble creatures, with a lifespan which nobeast can equal.

So, that only leaves two, Auma and myself, Rollo bankvole, who have lived and prospered in bygone seasons. The others have gone to their well-deserved rest, including Mattimeo and Tess Churchmouse whose son, Martin, is now our Abbey Warrior. Peacefully they went in the certainty that the wisdom and knowledge they gave to this great Abbey is still held strong in the stone of Redwall and in the minds of its creatures who carry on the wonderful tradition . . . Great seasons! How I do wander off, I should have been called Rollo of the roving quill pen. Where was I? Oh yes, I was telling you of the outdoor feast our Abbot had planned. Well, needless to say, as soon as a few tables were carried out to the orchard and some benches to sit upon, swoosh, down came the rain! However, I must own up to the fact that I was not totally unhappy. The Great Hall inside our Abbey is a comfortable place for feasting, far better for my creaky bones than a draughty orchard in early spring.

Foremole, the leader of our Abbeymoles, has convinced the Abbot to commence festivities late this afternoon. This will give Foremole and his crew time to create a huge turnip'n'tater'n'beetroot pie, a most homely delicacy. Actually, I think my paw rheumatism is playing me up a bit, so here I'll end my daily recording and pop off over to the kitchens, where I can savour the sights and smells of the good food. Not that I'm a greedy creature, you understand, merely appreciative, and slightly peckish too. My warm old cloak will give me sound protection in this awful rainstorm, the walk from gatehouse to Abbey seems to get longer as I get older . . .

Rollo the Recorder donned his cloak and stirred the fat otter curled in slumber on the hearthmat by the gatehouse fire.

'Wullger, come on, matey, wakey wakey. Let's pay the kitchens a visit and see how the feast preparations are progressing.'

Wullger yawned, stretched and blinked in one movement, then, scratching his rudderlike tail, he stood up. 'Wakey wakey y'self, Rollo. I wasn't asleep, jus' closin' me eyes 'cos yore scratchy pen was annoyin' me. Hah! Look at y'self, you got more skins on than an onion!'

The bankvole sniffed airily. 'Young snip! You'll learn as y'get older that comfort outweighs fashion. I need to wrap up warm until 'tis early summer!'

The two friends bent their heads against the wind and rain as they left the gatehouse, still keeping up a friendly banter.

'Lissen, you need all that wrappin', matey, stops yer blowin' off like an ole autumn leaf!'

'Know your trouble, fatty tail, no respect for your elders. It makes me shiver just looking at you, trolling round wearing little else but belt and tunic.'

'Gah! Fresh air an' a spot o' rain never 'urted anybeast. Come on, wrinklechops, step out smartlike!'

The kitchens were a bustle of steam, noise and merriment. Teasel, the hogwife of Higgle Stump, was crimping the edges of an apple and damson pie, prior to putting it in the oven. She was about to open the oven door when a little molemaid called Diggum bumped into the back of her with a flour trolley. Teasel fell backward with a whoop, holding the pie, and landed on top of the trolley. Diggum shot off regardless, head down, pushing the trolley at full speed. Foremole saw them coming, swiftly threw down a barrel wedge and flung wide the oven door where his deeper'n ever pie was cooking. The trolley stopped with a jerk, Foremole grabbed the back of Teasel's apron as she let go of the pie, and it shot from her paws to land neatly in the oven alongside Foremole's creation.

He grinned and nodded at her, rumbling in the curious molespeech, 'Thurr yew go, marm, bain't no sense a wasten oven space, hurr hurr!'

Diggum dusted flour from her smock and blinked. 'Thankee, zurr. Can oi use ee uther oven furr moi chessberry flan?'

Foremole raised a cloud of flour as he patted her dusty head. 'Whoi, surrpintly ee can, liddle missie, but wot be chessberries?'

Diggum twitched her button nose in despair at Foremole's ignorance. 'Whoi, chessnutters an' blackb'rries, zurr, wot else?'

Teasel the hogwife hid a smile as she took Diggum's paw, saying, 'Chestnuts an' blackberries, indeed. Come on, we'll make it t'gether, I'll roll the pastry.'

Diggum curtsied prettily. 'Thankee, marm, an oi'll eat any blackb'rries wot be a wrong size.'

Friar Higgle Stump was topping off a multicoloured woodland trifle with yellow meadowcream, roaring orders all about as he did.

'Hoi, Piknim, see that mushroom soup don't boil, keep stirrin' it.'

'Stirrin' hard as I can, Friar – shall I throw chopped carrot in?'

'Aye, do that, missie. Gurrbowl, be a good mole, nip down the cellars an' see if my brother Furlo 'as broached a new barrel of October Ale. Tell 'im I could do wi' a beaker to liven up my dark fruit cake mixture.'

'Roight ho, zurr, tho' you'm sure et ain't to loiven up yurrself?'

'Get goin', y'cheeky wretch! Craklyn, see if you can get some o' that dried mint down off the rafter 'ooks, I need t'make tea.'

The squirrel Craklyn shot off like a rocket; she bounced from a stove top to a high cupboard and leapt up to the rafter hooks, skilfully plucking a bundle of dried mint. Cutting a somersault she landed next to Friar Higgle, dropped the mint in his paws, scooped a blob of meadowcream from the mixing bowl and vaulted off licking her paw.

Abbot Durral watched her admiringly as he carried a deep dish to place in front of Higgle. 'What an acrobat our Craklyn is, eh, Friar? Taste that and tell me what you think, my old friend.'

With a knifetip, Higgle sampled a morsel from the dish edge. 'Mmmm! Now that is what I call a real honey rhubarb crumble!'

Durral shuffled his footpaws in embarrassment at the praise given to his simple offering. 'Oh, it's just something I made up from an old recipe. Shall we have the tables laid for around twilight? I've lit a good log fire in Great Hall, that'll warm it through nicely.'

Higgle, topping his trifle, nodded agreement. 'Good idea, Father Abbot. Have you seen Martin about?'

Abbot Durral scratched his chin thoughtfully. 'Can't say I have. Perhaps he's up in the infirmary with Sister Cicely. I'll go and take a look.'

Wind and rain shook the treetops of Mossflower until they swayed and undulated madly; howling gales sang a wild dirge between the weighty treetrunks. Paw in paw, fighting for breath, Tansy and Arven staggered doggedly on towards the forest fringe. Both of them were weary and pawsore and, driven by fright, they had partially lost their way. Then Tansy spotted the tall spire of Redwall through a gap in the woodlands. Staggering, the pair ran; slopping through a narrow ditch, fighting against whippy spring brush and squelching through rain-drenched ferns. Heedless of young nettles lashing at their footpaws they rounded a massive three-topped oak. Straight into the paws of a dark-cloaked form.

'Yeeeek!'

The baby squirrel and the young hedgehog maid squealed aloud in fright as they felt themselves held by strong paws.

'Whoa now, my little ones – here you are!'

The strong kindly face of Martin, the Warrior of Redwall, smiled reassuringly down at them. With a shriek of relief, Tansy and Arven buried their faces in Martin's cloak. Perching Arven on his shoulder and taking Tansy by the paw, Martin strode back towards the Abbey.

'Sister Cicely was getting quite worried about you two,' Martin said gently. 'You should have been back at the Abbey hours ago, when the storm broke. Where in the name of seasons have you been, all muddy and scratched, with your clothes torn like that?'

Arven was not afraid of anything now that Martin had found them. He had perked up considerably. 'Me found a skallingtung inna rocks!' he cried.

Martin chuckled. 'A skallingtung?'

'In the sandstone rocks, sir,' Tansy explained, 'down a deep crack, there was a skeleton of somebeast. Ugh! All white an' bony an' raggy!'

Martin saw the young hogmaid was bone weary. He let her lean against him and shielded her with his cloak. 'Well, you're safe now,' he said. 'You can tell the elders about it when we get back to the Abbey. Oh! I forgot to tell you, there's to be a surprise spring feast in Great Hall this evening. How d'you like that, eh, young 'uns?'

But they were both dozing, almost asleep with fatigue.

Sister Cicely put both Arven and Tansy straight to bed when Martin delivered them back to her at the sick bay. They had been sound asleep before Martin arrived at the Abbey gate. Spreading his cloak by the hearth to dry, Martin accompanied Cicely downstairs, explaining as he went. 'Something frightened them in the woodland today. I'll tell you about it when we're with the elders.'

Nobeast could be quite sure what made the spring feast such a success, the food or the fun. Martin and Cicely sat at the table with the Abbot, Foremole, Higgle, Auma and some other elders. They watched in amusement as the younger ones sat with their food on a thick rush mat, eating and providing their own entertainment. The smallest Abbey babes, the Dibbuns, ate all in sight with growing appetites.

'Oi thurr, Garffy, pass oi yon fruitycake. Yurr, you'm c'n 'ave some o' this plum pudden, 'tis turrible tasty!'

'Well thankee, my ole moleymate, I didn't know it were you be'ind those cream whiskers. Father h'Abbot, sir, would you like some o' my strawberry rolypoly?'

Smiling, the Abbot shook his head. 'No thank you, Durgel, I baked that specially for you and Garffy. Besides, I'm enjoying my salad. Nothing like fresh spring salad after the winter – what d'you say, Auma?'

The badger Mother held up a piece of cheese in her huge paw. 'Aye, Durral, and when there's soft white cheese and hot baked oatbread to go with it, well, I'm happy.'

Martin looked up from a steaming mushroom and leek pastie. 'I've never seen you sad when there's food about, Auma!'

Amid roars of laughter at her huge appetite the badger winked at Martin. 'Well, sir, I'm only making up for all the food that you used to scoff from in front of me, when you sat on my knee as a Dibbun!'

Furlo Stump the cellar-keeper poured himself a beaker of October Ale. 'Be you not careful, marm, an' Martin'll sit on yore knee agin an' scoff all that bread'n'cheese, I'll wager!' he chortled.

Rollo put aside a platter which had contained chestnut and blackberry flan and banged the tabletop with a soup ladle. 'Come on, you young 'uns, how's about a bit of song and dance for your poor elders before we fall asleep from boredom!'

In a flash Piknim the mousemaid and Craklyn the squirrelmaid were up and bowing to each other as they warbled an old ballad.

'Oh, look out, it's the terrible two!' Sister Cicely murmured in Martin's ear.

Piknim and Craklyn sang alternate verses at each other.

As I strode out gaily, one morning in spring,
I spied a fair mousemaid, who happily did sing,
She sang just as sweet, as a lark's rising call,
For she wore a green habit, and she came from
    Redwall.

I walked alongside her, and bade her good morn,
And her smile was as pretty, as rosebuds at dawn,
She captured my heart, and she held it in thrall,
For she wore a green habit, and she came from
    Redwall.

I said, 'Lovely mousemaid, where do you go to?'
'To Mossflower Wood, sir, for flowers of blue,
To decorate my bonnet, at the feast in Great Hall,'
For she wore a green habit, and she came from
    Redwall.

To the woodlands we went, and 'twas there in
    a glade,
I gathered wild bluebells, for my young mousemaid,
Then I walked her back home, lest she stumble or
    fall,
For she wore a green habit, and she came from
    Redwall.

'Pray sir,' said the mousemaid, 'be my gallant guest.'
O how happy was I, to take up her request,
For I never will leave, that old Abbey at all,
Now we both wear green habits, and we live at
    Redwall!

Piknim and Craklyn flounced about, grinning broadly and curtsying deeply at the cheers and applause they received.

Auma chuckled, watching mouse and squirrelmaid milking the ovation for all it was worth. 'Those two, what a pair! Hi there, Gurrbowl, what about a reel?'

The little mole took up his drum and thrummed at it with his heavy digging claws, calling to Friar Higgle, 'Coom on, zurr 'iggle, owt with ee 'ogtwanger!'

The Friar produced his hogtwanger, a curious three-stringed instrument which had belonged to his father, Jubilation Stump. Holding it strings-down over his head, he began humming a tune and nodding oddly. As he did, his headspikes struck the strings in time to the nodding and humming. Hogtwangers can only be played by hedgehogs, and Friar Higgle Stump was an expert.

Recognizing the lively reel, Abbeybabes and Dibbuns sprang up and jigged about furiously, calling aloud, 'Frogs inna gully! Frogs inna gully!'

Auma sat watching, great footpads tapping until she could restrain herself no longer. Then the big badger Mother of Redwall lumbered out to join the dance, clapping her paws and whooping, 'Frogs in the gully! Frogs in the gully!'

Martin and the elders remained seated, helpless with laughter at the sight. Gurrbowl stepped up the drumbeat and Higgle kept pace on his hogtwanger; faster and faster they played. Hopping, skipping and leaping, the dancers whirled, hallooing loudly.

While Auma made her own hefty pace, exhausted Dibbuns perched on both her footpaws and were bumped up and down. Then, dropping to all fours, Auma let the tiny creatures climb onto her broad back. When she was fully loaded the crafty badger danced off in the direction of the dormitories, followed by Higgle and Gurrbowl, still playing as they shepherded the other young ones up to bed.

Later, when she had rejoined the elders at table, Auma sat back and sighed wearily. 'Phew! I'm getting too old to do that much longer!'

Martin patted her striped muzzle affectionately. 'You're a sly old fraud, Auma, you enjoy it more than the Dibbuns.'

He poured her a beaker of cold mint tea, his voice growing serious. 'Little Arven and Tansy were in a dreadful state when I found them in Mossflower Wood today: dirty, ragged, weary, and very frightened.'

'Indeed they were,' agreed Sister Cicely, 'both so exhausted they couldn't speak. I popped up to see them in the sick bay not an hour back – fast asleep, the pair of them. Strange though, Tansy is a proper little rock of good sense. Did she say what had frightened them, Martin?'

Martin looked around the expectant faces of the elders, and said, 'They found a dead creature in the woodlands . . .'

'A dead creature in the woodlands?' Abbot Durral repeated in hushed tones.

Questions followed from around the table.

'What sort of creature was it?'

'Where did they find this creature?'

'I wonder how it got there?'

The Warriormouse held up a paw for silence. 'Please, let me explain. This was not a recently dead beast. Tansy said it was a skeleton, clad in rotten rags, so evidently it had been there for some time. They came upon it down a crack in the sandstone rocks of the woodlands. I know the place well, actually they weren't far from the rocks when I found them, so they must have been running in circles since they were caught in the thunderstorm. Poor Tansy, she was terrified, but doing her level best to protect little Arven and get him back to Redwall.'

Foremole nodded from behind a large beaker of October Ale. 'Ho aye, she'm a liddle guddbeast awroight.

May'ap you'm goin' thurr on the morrow to see furr-eeself, zurr Marthen?'

Martin pushed back his chair and stood up decisively. 'Why leave it until tomorrow, friends? The night is fine now, I'll go and be back before dawn. No need to upset our Abbey creatures by starting an expedition in full daylight. Besides, I can't sleep at all if there's anything bothering my mind, so it's best that I investigate it this very night.'

'Aye, with me by yer side, mate, soon as I finds me ash stave!'

No sooner had Wullger the other gatekeeper spoken than the others were all including themselves.

'Hurr, oi too, ee may 'ave need o' a gudd digger, zurr!'

'I'll bring a long stout rope from the winecellar!'

'Right, an' I'll fetch lanterns, we'll be in need of light!'

Martin hesitated a moment, then nodded. 'So be it. I'll get the sword. Meet back here as quickly as you can. Auma, will you stay behind and watch the main gate?'

'Gladly, friend. I don't feel much like charging around woodlands after our spring feast this evening.'

5

The Redwallers set off north up the path, Martin in the lead with the sword buckled about his middle. This was the fabulous blade which belonged long ago to Martin the first Warrior, he who had helped build Redwall Abbey and establish the order of Redwallers. The spirit of this brave mouse was said to help the Abbey creatures, appearing in dreams and offering wise counsel in troubled times. For countless generations the sword had been lost: it was Matthias, father of Mattimeo and grandsire of the present Martin, who had found the sword and restored it to Redwall Abbey.

Silent as shadows, the little party slipped into the night-darkened trees. They were skilled in the ways of woodlanders and knew that stealth and care combined with speed was the rule of safety, even in their own beloved Mossflower. There was no moon to light the way east, but Martin was an expert leader. Skirting thickets, bypassing brambles and staying close to the deep shadows, he led his companions to the clearing where the sandstone rift could be seen, poking up at an angle out of the ground.

Martin signalled quietly for Wullger and Foremole to accompany him, indicating that the rest should stay in the tree shelter at the clearing's edge, ready to come running should they be needed. Drawing his sword, the warrior edged forward; the mole and otter followed, carrying rope and lantern. The rain had stopped, though a sighing wind was still blowing up from the south. Mounting the rocks, Martin waited whilst Foremole put flint to tinder and lit his lantern. Shielding the light in the cowl of his cloak, Martin led his friends across the ridged surface. As they came upon each cleft, the lantern was lowered down on the rope to explore its darkness. They had nearly covered half the area when Foremole, shuffling backward away from a small fissure, disappeared with a gruff bass yelp.

'Whurrhumm!'

The lantern was swiftly lowered as Wullger called down to him. 'You all right, matey, not 'urted are yer?'

Wiping his paw disgustedly upon his smock, the good mole wrinkled his snout. 'Yurr ee is, zurr, oi foinded ee skallertung. Yurkk!'

Martin dropped swiftly into the crevice, landing lightly beside Foremole. He held the lantern close, illuminating the gleaming white bones that poked through rain-sodden rags.

Wullger peered down at the skull, fixed in its death grin. 'Poor wretch, fancy dyin' down there all alone.' There was compassion in the otter's tone.

Martin knelt and retrieved something from the flesh-less claw of what had once been the creature's right front paw. 'Aye, poor beast, what was it that brought him here?'

A low whistle from the tree fringe caused Wullger to throw himself flat upon the rocks. 'Hearken an' hide that lampglim, we've got visitors!'

Swiftly Martin pulled off his cloak and gave it to Foremole. 'Stay down here, keep that light covered. Hang on to the rope, Wullger, I'm coming up!'

Sheathing his sword, the Warriormouse clambered

paw over paw up the rope, with Wullger taking the strain. 'Remain here with Foremole, stay low!' Martin whispered.

Wraithlike, Martin appeared beside Rollo among the trees. The Recorder squeaked with fright. 'Oo! Don't sneak up on me like that!'

The Abbot pointed a paw north into the dark tree masses. 'Over yonder, Martin, I thought I heard voices and saw two white shapes. See, there they go!'

They caught a fleeting glimpse of whitish forms moving among the trees.

Martin nudged Higgle Stump, saying, 'Bring the ash stave and follow me, Friar.'

Crouching low they threaded off, carefully avoiding dry twigs beneath the tree cover. Judging the path the intruders were taking, Martin halted between a beech and an elm, signalling his intentions to Higgle. Martin crouched behind the beech and grasped one end of the stave. The Friar stooped behind the elm and took the other end.

The Warriormouse whispered across to his companion, 'They're coming this way; hold the stave low until I give the signal!'

As the shapes drew closer voices could be heard.

'There's nothin' dark as the dark, me ould mother used t'say.'

'Really? Well, that was jolly observant of her, wot! I'll wager she used to go on about how flippin' light the day was. Owooop!'

Martin and Higgle had raised the stave a fraction so that the speaker tripped, sprawling flat in front of them.

Immediately, Martin saw that the other shape was some type of great bird. Snatching Higgle's cloak he flung it over the creature, bringing it to the ground. The others dashed across and flung themselves upon the beast who had tripped, trying to pin it down as it yelled and kicked wildly.

'Ambush, chaps! Bring up the regiment, tell mother I died fightin'!'

Martin bounced along the ground, towed by the cloaked bird. Then he banged into a tree and was forced to let go. Recognizing the other creature's voice, he dashed back to his companions, yelling, 'It's all right, release him, it's a hare!'

The hare, whose long legs had kicked most of them flying, leapt up indignantly, dusting himself down and muttering, 'Flamin' cheek! Of course I'm a hare, what'd you think I was, a long-legged tadpole out for a bloomin' walk?'

Brushing irately past Martin, he uncovered his travelling companion, a great barn owl, all ruffled and blinking furiously. The hare was half white: a mountain hare, patching into his brown spring coat. Striking a heroic fighting pose, he challenged them.

'Blackguards, ruffians! Attackin' poor wayfarers, eh! Well, let me tell you blather-pawed bandits, y've picked on the wrong pair this time. Right! Defend y'selves sharpish now! I'll teach you a thing or three about the jolly old noble art, wot! C'mon!'

Prancing about in the most ridiculous manner, he blew fiercely through his whiskers, wobbling, ducking and flicking his paw against the side of his nose in a businesslike manner.

'C'mon c'mon, shape up, you cowardy custards! Oi, mattressbottom, you take those six an' I'll deal with the other ten!'

The hare twirled and weaved comically, throwing punches in mid-air, until by accident his nose collided with an overhanging branch. Immediately he went into a mock state of collapse, and staggered, throwing his paws wide as if appealing to a referee. 'Did y'see that? Beastly foul play, sir! Low underpawed trickery! Sneakin' up on a chap like that! Highly unprincipled, deduct ten points, ten points I say, sir!'

He stopped and turned to the owl, who was unruffling his feathers and blinking furiously. 'Well, you're a great help, I must say, foozlin' great flock-filled featherbag! Don't stand there blinkin' like a toad with toothache, assist me against these vile villains!'

Trying his level best not to burst out laughing, Martin held forth the paw of friendship. 'I'm sorry. Please accept our apologies, sir, and your friend too. We thought *you* were the villains, but as it turns out neither of us is. However, I'm sure that you'll agree with me nobeast can be too careful abroad in woodlands on a moonless night.'

Immediately the hare's attitude changed. He shook Martin's paw, chuckling as he bowed to the other Redwallers. 'Friends, eh? Well, I knew that all along, just testin', wot! Allow me to introduce m'self, ahem! I'm Cleckstarr Lepus Montisle, of the far northern Montisles that is, known to all an' sundry as Clecky. My erstwhile companion of the road you may call Gerul, simple t'remember, y'see, Clecky an' Gerul. As you may've prob'ly observed, Gerul is an owl, though not of the wise old variety, more the silly young type I'd say, bit of a duffer, wot!'

Gerul blinked his great eyes at the assembly, saying, 'Ah well, 'tis nice t'see ye, sirs, so 'tis, a rare ould pleasure!'

Clecky shook his head despairingly. 'Would somebeast put the cloak back over his pudden head, we were gettin' more sense out o' the bird when he was silent. Oh I say, look, there's a small fat mouse on fire!'

Foremole and Wullger had joined them, Foremole holding the lantern. He tugged his nose in greeting to the hare, saying, 'Hurr hurr, you'm be a gurt joker, zurr, oi bain't no mouse afire, oi'm nought but a mole wi' a lantern!'

General good humour prevailed and, amid introductions all round, the two wayfarers were invited back to Redwall.

The little party proceeded to the Abbey with Foremole in the lead carrying his lantern; Martin and the Abbot brought up the rear.

Abbot Durral had retrieved Tansy's basket. He checked the contents, saying, 'Old hogweed stalks, young angelica, see, she even managed to find some newgrown wintergreen. What a dutiful creature little Tansy is. A pity she was frightened by the sight of a deadbeast. Did you recognize anything about its remains, Martin?'

The Warriormouse drew his cloak close against the night wind. 'Very little, apart from the fact that he was a weasel once, some kind of corsair too, if the rags he had on were anything to go by. Strange though, he was clasping this in his paw, Fermald's spoon. That weasel must have been inside our Abbey!'

The spoon was old, beautifully carved from the wood of a buckthorn bush. Martin passed it to the Abbot, who also recognized it.

'You're right, this was the spoon Fermald the Ancient used to carry about with her. Aha! Now I know. The creature you found was Graylunk the weasel, he came to us two autumns ago!'

Martin rubbed his chin, obviously puzzled. 'Two autumns back? Why didn't I see this Graylunk?'

The Father Abbot paused, then held up his paw. 'Of course, you wouldn't know! That was the season you spent away from Redwall, helping the Guosim shrews against robber foxes.'

Upon reaching the Abbey most of the elders sought their beds. Martin, Rollo and the Abbot busied themselves, adding logs to the fire in Great Hall and putting together a sizeable repast from the remains of the spring feast for the owl and hare.

Clecky poured himself a beaker of strawberry cordial, heaped a platter high with deeper'n ever turnip'n'tater'n'beetroot pie, topped it off with two wedges of cheese and a massive portion of fresh spring salad, and wiped away a tear of joy with the corner of his white tunic.

'Oh corks! I say, you chaps, what a spiffin' spread! Tell me I'm not dreamin', wot!'

Gerul the young barn owl speared a carrot and mushroom flan with his powerful talons. 'Arrah, away with yeh, flopears, nobeast c'd imagine you a dreamin' with vittles in front of ye, y'great long-legged gutbag. Why, I've seen turnips uproot themselves an' run from yeh with me own two eyes, so I have!'

Seated by the fire with Rollo and the Abbot, Martin smiled as he watched the two ravenous newcomers. 'Friar Higgle won't need any leftover recipes with those gluttons about. Right, tell me all you know about the weasel who visited here in my absence, Rollo.'

Using his journal as a reminder, Rollo the Recorder related the incident.

'A weasel called Graylunk came to our Abbey gates in mid-autumn. He was a villainous-looking vermin, but quite harmless due to a dreadful skull wound he had received, probably from one of his own kind. Graylunk was weak and ill, and not in his right mind. We took him in out of pity, gave him food, warmth and shelter, doing what we could for his injury. I recall that he seemed to be terrified of many things, from the merest shadow to the sight of a bird flying overhead. He would often be found crouched in a corner moaning things like, "Mad Eyes will find me, his claws stretch beyond sea and land! Fools that we were to take the Tears of all Oceans, death follows wherever they go! Witless beast that I am, woe to me, 'tis useless to try to escape the vengeance of Mad Eyes!"'

Here, Martin interrupted. 'Hmmm, very strange. It may be nonsense, but on the other hand it may not. Tears of all Oceans; Mad Eyes; claws stretching beyond sea and land? Sounds like a riddle to me – as if this Mad

Eyes is after those Tears, whatever they are. And why was Graylunk out there with Fermald's spoon?'

'I remember that dirge too,' said the Abbot. 'The weasel carried on moaning and whining in such a manner, until even the most patient Abbeybeast grew tired of his ceaseless dirge. There was only one who had any sympathy for Graylunk, and that was Fermald the Ancient.'

Martin polished the buckthorn spoon fondly upon his sleeve. 'Ah yes, poor old Fermald, may fates rest kindly upon her. What an odd little squirrel, always saying verse and talking in riddles. I've heard it said that overlong seasons may sometimes do that to a creature. Fermald retreated into the curious world her mind had created. Maybe it was a nice place for her to be, she was always smiling and contented. She lived alone in the attics above the dormitories; perhaps the answer to this mystery lies somewhere there. Oh, I'm sorry, Rollo, please carry on.'

The Recorder put aside his journal, shrugging. 'There's not much more to tell. Fermald took Graylunk up to her attic, they ate, talked and slept there. Hardly anybeast in Redwall recalled seeing the weasel for six or seven days. Then one morning Fermald came to the kitchens for food and took only sufficient for one.'

Again the Abbot recalled the incident. 'Ah yes, excuse me, Rollo, I was there that day helping Higgle to make an upside-down cake. So I asked Fermald why she was not taking food for her guest, and she replied just one word. Gone! Remembering the deep skull wound Graylunk had, I asked her if he were dead and gone. Her answer was very cryptic.'

Martin leaned forward in his chair, saying, 'Do you recall what she said, Father Abbot?'

Durral sat back, folding both paws into his wide sleeves and closing his eyes. 'Indeed I do,' he said. 'Fermald spoke in rhyme. The lines stuck in my mind for no good reason.

41

Dead and gone, no, gone to be dead,
Following the crack that runs through his head.
From beyond the sunset, they will appear,
Tell them, the weasel was never here,
Remember my words and use them someday,
To keep the wrath of Mad Eyes away!'

In the silence that followed there was a noise from the far corner by the stairs. Swiftly Martin held a paw to his lips and moved quietly across Great Hall, followed by Rollo. They were almost halfway to the source of the noise when Clecky went dashing past them, paws slapping noisily on the stone-paved floor. Reaching the stair bottom, he held up two pieces of a pottery platter.

'Plate fell down the stairs, wot! That's all the noise was,' he chortled. 'Us hares don't miss a bally thing, even when we're scoffin'. I say, you chaps were a bit tardy there, tip-pawin' about like shrimps in a swamp, wot, wot?'

Martin went straight up the stairs at a run, while Rollo stood glaring frostily at the hare, explaining between gritted teeth, 'Thank you very much, sir, for frightening away whoever was on those stairs listening to our conversation! Your great lolloping footpaws sent them off upstairs before we had a chance to see who it was!'

The mountain hare wiggled his long ears huffily. 'Tut tut, sir! If you'd been a touch quicker, like I was, then you'd have the culprit by the jolly old heels!'

Rollo clenched his paws tightly in frustration.

'But you didn't get the culprit by the jolly old heels, did you? No, you ruined our chance to catch the eaves-dropper quietly.'

Clecky smiled disarmingly at the irate Recorder. 'No cause to get upset, old feller, we all make mistakes. P'raps next time you'll take my advice an' nip along smartlike, eh!'

Then the outrageous hare went speedily back to the

table, berating his dining partner. 'I say there, shovelbeak, go easy on that woodland trifle! I've only had two portions yet. Think of others beside y'self, y'great feathered famine-fetcher!'

Martin came back down the stairs shaking his head at Rollo and the Abbot. 'Couldn't see anybeast about up there. The young 'uns are all fast asleep and snoring. One of them may have left the plate on the stairs at bedtime; maybe it was balancing on a stair edge and it only took a slight draught to topple it.'

Gerul the barn owl wiped meadowcream from his beak with a wingtip. 'Arr, that's what meself thinks has happened, yer honour, sure a good puff of wind can blow even an owl tip o'er tail if the creature's not stood up properly, an' that's a fact, so 'tis!'

Abbot Durral put his paws about the shoulders of Martin and Rollo. 'Perhaps friend Gerul is right. Now what we need is a nice gentle breeze to waft us upstairs; time for sleep, I think.'

Martin fought back a yawn. 'Good idea, Father Abbot,' he agreed. 'We'll talk more tomorrow over breakfast.' He looked at the two visitors. 'When you two have finished eating perhaps you wouldn't mind sleeping on that rush mat by the fire for tonight. I'll have Brother Dormal fix proper accommodation for you tomorrow.'

The owl waved a soup ladle at the retreating trio. 'I thank ye kindly, sirs, the mat'll be fine fer the likes of us!'

Clecky put aside the trifle bowl he had been licking clean. 'The likes of us indeed? Speak for y'self, cushionbottom, I'm puttin' me paws up in that big Abbot's chair yonder. Likes of us! Blinkin' draughty barn is all you're used to!'

'Aye, an' that's the truth, so 'tis. Me ould mother used to say better to be an owl in a barn than a prince in a palace, so she did.'

'An' what, pray, did your old mother mean by that?'

'Sure how would I be knowin'? Sounds grand, though, doesn't it?'

'Oh, go an' boil your fat head. Goodnight!'

The Abbey was quiet and still as the fires burned low. Outside chill winds sighed and whined against Redwall's immovable stone. Though it was less than four hours to dawn, Martin lay awake, his mind picking over that evening's events. Graylunk's skeleton in the rocky fissure, Fermald's spoon, the Ancient's rhyme, an unknown creature called Mad Eyes and the mysterious eavesdropper who had listened to the conversation in Great Hall. What did it all mean?

6

Conva the corsair had spent a perilous night in the Monitor barracks, huddled in a corner, shivering and hungry. The long-tongued lizards constantly watched him, their flat reptilian eyes appraising his trembling form. He did not know whether to feel fear or relief when two of them entered the barracks and hauled him off for an audience with the Emperor.

He was ushered into an upper room. The pine marten lounged on the sill of a broad window, open to the warm tropical noontide. Behind Ublaz, four great black-backed gulls perched on the window ledge. They were fearsome-looking birds, each with the characteristic red spot of their species adorning the tip of its heavy amber bill.

Mad Eyes' cruelty was legendary. Conva went rigid with terror, and his footpaws scrabbled against the floor as he resisted the Monitors dragging him into the room.

Ublaz was in no mood to be delayed. Fixing the corsair with a stare of icy contempt, he rapped harshly, 'Cease struggling, idiot! If I wanted you dead you'd have been crabmeat yesterday. Sit at that table and do as I command!'

Quickly Conva seated himself. Ublaz leaned over, his

silver dagger blade tapping a bark parchment and char-coal sticks which lay on the table in front of the corsair. 'You saw the six pearls, did you not, felt them, noted their shape, held the shell in which they were kept?' he snapped.

Conva nodded. 'Aye, Mightiness.'

The dagger blade tapped the corsair's paw lightly. 'Good, then you can draw them for me, the pearls and the shell.'

Conva picked up a charcoal stick hesitantly. 'But I don't know if I'm any good at drawing, Sire . . .'

Lifting Conva's chin with the blade, Ublaz said gently, warningly, 'Perhaps you didn't hear me right, seascum. I said draw. If you wish to continue living . . . then draw!'

Hastily Conva began sketching, answering the Emperor's questions as his paw guided the slim charcoal stick.

'None of the pearls was flawed or marked in any way?'

'No, Sire, all six were perfect, smooth and round.'

'Were they of different sizes, some smaller than others?'

'Each was exactly the same size, Sire, bigger than any pearls I have ever seen, something like this.'

As Conva outlined the six orbs, Ublaz watched approv-ingly, saying, 'See, you can sketch. Now, the colour of these beauties?'

'Mightiness, they were a pale pink, not bright. In daylight they appeared soft and creamy, but by lantern light the pink showed warmer, like a budding rose.'

'Very poetic, my friend. You are doing well. Tell me about the scallop shell they were kept in?'

'It was a big deep-sea thing, Sire, both sides well ridged and whitish yellow. Some skilled beast had given it hinges and a clasp carved from hardwood. Inside, the shell was lined with soft red cloth. There were six cuplike dents to hold the pearls – as I recall, it looked like this.'

When the corsair had finished sketching, Ublaz took the parchment. After inspecting the drawing he placed it in front of the four gulls on the window ledge. They gazed unblinkingly at the work.

Ublaz stared into the eyes of Grall, the leader of the black-backed gulls, concentrating all his mesmeric powers upon the huge bird. In a short time Grall was completely under the influence of the mad eyes and sinister voice.

'Fly east to the shores of Mossflower land, and find the place called Redwall. Stay there and watch. Should you see the pearls or the case, seize them and bring them here to me! If you cannot do this then stop in the area, and wait until you sight Lask Frildur and those under his command. If they find the pearls give this token to him.'

Ublaz took a pawring surmounted by a polished jetstone, and looped it on a thong around Grall's neck.

'My Monitor General will know this comes from me. Get the pearls from him and fly back here to Sampetra. Go now, ride the winds, make your wings fly faster than the waves of the sea. When you return I will reward you and your kin. Fly!'

'Kreeeehaaarkaa!'

With a long wailing cry the gulls took to the air, swooping off over the main, eastward.

The pine marten smoothed his creamy throat fur, gazing at his reflection in a burnished bronze wall mirror. He turned to Conva, who sat trembling at the table. 'And you, my friend,' he said, 'what shall I do with you?'

The charcoal stick crumbled in the corsair's shaking paw as he tried to tear his gaze from the pine marten's frightening eyes. 'Mighty One, let me live!' he whimpered.

Ublaz gripped Conva tight by his ears and stared down at him. 'A simple request, but one I am unwilling to grant. You have seen and heard too much, Conva, far too much. Look into my eyes!'

*   *   *

Slashback the searat captain heard the clatter of paws and trident butts upon the jetty. He inched open the cabin door and peered out.

'Rats! Trident-rats!' he yelled. 'The jetty's crowded with 'em! We're trapped aboard this boat, mates!'

Barranca grabbed his sword and made for the door, snarling, 'We'll see 'ow they likes the taste of cold steel, eh, mates!'

Slashback slammed the door shut. 'Stay yer paw or y'll get us all carved up. There's too many of 'em, we'd be fishbait afore we got 'alfway along the jetty!'

The stoat captain Rocpaw slumped down and refilled his beaker. 'Hah! This is a great start to an uprisin', us trapped aboard ship, an' our crews all ashore separated from their cap'ns. Now's the time fer bright ideas, anybeast got one?'

Slashback had cracked open the door again to watch what was going on outside. 'Well, they ain't made a move yet, just stannin' there, an' Sagitar lookin' well pleased with 'erself,' he said. 'Ahoy, 'ere comes ole Mad Eyes 'isself with a gang of 'is Monitors.'

Barranca still had his sabre at the ready. 'Let's sit tight 'ere an' 'ear wot Ublaz has t'say. I ain't goin' out there fer a starin' match with that one!'

There was a pause in the proceedings, then the sound of the Emperor's voice reached the rebels in the cabin. 'Friends, brethren of the seas, have you got grievances? Come out here and tell them to me!'

Barranca half opened the cabin door and shouted back, 'Ho, we got grievances all right, but we ain't stupid, we can state 'em comf'table from 'ere! We ain't takin' no more orders from you, Ublaz. Our crews outnumber you an' yer gang!'

'Be reasonable, friends, fighting will get us nowhere,' Ublaz replied, signalling Sagitar to start the Trident-rats moving further up the jetty towards the ship. 'Come up to my palace. I will lay on a feast while we talk things out . . .'

Suddenly Barranca burst out onto the deck waving his sabre and yelling, 'Ahoy the taverns! Corsairs ahoy!'

The bold move was successful. In an instant, searats and corsairs began piling out of the waterfront dens adjacent to the jetty.

Ublaz turned, pointing his silver dagger at them. 'Stay back, keep out of this! It concerns only me, Ublaz, and those aboard the *Freebooter*!'

Bilgetail the weasel captain came out on deck followed by the other captains. In a booming voice, the tall sombre weasel called to the crews, 'Stand by to rush 'em, buckoes! If they puts a single paw t'this deck, then charge!'

Barranca and Rocpaw had positioned themselves fore and aft; they stood by the head and stern mooring ropes, swords drawn. Barranca knew that Ublaz had lost the element of surprise, but he had also figured that if the vermin crews charged they could be easily fended off by Trident-rats defending the narrow jetty. Moreover, if an attack were mounted, Ublaz and the front ranks of Monitors and Trident-rats would swarm aboard and slaughter the captains before the crews could get to them.

Barranca's brain was as nimble as his paws. Keeping his face averted from Ublaz, he called out his demands. 'Order yore soldiers not to make any sudden moves an' we'll tell our crews t'do likewise. But we're finished payin' tribute to you, Ublaz. As for the timber stocks yore holdin' – share 'em out atwixt the cap'ns. Oh, an' you kin release my brother Conva, now! Yore days of imprisonin' us is over!'

A cold fury gripped the Emperor. He pointed his dagger at Barranca, snarling, 'This is my island. I alone rule here. I am Emperor Ublaz and none dare look at my eyes! Seascum do not dictate terms to me, Barranca. Ask your brother – he is an even bigger fool than you!'

Ublaz signalled to his Monitors. Four of the lizards strode forward with a sailcloth-wrapped bundle, and slammed it down on the jetty. The bundle burst open, revealing the mangled carcass of Conva.

The mad-eyed Emperor laughed coldly, and said, 'This one thought he was a bird. I merely looked at him and he tried to fly out of a high window!'

Barranca was still with horror for an instant, then he roared his hatred at the pine marten. 'I'll live to close those evil eyes of yores fer good, Ublaz! This is war! Cut 'er loose, Rocpaw, 'tis *waaaaaar*!'

Rocpaw slashed down twice on the stern rope as Barranca sliced through the headrope with a single blow of his sabre. The ship *Freebooter* drifted out from the jetty on the ebbing tide, sailing free as the captains loosed her sails. Bilgetail bellowed to the vermin crews milling about on the waterfront. 'Retreat to the hills, arm yerselves an' wait 'till we give the word, cullies! We'll take Sampetra fer ourselves, mates – 'tis war!'

Whooping and screeching, the wave vermin dashed off behind the harbour into the high ground.

Ublaz placed a restraining paw on the shoulder of Sagitar. 'Let them go, they are nought but a rabble without leaders. Take a crew of Trident-rats and commandeer Slashback's ship, the *Bloodkeel*. Hunt Barranca down, slay the other captains, but bring Barranca to me. I want him alive!'

7

Grath Longfletch notched another shaft to her bowstring and waited for the next searat to emerge from behind the longboat hauled high above the tideline. From where she sat in the rocks the deadly otter commanded an uninterrupted view of the shore for miles around. She had slain five searats. Their bodies lay on the sands by the boat, each transfixed by a green-feathered arrow. Now only two more rats crouched behind the beached vessel.

Grath held the great bow firmly. Allowing its string to touch her cheek, she gazed down the arrow shaft, singing softly to herself as she waited for the quarry to materialize.

'Run from me, hide from me,
Still my shafts will find you,
All you vermin of the sea,
I must bring swift death to.
Lutra's Holt has not yet gone,
By my bow I swear it so,
I alone will carry on,
Wreaking vengeance where I go.
Run from me, hide from me,
Hear my longbow singing,

51

Grath of Lutra's family,
Sleep to you is bringing.'

Sculrag the searat captain and his steersrat Karvil lay
flat on the sand behind the stern of the single-sailed
longboat that had once served as ship's dinghy for
Sculrag's vessel, *Sprayraider*.

Karvil whined continually. 'Lookit, the tide's comin'
in, an' we ain't got a crab's chance of gettin' off this
shore. Why'd you tell 'em t'pull the boat up beyond
the tideline. Why?'

Sculrag hurled a pawful of sand at the steersrat, but
the breeze whipped it away before it found his face.

'Because the tide would've drifted it away while we
was lookin' fer shellfish on those rocks, block'ead, that's
why! Oh, an' while we're talkin' about rocks, who was
the witless buffoon that ran me ship onto the rocks an'
wrecked 'er . . . You!'

Sculrag kicked out viciously, catching Karvil painfully
in his side, and raged on at the hapless steersrat. 'A good
ship an' two seasons' plunder lost! Huh, steersrat? I
wouldn't let you steer a beaker round a bowl of grog!
Twenty days in an open longboat, twenty days without
vittles, livin' on barnacles an' rainwater! If I ever gets
outta this mess I'm goin' to 'ang you upside down over
the sea an' let the fishes nibble yore 'ead off, though
they'll be out o' luck if they expects to find any brains
in there!'

Quite unexpectedly Karvil kicked back, catching Sculrag
square in his flabby stomach. The searat captain glared
at his attacker as he fought for breath, and croaked, 'Yer
mutinous toad, 'tis the death penalty fer strikin' a ship's
master!'

Sneeringly, Karvil avoided Sculrag's flailing paw and
drew a dagger. The fact that he had hurt the searat made
him bolder. 'Yore no ship's master, slimeguts, you ain't
got a ship no more! I'm sick of takin' orders from yer,

see. Jus' try strikin' me once more an' you'll feel this 'ere blade!'

Sculrag kicked swiftly, sending the dagger spinning out onto the sand. Karvil kicked back, but Sculrag grabbed his footpaw and bit it hard. The steersrat screeched in agony as he pulled away, grabbing for the dagger. Breaking free, he scrambled out onto the sand and retrieved his blade.

Sssssthukk!

Karvil fell backward, the green-flighted shaft between his eyes.

Desperately Sculrag looked over his shoulder at the incoming tide. The longboat was fully twice its length away from the tideline. Reaching over the after end, he groped madly about until his paw encountered the stern rope. It was made fast to the back seat. Sobbing with relief and panting, the searat captain began dragging the longboat backward, towards the sea and freedom. It was tough going. He dug his footpaws into the sand and, still lying flat, he tugged the longboat, inch by painful inch, its flat bottom scraping the shore. For interminable minutes he sweated, puffing, tugging and heaving, spitting sand from his mouth and wiping sweat from his eyes.

Sculrag was fat, but he was strong. Rewinding the rope around his shoulders, he dragged hard, digging his footpaws deep to gain purchase until he felt the waves lap at them. Sculrag smiled then, the wreck of his ship and the crew that was lost on the reef all forgotten. Whoever it was up in those rocks, they would not be adding him to the list of the slain. He, Sculrag, would escape and, once the longboat was in the sea and he could hoist the single sail to catch fair wind, he was certain nobeast alive would catch him. One more tug, just one more! His footpaws hit something solid and he glanced over his shoulder. Sculrag's blood ran cold as he stared into the vengeful eyes of Grath Longfletch.

Moonlight glimmered and danced across the restless

waves as the longboat skimmed lightly south on the open seas. Grath was now captain of her own little vessel.

Every scrap of *Waveworm*'s canvas was stretched tight; she dipped her bows deep to the troughs of great waves. Spray hissed as she forged over the surface of endless deeps, leaving behind a silvery wake, like the track of a giant snail.

Bladetail the steersrat wiped seawater from his eyes. He leant hard on the long wooden tiller to keep the vessel on course, east, always east, to where the sun rose each dawn. Romsca the ferret stood at the helm, eyes on the horizon. She had been Conva's first mate; the Emperor Ublaz had promoted her to captain for this voyage. Romsca was as tough and fierce as any sea vermin; but she was under no illusions. She knew that she was dispensable. If Lask Frildur brought back the Tears of all Oceans, Ublaz would not bother what price had been paid to obtain them.

Romsca joined Bladetail at the tiller; glancing through the scupper slits, she watched the rate at which the waves passed by. 'Well under way an' makin' good time, mate, like as if we're in an 'urry t'rush to our deaths, eh?'

The steersrat glanced nervously around. 'Stow that gab, there might be Monitors cockin' a lug t'yer.'

Romsca smiled thinly as she shook her head, saying, 'Not today, messmate. I may be feared o' those lizards, an' that Lask Frildur, every time he looks at me my blood runs cold. But I ain't daft, we can gab away up 'ere an' they won't be bothered t'lissen in on us. Know why?'

Bladetail put a harness on the tiller to stop it wandering. 'No, why?' he said.

Romsca tapped the side of her muzzle and winked. 'Well, there's two reasons, see. I figgers it out fer meself when we first took those lizards aboard. One, they're lubbers, they been ashore all their lives an' this is their first voyage. Two, lizards like them are born in tropical parts, so it stands ter reason, they can't abide the cold. Now me'n'you an' all the crew, why, we love the feel of a rollin' deck 'neath our paws, an' as fer weather, we've been through it all, foul'n'fair as well as 'ot'n'cold!'

Bladetail looked at her blankly. 'I don't see 'ow that 'elps us.'

The ferret explained. 'Good job y'got me t'look after yer. I put the Monitors in the best cabins, up for'ard, hahaha, where they gets the real buck an' pitch of the ship, up an' down, up an' down, night'n'day. If you wants ter see a sick green lizard, take a look in the for'ard accommodation. Lask Frildur an' his gang are all laid out there, moanin' an' groanin' like they wanna die.

'Now, as we sail further east the weather gets colder, it ain't tropical no more. Ole Mad Eyes never thought o' that, but I did. So, mate, we won't 'ave no lizards bossin' us about on this trip. No sir, lizards like them can't stand the cold, take my word fer it!'

Bladetail thought for a moment, then the logic of Romsca's words hit him, and the steersrat started to guffaw aloud.

'Ahawhawhaw! Yer a canny one, Cap'n, hawhaw!'

Romsca kicked his footpaw suddenly, muttering low, 'Stow that cackle, 'ere comes ole Lask 'isself!'

The Monitor General's skin, which was normally grey-blue, had a definite tinge of unhealthy green to it. Hauling himself painfully over the for'ard cabin coamings, he staggered, shivering and holding tight to the deckrails.

The big Monitor's dull muddy eyes stared accusingly at Romsca. 'It'z not good on waterz,' he said. 'Me and my Monitorz much ill. How far to Mozzflower, tell me!'

Romsca paced the heaving deck nonchalantly, gazing up at the sky and testing the wind with a dampened paw. 'Oh, I'd say quite a stretch o' time yet, though if'n we lose this fair wind or run into proper rough seas, then who c'd say?'

'Proper rough zeaz!' Lask Frildur's eyes glazed over, and his jaw sagged visibly. 'You mean it can get rougher than thiz?'

Bladetail was enjoying himself. 'Bless yer scales, Gen'ral, you ain't seen rough water yet,' he said jovially. 'Why, the sea's as still as a millpond today, ain't that right, mate?'

Romsca agreed wholeheartedly. 'Aye, 'tis so, but don't you worry, sir. The Emperor said to deliver you an' yore Monitors to Mossflower shores, an' I gave 'im me solemn oath that I would. The seas'll get big as mountains an' there'll be blizzards with ice thick on the riggin's, but don't you fret yer scaly 'ead, we'll get yer there one way or t'other. You take a seabeast's advice now, sir, go an' lay down in yer cabin. Let these gentle waves rock yer t'sleep. I'll send Rubby the cook along later with yore dinner, some nice fish guts boiled in ole tallowfat . . .'

'Bloooaaargh!'

Lask Frildur clapped both paws to his mouth and staggered off miserably to his cabin, bowed and shivering.

Romsca and Bladetail leaned against the tiller, cackling helplessly.

'Wohawhawhaw! Fish guts boiled in tallowfat, that's a good 'un!'

'Haharrharrharr! Follered by a cold pan o' greasy skilly, that should bring the roses back to 'is scaly ole cheeks. Haharr!'

8

Bright spring dawn, with no traces of the night's gale, was scarce an hour old over Redwall when little Arven flung himself on Tansy's bed in the sick bay and began buffeting her with a pillow.

'Wakey up, Tanzee, sleepyspike, dozypaws!'

With a bound the young hedgehog maid was out of bed and attacking back with her pillow. 'Dozypaws, eh, you little maggot! Take that, an' that!'

The pillowcase caught on a bedpost and ripped; downy feathers flew about like snowflakes in a breeze. They both fell back on the bed giggling helplessly amid the whirling cascade.

'So, this is how villains behave in my sick bay!' said Sister Cicely, standing in the open doorway, paws akimbo. 'I was going to bring you both breakfast in bed. Silly me, to think that you were still sick and exhausted and needed rest.'

Tansy was about to speak when a feather tickled her nose and she sneezed. 'Ah, a, a, choooo!'

Arven smiled innocently at the indignant mouse Sister. 'I fink Tanzee gotta cold.'

The good Sister's paw was wagging furiously at the miscreants. 'That's enough of your impudence, Dibbun.

No breakfast for either of you until this mess is cleared up! Arven, get a broom and sweep up those feathers. Tansy, get needle and thread, repair that pillow and stuff those feathers back into it, this instant!'

Cicely stood over them as they went to work, still scolding. 'When you've done that I want to see those beds made, properly! Oh yes, and while you're up here you can shake out the rush mats at the window and dust the shelves and cupboard tops!'

She stormed out, slamming the door. Immediately Arven placed his paws on his sides and began imitating Sister Cicely. 'Tanzee panzee brush uppa floor, worra mess I never see'd in my life! Dearie grayshuss, likkle villains!'

Tansy shook with laughter and sneezed until tears were running down her cheeks. Then a knock sounded upon the door.

'Can't come in 'less you a villain or a maggit!' Arven called cheerfully.

Teasel the hogwife popped her head around the door-jamb. 'Great seasons, m'dears, what's bin goin' on up 'ere?'

Tansy stopped sneezing and regained control of herself. 'Oh, nothing really, missus Stump, it was an accident, but Sister Cicely said we've got to clean the whole sick bay before we're allowed any breakfast. Come on, Arven, get sweeping.'

Teasel chuckled as she watched the youngsters floundering about amidst the feathers. 'You'll be 'ere this time tomorrer at that rate, young 'uns. Get you down to brekkist, I'll clean up 'ere. 'Twon't take long.'

Arven and Tansy hugged the kindly hogwife gingerly, careful of her spikes. Teasel patted their heads, saying, 'Go on with you, be off afore I changes me mind!'

The pair fled downstairs, yelling their thanks.

Tansy and Arven joined the serving line at the kitchen doorway. Clecky, who was before them, turned to Gerul and remarked, 'D'you see what I mean, strange creatures in this place, wot? Look here behind me, a little hedgehog bird, jolly odd, eh?'

Tansy, picking feathers out of her headspikes, said, 'I'm a hedgehog, sir, my name's Tansy, and he's Arven, my friend.'

The brown and white mottled hare made an elegant leg and bowed. 'Pleased t'meet you, I'm sure. My name's Clecky and this chap is known as Gerul.'

Tansy nodded. 'I know.'

Clecky wrinkled his nose inquisitively at her. 'Oh? An' how pray did you know, missie?'

Tansy was taken by surprise. 'Er, er, I think somebeast told me . . .' Thinking quickly, she took Clecky's mind off the enquiry by saying, 'You're next, sir, you'd better jump to it if you want breakfast!'

The mention of food distracted the hare, who began jostling Gerul. 'Not so fast, y'feathered frump, it's my turn t'get bally well served, don't fret y'beak, there'll be plenty left for you!'

The owl lost out; he was forced to step aside as his companion loaded up an oversized platter. 'Plenty left fer me, d'you say? Ah, I'm not so sure with you helpin' yerself to all an' sundry, sir.' He turned and winked at Arven. 'Sure he's a turrible creature at eatin' that one is, 'tis a fact.'

Tansy steered Arven to a back bench, well out of the way of Sister Cicely. They sat between the molemaid Diggum and Viola bankvole. Tansy kept her head down, applying herself hungrily to hot oatcakes, honey and a beaker of greensap milk.

Viola sipped mint tea, not looking at Tansy but pointedly remarking aloud to others within hearing range, 'I've heard that certain creatures won't be allowed to take Dibbuns out into Mossflower Wood again, 'cos they get into trouble and come back home very, very late, and filthy too, smocks torn, dirty paws'n'faces. Anyhow, that's what I've heard!'

Diggum looked up from a bowl of barleymeal. 'Hoo urr, who'm tol' ee that, missie Voler?'

Viola pursed her lips prissily. 'That's for me to know and you t'find out, so there!'

Arven gave a wink to Diggum; the mole twitched her nose knowingly in return and pointed across to another table further up. 'Wurr et thatbeast oo tol' ee, that 'un thurr?'

Viola turned to look, craning her neck. 'Where?'

As she turned away, Arven slid Diggum's bowl of warm barleymeal porridge to one side, pointing and saying, 'There, tha' likklemouse, can't y'see 'im?'

Viola slid off the bench and stood on tip-paw. 'Where, which creature do you mean, silly?'

Arven quietly placed the porridge bowl in the spot where Viola had been sitting, and said, 'Too late, 'e finished an' gone now.'

Viola heaved a sigh of exasperation and sat down with a flounce.

Splodge!

Martin, who was sitting at the top table with the elders and Redwall's two latest guests, heard the wail set up by Viola bankvole.

'What's going on over there?' he said, starting to rise from his seat.

Auma pressed him back down with a firm paw. 'Only Dibbuns and young 'uns fooling about, I'll attend to it.'

Rollo peered over the top of his glasses. 'It's Viola, I might have known, if she sits next to Tansy there's bound t'be trouble,' he said.

The hedgehog maid's name stirred Clecky's memory, and he leaned across to Martin. 'A word in your shell-like ear, old chap,' he said. 'I was just thinkin', I introduced meself an' Gerul to that pretty hogmaid this mornin' in the breakfast line. Funny thing, when I told her our names she said she already knew them. Well, I jolly well asked her how, an' she muttered summat about already bein' told by some bod or other. Point is, all your young 'uns were abed by the time we reached the Abbey. How could she have known my name if she was fast asleep?'

Martin stroked his chin pensively as the answer became clear. 'Hmmm, our little eavesdropper on the stairs last night.'

Gerul gazed owlishly at a half-demolished cheese flan on his plate. 'Hah! Yer right, sir, indeed y'are. Like me ould mother used t'say, a hog on the stairs is worth two hares in a hamper, an' that's a fact, so 'tis!'

Martin smiled at the irrepressible owl. 'Your mother must have been a very wise bird, Gerul. Hush now, here's Auma bringing the culprits for sentence.'

The badger Mother led Viola and Tansy up to the main table, halting them both in front of Abbot Durral. 'Stand up straight now, both of you, don't slouch,' she said sternly. 'Tell the Father Abbot what you've been up to, the truth mind!'

Viola's voice was a tearful whimper. 'She made me sit in a bowl of porridge, Father Abbot!'

Tansy's voice was indignant. 'No I never! Even though you were teasing me!'

Hiding a smile, Abbot Durral stroked his whiskers slowly. 'Fighting among yourselves, little maids, this is very serious! What d'you say, Martin?'

The Warriormouse kept his face straight. 'Make them promise never to do it again. Kiss and make up, I say.'

Tansy was just about to protest again when she happened to glance at the table where Arven was shifting from paw to paw looking decidedly uncomfortable.

'Well, all right,' she said stiffly, giving Viola a swift peck, 'I'm sorry I made you sit in the porridge. I'll never do it again. Sorry!'

Auma shook a huge paw at Tansy. 'Wipe that smile off your face, miss. Viola, apologize to Tansy.'

The bankvole kept her lips pursed tight as they brushed her enemy's face. 'Sorry for teasing you, never do it again!'

'There!' said Martin, sitting back, satisfied that justice had been done.

Auma gave him a look that would have curdled milk. 'Is that all?' she demanded.

Glancing meaningfully at Martin, Rollo the Recorder interrupted. 'We can't have young maids arguing and teasing and sitting in good porridge. I think they should be taught a lesson.'

Then Arven and Diggum wandered up sheepishly paw in paw. They had decided to own up to their part in the trouble.

'Zurr h'Abbot, et wurr moi porridge as she sitted in.'

'An' I'm a maggit, I maked 'er look away so she din't see.'

Abbot Durral made a swift decision. 'Right, I sentence you both to play in the orchard all day; and for arguing, Viola can clean the gatehouse from top to bottom and Tansy can sweep the dormitory stairs.'

After breakfast Martin took a stroll in the Abbey grounds with Rollo, Clecky and Gerul. A high sun was warm on their backs as they enjoyed the fine spring morn.

Martin threw a paw across the old Recorder's shoulders. 'I've been thinking. Tansy is alone near the dormitories. If she *was* the listener on the stairs, I'll wager she goes up to Fermald's attic.'

The mountain hare winked at Martin. 'Well, what d'ye think, Warrior, time we sneaked upstairs to see what young miss Tansy's about, eh?'

He strode off jauntily in the direction of the Abbey. As they followed, Rollo commented to Martin, 'It's good to have a hare in our Abbey again. There's not been one since old Basil in the time of your father, remember him?'

Martin smiled at some half-forgotten recollection. 'Aye, just about. I recall my father telling me that despite how they look, hares are dangerous and perilous beasts. Let's hope Clecky lives up to the reputation if trouble ever visits us.'

9

The spiral stone staircases, from Cavern Hole and Great
Hall, up to the Abbey dormitories, needed only the
lightest skim with a broom; they were passably clean
before Tansy began her chore. It was the stairs above,
from dormitory to attics, which intrigued the young
hedgehog maid. She swept her broom along the bedroom
corridor, glancing nervously to where the upper stairs
were situated at the end of the passage. Curving up
into the darkness, they looked very forbidding and
gloomy. Tansy brushed the first three steps, conscious
of the echoing swish her straw broomhead made in the
eerie silence. Finally curiosity overcame her fear and,
abandoning her work, she gripped the broomhandle like
a quarterstave and trod silently, keeping to the broad
edge of the spiralling wedges of stone, upward into the
dim dusty attics.

Peering down a passage, Tansy saw a pale shaft of
light, and crept forward to investigate. She came to a
long, low-ceilinged room, with light filtering through
a high cobwebbed window of chunked crystal. Picking
her way through the jumble of musty furniture, Tansy
knew she had found the dwelling of Fermald the Ancient.
Locating lamp, flint and tinder, the hogmaid soon had

better illumination for her exploration. It was a sad and lonely place, furnished by the old squirrel with forgotten odds and ends she had found in this and other attic chambers. Dust rose in a small cloud as Tansy plumped down into a battered armchair.

'Found anything interesting, missie?'

Unable to stifle a shriek, the hedgehog maid leapt up.

Martin and Rollo strode into the attic, followed by Clecky and Gerul. Tansy began stammering and sweeping, avoiding the eyes of the Warrior and the Recorder as she tried to make up excuses. 'I was . . . er, I just . . . atting the brushic . . . er, I mean brushing the attic . . . !'

Rollo held a sleeve across his nose and mouth, saying, 'Will you stop stirring the dust, missie! Put that broom down!'

Martin sat in the armchair, bringing his eyes level with Tansy's. 'Why were you sneaking about on the stairs last night, listening in on our conversation?'

The hogmaid fumbled with the corner of her apron. 'I wasn't sneaking, sir. I woke up in the sick bay, it was dark and I was hungry. Then I remembered, as you were taking me and Arven back home through the woodlands, you said something about a feast. So I came downstairs; it was very quiet and I heard voices. I peeped around the stairs and saw the feast was over. I couldn't help hearing what you were talking about and I didn't want to disturb you, but then I trod on a plate that some Dibbun had left on the stairs and it broke and clattered down. So I dashed straight back up to bed . . .'

Rollo perched on the chair arm. 'But you obviously heard all that we said, about Graylunk and Fermald and the time they spent together up here.'

Tansy stared miserably at the dusty floor. 'Yes sir, I couldn't help but hear, it sounded so interesting and exciting, that poem the Abbot recited and all. I wanted to come up here and look for clues. I was only trying to help.'

Martin felt sympathetic to the little maid. He patted her paw and said, 'Yes, I'm sure you did, Tansy, but there's not much up here to see, is there? A few old sticks of furniture and lots of dust, and you shouldn't be up here really, should you? It was your job to sweep the dormitory stairs. Obedience is one of the first things young 'uns learn at Redwall.'

A light of indignation arose in Tansy's eyes. 'But I did sweep the dormitory stairs, both flights. You must have noticed that when you came sneaking up here after me. Sir!'

Clecky burst out laughing at the hogmaid's pert reply. 'Hahaharr! She's got y'there, Martin, those stairs looked clean enough t'me, wot! By the left, marm, you're a snippy little 'un an' no mistake!'

Rollo was smiling too. 'She's right, Martin, we did come sneaking up here after her; and give Tansy her due, the stairs are well brushed. Righto, missie, your chores are done for the day. Away with you now and play out in the sunlight. Dirty old attics are no place for a pretty one like you on a bright spring day.'

Martin took Tansy by the paw, as she seemed reluctant to leave the attic. 'Come on, Tansy pansy, I've got another job for you. If I recall rightly this is Abbot Durral's seventh season as Father Abbot of Redwall. Here's a good idea: supposing you and our two guests here went to the kitchens and baked him a surprise cake!'

Clecky rubbed his paws with delight. 'I say, what a spiffin' wheeze! I bet ole Abbot Thingummy'd be highly jollificated to get a surprise cake, what d'you think, Gerul?'

The owl blinked furiously. 'Aye, that he would, sir. Me ould mother always said, there's nothin' like a surprise when yer not expectin' it, 'tis surprisin' how it can surprise yer!'

Clecky led the way downstairs enthusiastically. 'Oh,

tickety boo! I've never made a cake before, you'll have t'show me an' Gerul how it's done, young hog m'gel!'

Tansy found herself as excited by the prospect as her companions. 'Well, the first thing you need is spotless clean paws, then we'll ask Friar Higgle to give us an oven to ourselves an' a big table. We'll need fruit an' nuts, cream too, lots of it, oh, honey as well, an' a beaker of October Ale to go in the mix – Father Abbot likes good dark cake, nice an' moist . . .'

Martin winked at Rollo as the happy voices receded downstairs. 'Sounds like fun, shall we go down and watch?'

The Recorder slid from the chair arm into the seat vacated by his friend. 'No, you go, Martin. I want to stay up here a bit and have a think and a glance around.'

When the attic was quiet, Rollo sat alone in the armchair. He sighed and leaned back, then, closing his eyes, he let his paws stray down the sides of the seat cushion.

Tansy stood on a stool, checking the ingredients spread around the tabletop next to the oven.

'Hmm, I think that's everything. Gerul, would you tip the flour into the bowl, please? Mister Clecky sir, stop that!'

'Yowch! I say, that jolly well hurt!'

Tansy brandished the wooden mixing spoon under the hare's nose. 'Then stop pinching the hazelnuts! They're supposed to go in the cake mix, not into your fat tummy! That's enough flour, Gerul; now you add the greensap milk slowly and Clecky can stir. I'll dribble the honey in bit by bit like this. Oh, and just let me catch you trying to lick that spoon, Clecky flopears!'

The hare stirred vigorously, muttering rebelliously to himself. 'Humph! Lick the spoon indeed, bossy little spikebonce, what's the point of makin' a cake if a chap can't lick the bally old spoon once in a while, prickly little slavedriver!'

Hazelnuts, chestnuts, almonds and beechnuts were added to the mix under Tansy's watchful eye, though she missed Gerul taking a quick swig of October Ale because she was busy checking on the hare pouring in a small noggin of dark elderberry wine. Friar Higgle chuckled as he watched Tansy's efforts to supervise the gluttonous pair whilst concentrating on her mixture.

'Tch, tch, Gerul, take those dried apple rings off that talon!'

'Mmm, I say, these little purply things are just the job!'

'You villain! Stay away from my dried plums. Mind out, let me get this crystallized fruit in the bowl before you two get your thieving paws into it!'

The cake mix was finally emptied into a circular oven dish that had been lined with thin maple bark soaked in vegetable oil to prevent the cake sticking. Tansy allowed the hare and owl to place it in the oven whilst she got the covering ready.

Clecky's ears stood up and his nose twitched. 'What ho, m'gel, is that cream an' marchpane I see, wot?'

Narrowing her eyes fiercely, Tansy shook the ladle at them both. 'Yes it is. Keep your distance – go and get more charcoal for the oven fires – do something useful!'

Clecky sniffed indignantly. 'Tchah! Have a care, marm, we're chefs, not stokers. Here you, small molechap, more fuel for the oven fires, smartly now!'

The young mole whom Clecky addressed was quite taken aback. He saluted the hare and dashed off to get charcoal.

Gerul clacked his beak admiringly, remarking to Friar Higgle, 'Isn't he the good one at the givin' of orders, sir? Why, if I wasn't so disobedient to him I'd obey him meself so I would!'

Higgle stepped in and came to Tansy's rescue. 'You carry on mixin' the cream, missie; I'll set these two to rollin' out marchpane.'

The good Friar instructed them both in the use of the doughy golden mixture. 'This 'ere's marchpane, see. 'Tis made from ground almonds, stiff comb honey an' sweetchestnut flour. Mister Clecky, you take this roller an' roll it out flat, so's it'll go over the cake afore Tansy tops it off with meadowcream. Now, Gerul sir, I wants you t'make seven lovely round balls with this lump o' marchpane. They'll go atop of the cake for Father Abbot's seven seasons. Look busy now, sirs, an' mind, no nibblin'. Martin, will you stand by with yore great sword an' keep an eye on 'em?'

The Warriormouse chuckled. 'Oh, I won't need my sword, Higgle, this copper ladle should do!'

10

Rollo knew from experience how many times he had lost things only to find them again down the sides of his armchair in the gatehouse. He smiled, producing a parchment scroll from a gap between cushion and chair. Fermald the Ancient had not been very different from him when she lived. Balancing his lantern on the chair arm and donning his spectacles, the old Recorder carefully unfastened the ribbon from the parchment and unrolled it. The writing was thin and spidery, but quite legible.

Unusual it is to call a vermin friend, but this weasel Graylunk, a poor lonely creature whose mind was sore troubled by his past, I call him friend. But why? Have not the vermin, more so those who come from the seas, always been the foebeast? I call Graylunk friend because he called me friend. Creatures below stairs did not understand him, they grew weary of his constant weeping. But I knew by the deep wound in his head that he could not help behaving in the way that he did. Ah, cruel wound! to cut short the seasons of one still young.

Death is no stranger to me, I could see its mark upon

Graylunk and I did all in my power to make his last days comfortable. He told me of many things; together we sat in this dusty attic, I listened to his words and in my mind I was transported, far over the seas to where there is no winter. In my imagination I saw the surf booming against the warm coast of Sampetra and learned of the Emperor Mad Eyes. My friend had led a wicked life, but in his final days he repented of all evil. Though I tried to set his mind at ease, he was troubled, frightened of the vengeance which would stretch across the ocean to claim him. Graylunk told me a secret and begged me to speak of it to no living creature.

One morning I awoke and he was gone, fled from this Abbey to die alone someplace, where he would not bring evil upon me, his friend. One day, if I still live, I will stand before those who follow him from afar and I will do as my friend told me, I will deny that ever I knew of him, I will say Graylunk was never within the walls of this Abbey. In this way I will try to keep Redwall safe, for it is my home.

As for the secret my friend imparted to me, I will keep my promise and never speak of it to any living creature. I will not speak, but I will write, lest the Tears of all Oceans remain for ever lost. Someday they may be needed for a great purpose. Graylunk left the Tears with me, a final gift to his only friend. When I am gone the only one to possess them will be the creature with the wit and wisdom to find them. The Tears would only bring grief and death to a beast with little sense. I have spoken in my dreams to the spirit who long ago founded Redwall, Martin the Warrior of old, and I know what I do now is right.

To the goodbeast whose name I do not know, nor never shall, I say this. Seek and find the Tears of all Oceans, be not blinded by their beauty, use them wisely.

Look not up, nor to the four main points,
But where our paws do tread, the dead oak
   joints.
There wrought by mother nature 'neath the main,
Lies that which holds the beauty, or the bane.

Rollo folded the parchment carefully, concealing it within his wide habit sleeve. Then he took the lantern and made his way downstairs. The old Recorder's mind boiled with Fermald's testament, unanswered questions, and the baffling rhyme. He joined Martin in the kitchens where, in low tones, a brief conversation was held.

'Martin, I found a strange parchment, written by the Ancient.'

'I knew you'd find something, Rollo, that's why I left you up there on your own. Where was this parchment hidden?'

'Down the side cushions of Fermald's armchair, though I don't think the rest of this mystery is going to be so easily solved.'

'Hmm, only what we'd expect, I suppose. Fermald was a quaint and devious creature. We must investigate it fully, but later, not now. Take a look at the antics of our cake-making crew; they've had these kitchens in uproar since they started.'

All Redwall kitchen work had ceased; Friar Higgle and Teasel with the rest of their workers watched with much merriment as Tansy supervised her unruly helpers. The cake had baked perfectly, and now stood cooling on a stone ledge. Tansy had beaten the meadowcream until it was right for spreading.

Gerul helped her to lift the cake down onto the table, saying, 'Great seasons, missie, sure an' I never smelt anythin' as wonderful as this cake in all me life! 'Tis a tribute to ye!'

The hedgehog maid smilingly thanked the owl for his compliment, rounding on Clecky in the same breath.

71

'Why, thank you, Gerul. Mister Clecky! Put a paw near that bowl of cream and I'll chop it off!'

The rascally hare bowed low, the picture of nobility and injured innocence. 'For shame, marm, how could you accuse me of such foul deeds? Why, I'd chop me own paw off before I'd use it to steal cream!'

Swiftly Tansy turned on Gerul, judging by the laughter behind her back that something was going on. 'Gerul, take those talons out of that marchpane this instant!'

'Who, me, marm? I was only makin' pretty liddle patterns on it!'

Taking advantage of Tansy's back, Clecky scooped a glob of meadowcream with the tip of his ear, bending it skilfully into his mouth. The assembled Redwallers fell about laughing, but Tansy was not amused.

'I told you I'd chop those paws off if you put them near my cream,' she snapped.

Clecky appealed to the onlookers. 'I say, what a vile accusation! Did anybeast see me put a paw near that bally cream bowl? No! So, miss fussyapron, what proof have you that I've been anywhere near your blinkin' cream, eh?'

Tansy pursued him round the table with a ladle. 'What proof? It's all over your whiskers, you fuzzy-faced fraud!'

Friar Higgle stepped in and restored order, then he helped them to drape the marchpane over their cake and trim it neatly. Teasel took a flat palette knife and spread the meadowcream expertly over the marchpane, then she wrapped the seven balls of marchpane in pink rose petals preserved in honey. There were gasps of admiration from the kitchen helpers at the finished confection. The cake was an absolute beauty, standing on a large tray surrounded by pale flaked almonds, candied angelica leaves and preserved damsons. Teasel had whirled the meadowcream artfully in waving patterns around the cake, leaving it flat and smooth on top. Everybeast watched breathlessly whilst Tansy gingerly placed the seven pink petal-wrapped marchpane balls around the top of Abbot Durral's cake.

'There, one for each of Father Abbot's seven seasons,' she said. 'Now, let's hide it over in the gatehouse until this evening.'

Carrying the tray between them, Tansy and Higgle walked carefully out of the kitchens towards the Abbey door. Clecky and Gerul hovered about them, shouting needless orders.

'Steady there, chaps, hold your side level, missie!'

'Hey, you there, keep out of the way. Somebeast open the door!'

When they were outside on the Abbey lawns, Tansy finally lost her temper with Clecky and Gerul's harassments.

'Look, go away, begone, the pair of you. We'll be bound to drop this cake if you keep hovering round and getting in the way!'

As they turned to go, Friar Higgle noticed the hare was eating something. His suspicions were confirmed as he took a swift count of the rose-petal-covered marchpane balls.

'I knew it, there's only six here! That rogue has stolen one an' scoffed it!' the Friar announced.

Tansy nearly dropped her end of the tray as she wailed aloud, 'Oh, the beastly glutton, my surprise cake is ruined!'

'Well, at least we've got rid of those two now,' the good Friar comforted her. 'Don't worry, missie, there's enough marchpane an' petals left to make another. I'll do it as soon as we get back to the kitchens, don't fret.'

Martin and Teasel remonstrated with the hare as he loped chuckling into the Abbey followed by Gerul.

'We saw you from the doorway, Clecky, that was a pretty swift trick!'

The hare swallowed the remains of his plunder guiltily. 'Who, me? There's nothing in my mouth, take a look, old chap.'

'Yore a villain an' a glutton, mister Clecky, an' I don't know which is the worse o' the two!' So saying, Teasel shook a pudding spoon angrily under the hare's nose, but before she could say more there was a shrill screaming, squawking and shouting from down by the gatehouse.

Martin leapt into action. 'What'n the name of fur's going on out there?' he shouted, and dashed out, followed by Clecky and Gerul.

Tansy and Friar Higgle were only a short distance from the gatehouse when the attack took place. Four big black-backed gulls dropped out of the sky onto them, knocking the cake to the grass. Two gulls flew at Higgle and Tansy, beating with wings, webbed talons and huge beaks, while the other two pounced on the cake and began snatching the rose-coloured orbs from it, their harsh cries of triumph ringing out.

'Kaareeeaaah! Kreeeghaaa!'

Suddenly Gerul was amongst them like a thunderbolt. At the sight of the hulking young barn owl the two gulls immediately left off despoiling the Abbot's cake and took wing. Gerul hurled himself upon the gull that had Tansy upon the ground, and locked talon and beak with the invader as it tried to fly off. Martin came speeding to the rescue of Higgle, closely followed by Clecky. Grabbing the elmboard cake tray the Warriormouse broke it in half over the gull's back; Clecky swiftly gathered Tansy and Higgle to him and threw them down, shielding them with his body. Martin managed to get one more crack at his gull with half the cake tray before it hopped off and flopped awkwardly into the air.

The bird Gerul had taken on was not so lucky; the owl's powerful talons and savage hooked beak did their work with blurring speed, and the gull lay slain by the gatehouse door.

Redwallers poured out of the Abbey and across the lawns. Headed by Auma the badger Mother and Abbot

74

Durral, a crowd arrived at the scene in front of the gatehouse. Everybeast was shouting at once.

'Oh woe, what's happened here?'

'Was it eagles or hawks, did anybeast see?'

'Go 'way, silly, can't y' see that's a dead seagull!'

'Hurr, seagully burd, ee'm a gurt big 'un, boi ecky ee is!'

Between them, Auma, the Abbot and Foremole restored order.

'Stand back there, please, keep those Dibbuns away from that bird!'

'Yurr, coom out o' ee way. Froir 'iggle, missie, be you'm 'urted?'

Auma inspected Friar and hogmaid. 'Yes, they're both a bit battered and scratched one way or another. Dormal, Wullger, you others, carry them both up to Sister Cicely in the sick bay. Martin, what is that creature?'

The Warriormouse was inspecting the bird's body. He shook his head and scanned the sky. 'It's a gull, but I've never seen any this big come as far inland as Redwall. There were four of them altogether – no sign of the other three now, they got out of here fast. Friend Gerul put paid to this one, he's a fearsome fighter all right!'

The owl blinked several times. 'Ah well, d'ye see, sir, as me ould mother used t'say, there's not a bit of use shakin' claws with the other feller. If yer goin' t'fight then best get it done with proper so's yer foe don't come back fer more.'

Clecky was eyeing the cake on the grass, inching towards it. 'Well said, old pillowfeatures, your ma must've been quite a bird in her time, wot!'

Teasel nudged Clecky hard in his midriff. 'Aye, an' you'll find me a bit of a pawful if y' don't keep away from yon cake, sir. There ain't too much damage done; I can dust it down an' fix it up good as new. Though we'll need a new tray, Martin.'

Echoing around the woodlands into an unusually warm

spring evening, the Abbey bells tolled supper. Red-wallers gathered in Cavern Hole, which was smaller and less stately than Great Hall. The meal was a serve-yourself affair: cress and watershrimp soup, celery and leek turnovers, strong old chestnut cheese, barleybread, greengage flan, latticed redcurrant tart and October Ale or maple cordial to drink. The Abbey creatures sat in wall niches, sprawled on rush mats, or just set down wherever they pleased to chat and eat.

Abbot Durral sat with Martin and the elders on a dry, fern-strewn rock ledge which ran along one wall. When the Father Abbot stood up to speak there was complete silence; everybeast was curious as to what he was going to say.

'Friends, there is little use my reporting to you what happened today, as you already know. Why four gulls should attack two perfectly harmless creatures is a mystery, both to me and to your elders. However, our good friend from Mossflower, the Skipper of Otters, has volunteered to set up a patrol around the top of the outer wall. His otters will be armed with slings and stones, in the event of another unwarranted attack.

'But for the next few days I would ask you to stay indoors as much as possible; make sure that if you do go out of doors it is for a necessary chore and not just to stroll or play. Oh, and keep a keen eye on our Dibbuns – little ones do not know the danger, and it is our duty to protect them. One last thing: thanks to our friends Clecky and Gerul for their quick and brave action today, helping Martin out.'

A round of applause was called for. Gerul modestly buried his beak in a wedge of old chestnut cheese, but Clecky bowed and strutted in an outrageous manner, acknowledging the plaudits.

'Forward the whites, wot, wot! Only doin' me duty, savin' hogmaids, slayin' seagulls an' whatnot, all in a day's work, chaps!'

Rollo, who was sitting next to Martin, turned his eyes upward at the hare's shameless display. 'By the fur an' cringe, Martin, I can't take much more of that doodle-eared windbag. Let's get out of here. I know, we'll take a tray of supper up to Tansy and Friar Higgle, and see how they are.'

'Right,' the Warriormouse agreed, 'but don't mention trays to me. The one I smashed over that seagull was Hogwife Teasel's best tray – she's not going to let me forget that for a while!'

Friar Higgle and Tansy were pretending to be asleep, but Sister Cicely still prattled on as she set a bowl apiece beside their beds.

'Warm nettle broth, best thing in the world for shock and minor injuries. I'm going down to supper now. Make sure you finish it up, every drop; I'll be checking those bowls later.'

Rollo and Martin entered, bearing the tray of food. Cicely pursed her lips severely at them. 'Hush now, you two,' she said, dropping her voice to a whisper, 'my patients are asleep. Er, I hope that food isn't for them, they're restricted to a diet of my nettle broth.'

Martin smiled winningly at her, and whispered, 'This food? Great seasons no, Sister, this is *our* supper. Rollo and I thought we'd just nip up here and sit awhile with Tansy and Higgle. If they wake we'll see that they take all their broth.'

Sister Cicely smiled back and curtsied. 'Thank you, Martin, I know they'll be safe in your sensible paws.'

She slid silently out, closing the door softly after herself.

Higgle sat bolt upright, paws clenched and teeth grinding. 'Grr, that ole Siss Cicely, I'd as like chuck meself in the Abbey pond wi' a boulder tied to me footpaw as lay up 'ere another day! Open that window, Rollo, 'ere, sling this filthy nettle broth out afore it makes me any sicker!'

Tansy sat up and clapped her paws with joy. 'Look,

77

Friar, real food! Turnover an' cheese, redcurrant tart an' maple cordial! Thanks, pals, you've saved our lives!'

Martin could not help smiling at the irrepressible little hogmaid as she tucked into the supper. 'So, how are you feeling now, Tansy?' he asked.

The answer came from around a mouthful of celery and leek turnover. 'Hah! Fit as a firefly an' brisk as a bumblebee, sir. Heeheehee! I heard that Viola bankvole saw what happened as she was cleaning the inside of the gatehouse windows. Wullger said she went down in a swoon an' had to be revived by sniffing burnin' feathers, hahaha! I hope the smell made her dreadful sick!'

Friar Higgle munched thoughtfully on a wedge of cheese. 'Silly really, isn't it, why should four great birds attack us?'

Rollo shrugged, saying, 'From what I heard only two attacked you, the other two were after Abbot Durral's cake. Going for you and Tansy like that was merely a diversion, so they could steal the cake.'

Martin waited until the hogmaid had taken a drink of cordial, then asked, 'Hmm, what do you think, Tansy?'

The young hedgehog looked serious. 'It sounds strange, I know, but they didn't really seem interested in the cake, or even us. The only other thing was the marchpane balls, but why?'

'Another mystery!' said Martin, turning to Rollo who was deep in thought.

Rollo shook his head worriedly. 'Mysteries and riddles,' he sighed. Then he jumped, startled. 'Riddles! Goodness me, in all the excitement I'd quite forgotten!' From his sleeve he drew forth Fermald's parchment, saying, 'Listen to this . . .'

The Recorder of Redwall sat reading Fermald's note aloud in the sick bay whilst Friar Higgle Stump carried on eating his supper. Tansy had forgotten all about food. She and Martin hung on every word that was read out to them.

11

Corsairs and searats roaming the hills of Sampetra did not bother Ublaz unduly – they would be taken care of when he had dealt with their ringleaders, the captains. Slouching on his throne, sipping wine and nibbling on a roasted bird's wing, the Emperor turned over events in his mind. Barranca was the one who had started all this, accordingly he was the one Ublaz intended to make an example of. The other captains were not so important. If Sagitar did not slay them, then he, the Emperor, would sooner or later. However, next time he would promote Trident-rats to be captains: good, loyal, Emperor-fearing Trident-rats. As for the vermin horde who had taken to the hills, well, they would soon jump back into line when they witnessed the punishment he intended meting out to Barranca. It was an old cure for rebellion – cut off the snake's head and the rest ceased wriggling. The snake!

Ublaz tossed aside the meat and strode briskly from his throne room, towards the cellars carved in the rocks beneath the escarpment.

Two Monitors stood at attention in front of a heavily barred door in the cellars. Ublaz pointed with his silver dagger blade, ordering, 'Open it!'

The lizards obeyed with alacrity, throwing the door

79

wide. Pulling a torch from a wall bracket Ublaz swept inside, leaving the door ajar so the guards could watch him. The pine marten sighed aloud with pleasure as he went to a stone plinth and lovingly picked up the crown from it. Made to the Emperor's own design, the thick gold band fitted his head perfectly. Studded almost halfway round with purply red garnets, it was a crown fit for an Emperor. But with something missing. Six empty claw settings on the circlet's front lacked the six rose-coloured pearls to fill them. When he possessed the Tears of all Oceans his crown would be complete.

A damp rustling and a loud hiss caused the Monitor guards to shuffle fearfully away from the door. Fixing them with a glare of his strange eyes, Ublaz rasped, 'Stand still! Watch and witness the power of your Emperor!'

Mutely they obeyed, reptilian eyes unblinking as they viewed the eerie scene beyond the doorway.

The entire chamber flickered with gold light, reflecting from the pine marten's torch and highlighted by his shining crown. A long shallow trough built into the floor, filled with water, cast shifting patterns of golden lights around the walls. Gliding sinuously out of the trough and across the floor, the snake came hissing towards Ublaz. It was a dull ivory colour, but the water rippling on its scales caught the light, turning the serpent into a long moving stream of liquid gold.

Rearing up, the creature quivered and hissed menacingly as it faced the intruder. Few snakes in the world are more highly venomous and unpredictable than the coral water snake. As Ublaz concentrated all his powers upon the angry beaded eyes confronting him, the reptile arched, preparing to strike, mouth open wide, a crimson cavern with dark flickering tongue and poisonous fangs.

Ublaz began chanting in a high steady cadence.

'Golden guardian of my wealth,
Hear me now, be still,
Deathly fang and coiling stealth,
Bend unto my will.'

Over and over the Emperor repeated his dirgelike
chant, swaying from side to side in time with his
adversary. Wide and unblinking, the mad eyes of Ublaz
radiated all their power. He moved slowly forward as
he chanted and swayed, until the snake's damp breath
wreathed his nostrils. With his head a hairsbreadth from
the serpent's, he strove to pierce it with his strange hypnotic stare. Side to side the two heads moved, challenging
and seeking in unison with the cadence.

The snake began to subside, its mouth closed. The
stiffened head relaxed and sank slowly into its bunched
coils, both eyes filming over with a clouded membrane.
Ublaz moved with it, down to floor level, still staring
and chanting, until the venomous reptile lay still and
subdued, conquered by his power. He stroked its head
lightly then ceased chanting.

Ublaz stood upright, turned his back on the snake and
faced the awed Monitor sentries. 'Now you have seen the
power of your Emperor!' he hissed.

Then he swept past them and strode upstairs, knowing
that tales of the sight they had witnessed would spread and
grow in the telling. Ublaz knew that mightiness brought
dread, and total fear and respect were based upon a frightening reputation. Soon even the sea vermin ranging the hills
would realize that resistance was futile against his power.

Ice hung from the rigging of *Waveworm* as she nosed into
a thick fogbank. The crew had long oars to manipulate
port and starboard; they rowed wearily. Romsca strode
up and down the welldeck, swinging a knotted rope's
end at anybeast she saw slacking.

'Bend yer backs, ya barnacle-pawed swabs! Come on now, pull! It's row or die in this weather, an' this ferret ain't goin' t'die! Put some backbone into it, ya spineless seaslugs. Row!'

Rubby the cook was up in the bowsprit, on the lookout for rocks or the great lumps of ice that sometimes cruised the seas in the cold latitudes. Cupping his paw, he called back to Bladetail, 'Clear ahead, mate, steady as she goes!'

The steersrat wiped frosty rime from his lips as he answered, 'Aye aye, steady she is, dead ahead!'

Lask Frildur was wrapped in any available stitch of material he could lay claws on. The Monitor General sat dull-eyed and almost rigid in front of a miserable charcoal glow from a brazier in the for'ard cabin. As Romsca entered the foul-smelling accommodation, he winced, saying, 'Cloze that door, I'm freezing to death, it'z cold, cold!'

Romsca slammed the door and stood grinning at the lizard. 'What are you bellyachin' about now, scaleface? There ain't a wave out there t'day! It's smooth as a babe's fur!'

The Monitor's head shook spasmodically. He had to wait for his teeth to stop chattering so that he could talk. 'L-l-look, half of my Monitorz dead, frozen, iz no warmth, iz only d-d-death for uz unlezz zun shinez again!'

Romsca waved a paw on high. 'Oh, well, why didn't yer say, matey? I woulda tole the sun t'come out an' shine all day if yer'd mentioned it!'

The dark muddy eyes of Lask Frildur glared hatred at the corsair. 'Emperor Ublaz will hear of thizz inzult, ferret!' he spat.

The corsair ferret captain laughed harshly. 'Lissen, dead'ead, yer out at sea, in blue water! There ain't a thing you, me, or the Emperor can do about the weather, get that inter yer thick skull, lizard! We're all in the paws o' fate, see, and luck'n'judgement is all I got. Right now I don't know if'n we be sailin' south, east, or north. No stars, sun or wind, just fog everywhere, an' it ain't my fault!'

Lask buried his huge head in frost-numbed claws. 'You loze the way, the ship iz lozt!'

Romsca's voice dripped sarcasm. 'Clever ole reptile, the acorn's finally dropped, eh! Right, matey, 'tis about time yer realized, none of us might get out o' this liddle fix alive, an' I doubts if I could make it over t'this Mossflower shore an' then back to Sampetra, 'cos I ain't 'alf the cap'n that Conva was. Aye, Conva, now there was a stoat wot knew 'is way about the seas. But where is Conva now, eh? Prob'ly rottin' in some dungeon 'cos yer precious Emperor didn't like 'is face!'

'Land ho to starboard an' clearin' weatheeeeer!'

Rubby's shout from his position as lookout in the bows sent Romsca hurtling out on deck as *Waveworm*'s vermin crew yelled in joy and relief.

'Land ho! We made it, mates, land ho!'

The shoreline could be seen through the thinning mists and pale watery sunlight. Romsca vaulted nimbly up to the bowsprit beside the jubilant Rubby.

'Haharrharr! We did it, Cap'n! Ain't it a pretty sight?' Rubby cried.

The ferret narrowed her eyes, peering hard at the rocky coast. 'Aye, any land's a pretty sight, mate, even if it ain't Mossflower.'

Rafglan, searat bosun of the *Waveworm*, scrambled up beside them. 'If this ain't Mossflower, then where'n the name o' blood'n'fangs are we?'

As she stared at the approaching land, realization dawned on Romsca. 'This is far north, where we slew the otters, all for those accursed Tears, on our last voyage. Hah! I know where Mossflower is from 'ere. Bladetail, bring 'er 'alf round t'port! Ship those oars, mates! Rafglan, break out sails! Step lively now, buckoes, we'll beat down the coast south'ard to Mossflower an' the sun!'

By mid-noon a stiff breeze had sprung up. *Waveworm* had left the foggy regions far in her wake. The sun was out, though the weather remained brisk and nippy. Romsca helped Bladetail at the tiller as the vessel chopped and crabbed against the white-crested coastal rollers. The corsair ferret watched the rocky coastline.

'Another few days an' we'll be keepin' our eyes peeled fer that freshwater stream runnin' out o'er the shores. That's 'ow I'll know Mossflower – I remembers that stream well, mate.'

The for'ard cabin door slammed open and Lask Frildur stumped heavily out, still swathed in wrappings, but with a glint of the old imperiousness back in his eye.

'You, Romzca! Make arrangementz for my ten dead Monitorz!'

In a flash the corsair had drawn her curved sword. She let go of the tiller and approached the Monitor General, a tic in her left eye quivering with rage.

'It's Cap'n Romsca t'you, an' I've got a ship t'run on yore Emperor's orders! My crew's got other things t'do, so go an' give yore commands to yer own kind. You've got enough livin' lizards to shove ten o' their dead mates overboard. Don't try pushin' me round, Lask, I warn yer. I'm in command on this ship!'

Lask Frildur bared his lethal yellowed teeth at the corsair. 'I hear you, Romzca. You are in command . . . until we reach the land of Mozzflower!'

The corsair roared at the Monitor as he strode away to his cabin. 'Until we reach Mossflower, eh? The day ain't dawned yet when Romsca the corsair is afeared of a lizard! Just you give the word when yer ready, an' I'll show ye the colour of yer insides!'

Ever since the lizards had begun to show their weakness at sea, the ferret had grown in confidence.

Bladetail nodded in admiration of his captain. 'Haharr, that's the stuff, Cap'n. Let's 'ear yer brag, go on, like you do in the tavern at Sampetra.'

Romsca felt her good humour return. Waving her curved blade she danced around the welldeck, throwing out the traditional corsair challenge while the crew cheered her on.

'I'm the babe of a bloodripper,
Born in the teeth of a gale,
I'm the one who wields the sword,
An' makes the foebeast wail.
I'm as sharp as the reef rock,
I carry death in me paw,
Go where I like, slay who I will,
That's the corsairs' law!
Blood's me favourite colour,
Swifter'n lightnin' aye,
Stand out me way, stand out I say,
Step aside now, or die!
'Cos I'm the spawn o' nightstorm,
An' death sails in me wake,
I sheath me blade in innards,
An' what I want, I take!
Come one, come all, I'm waitin',
I'll flay yer carcass bare,
So everyplace I go they'll say,
"Ahoy, you bold corsaaaaaaiiiiiirrrrr!"'

Lask Frildur crouched over the charcoal embers in his cabin, listening to the roistering sea vermin applauding Romsca. The Monitor General also heard the dull booming splashes as his lizards jettisoned their companions' dead bodies astern into the restless sea. Lask gritted his teeth until they hurt, muttering, 'Enjoy yourzelf, corzair! One day I will danze on your grave!'

Evening came with long rolling purple clouds tinged beneath with gold from the setting sun. *Waveworm* beat a course slowly south, following the darkened coastline which led to Mossflower country.

12

Night brought with it the rain, drizzling at first, then a distant rumble of thunder and a faraway lightning flash that illuminated the dark horizon. Grath Longfletch shook water from her eyes as the rain increased. Her little longboat rode the rollers bravely, tacking south down the coast. The otter sat astern, guiding the small tiller lightly, watching the prow plunge up and down as it met each wave's onslaught. Easterly wind buffeted the boat's single square sail, pasting its middle to the slender rowan mast then pulling it away, allowing the canvas to flap wetly, driving the frail vessel towards the rocky shores.

Knowing it was dangerous to be caught out in a storm on a coastline peppered with reefs, Grath steered for the shore, silently hoping that her boat would not encounter any hidden rocks. She leant on the tiller and let the sail blow full out. Sideskipping the eastering wind, her longboat skimmed the floam-flecked wavetops, running for shore like a swift to its nest. Thunder boomed and in the lightning flash that followed Grath saw the cove – small, shingled and dead ahead. Rain-battered but exhilarated, the soaking otter clung tight to the tiller, sending her craft straight as one of her arrows, prow on into the cove and safety from the storm.

Leaping into the shallows Grath grabbed the headrope and began pulling her boat up the tideline, when a cheery voice rang out above the gale.

'Lend a paw there, y'slab-sided shellackers, give the seabeast some 'elp t'beach that craft!'

A lantern glimmered high in the cliff surrounding the cove, and ten or more small raggedy furred creatures with brightly coloured headbands came dashing down and seized the headrope. With their aid Grath soon had the boat high and dry above the tideline. The small fat creature carrying the lantern approached her. He was obviously the leader; he carried a small rapier tucked into his waistband. He held out a paw to the otter.

'I'm Log a Log, Chieftain of the Guosim shrews!' he announced.

The paw was taken willingly. 'Grath Longfletch, last of the Holt of Lutra!'

Log a Log set about gathering Grath's few possessions from the boat. 'Hah! You would've been nought but a drowned otter if ye stayed out at sea in that little lot, matey. Dabby, Curlo! Take this big bow atwixt ye afore it knocks me flat. Come on, Grath, 'tis no fit night for beast nor bird to be out in the open. Follow me.'

Halfway up the cliffs, sheltered from the sea by a protruding rockrift, Grath sat snug in a cave with her new-found friends. She drank shrewbeer which had had a red hot rapier thrust in to mull it, and the one called Dabby served her with a bowl of seafood soup from a cauldron bubbling at the edge of a seacoal and brackenwood fire. Grath ate with an appetite that amazed the shrews, tearing off hunks of flat barleybread to dip in her broth. As she satisfied her hunger, the otter related her tale.

When she had finished, Log a Log patted her broad, scarred back, smiling. 'Well, at least you lived through it, Grath, an' you eat like you survived a seven-season famine, mate. Lucky we found you. We're the Guosim shrews

– stands for Guerilla Union of Shrews in Mossflower, though we're a long way from that place up 'ere. Guosim like to wander, y'see. Every spring we come up to the coast an' feed off its bounty. We fish a bit, gather seaweed an' collect shellfish. Guosim are river shrews; our boats are back inland a piece, moored in a creek. Nobeast knows the rivers'n'streams like we do, eh, mates!'

An old shrew began tootling on a flute. Log a Log nudged the young female called Curlo. 'C'mon, sleepychops, stop noddin' off in front o' that fire an' sing a ditty fer our new pal Grath!'

Curlo had a lively gruff voice, and she sang out with a will.

'Guosim! Guosim!
Sail 'im, dip 'im, douse 'im,
If'n you see a shrew in river or stream,
Who can jump like a trout an' swim like a bream,
Fight like a pike an' sing like a lark,
An' paddle a boat from dawn 'til dark . . .
Yer lookin' at a Guosim!
O Guosim! Guosim!
Sail 'im, dip 'im, douse 'im,
If'n you see a shrew who c'n cook up a stew,
Brew dark beer an' bake bread too,
An' bend 'is back an' pull an oar,
Row all the day an' shout fer more . . .
Yer lookin' at a Guosim!
O Guosim! Guosim!
Sail 'im, dip 'im, douse 'im,
Not an otter or a waterdog,
No nor a spiky ole 'edge'og,
Even a warty toad or frog,
So it's three cheers for our Log a Loooooooooog!
We're Guosim Guosim Guosim!'

The merry song was so catchy that Grath laughed

aloud and asked Curlo to sing it again, which she did whilst two old shrews leapt up and gave the lie to their long seasons by dancing a merry jig to the tune.

Log a Log refilled Grath's beaker, saying, 'You've got a great laugh, friend. Y'should use it more often!'

The big otter stared into the fire. 'There's not been much to laugh about the last few seasons, matey.'

Curlo tugged at Grath's big calloused paw. 'Will you sing a song fer us, marm?' she asked.

The otter shook her head at the disappointed shrew-maid. 'I'm not a very good singer, but I'll do some magic for you.'

'Magic, what sort of magic?'

'With my bow, I'll shoot a star for you!'

All eyes turned on Grath, who winked secretly at Log a Log.

The shrew Chieftain nodded sagely. 'Aye, she looks like a magic otter t'me. Trimp, Dimple, fetch our friend her big bow an' quiver.'

The shrews watched intently as Grath strung the great longbow and chose an arrow. Then she passed her paws over the bow, murmuring, 'Magic arrow travel far, I will shoot a bright night star!'

Grath stepped outside onto the ledge in front of the cave, surrounded by curious shrews.

'Which star do you want me to shoot?' she asked Curlo. 'Point it out.'

With a hearty gruff giggle, Curlo pointed. 'That'n up there!'

'Which one, that bright twinkly one?'

'Aye, that's the one, marm, but even a bigbeast like you with a great bow like that'n couldn't shoot so far!'

With a mock serious face, Log a Log shook a paw at her. 'I see you don't believe friend Grath. Right, go on, mate, show 'er!'

Grath sighted on the star, and bent her bow full back, the arrow tight on the tautened string. Whipping the bow aloft, she loosed the green-feathered shaft, and in seconds it was speeding upward, lost in the vastness of the night sky.

'Quickly, everybeast inside!' Grath shouted.

The shrews dashed into the cave, with Grath behind them yelling, 'Stand well back from the fire then look at it hard for a few seconds.'

After a short interval the otter called to them, 'Close your eyes tightly, keep them closed and come outside!'

Doing as they were bidden, the shrews filed outside, clasping each other's paws with their eyes screwed shut.

'Now, turn your faces to the place where the star was in the sky,' Grath announced in a loud, mysterious voice. 'Open your eyes quickly and blink once!'

Roars of wonderment went up from the Guosim shrews.

'She did it! She did it!'

'The star burst in a great flash of light!'

'I can still see it bursting, there's lights everywhere!'

One tiny shrew ran round shrieking, 'I saw the arrow hit the star, miss! Grath is magic!'

Later the wind abated, and the thunder and lightning ceased. Outside the rain continued, but not so hard as before. Grath and Log a Log sat with their backs against the cave wall, watching the flickering firelight cast patterns over sleeping Guosim shrews and listening to the steady patter of raindrops on the rocks outside.

The shrew Chieftain yawned. 'That was a good trick, Grath. Have you got any more magic t'stop this lot snorin'?'

The otter chuckled. 'You want to try living in an otter holt sometime. It makes shrew snores sound like gentle music. They don't bother me, friend.'

Log a Log closed his eyes, paws folded on his fat stomach. 'Good! Then y'won't mind me addin' my snores to 'em, mate. Peace be upon your rest, Grath Longfletch!'

'Thanks for your hospitality, Log a Log. Peace be upon you also, and all of your Guosim this night!'

Grath closed her eyes and slept then. But peace would have been the last thing on her mind had she known that not half a league out to sea beyond the reefs, *Waveworm*, the corsair ship, was sailing parallel to the shrew's cave, bound south. It passed in the night, leaving only a broad wake which was soon swallowed up, lost in sweeping rain and the eternally flowing seas.

13

Up in the sick bay, Rollo finished reading Fermald's cryptic message. Tansy narrowed her eyes thoughtfully, then slowly repeated the strange little rhyme, having heard it only once. The hogmaid spoke out firm and clear.

'Look not up, nor to the four main points,
But where our paws do tread, the dead oak joints.
There wrought by mother nature 'neath the main,
Lies that which holds the beauty, or the bane.'

Martin raised his eyebrows in surprise. 'Well done, miss! What a curious tale Fermald the Ancient had to tell. Sampetra, where is it? Emperor Mad Eyes, what sort of creature is he? Graylunk's secret gift, the Tears of all Oceans, why are they so dangerous, what are they? I tell you, it's a riddle within a riddle!'

Rollo breathed hard on his spectacles and polished them with his sleeve, saying, 'Aye, Martin, it has me baffled too.'

Tansy tapped her paw on the unrolled parchment. 'Oh, let's get on and follow the clues,' she cried.

Rollo gave the hogmaid a severe glance over the top of his glasses. 'But do you feel well enough yet, Tansy?' he asked.

92

Friar Higgle glanced up from a slice of pie and chuckled. 'Hohoho! Well enough, did y'say? Just look at 'er. If'n I felt that well I'd be up an' cuttin' a jig. That one's as spry as a whippy willow in a breeze!'

Tansy leapt from the bed to prove her point. 'See! Oh, come on, please, please, or I'll make myself ill lying in bed thinking about it all. What d'you say, Martin sir?'

The Warriormouse tapped a paw against his chin. 'Mmm, maybe . . . But what if Sister Cicely comes back and finds one of her patients gone, what then?'

Higgle licked redcurrant from his paws. 'Then I'll sling 'er into bed an' feed 'er warm nettle broth, an' see as 'ow she likes it! Hohohoho!'

Amid the general laughter at Higgle's outrageous suggestion, Rollo and Tansy clasped paws with Martin, their eyes shining as he spoke the words they were waiting to hear.

'Right, let's go and solve this thing, friends!'

Three lanterns illuminated Fermald's chamber as the trio set about their search. Rollo sat in the armchair and read out the first two lines of the rhyme.

'Look not up, nor to the four main points,
But where our paws do tread, the dead oak
    joints.'

A faint smile hovered on Martin's lips as he questioned Tansy. 'Now, missie, tell me. Which are the four main points?'

'Easy: north, south, east and west.'

'Good! So if we can't look north, south, east or west and we can't look up . . . Where else can we look?'

'I'd say down, Martin.'

'Well done! And where do our paws usually tread?'

'On the floor?'

'Indeed they do. So, when an oak is dead our carpenters cut it lengthwise into long planks and joint them together into floorboards. D'you think we should look into the walls?'

Tansy giggled. 'You're being silly now, Martin, we should look under the floorboards, of course!'

Rollo spread wide his paws. 'All very clever, but this is a big attic, so where under the floorboards do we start looking?'

It was decided that they start at the far wall and together, working slowly, cover every bit of the attic floor. On all fours they went, pushing their lanterns ahead as they searched.

About a third of the way down the attic Rollo got up with a sigh and went to sit in the armchair, saying, 'I've had enough for one night, friends. My old back is killing me and these eyes of mine aren't what they used to be.'

Both Tansy and Martin remonstrated with the Recorder.

'Oh, come on, Rollo, you're no fun at all, you old grouch!'

'Yes, please, mister Rollo, don't fall asleep in that armchair.'

'Up on y'paws now, or we'll take you to the sick bay and let Sister Cicely feed you warm nettle soup!'

'I'd help us if I were you, Rollo; that warm nettle soup tastes awful, it's like trying to drink dirty ditchwater!'

But Rollo refused to be moved. 'No, my mind's made up. You're strong, Martin, and Tansy's young, you carry on, I'm too old . . .'

Martin had been creeping up behind the armchair as Rollo spoke, and suddenly he gave it a mighty shove. Rollo squeaked out in surprise; so did the little caster wheels as they rumbled along the floor, stopping just short of the far wall. Martin wagged a warning paw. 'Now will you get up and help us, you old fraud?'

'Look, see here!' Tansy was on all fours inspecting the floor where the armchair had formerly stood. Rollo leapt from the chair to join Martin and Tansy at the spot.

'Where, what is it? Hold the lantern closer!'

It was a crude black ink drawing, sketched at a joint lengthways where one floorboard ended and another began: a simple picture of a spoon.

Martin forestalled their enquiries. 'Before you ask me . . . Yes, I have Fermald's spoon right here in my belt.'

He produced the polished buckthorn spoon and inserted it into the crack between both floorboards, muttering, 'What am I supposed to do with it now, lever the board up?'

'No, sir, the spoon is too fragile. It'd break.'

'Hmm, you're right, Tansy. Any ideas?'

'Perhaps if you wiggled it from side to side,' Rollo suggested.

Martin tried, but nothing happened. He sat pondering the problem until Tansy said, 'Try pushing it down, sir.'

The Warriormouse pushed the spoon firmly into the crack. 'Good try, Tansy, but there's still nothing happening.'

Rollo peered at the problem from all angles. 'Maybe if we all *moved off* the floorboard – come this side of it, you two. Try pushing the spoon in now, Martin.'

Martin did. There was a click and the floorboard lifted slightly, just enough for the Warriormouse to get a grip with his paws. He lifted and the board came out easily. Tansy scooped a small linen flourbag out of the space beneath.

'Hahah! Got it, good old Rollo!'

The Recorder beamed with pleasure as he inspected the empty space. 'Yes, 'twas rather clever of me, wasn't it? The floorboard would never have risen while we were all kneeling on it. See, it was just a simple lever, the spoon pushes one end and the other end further along rises up and moves the floorboard. Shall we adjourn downstairs where we can sit comfortably by the fire in Cavern Hole? Everybeast should be abed by now. We

95

can look at what we've found in peace and comfort; it's a bit chilly up here.'

They were halfway along the dormitory corridor when Viola bankvole came bursting out of the main bedrooms. She was quaking and sobbing. Martin and Rollo caught hold of her.

'Viola, what's wrong, miss? Why are you so upset?'

The bankvole snuffled tears onto her nightgown sleeve. 'The big bird, it was horrible! It came right against the gatehouse window and nearly got me, it had a sharp beak and great eyes and it was screeching. Waaahaaah!'

Tansy led her to the sick bay, comforting her. 'Hush now, Viola, there there. It was only a dream. You can sleep in my bed, it's nice and quiet in the sick bay. There's only Friar Higgle and he's fast asleep. Lie down now.'

They left a lantern by the bed to reassure Viola.

Walking back out into the corridor, Rollo gave a start and leaned fearfully against Martin. A small white-clad figure had materialized out of the gloom.

'Toogle doo Tansy pansy, I'm a likkle maggit!'

It was Arven, in a long white nightshirt. He tripped giggling into Tansy's outstretched paws. The hedgehog maid chided him. 'You should be fast asleep. What have you been up to, eh?'

Arven drew two big gull feathers from his nightshirt. 'A been ticklen Vola bankee onna nose. Heeheeheehee!'

Martin took the two feathers from the tiny squirrel. 'You dreadful creature, so it was you frightening poor Viola into having nightmares! What are we going to do with you?'

Arven shrugged nonchalantly. 'Phwah! Can't do anyfink wiv Dibbuns, not choppa tail off wivva big sword, ho no, Arven on'y likkle!'

Rollo shook his head despairingly. 'He's right, y'know, there's not a lot we can do to a naughty Dibbun. There's only the fun things, like letting Mother Auma give him a good bath. It's nice when the soapsuds go up your nose and down your mouth and your eyes smart and you have to be still while she scrubs your tail with that hard brush and . . .'

The rest of Rollo's words were lost on Arven as he wriggled out of Tansy's grasp and fled back into the dormitory, muttering, 'Nono, I be good, I be good now, not lerra m'Auma get me inna baff.'

As they went through the kitchens, they found that Teasel the hogwife had left a big parsnip and mushroom pastie to cool for morning before she went to her bed. Safe inside Cavern Hole, Martin grinned as they divided a slice between them. 'I haven't stolen a slice of pastie since I was a Dibbun, huh, us three are worse than little Arven!'

Tansy blew on a slice of pastie to cool it, licking the dark rich gravy from her paws. 'Wrong, Martin, if there were ten of us we couldn't make more trouble than that maggot. He's the terror of all Dibbuns, take it from one who knows!'

Rollo burnt his tongue on the hot pastry. 'Whooh! Excuse me, but are we going to sit here discussing Abbeybabes or is somebeast going to open that bag tonight?'

Martin twirled his paw towards Tansy. 'The honour is all yours, my friend!'

Inside the flourbag was the shell of a scallop, a huge one. Deep ridges on both sides met where the shell closed in a perfect watertight seal. At some time a clever and artful creature had created darkwood hinges to the shell's back flanges and a cunning clasplock on the front. As Tansy opened the shell, she recited the second half of the rhyme:

'There wrought by mother nature 'neath the main,
Lies that which holds the beauty, or the bane.'

Both halves of the scallop shell fell open before their eager eyes. The interior of the shell was lined with soft red cloth. One perfectly round ball of thin fine parchment nestled in a holder; five more holding spaces were empty.

Rollo sighed with disappointment. 'I told you, Martin, this is only the beginning of a wild goose chase. What a tricky and aggravating squirrel Fermald the Ancient was – though fates preserve her memory.'

Martin heard Rollo, but he was staring at Tansy. 'What's on your mind, missie? You seem very pensive.'

The hogmaid let her paw stray across the five vacant holders. 'Sea shell, sea birds . . . oh, I don't know. What is sure is that there are five empty spaces, which must mean that there are five missing balls of paper.'

'Well, let's not waste any time,' said Rollo. 'Let's open the one we've got and see where fortune leads us.'

Rollo's paws shook as he worked, carefully peeling the delicate tissue of the flimsy orb open. 'Gently does it, I don't want to rip the paper. Ah, there!'

The three friends scanned Fermald's spidery writing.

For you my old friend Higgle,
I shed a single tear,
The kindnesses oft showed me,
Your food and smiling cheer,
Go, find my gift, good Friar,
This tear is given free,
Not hid away in secret,
But there for all to see!

Rollo stared into the fire, watching the intricate flame-dances around log and charcoal. 'Tears, tears, always tears,' he said.

Tansy could not resist a little joke. 'If tears are the answer you need go no further than Viola bankvole; she's always weeping and whining about something or other. Let's try her!'

Martin gave the hedgehog maid a sideways glance.

'Probably because she's easy to pick on. I'm surprised at you, Tansy, making fun of the misfortune of others.'

The regret Tansy showed at her ill-chosen remark was sincere. 'I'm sorry, sir, I'll try to be kinder to Viola in future.'

Rollo patted her paw cheerily. 'Well spoken, young 'un, that's the true Redwall spirit. Here, finish this pastie off before it grows cold.'

Tansy needed no second bidding; Teasel's pastie was delicious.

For a long while the three friends sat in silence, staring at the thin scrap of parchment and pondering its meaning. Cavern Hole was peaceful and warm, and soon Rollo's glasses started to slip further down his nose as his head began to slump forward. Martin winked at Tansy and nodded towards the drowsing old Recorder, then he blew gently on Rollo's eyelids.

The bankvole blinked several times and sat up straight, as if he had never dozed off, saying, 'Ahem! Right, where are we, still studying this rhyme, eh?'

Martin kept a straight face as he replied, 'Aye, still studying. Have you come up with any good ideas?'

Rollo's paw shot up decisively. 'I've got it. Here's what we must do next!'

Martin and Tansy exclaimed together, 'What?'

A twinkle shone in Rollo's tired old eyes. 'Go straight to bed before we all fall asleep here and wake up with stiff necks and rickety backs. Now don't start pouting, miss, we've got to sleep sometime. Tell her, Martin.'

The Warriormouse rose and stretched. 'He's right, Tansy. You'll see, a clear morning after a sound night's sleep and a good breakfast always improves a creature's brainpower. You'd best sleep in the dormitory, Viola is in your infirmary bed. Come on now, up you go!'

Despite her protestations that she was not the least

bit tired, Tansy found the dormitory bed soft and comfortable. Sleep stole up, gently closing her eyelids and leading her into the realm of odd dreams.

Martin appeared, but he was not quite like the Martin she knew so well, and he was wearing a magnificent suit of armour. Tansy realized that this was the other Martin, the Warrior Founder of Redwall – the same mouse whose likeness was woven into the tapestry which hung in Great Hall. He wore the same sword she had often seen the present Martin wearing.

Tansy felt happy in the presence of the Warrior. He radiated strength, safety and confidence, and his voice was soothing when he spoke.

'Maid of Redwall, search and never give up hope. You will find joy, frustration and sorrow in your quest. Never forget that friendship and loyalty are more precious than riches. Remember these words on the day you must return the Tears to their true owner. Happiness can be brief, but it knows no time in the land of dreams. Sleep on and I will show you.'

The Warrior's image faded and Tansy went deep into the most pleasant dream. Like a leaf she was borne upwards, and she wandered with the breeze through quiet summer woodlands, resting in sunlit coppices, drifting on margins of still water meadows and dancing lightly over faraway flower-clad hills.

14

Friar Higgle Stump was up and about early the next morning. He trundled down to his beloved kitchens, grumbling to himself.

'I wager breakfast ain't but 'alf started yet, best be about my business, 'ungry mouths t'feed. That Sister Cicely, she'd 'ave a body lyin' abed all season for no good reason. Us Stumps're made of stern spike, 'tis plain no seagull can bother me!'

He strode boldly into the kitchens, only to be met by his wife Teasel's accusing eye.

'I knowed there weren't nothin' wrong wi' you, 'iggle, I 'spect it was you sneaked down last night late an' took a slice of that parsnip an' mushroom pastie I left out to cool afore I went abed!'

The good Friar brushed past her stiffly, saying, 'Shame on you for even thinkin' such a thing about me, marm! When did I ever filch food from me own kitchens, eh?'

He set about measuring oatmeal and barley into a mixing bowl before livening up the oven fires with fresh charcoal. Teasel took a tray of nutbread rolls down from her cooling shelf, her muttering blending with that of Higgle. Both hedgehogs chunnered to themselves as they went about their cooking chores.

'A pastie that eats itself? Ain't nought but mysteries of late in this 'ere Abbey, mysteries an' mischief!'

'Huh! This honey's stiff as glue, I'd best leave it atop the oven t'warm through. Parsnips don't agree with me, why should I want to eat 'er pastie?'

'We're goin' t'need more white cheese afore the mornin's done, aye, an' this oven fire needs a good rakin' out . . .'

Abbot Durral had also risen early. He strode into the kitchens rubbing his paws in a lively fashion. 'Good morrow to you both, can I lend a paw? Here, that fire needs raking out, Teasel – let me do it!'

The three friends went about their work as the atmosphere lightened and mouth-watering aromas began pervading the air. Durral helped Higgle to carry a small churn of greensap milk from the cooling slab to the mixing bowl, explaining his day's plans as they measured it into the oatmeal and barley.

'I thought I'd take a stroll into Mossflower woodlands today, collect some coltsfoot and brooklime, maybe find a clearing where some red clover is showing. It's going to be a nice warm day, I feel we'll soon have a hint of summer.'

Friar Higgle winked knowingly at his friend, and said, 'Who knows, may'aps I'll be able to make you some pastilles if'n you collects enough o' those plants, Father Abbot.'

Durral hid a smile, putting on a mock-defensive tone. 'Coltsfoot pastilles are good for the young ones, keep them fit, good for coughs and any number of small ailments.'

Teasel had been eavesdropping on the conversation, and now she tapped the Abbot's paw lightly with her ladle. 'I don't suppose it'd 'ave anythin' t'do with a certain Abbot o' Redwall who likes to carry a liddle bag o' coltsfoot pastilles to suck. Some elders are worse'n Dibbuns, I say!'

Durral lifted the warmed honey from the oven top, protecting his paws with a cloth. 'You would say right, Teasel. I've been dreaming lately of having a good pocketful of nice sweet coltsfoot pastilles.'

During breakfast, the Abbot called Tansy to his side and whispered in the hogmaid's ear, 'I'm off into Mossflower today, collecting plants. How'd you like to come with me? It will be mild and sunny – we could take lunch with us. What do you say?'

Much to his surprise, Tansy refused the offer. 'Thank you very much, Father Abbot, but maybe you'd like to give someone else a chance. Take poor Viola bankvole with you.'

The kindly old mouse was pleased, but perplexed. 'Certainly, missie, but why Viola?'

'Because I feel sorry for her and I think we should be friends. Last night Viola had bad dreams, so I put her in my bed at the sick bay. I thought I was helping her, but Sister Cicely came in during the night and made her drink a big bowl of warm nettle broth. Poor Viola, she's sitting over there unable to touch any breakfast. See, she looks a funny colour to me.'

Abbot Durral looked up from his mint tea. 'You're quite right, Tansy, a walk in the woodlands and a picnic lunch will do your friend a power of good, I think. But what will you do with yourself all day?'

Tansy's voice dropped to a secretive whisper. 'I've got business with Martin and Rollo. We've a riddle to solve. Very important.'

The glorious spring morning rolled on into early noon-tide, with Redwall Abbey abuzz as creatures went about their chores and young ones played across the lawns. Skipper of Otters and his stalwarts patrolled the ramparts, striding along the high battlemented outer wall, ever alert for the slightest sign of invading gulls.

At the woodland's edge on the north path, a mass of cow parsley, with white flowering buds, stirred, which was odd, because there was not the slightest breeze to move it. The corsair ferret Romsca popped her head up momentarily, before dropping back out of sight.

'Last time I saw that place I was with Cap'n Conva an' we was on the trail of ole Graylunk. That's Redwall Abbey right enough!'

Despite the warmth of spring sunshine, Lask Frildur was still shivering from a cold night spent wandering through the damp woodlands. He was not in the best of tempers.

'Why not raize your voize a bit louder zo they can hear you properly, addlebrain!' he snarled, drawing a heavy cloak tight about his quaking body.

Romsca leaned towards him, her voice contemptuous. 'Button yer lip, sloptongue. I'll talk when an' 'ow I like, see! Hah, it don't matter if they 'ears us, the moment those Abbeycreatures catches sight of you they'll be dumbstruck fer sure!'

Lask loosened the cloak and puffed out his throat airily. 'You zpeak nonzenze, fool!'

Romsca snorted as if in despairing amusement. 'Lissen to 'im, messmates; every time 'e opens that gob 'e treads on 'is tongue! Let me tell yer somethin', Monitor, a fact you'n'the Emperor overlooked. Them Abbeybeasts can't abide searats, corsairs an' suchlike, so imagine 'ow they'll take to the sight o' you an' ten other reptiles, great flesh-eatin' lizards from the tropics beyond the sunset. Haharr, never thought o' that, did yer? They ain't never seen the likes o' you before. Wot d'yer think they're goin' t'do, invite yer inside fer cakes'n'wine? Tchah! They'll slam the gates tight in yore face, give those Monitors a volley of spears, an' send the lot o' ye packin' up the road! Just like any right-minded creature would, I'll take me oath on that, matey!'

Deflated, the Monitor General drew away with his ten

remaining Monitors, and went deeper into the woodland where they could hold a conference. Romsca had left a guard of six vermin aboard *Waveworm*, but her corsairs were still three times the number of Lask's force. They too drew back into the wood, but only to light a small fire on which they could cook their supplies, supplemented by whatever roots and fruits they had foraged from the countryside.

Rubby the cook held out a young turnip he had spitted and roasted on his cutlass blade. Romsca accepted it and lounged nonchalantly in the sunlight.

Rafglan the bosun joined her, munching a stalk of wild celery. 'So, wot are y'goin' t'do now, Cap'n?' he said.

Romsca spat out a tough piece of turnip. 'Do? I ain't doin' nothin', matey. Ole scaleguts is in charge o' the land party, let Lask do all the doin'.'

Rafglan cast a glance through the bushes. 'Ahoy, 'ere comes ole Lask 'imself, looks like 'e wants to talk.'

The Monitor General dismissed Rafglan with a nod and seated himself next to Romsca, saying, 'Perhapz what you zay iz right, my friend.'

Romsca flung the half-eaten turnip away and wiped her mouth. 'Oho, friend, is it? You've changed yer tune, lizard. So tell me, what's the plan?'

Abbot Durral sat on the bank of a small stream with Viola bankvole. They ate nutbread rolls and cheese, washed down with sips of old cider, for lunch. The Father Abbot kicked off his sandals and lowered his footpaws gingerly into the cold clear water with a long sigh. 'Aaaaah, that is truly delightful. Nothing like streamwater for refreshing the footpaws. You should try it, Viola.'

The bankvole maid stared doubtfully at the gurgling stream. 'But I don't like getting my footpaws wet, Father, and besides, there's no towels to dry them.'

Durral smiled benevolently at the prissy little creature. 'Grass, soft moss or dead ferns are as good as any towel,

Viola. Come on, you'll never know what it's like until you try it.'

Slipping off her sandals, the volemaid lowered her footpaws into the water. She shuddered, then giggled. 'Heeheehee! It tickles and it's cold, but you're right, Father, it does feel good. I think I'll stand up and have a paddle!'

Lussak and Fraddle, two of Lask Frildur's Monitors, had been unsuccessfully trying to catch birds with a net. Finding the stream, the two lizards had followed its course, searching for a likely spot where fish might be found.

Fraddle suddenly held up a heavily scaled claw, saying, 'Hearken, lizzen, I hear voizez!'

Crouching low, they wriggled silently forward. From behind a screen of hemlock and dropwort they watched two creatures clad in green habits, an old mouse and a young bankvole, prancing in the stream shallows, laughing and splashing.

Lussak's dark tongue snaked out hungrily. 'Food at lazzzzt!' he breathed.

Fraddle's claw shot out as Lussak started to creep forward. Seizing him tight by the loose jawflesh, he dragged until it threatened to tear. 'No, theze will be prizonerz for General Lazk!'

Viola and the Abbot sat on the streambank, rubbing their footpaws in the sunwarmed grass.

'Oh, Father Abbot, what fun! You were right when you said tha— Eeeeeek!'

The tough twine meshes of a ship's net trapped them both. They were pulled backward and hauled up the bank. Terrified, wordless and stiff with fright, the old mouse and the young bankvole found themselves staring into the foul-breathed faces of two reptiles they could not have imagined in their worst nightmares.

'Be ztill or be zlain!'

15

Apart from a few helpers, the kitchens were quiet after lunch had been served. Martin and Rollo sat on grainsacks with Tansy, questioning her closely.

'Are you sure you can remember no more of your dream, Tansy?'

'I wish I could, Rollo, really I do! I can remember seeing Martin the Warrior of ancient times, and he said many things to me, though it all seemed so fuzzy this morning. It was something about searching and never giving up hope. Then more words about friendship and loyalty . . . Oh! and he mentioned about one day giving the Tears back to their true owner. I'm sorry, but today my mind doesn't seem to be working properly. Oh dear, it makes me so irritable when I can't remember exactly what he said!'

Martin said understandingly, 'No matter, Tansy, all will become crystal clear when our Warrior's spirit wishes it so. The main thing at this moment is to solve the riddle. Would you read it again, please, miss?'

Tansy unfolded the flimsy parchment scrap.

'I think the relevant part is in these last four lines – listen:

'Go, find my gift, good Friar,
This tear is given free,
Not hid away in secret,
But there for all to see!'

Rollo donned his glasses and stared at the rhyme, saying, 'Fermald meant this for Friar Higgle, really. Don't you think we should go to him and ask for his help?'

At that instant Foremole and Higgle emerged from the winecellar ramp, rolling a small cask of elderberry wine between them.

Foremole unbent and grunted, 'Yurr, zurr 'iggle, us'll take et o'er to ee corner thurr.'

Rollo called over from his perch on the grainsacks. 'Friar Higgle, can you spare us a moment, please?'

Leaving Foremole to trundle the cask, Higgle came over, his homely face wreathed in a big smile. 'Whew! We none o' us're as spry as we used t'be, friends; good job I got Foremole to 'elp me. Now, wot can I do to 'elp you?'

Skipper of Otters was a big, tough-looking beast. He turned on the walltop as one of his otter crew called across from the south ramparts. 'Nary a sign of gulls again today, Skip!'

Skipper's deep gruff voice rang back in reply. 'Keep yore eyes peeled though, Glenner, we'll give it another day or two yet; may'aps they're watchin' us from afar.'

As he took his eyes away from the cloudless blue noon sky, Skipper saw a ferret emerge from the woodland fringe. Everything about her, from the brass earhoops to the tattooed paws and ragged silks she wore, branded her as sea vermin.

She waved in a cheery fashion at the big otter. 'Ahoy there, ruddertail, is this the place they call Redwall?'

Skipper became immediately alert. 'What if it is, snipenose? What's yore business 'ere?'

'Oh, just some information. No need t'get offended.'

Skipper chuckled, amazed at the ferret's impudence. 'Bless yer 'ide, matey, I'm not offended at a corsair callin' me ruddertail, though if'n I was down there now I'd give yer such a clout you'd land up in the middle o' next season!'

Romsca laughed back, giving as good as she got. 'Yer a big saucy beast, talkin' all brave from up there. Why not come down 'ere an' try yer luck, riverdog?'

Skipper wagged a hefty gnarled paw at her. 'My ole mother never raised no fools, corsair. Where's yer sword an' daggers, lyin' in the undergrowth with the rest o' yer slimy crew? Now say yore say an' begone, quick an' sharpish!'

The hogwife Teasel arrived up on the walltop carrying a basket. 'Good afternoon, mister Skipper. I brought up a snack for you an' yore crew . . . Who's that creature down there?'

Skipper peered into the basket, his face lighting up in appreciation. 'Nothin' to worry yore good 'ead about, marm; thankee for the vittles, though. Beg yore pardon whilst I deal with this villain.' Immediately the Skipper of Otters became serious, whirling his sling until the thongs hummed. 'Say yore piece, scum, or stand by to eat stone!'

Romsca spoke out smartly. 'Where's Graylunk? I wants ter speak with 'im!'

'Yore wastin' yore time, there ain't no Graylunk 'ere!'

'Arr, cummon, you c'n do better'n that. Either bring the weasel out or return wot 'e stole!'

Skipper and his crew were infrequent Abbeydwellers, living mainly in Mossflower's woodlands and waters, and he had no idea what Romsca was talking about. And he was not a beast to stand arguing.

Whokk!

The slingstone bounced off a sycamore trunk a hairsbreadth from the corsair's skull.

'Next one goes down yore throat, vermin – now clear off!'

Romsca leapt behind the sycamore trunk, shouting, 'We know you've got Graylunk in there, an' the pearls. It'd be a lot easier on yer if you brought 'em out!'

Hogwife Teasel popped her head over the battlements, and cried, 'Graylunk left 'ere seasons ago – they found 'is remains not two nights back in the woodland rocks, the red ones east of 'ere. Graylunk's dead long ago, so be off with you!'

'So you say. I'll be back again at this time tomorrow!' Romsca yelled.

When it was obvious Romsca had gone, Skipper chided Teasel gently. 'You should've told that'n nothin', marm. I'd advise you to find Martin an' tell 'im all that 'appened.'

Back in the kitchens, Friar Higgle had been shown the rhyme and told all about the situation. He shrugged.

'Alas, I know nothin' about any gift; old Fermald never gave me nothin' but smiles. I wish I could help you, but I can't. A tear for all to see? That's a real poser, friends. I must start bakin' for supper now. You'll 'ave to excuse me, but good luck to you.'

Feeling defeated, the three wandered about the kitchens on a futile search. Then Clecky ambled in, followed by Gerul. The mountain hare looked about hungrily.

'I say, chaps, is it nearly teatime? I'm famished. Sorry, are you lookin' for eatables too, wot?'

Rollo walked around Clecky, investigating the shelves behind him. 'No, we're not, you great famine-fetcher. We're looking for a tear that is in plain view.'

Gerul blinked several times, shifting from one talon to another. 'Ah well now, if me good friend Clecky here doesn't get sumthin' to devour soon, no doubt you'll see plenty of tears in plain view, sirs, an' you too, miss.

Ould Clecky here can blubber up a storm if the food isn't forthcomin', indeed he can!'

Tansy fidgeted with her apron restlessly. 'Oh bother! How can you hide something and yet leave it in plain view? It doesn't make sense!'

Friar Higgle looked up from the rhubarb crumble he was making. 'Aye, 'specially when you don't know what it is you look for!'

Clecky knew what *he* was looking for. The hungry hare had spotted a box of candied chestnuts on a far corner shelf. He sidled slowly over and tried to snatch some of the delicious sweets. Unfortunately there was a huge ornate wooden candlestick standing between Clecky and the shelf. The immense candle it held was lit only once every four seasons, at the first summer feast. Wax had melted upon wax over the seasons, crusting the top of the carved holder. Clecky stood with his back against the candle, trying to appear as though he were doing nothing. However, behind him his paws were working furiously. With one paw around each side of the candlestick, he grappled and grabbed furiously, trying to reach the box standing on the shelf behind the giant candle. As Tansy and her friends wandered about searching, Friar Higgle became alerted by the scrabbling noises. He looked directly at Clecky.

'What are you doin' over there, sir?'

The hare stood with both paws searching madly behind his back for the box as he tried to stand still, smiling casually. 'What, er, who, me? Er, ahaha, old feller, nothin' at all, nice an' snug in this corner, doncha think, wot wot?'

The Friar advanced on him, shaking a ladle threateningly. 'Yore up to some prank, I know it! Now get out o' my kitchen; tea'll be ready when I've made it!' He grabbed hold of Clecky's tunic and pulled sharply. 'Come on, out I said!'

But the hare had hold of the box in both paws

and was unwilling to let go. He tottered forward and overbalanced, shouting indignantly, 'I say, leggo, y'great foozlin' Friar! Yaaaahah!'

Higgle dodged to one side as the hare fell, bringing the candlestick crashing down to the floor with him. Candied chestnuts from the fractured box rolled around the kitchen floorstones. Martin and Higgle helped Clecky up. The Friar was furious.

'Now lookit what you done, an' all through sheer greed for a few chestnuts. The great summer candle is broke, snapped clean in two pieces! You'll pay for this, sir ten-bellies!'

Rollo, Tansy and Gerul were gathering up the spilled nuts. Tansy could not help grinning as she nudged the old Recorder. 'Rollo, shame on you, don't eat them, put them back in the box. Really, a vole of your seasons pinching candied chestnuts like a Dibbun, you're worse than Clecky . . . Hello, what's this?'

By accident, she had trodden on a lump of the congealed candlewax, which had broken from the holder in its fall.

As the candlewax broke under Tansy's paw, a large pink globe rolled out across the floor.

Martin stared at it in wonder. 'A pearl,' he whispered. 'A perfect pink pearl.'

'So that was it,' said Rollo. 'Hidden in plain view! Fermald pushed the pearl into the molten wax and it set around it. Clever!'

Rollo sat flat upon the floor, watching Tansy breaking up the rest of the hardened wax globules. 'Tears, the Tears of all Oceans – we're hunting for *pearls*! Why didn't I think of it before? The most precious thing to come out of the great waters; though I've never heard them referred to as tears of oceans before. What a charming description! Tansy, you're making a dreadful mess breaking up all that wax over the floor. What are you doing?'

The young hedgehog maid produced a greasy ball of rolled-up paper, the same size as the pearl, from among the wax pieces.

'Hah! I found it, the clue to the second pearl!' she cried.

Clecky tried to look as if he was not chewing three chestnuts as he swaggered about dusting himself down. 'Mmmff snch! Knew I'd be able to help you chaps, mmf glupp! Takes an eagle eye an' a sharp brain t'hunt the jolly old pearls y'know, gronnff snch! No need to thank me, all in a day's work, wot? Youch!'

Friar Higgle's ladle caught him smartly on the tail, and he fled from the kitchens, yelling amid the laughter that followed him, 'Base ingratitude. Yowp! Desist, sir, I say. Owch!'

16

Of all the seagoing vermin frequenting Sampetra, Rasconza was the only fox. He was bosun to Slashback, searat captain of the ship *Bloodkeel*. Rasconza was tough, ambitious and smart; after the captains' revolt he had appointed himself leader of the rebel crews roaming the island's high hills.

The fox was a renowned blade thrower, having about him no fewer than ten daggers which he would use at the drop of a paw. None of the other vermin challenged his position.

Rasconza crouched on a hilltop at the isle's northwest tip. Behind him in a hollow the vermin crews lay about, eating fruit, roasting fish and dozing in the warm tropical noon. But the fox was alert, watching the sea before him.

Barranca and the captains were sailing the *Freebooter* towards the inlet below, unaware that Sagitar with a full crew of Trident-rats was following in the *Bloodkeel*. Barranca had taken the open sea route, but Sagitar had followed at a distance, hugging the coast. *Bloodkeel* was now lying in wait around the high curving hills of the headland. Once Barranca sailed his ship into the inlet, Sagitar could slip around and block the exit with her vessel, trapping *Freebooter* and the captains. It would be the perfect ambush.

Rasconza's sharp brain and keen eyes took in the situation at a glance, and he laid his plans swiftly. Slipping away from the drowsing rebels was but the work of a moment. Once out of their sight the fox dashed headlong down the cliff towards the inlet and arrived in time to hail Barranca as *Freebooter* nosed into the shallows.

'Cap'n, 'tis I, Rasconza. There's a shipload of Trident-rats lying in wait for ye, they'll round the point soon an' trap yer!'

Barranca glanced around the narrow inlet, realizing it was too late to back water and turn for an open run out to sea. 'We'll 'ave to stand an' fight 'em! Are the crews close by, mate – we're goin' t'need 'elp!'

Rasconza put on his steadfast and honest face and saluted Barranca. 'Leave it t'me, Cap'n,' he said, voice grim and determined, 'I'll muster 'em an' get back 'ere in a flash! You 'old those Trident-rats off, I won't be long!'

Barranca returned the salute as Rasconza trotted off. 'That's the spirit, messmate – together we'll give 'em a drubbin' they won't fergit!'

Rasconza ran puffing and panting uphill until the ships below looked like toys. Slowing down, he crept into the hollow where the crews lay asleep around the ashes of their fires. The fox cocked up both ears and listened, satisfied that he could hear no noise from far below. Then, retrieving half a roast fish from the paws of a sleeping searat, he began eating slowly, mentally calculating the wait before putting the next stage of his plan into action.

After what he deemed an appropriate interval, Rasconza stood up, kicking those about him into wakefulness. 'Our cap'ns are bein' massacred down there, look!' he yelled.

He dashed to the hilltop and pointed down to the inlet.

Wave vermin rubbing sleep from their eyes joined him, yelling outrage at the scene below.

'Trident-rats! They've got the cove blocked off!'

'Scum, they've overrun the *Freebooter*!'

'Let's get down there an' rip into 'em!'

'Aye, we'll make the waters run red t'save our cap'ns!'

Rasconza strode to the fore, bellowing, 'Too late to save those cap'ns now, mates. I got a plan, lissen! We split into three groups. Baltur, you take one lot down there to the left, bypass the Trident-rats an' board the *Bloodkeel* from 'er stern! Gancho, you take another lot to the right an' board 'er from the for'ard end, that way we've got ourselves a ship! I'll take the rest straight down the centre an' attack the Trident-rats – I'll make 'em pay fer slaughterin' our cap'ns!'

A roar of approval went up from the crewbeasts.

Sagitar had not thought it would be so hard to slay six captains and take one prisoner, but it had been a long and bitter fight. Once she had blocked the inlet by anchoring *Bloodkeel* across it she ordered her Trident-rats to attack. They went overboard and had to swim until the water was shallow enough for them to wade.

The captains were waiting for them. Having armed themselves with pikes and boathooks, they dashed around *Freebooter*'s rails, hacking and stabbing at every head that appeared over the side. But numbers began to tell. Urged on by Sagitar, the Trident-rats fought their way aboard. Immediately Barranca and his companions abandoned ship and, wading ashore, they speared viciously at the foebeasts in the shallows. Then Flaney fell to a trident thrust, followed by Rippdog and Rocpaw. Back to back, Slashback, Bloodsnout and Bilgetail kept off the advancing Trident-rats. Barranca joined them, blood streaming from him as he slashed about with his sabre, shouting, 'Where's that fox got to with our crews?'

There was nothing left but to turn and run. Bilgetail and Bloodsnout went down, pierced by tridents. Slashback staggered on uphill, mortally wounded, Barranca supporting him. Finally Slashback fell sideways, knocking Barranca over as he did.

Surrounded by Trident-rats, Slashback breathed his last words into the corsair stoat's face. 'What 'appened . . . Where's fox?'

Barranca was dragged upright roughly. 'So, corsair, Sagitar sneered at him. I told you that you'd have me to deal with, but you were too clever to heed my words. How d'you feel now, scum!'

Barranca laughed harshly at his captor. 'Yer lily-livered cur, you should've been within reach o' my blade, instead of leadin' yer army from be'ind!'

Sagitar ignored the jibe. She turned to her Trident-rats and ordered, 'Scuttle the *Freebooter* in the shallows, her sailing days are over. The rest of you get aboard *Bloodkeel* and prepare to get under way!'

Scarcely had the Trident-rats opened *Freebooter*'s seacocks when a mighty yell arose from the rebel crews, who had succeeded in boarding the *Bloodkeel*. Sagitar wheeled in dismay to see Baltur and Gancho and hordes of wave vermin at the rails, yelling and roaring.

'Come on, buckoes, make crabmeat of 'em!'

'Haharr, give 'em steel an' take no prisoners!'

Stranded on the shore with a mere ten rats to guard herself and control the captured Barranca, Sagitar's last shred of courage deserted her at the sound of more bloodcurdling yells from behind. She turned and saw Rasconza leading a pack of vermin downhill, straight at her. The Emperor's Chief Trident-rat fled the scene, dashing off southward at a tangent, into the hills.

Barranca whooped triumphantly and, breaking free of his guards, he ran with open paws towards Rasconza.

'Ho, ho, yer a sight fer sore eyes, matey!' he cried.

As the corsairs threw themselves upon the ten Trident-rats, the fox grabbed Barranca in a tight embrace.

'Aye, Cap'n, yer worries are over now!' Rasconza said

as, smiling slyly, he slew Barranca with a single knife thrust. Then, sheathing his blade quickly, he cried out, 'They slew Cap'n Barranca, the scum! Finish 'em off, buckoes! I'll get Sagitar if'n it takes me last breath!'

He sped off after the Chief Trident-rat.

Sagitar threw a fleeting glance over her shoulder. The fox was hot on her trail. Stumbling and panting, the Trident-rat gained the hill summit and staggered southward, hoping to reach safety at the palace of Ublaz. Rasconza pursued her relentlessly, grinning as he closed in on his quarry.

Sagitar's paws felt leaden. She blew for breath as she started downhill. Chancing another quick look behind, she tripped and went rolling head over tail down the grassy slope. Rasconza bounded lightly alongside the Trident-rat until she came to rest, half in and half out of a gurgling stream.

Helpless and unarmed, Sagitar lay with the fox's knife at her throat, expecting no pity from him.

Rasconza flicked his bladepoint teasingly under her chin. 'Well now, me beauty, what's t'be done with you?'

Sagitar broke into a sobbing whine. 'Mercy, spare me!'

Standing upright, the fox kicked the Trident-rat contemptuously. 'Quit yer snivellin', rat, I'd like nothin' better than t'gut ye, but I've got plans fer you, so lissen good!'

Wide-eyed with surprise, Sagitar lay staring upwards at Rasconza as the devious fox relayed his information to her.

It was high noon of the following day. Ublaz sat atop the timber piled at the rear of his palace, and below him on the sunbaked ground Sagitar crouched, not daring to raise her eyes as she related the fox's message.

'Mightiness, the fox is called Rasconza. He said to tell you that it was he who slew Barranca and now he alone rules the rebel crews. Even now he is on his way here in the *Bloodkeel*. He wants to meet you tomorrow morning on the heights above the north inlet. You may bring armed guards with you. He says he wants to talk peace.'

The Emperor whittled pensively at a sliver of wood with his silver dagger. 'Rasconza, eh?' he said. 'This fox sounds like one I could do business with. I think we'll take him up on his offer. Pick fifty of your best Trident-rats and a score of Monitors to accompany me. Oh, and Sagitar, you know what will happen should you ever fail me again?'

Avoiding the mad eyes, Sagitar stood trembling, head bowed. 'Mightiness, I will never fail you again!'

Ublaz smiled thinly; his voice was like oil flowing over ice. 'I would hate to be in your skin if you did.'

17

Log a Log inspected Grath's longboat.

'You've got a couple o' boards cracked 'ere, matey,' he announced. 'I'll get some o' my shrews to turn 'er over an' we'll patch 'er up again.'

The longboat had shipped water, and now she was over a quarter full. Six Guosim shrews heaved and huffed as they tried to turn the vessel over in the shingled cove.

Grath waved them aside. 'Save yore strength, mates, I can do that.'

She dismantled the mast and sail, placing them safe, then, digging her powerful paws under the shingle, she found a hold and lifted. In one move she turned the longboat upside down in a rush of water.

The shrew named Dabby wrinkled his nose in admiration. 'Now that's wot I calls a strongbeast!'

Pine resin was melted over an open fire. Skilfully the Guosim applied it, alternating layers with tough vegetable fibres, until a proper repair was effected on the cracked boatribs. Other shrews had sewn and patched the torn sail, double-strengthening it on all four corners.

Finally, Grath set the longboat upright, and said, 'Log a Log, I thank you and your Guosim for the help and kindness you've shown me. True friendship can't be properly expressed by just words, but, matey, I'll never ferget you!'

The shrew Chieftain kicked awkwardly at the pebbled shingle. 'Oh, 'twas nothin', mate – wot use are friends if'n they can't 'elp one another? You be on yore way now, afore this tide ebbs. Trimp, Dimple, load those vittles aboard fer our mate!'

Two bags of provisions and a couple of canteens filled with drink were stowed under the stern seat. Aided by a gang of shrews, Grath pushed the longboat into the shallows and jumped aboard. Looking back at her new-found friends on the shore she sniffed, and rubbed a paw across her eyes as she began setting the sail to catch the fine spring breeze.

Log a Log waded out and shook the lone otter's paw firmly. 'Ahoy, what's all this? No time fer weepin' now, missie, the tide'll ebb away! Go on, off y'go, Grath, an' may good luck an' fair winds follow ye, matey!'

Heading out to catch the south current, Grath leaned over the stern, waving to the Guosim as they sang her on her way from the shore. Deep gruff shrew voices rang out across the waves into the bright sunny morn.

'Hey la ho, hey la ho,
Our hearts go with you where you go,
Hey la hey, hey la hey,
Maybe we'll meet again someday.
Like a feather on the breeze,
Blown to wander restlessly,
Out upon the open seas,
Travel speedily and free.
But as the earth turns,
And our fire burns,
And the moss grows on the lee,
When long day ends,
Think of old friends,

121

In whatever place you be.
Hey la ho, hey la ho,
Fortune follow you where e'er you go,
Hey la hey, hey la hey,
May sunlight warm your back upon the way.'

Late afternoon sun cast lengthening shadows over Moss-flower. A fire burned in a sheltered glade, and Lask Frildur sat warming his claws, watching his ten Monitors prowling restlessly around the two pitiful figures bound to the trunk of an elm. Long tongues snaking out, cold predatory eyes fixed on both mouse and bankvole, the lizards circled close.

Abbot Durral felt a scaly claw caress his footpaw; closing his eyes tight, he shuddered. Viola, rigid with terror, huddled as close to Father Abbot as her bonds would allow. Durral spoke reassuringly to her.

'Don't be frightened, little one, had they been going to harm us they would have done so long before now. We'll face them together and show them that Redwallers are brave creatures.'

One of the Monitors brought his face close to Viola. She smelt the lizard's rancid breath as it bared sharp teeth and hissed, and she shrieked in fear.

The Monitor General far outstripped his lizards in size and strength. He bounded over and dealt the offending Monitor a savage blow with his tail that sent the reptile crashing into a nearby bush. Then turning to the others, Lask Frildur stood to his full height and snarled menacingly, 'Eat birdz, eat fizhez, I zlay any who go near theze two!'

Abbot Durral addressed Lask in a reasonable and friendly tone. 'Who are you, sir? Why have you bound us up like villains? We are creatures of peace . . .'

The Monitor General rounded on him contemptuously. 'Keep your ztupid mouth clozed, mouze!'

Viola plucked up her courage, shouting shrilly at Lask.

'Don't you dare talk to him like that, he is Abbot Durral, the Father Abbot of all Redwall Abbey!'

A slow smile lit up the Monitor General's cold features. 'Good, good, thiz iz very uzeful to me!'

Durral leaned back against the tree, sighing. 'I wish you had not told him that, Viola. It has put both us and Redwall in a very dangerous position.'

The volemaid wept bitterly at the realization of what she had done.

Durral was immediately sorry he had chided her. 'Hush now, little one, here, turn your head and wipe your eyes on my sleeve. It wasn't your fault really, you are young and know nothing of situations like this. Hush now, don't cry.'

A short time later Romsca strode into the glade at the head of her crew. She pointed to the prisoners. 'Aye aye, what've we got 'ere?'

Lask ignored the question. He spoke without turning from his fire. 'You have been gone long, corzair, why iz thiz?'

Squatting by the flames, Romsca speared an apple on her sword and began roasting it. 'I've got news for you, matey. Graylunk's long dead. I found 'is bones, me'n'my crew, over in a pile o'rocks east of 'ere.'

'What elze did you find, Romsca?'

'Nothin'. Not a single thing, no sign of any pearls, jus' ole Graylunk's bones an' the rags 'e wore.'

'Did you talk with the creaturez at Redwall Abbey?'

'Course I did, that's how I knew where t'find what was left o' Graylunk. But mark my words, Lask, those beasts at Redwall ain't soft, they can fight, I know! If the pearls are anywheres you can lay a belayin' pin to a bobbin they're inside o' that red-walled Abbey somewheres. So, matey, yore in charge o' shore operations, what are y'goin' to do about it?'

The Monitor General did not attempt to hide a triumphant smirk. 'I have two captivez. The old mouze iz Father Abbot of Redwall!'

Romsca nibbled at the steaming apple. 'Well, ain't you the lucky lizard! But watch yore step, Lask, if those Redwallers find out you've got their Abbot, they'll come searchin' fer 'im in force an' tear these woodlands apart! I tell yer true, they've got tough, full-growed otters an' beasts who ain't scared of battle. Conva reckoned he saw a great badger roamin' the walltops last time we was 'ere. You might find ye've bitten off more'n y'can chew, takin' an Abbot as 'ostage!'

Lask Frildur stood up decisively. 'I zerve my Emperor, Ublaz. I will do what I muzt! We will divide our forzez, half to take the prizonerz back to *Waveworm*, the other half to remain here under my command.'

'Aye, that's good thinkin', matey,' Romsca agreed, only too glad to be away from the hated Monitor General. 'I'll take the 'ostages an' my crew back t'the ship . . .'

Lask gripped Romsca's paw so tight that she winced. 'You take half your crew and five of my Monitorz, that way there will be no trickz played. I keep half your crew here with my other five Monitorz.'

The corsair managed to pull herself from the lizard's grip and stood fuming, paw on sword.

'All right, so be it, you don't trust me an' I don't trust you! Permission t'go, yer 'igh mightiness, or will there be anythin' else whilst I'm 'ere t'do yer biddin'?'

Smiling thinly, Lask produced a slim bone whistle and blew it. 'Oh yezz, I had vizitorz while you were gone. They will accompany you back to your vezzel, juzt to keep an eye on thingzz!'

Grall the great black-backed gull and his remaining two companions, looking much the worse for wear, came padding through the trees.

As soon as Hogwife Teasel had told Martin about the corsair ferret and her questions about Graylunk and the pearls, he joined Skipper and his otters on the walltop, a look of concern clouding his face.

Skipper seemed unconcerned, however. 'Oh, it was a corsair, no doubt o' that, an' I wager there's others waitin' orders in the woodlands. But wot's a crew o' seascum an' vermin to us, Martin? We'll teach 'em a lesson they'll never ferget if'n they comes too close t'Redwall!'

Leaning over the parapet, Martin peered into the silent woodlands.

'I wish it were that easy, Skip, but Tansy told me that the Abbot is out there with young Viola. They should have been back by now.'

Dismay showed on Skipper's tough face. 'Wot d'you suggest we do, Martin?'

'We'd best get the elders together and hold a quick council of war.'

Tansy and Rollo caught up with Martin as he crossed the lawn with Auma the badger Mother and Foremole.

'Martin, what can we do to help?'

The Warriormouse paused a moment before he entered the gatehouse where the other elders were waiting. 'Keep on with the search for the other five pearls, you two. I've a feeling we may need them!'

Tansy pulled Rollo towards the wallsteps. 'Let's sit out here, it's a nice afternoon, maybe we'll think better out in the fresh air.'

Rollo read out the rhyme from the waxy paper for the fourth time. Like all Fermald's poems it seemed to make little sense.

'I shed my second tear, into the cup of cheer,
But look not into any cup, the answer's written here!
My first is in blood and also in battle,
My second in acorn, oak and apple,
My third and fourth are both the same,
In the centre of sorrow and twice in refrain,
My fifth starts eternity ending here,
My last is the first of last . . . Oh dear!
If I told you the answer then you would know,

'twas made in the winter of deepest snow.'

Tansy drummed her paws in frustration on the steps. 'Ooh, that Fermald! If she were still alive I'd give her a piece of my mind! This rhyme's twice as tricky as the last one!'

They sat in silence, racking their brains until the Abbey bells tolled four times. Rollo had started to doze, but the bells woke him, and he said, 'Come on, Tansy, let's go for tea!'

It was such a nice afternoon that Brother Dormal and Teasel had arranged tea in the orchard. Rollo and Tansy took scones, crystallized fruits, cream and steaming rosehip tea and sat with Piknim the mousemaid and Craklyn the squirrelmaid beneath the spreading boughs of an old gnarled apple tree. No sooner had Tansy sat down than Arven's face appeared upside down in front of her. He wrinkled his nose and stuck out his tongue.

'Tansy pansy toogle doo . . . Boo!'

The little squirrel was hanging by his tail from a bough. Tansy unhooked him and lifted him down.

'You little maggot, you'll fall on your head one day!'

Arven helped himself to a pawful of cream and ran off, giggling at the clever trick he had played.

Piknim looked over Rollo's shoulder at the waxy paper. 'What's that, mister Rollo, the words of a song?'

The Recorder threw up his paws in despair. 'I wish it were, miss, it's a riddle.'

'Ooh, a riddle, lovely!' Piknim and Craklyn chorused in a single voice.

Rollo looked at them over his spectacle tops. 'You mean that you like riddles? Are you any good solving them?'

The two friends immediately broke out into:

'If string cannot sing then answer this riddle,
What sings as sweet as the strings of a fiddle,
The fiddlestring sings, but it never can throw,
An arrow so far as the string of a bow,

126

But a bow plays a fiddle and I'll marry thee,
If you give a bright bow of ribbon to me!'

They curtsied prettily as Rollo applauded, saying,
'Well sung, misses, you can help us solve our riddle!'

Piknim and Craklyn read the rhyme twice then began
tittering and winking at each other. Tansy looked from
one to the other. 'You've solved it, haven't you?' she
demanded.

They began teasing.

'Well yes, but then again, no!'

'We've solved it, but not all the rhyme.'

'But we know what the main part means!'

'Oh yes, it's a six-letter word!'

Rollo could restrain himself no longer. 'Well, in the
name of seasons and summers, tell us!'

Piknim and Craklyn were real teasers. They went off
into gales of tittering and giggling until they were unable
to talk.

Tansy placed a restraining paw on the irate Recorder.
'Leave this to me, Rollo!' Scooping up two large globs of
cream, she faced the laughing duo.

'If you don't tell me by the time I count three, stand
by for a creamy facewash. One . . . Two . . .'

They both yelled out, 'It's a barrel, it's a barrel!'

Still holding the pawfuls of cream, Tansy commanded
them, 'Right, show us how you arrived at the answer.'

Piknim and Craklyn talked like a double act, one after
the other.

'Well, we don't know what the first two lines mean,
all that stuff about cup of cheer and shed a tear.'

'But that line, my first is in blood and also in battle.
Only two letters appear twice in both words, the B
and the L.'

'Yes, and the next line's easy. Acorn, oak and apple
have only one letter in common, the A.'

'Now, look at these lines, my third and fourth are both

127

the same, in the centre of sorrow and twice in refrain. The middle of the word sorrow contains the letter R twice, and R crops up twice in the word refrain. So it's R and R.'

'Correct, now the next line. My fifth starts eternity ending here. Simple, what starts the word eternity and ends the word here, the same letter, an E.'

'The final one isn't too difficult either. My last is the first of last. Huh! The first letter of the word last is an L.'

'So, we've got a B or an L, then an A, two Rs, an E and an L.'

'And it's certainly not larrel, so it's got to be barrel!'

Piknim jumped up and down clapping her paws, squeaking, 'Oh, this is fun, can we help you some more?'

Tansy was musing over the word and gazing at the waxy paper. 'What? Yes, of course you can help. Hmmm, barrel, where in Redwall would we find a barrel?'

Rollo put his food to one side. 'In the winecellar?'

Piknim and Craklyn were off, running ahead of Tansy and Rollo. 'Last one to the winecellar is a jumpy toad!'

Rollo trailed on behind Tansy. 'Carry on, young misses, with your fleet young paws. I'll just take my time like any old jumpy toad!'

18

The Stump family had been in charge of Redwall's winecellars for many seasons. Friar Higgle Stump's brother Furlo was a strong fat hedgehog, conscientious and tidy in all things pertaining to his beloved cellars. He sat the three maids and Rollo down on a bench and fetched them a drink.

'This'll cool you down, fresh-brewed dandelion and burdock cordial,' Furlo said as he poured out four beakers from a big jug. It was cool, sweet and dark with a creamy foam head, and they drank gratefully.

Then the cellar-keeper dug his paws into his wide apron pocket, saying, 'Now, young 'uns, an' you Rollo sir, what can I do for ye?'

The Recorder wiped a foamy moustache from his mouth. 'I know this sounds silly, Furlo, but we're looking for a barrel.'

'Well, sir, I've got lots o' barrels down 'ere, which one'd you like?'

Tansy spread the waxy paper flat on the bench. 'Trouble is, sir, we don't know. Maybe if you read this it may help.'

Furlo Stump was a slow reader. He borrowed Rollo's spectacles and scanned the rhyme for what seemed an age. Then he scratched his huge spiky head in bewilderment. 'Dearie me, I can't unnerstand none of that, missie. 'ere, you 'ave a look round my cellars whilst I think about it.'

Rollo took them on a tour. He had worked in the winecellars on many an occasion when he was younger and had a fair knowledge of things.

'What a lot of barrels, mister Rollo!'

'They're not all barrels, miss Craklyn; those great giant ones standing in the corner, they're called tuns. Beetroot wine is kept in them. Barrels are these smaller ones, mainly for ale. Then there's the kilderkin, a bit smaller, for cordials and such, and smaller again, half the size, is the firkin, usually for wines. Any small quantities of strong wine are kept in these little casks.'

Tansy waved her paw around, indicating the cellar stocks. 'So we can rule out most of these, and just pay attention to the barrels, is that right, Rollo?'

The old Recorder shrugged. 'Who knows, maybe Fermald knew little of cellars and they all looked like barrels to her. Where are we then?'

Furlo approached them, still scratching his head and looking very unsure of himself. 'Beg pardon, Rollo sir, but I been thinkin' about the poem as was written down on that paper. There's somethin' a botherin' my 'ead, those words at the end o' the rhyme, the winter of the deepest snow. I remember when I was but a Dibbun, my father told me somethin' about a cellar-keeper name of Ambrose Spike, long afore my time, though what it was 'e told me I can't recall.'

Rollo halted him with an upheld paw. 'Ambrose Spike – I remember him from when I was a Dibbun. Piknim, you're the fastest runner, nip across to the gatehouse and ask Wullger to dig out the volumes of a Recorder named Tim Churchmouse. Craklyn, go with her, there may be more than one volume to carry. Bring them straight back here to me, quick as y'like now!'

The two young ones sped off out of the cellars, shouting. 'Last one to the gatehouse is a frumpy frog!'

As it turned out, neither of the young maids was a frumpy frog. They matched each other for speed all the way to the gatehouse and back to the winecellar, arriving breathless and burdened down with two volumes apiece. Furlo poured out more dandelion and burdock cordial for everyone. With tiny spectacles balanced on his nose end, Rollo pored through page after yellowed page, muttering to himself.

'Spring of the lesser periwinkle, hmm, later than that. Autumn of the late marjoram, hmmm, later I think. Summer of the rosebay willowherb, ha, I've gone too far, it was the winter before that. Yes, here it is, winter of the deepest snow, got it!'

The three young maids leaned over Rollo's shoulder eagerly. 'What does it say, sir, tell us?'

Rollo took a deep draught of cordial before reading, 'Ambrose Spike was lucky, he harvested all the rhubarb he had been growing alongside the west wall before the snows started. The snow is now so deep they have named this season the Winter of the Deepest Snow. The weather outside is harsh and gloomy, but Redwallers are merry and snug within our Abbey. I helped Ambrose in the cellars today; he is squeezing the rhubarb with great stone slabs and ale barrels as weights. The juice we mixed with clear honey and poured into a firkin; it is a beautiful pink colour. Ambrose Spike would not allow me to touch it, he says it will not be properly ready for at least two seasons, but when it is ready Ambrose is of the opinion it will be unequalled for taste.

'I left him to go back to my recording today. Ambrose was fitting the lid tight onto the firkin with soft willow withes. He had a brush and vegetable dye to paint the name on the firkin. I like the name he has chosen for this wine: the Cup of Cheer.'

Tansy repeated the first line of the rhyme aloud, 'I shed my second tear, into the cup of cheer!'

Rollo slammed the volume shut, sending up a small dustcloud. 'Of course, a pink pearl in pink wine!'

There were a lot of firkins, each one identical to the next. They stood on end, two high. Furlo bade them stand aside as he lifted each one down for inspection. Tansy and her friends could not help smiling at the fashion in which hedgehog cellar-keepers wrote the names on different firkins, though they did not laugh aloud for fear of offending Furlo Stump. The powerful hedgehog lifted down one firkin after another for their inspection, and Rollo translated the simple spelling.

'Persnup corjul, ahem, that'll be parsnip cordial. Pinnycludd win, er, that'll be pennycloud wine. What's this one – rabzerry viggen?'

Furlo chuckled. 'That's raspberry vinegar, sir. Us cellar 'ogs ain't the best o' scholars, but we know our own marks when we sees 'em!'

Tansy and Craklyn dusted off the bottom of a firkin which Furlo had laid on its side. Piknim read out the faint green lettering, 'Ambrows Spiks faymiss Kopachir?'

Tansy said the last word several times before it dawned on her. 'Kopachir . . . Kop a chir . . . Kup a chir . . . Cup o' chir . . . Cup of Cheer!'

Rollo stroked the aged wood reverently. 'This is the one, made long ages ago in the winter of the deepest snow. Ambrose Spike's famous Cup of Cheer!'

It took quite a while for the cellar-keeper to tap the bung. With his coopering hammer, he knocked a sharp spigot through the centre of the firkin bung without losing a drop of its contents. Then, with a mighty heave, Furlo lifted the firkin onto a table and began running the liquid off into an empty barrel. They watched the pink rhubarb wine splashing out in a shining stream.

Rollo caught some in a beaker and tasted it. 'Delicious, but very strong, perhaps Sister Cicely could make use of it in the sick bay for cold and chills.'

Tansy could not resist adding, 'Instead of warm nettle broth!'

When the firkin was empty Furlo removed both tap and bung and began shaking it; something clattered around inside.

Piknim had the smallest paw; she reached inside and felt around. 'Move it a touch this way, please, mister Furlo, a bit more . . . Ah, got it!'

It was a tiny stone beaker, of the type used for medicine doses. Its top had been sealed over with beeswax. Furlo cut the wax away with a small quill dagger, and out fell an exquisite pink pearl.

'My, my, that 'un's a fair beauty of a treasure,' the cellar-keeper remarked admiringly. 'Ain't never seen anythin' as 'andsome in all me born days!'

Tansy, however, was far more interested in the thin fold of paper lining the bottom of the beaker; she picked it out and unfolded it.

Auma looked around the worried faces inside the gate-house and spread her paws placatingly. 'Please, friends, let's not do anything hasty. There's still time for the Abbot to return yet. I've often known him to stay out far later than this.'

'But not when there are corsairs and vermin abroad in Mossflower,' said Martin.

The badger Mother turned her gaze on him. 'What do you suggest we do?' she asked.

The Warriormouse stared out of the window at the evening sky. 'I think the best thing is to wait until dark. If Viola and the Abbot are not back by then, something is surely amiss. I can lead a party out into the woodlands by night. We know the woods better than strangers do, and they will not be expecting us.'

Skipper seconded Martin's proposal. 'Yore right, matey. I'll go along with you. Hark, what's that?'

Wullger the gatekeeper knew immediately. 'Somebeast poundin' on the main gate outside. It ain't the Abbot, though, 'e knocks proper like a gentlebeast, always three taps. I'd advise you go atop of the wall to see whatbeast is makin' that sort o' din!'

Martin, Auma and Skipper raced out of the gatehouse and up the wallstairs. They stood on the main threshold over the gate, staring down at a band of creatures, the leader of whom seemed to make the rural twilight sinister and unclean with its presence.

Even tough Skipper was taken aback. 'Seasons o' slaughter!' he whispered to Martin. 'Am I 'avin' a bad dream, or is that thing real?'

Surrounded by half a crew of corsairs and searats, the Monitor General stood head and shoulders over his remaining five lizards. Lask Frildur made a horrific and impressive sight. His flat reptilian eyes watched the Redwallers as he pointed a monstrous scaled claw and rasped officially, 'Open your gatez, I have wordz to zay to you!'

The Warriormouse showed no fear. His voice rang out like steel striking an anvil. 'I command these gates, not you! Say who you are and what you want, but don't try giving orders to me!'

The huge Monitor puffed out his throat balefully. 'I am Lazk Frildur, Monitor General to the mighty Emperor Ublaz. I come here to collect zigz pearlz called the Tearz of all Oceanz. They were ztolen from my mazter – you will return them!'

Auma leaned towards Martin, her voice low. 'I don't like this. That reptile wouldn't turn up here demanding anything if he didn't have something up his sleeve.'

Skipper's lips barely moved as he muttered, 'She's right, matey, you'll 'ave to see if'n y'can bluff 'im!'

Martin kept his face grim and resolute as he murmured

134

to his friend, 'I certainly will have to bluff my way along; we don't have six pearls and it could be a long while until we do. Let's see if I can find out what's making this lizard so confident.'

Lask's tongue was beginning to flicker impatiently. 'I am waiting, mouze!'

Martin leaned carelessly against the battlements. 'Supposing we did have these six pearls to give you, what would we receive in return for them?'

'The livez of your Abbotmouze and a bankvole!'

Martin felt his heart sink, but he kept up a nonchalant attitude. 'You lie, lizard. How do I know you are holding them?'

At a signal from the Monitor General, one of the lizards hurled up a small bundle weighted with a stone. It clattered on the threshold. Auma seized it and tore away the vine-wrapped rags.

Martin felt his worst fears confirmed as he saw Skipper pick up two pairs of Redwall sandals, one pair slightly larger than the other. It was hard for the Warriormouse to keep his voice calm as he said, 'These are just two pairs of sandals, they could belong to anybeast . . .'

For the first time, Lask Frildur smiled, showing yellowed rows of evil-looking teeth. 'The Abbotmouze iz called Durral, Viola iz the maid'z name. You want more proof – here!' Lask's claw shot out as he hurled something up.

Auma swallowed hard. She picked up the delicate object, both finely polished crystal lenses smashed. 'Father Abbot's glasses. Look, Martin.'

Blood rose in the Warriormouse's eyes. Raging and roaring, he tried to tug free of Skipper and Auma, straining to climb over the battlements at his foe. 'Touch one hair of their heads and I will slay you, scalescum! You and all your rabble, I will send you to Hellgates!'

Lask had never seen such ferocity from any creature. He realized that Romsca's warning had not been an idle one: these Redwallers did indeed have warrior blood in their veins. Steadying himself, he called back to the raging beast on the walltop, 'Your friendz are unharmed, but they are far from here on a vezzel anchored out on the great waterz, you cannot rezcue them. Bring me the pearlz and I will releaze the captivez to you!'

Having delivered his ultimatum, Lask marched off quickly with his followers and dodged smartly into the cover of Mossflower Wood.

Auma held Martin tight. He was still struggling, tears of helpless rage flowing openly down his cheeks, and she had to exert all her strength to hold him.

'Skipper, let's get him back down into the gatehouse,' she said, 'we need to think this out calmly. Grab his footpaws, he has the power and wildness of a badger Lord. I've never seen Martin like this!'

Unaware of what had taken place on the walltop, Tansy sat with Rollo, Piknim and Craklyn in the cellars, puzzling over Fermald the Ancient's third, and what seemed to them most baffling, rhyme. Tansy read it aloud for the umpteenth time:

'My sad third tear is shed, for one who now
  lies dead,
A friendly foe it was to me, a cunning old
  adversary.
Now heed the clues and read my rhyme,
Patience pays but once this time.
Inside the outer walls I lie,
Without me you would surely die.
I am not earth nor am I stone,
No shape at all to call my own,
Not bird or beast or flow'r or tree,
Yet captives live within me free!'

Rollo removed his glasses and rubbed his eyes, sighing wearily. 'Is there any of that dandelion and burdock cordial left? Pour me some, please, Craklyn. This is a real poser and no mistake!'

The squirrelmaid offered a suggestion as she poured the drink. 'I wonder if Fermald was writing about the dead creature, Graylunk? See, the first line says, my sad third tear is shed, for one who now lies dead. What d'you think, Tansy?'

The hogmaid studied the slim paper scrap in front of her. 'No, it couldn't be. Graylunk's remains are outside in Mossflower, and this line states clearly, inside the outer walls I lie.'

The mousemaid agreed. 'Correct. What we're looking for lies within the walls of our Abbey. It's not much of a clue, but I think it means something not actually inside this main building.'

Craklyn thought about it, then seconded her friend's view. 'Aye, when we talk of things in the grounds we always say inside the Abbey walls. Not within the Abbey, but between the building and the outer wall.'

Rollo was tired, but the logic suddenly dawned upon him. 'Oh, I see! You mean outside – the orchard, the lawns and so on. Right, who do we know who lies buried out there?'

Furlo Stump was restacking the firkins back in place, listening to the conversation. Leaving his work he ambled over, wiping slowly at his strong paws with a damp cloth. 'Beg pardon, but don't mind me sayin', I thinks yore wrong lookin' for a he or a she. The poem says it were an it, not he nor she. A friendly foe it was to me the line says. I'm prob'ly wrong though, but I jus' thought I'd mention it.'

Tansy shook Furlo's paw heartily. 'Well done, mister Furlo. That was cleverly thought out! Sometimes we can get too smart for our own good and miss the clue, and that's when we need good common sense like yours, sir. Come on, let's take a look around outside, there's still time before dark.'

The friends had barely ventured outdoors into the gathering dusk when Auma came hurrying towards them, calling, 'Have you seen Martin or Skipper recently, are they inside?'

Tansy sensed something was wrong by the worried look on the badger's homely face. 'No, we haven't seen them, Auma. What's happened?'

Ushering them back inside, the badger Mother glanced about. 'Come, help me search for Martin and Skipper. I'll tell you as we go . . .'

BOOK TWO

Westward the Warriors

19

Pale white as watery milk, a spring moon cast its light over the still trees of Mossflower, patching light and deep shadows throughout the silent woodlands. Without the need of lanterns, Martin the Warriormouse strode abreast with the Skipper of Otters, Clecky the mountain hare and his companion Gerul the barn owl. Martin had sheathed the sword of his legendary namesake across his back; Skipper carried sling, stones and a light javelin, whilst Clecky had found a hare longbow and quiver of arrows in Redwall's armoury. Gerul had his formidable talons and fierce curved beak, weapons enough for any owl.

Telling only Auma of their plans, the four friends had slipped away from the Abbey, making a pact that they would only return in the company of Abbot Durral and Viola bankvole. Skipper and Martin were both experienced trackers. A broken twig, a crushed leaf or the slightest pawdent in the Mossflower loam was sufficient to tell them that they were right on the trail of Lask Frildur and the vermin crew.

It was long after midnight when they spotted the glimmer of campfire 'twixt the treetrunks. Martin waited with Clecky and Skipper, while Gerul flew to investigate, gliding like an elusive moonbeam through the high foliage.

They had not long to bide before Gerul returned. Fluttering down to the low boughs of an alder, the owl blinked and ruffled his breast feathers briskly. 'Ah, 'tis them all right, sir, bold as brass an' cheeky as chaffinches, squattin' on their hunkers an' gnawin' at pore dead birds. But the big lizard spoke truth, so he did. There's not a sign of the good ould Abbot, nor the liddle volemaid, he's hid them away on that ship he spoke of, the scurvy rascal!'

Martin unsheathed his sword. 'Skip, you go in from the left, Clecky, you and Gerul circle in from the right, I'll take the centre. Wait for my call, then it's straight in and give no quarter. But remember, we want to take the leader alive, so don't slay the big one called Lask. We need him to bargain for the Abbot and Viola. Go now and good luck be with you!'

A single vermin sentry had been posted on the left side. It was closest to the woodland edge, and Lask considered that the most likely place an attack would come from. Normally he would not have bothered with a sentry, but something in the maddened eyes of the Warriormouse had told him that this was no creature who would sit still and bargain whilst those under his protection were held hostage.

The sentry was a burly stoat called Skarbod, veteran corsair of many fights and battles. Hiding behind an elm trunk, Skarbod watched Skipper creeping noiselessly forward. The stoat stood well hidden by the broad elm as, drawing a scimitar, he waited for the otter to pass him.

Skipper heard the corsair's blade start whistling through the air; only speed saved the otter Chieftain's life. Throwing himself flat to the earth, he left the blade slashing night air, then, rolling over, he thrust upward like lightning with his javelin.

'Yeeeeaaagh!'

Skarbod's last scream was cut short as he fell dead on top of his slayer. As Skipper threw him off, pandemonium broke out.

Martin charged through the centre like a thunderbolt. 'Redwaaaaall!'

A searat who was not fast enough fell to Martin's blade. Lask Frildur immediately signalled his Monitors to follow him. Leaping back out of the firelight, he hissed at the corsairs, 'He iz only one, kill the mouze!'

Suddenly Martin was hemmed in by vermin swinging a variety of weapons; he cleaved a ferret immediately in front of him. A weasel behind him raised an axe, but before the vermin could strike a feathered shaft took it through the nape of its neck, and the time-honoured battlecry of hares and badgers rang through the glade.

'Eulaliaaaa!'

Clecky and Gerul stormed in at the same time Skipper hit hard on the opposite flank of the mêlée. Four more fell before the corsairs broke and scattered in all directions.

The fire had been scattered in the ambush. Clecky coughed and rubbed his eyes as he staggered about, shouting, 'Onward the buffs! Death before dinner! Stand an' fight!'

Skipper halted the hare, who had picked up a broad-bladed cutlass and was in danger of felling anybeast with it.

'Whoa there, mate, can't yer see they've fled!' the otter said.

As the smoke cleared it became apparent that the four Redwallers were alone. Martin stepped out of the cloud of choking smoke, saying, 'What happened to the lizards?'

Gerul beat the air with his wings to clear it. 'The blackguards never even stopped t'fight, sir, they were away through the dark like a half-dozen ould swallows flyin' south!'

Skipper had picked up the trail on the far side of the camp. 'They went this way, Martin, come on!'

Lask and his Monitors had a good head start. They emerged from the woodlands onto the path, where most of the panic-sped remnants of the crew joined them. The Monitor General found himself facing an angry searat brandishing a spear.

'Yew rotten coward! Slidin' away an' leavin' yore shipmates in the lurch! Yer a spineless, scale-faced . . . Unhh!'

Lask wasted no time. One great smash of his heavy tail left the searat lying with a broken neck. Scuttling across the path, Lask leapt into the ditch running along its west side. 'We muzt get back to the vezzel. Follow me, or ztay and die like he did!'

Wordlessly they piled into the ditch and splashed along behind the Monitor General, their flight made more desperate by the knowledge that the Redwallers would soon be on their heels.

Skipper was lagging behind. Martin waited for him to catch up, and saw that he was hobbling slightly.

'Skip, what's the matter, you old streamdog?' he asked.

The otter grimaced and lifted his right footpaw. 'Oh, I'll be all right, mate. Stepped on some vermin's fallen sword back there, 'tis only a scratch . . .'

Clecky inspected the wound. 'If y'call that a scratch, bucko, then I'd hate t'see what you call a real wound. Gerul, Martin, scout about, see if y'can come up with any herbs. Sit still, old chap, this shouldn't take long.'

Martin returned with dock leaves, but Gerul had found some young sanicle, of which he was very proud. 'Me ould mother always said sanicle's just the plant fer keepin' wounds from gettin' infected. She said 'twas also a grand remedy for the owl wumps an' spotty egg pimples, so she did!'

Martin tore a strip from his tunic sleeve, and Clecky used it to bandage the dock and sanicle tightly to Skipper's footpaw. 'There y'go! You'll never see an otter totter with a bandage like that on his jolly old paw, wot wot? An' y'won't have to worry about spotty egg wumps

144

or owl pimples, or whatever it was that burblebeak's old mum was always goin' on about. So that's you fixed up, me ole scout, good as new!'

Clecky was right. Skipper could get along on the bandaged footpaw as if it had never been injured.

Dawn was starting to streak the sky as the friends scoured the path for signs. It did not take Skipper long to discover Lask's plan.

'Hah! Ole scaletail thinks he's throwin' us off the scent by jumpin' in the ditch an' sloshin' through the water. Just look 'ere, Martin, bruised nettles, broken reeds, mud sloshed everywhere, it's plainer'n the nose on yer face!'

They walked along the edge of the ditch following the signs as the sun rose on a bright spring day.

20

Breakfast at Redwall that morning was a subdued affair. Tansy hardly noticed little Arven and the molemaid Diggum helping themselves slyly to the blackcurrant muffins on her platter. She looked up from a beaker of mint tea growing cold in front of her; Auma the badger Mother was rising from her seat. A gradual hush fell on the diners as Auma's paw went up.

'Friends, there is a lot of gossip and rumour abroad in our Abbey since last night, so let me set matters straight. Our Abbot and young Viola bankvole have gone missing; they are probably lost in Mossflower Wood somewhere. Martin has taken some companions and gone to search for them. I am sure that eventually they will all come home safe. Meanwhile our life at Redwall must carry on as usual, Abbot Durral would wish it so. Therefore I ask you to carry on with your work as you always do, look after the Dibbuns, do not wander outside the Abbey gates, see to your chores, and above all please do not indulge in gossip and scaremongering. That is all.'

Diggum absently took a gulp of Arven's pennycloud cordial. 'Worrum 'bout ee gurt blizzard, will ee cum back an' eat us oop?'

Arven considered this as he stole Diggum's nutbread.

'Naw, blizzards on'y eat h'Abbots an' voles's!'

Tansy wiped cordial from Diggum's chin. 'The word is lizard, not blizzard. And don't say such horrible things. What has Mother Auma just said about gossiping?'

Arven wrinkled his nose at the hogmaid as he climbed down from the dining bench. 'She din't say Dibbuns not gossip, we be likkle an' don't know no better. C'mon, Diggum.'

With their paws about each other's shoulders, the unstoppable pair ambled off chanting at each other, 'Gossip gossip gossip gossip gossip!'

Rollo joined Tansy, nodding in the Dibbuns' direction. 'What are those two up to?'

Tansy shook her head, smiling fondly at the retreating Dibbuns. 'Oh, they're just gossiping, they're too little to know any better.'

Rollo adjusted his glasses higher on his nose. 'Let us gossip a bit about these pearls. Auma tells me we need all six of them to ransom Viola and the Abbot from their captors.'

Tansy got up and accompanied Rollo outside. 'That's a lot easier said than done. This third rhyme has me well and truly stumped, Rollo. Did you dream up any solutions during the night? I know I didn't.'

Piknim and Craklyn were already outside, sitting on the ramparts over the gatehouse. Teasel the hogwife was with them, sipping at a large mug of dandelion tea.

'Mornin', Rollo, mornin', Tansy. My, wot a nice day 'tis. I'm just coolin' my ole paws out 'ere an' takin' tea, them kitchens gets so steamy 'ot after breakfast.'

Rollo and Tansy went up to the walltop and continued studying the rhyme with Piknim and Craklyn, whilst Teasel sipped tea and hummed to herself.

Tansy passed the thin paper to Piknim. 'Oh, here, you have it. I'm getting dizzy just looking at that rhyme and getting nowhere with it. My sad third tear is shed, for

147

one who now lies dead, a friendly foe it was to me, a cunning old adversary. Hmm, I can repeat it by heart now. Teasel, you knew Fermald the Ancient as well as any; what friends did she have to your knowledge?'

The good hogwife scratched her headspikes. 'Friends, y'say? I don't know as Fermald ever spoke of otherbeasts as friends, 'ceptin' that wounded vermin Graylunk an' maybe ole Grimjaw, an' that'n she spoke of as friend an' foe in the same breath. Aye, Fermald were a right ole strange 'un!'

Rollo looked up sharply from the rhyme. 'Grimjaw? Who in the name of autumn apples was Grimjaw?'

Teasel sipped at her tea, rocking back and forth. 'Fermald often told me about Grimjaw, though goodness knows wot she'd 'ave done with the thing if ever she'd 'ave caught it.'

Rollo blinked impatiently over his glasses at the hogwife. 'Really, marm, will you please stop talking in riddles and tell us what you know about this . . . this Grimjaw!'

Teasel blew huffily on her tea to cool it. 'Now don't you get all sharp wi' me, mister Recorder, or I shan't say another word. Politeness don't cost pear pudden, they say!'

Tansy smiled winningly, stroking the ruffled hogwife's paw. 'There! I'm sure Rollo didn't mean to be sharp, missus Stump. Please tell us about Grimjaw – it's very important that we know.'

Teasel cast a fond glance at the young hogmaid. 'Well, all right, missie. Never mind that ole grump, I'll tell you. Every time there was about t'be a feast or celebration, Fermald brought out her rod'n'line to fish the Abbey pond. She was forever tryin' to catch a big ole grayling that'd lived there for more seasons than most could remember. Fermald wanted that fish to grace the Abbot's table, but she never did manage to catch it. She'd stop out there from dawn till dusk, empty-pawed

148

an' 'ungry. Later, I'd serve 'er supper leftovers. Teasel, she'd say, that grayling is my best friend and my worst foe, the long hours I spent trying to catch that fish, she'd say, but he won't be caught, the old villain, he always escapes my line! That's wot she'd say.'

Suddenly everything became clear to Craklyn. She waved the paper, chanting,

'Inside the outer walls I lie,
Without me you would surely die.
I am not earth nor am I stone,
No shape at all to call my own,
Not bird or beast or flow'r or tree,
Yet captives live within me free!

'The answer is water! Without it anybeast would surely die. Water's not earth, stone, beast, bird, flower, or tree. It has no shape of its own. Fish swim freely in it, though they are really captives of whatever stretch of water they live in. Our water lies within the Abbey walls – I can see it from here, the Abbey pond!'

Teasel watched the young ones scampering down the steps and speeding over the lawns, with Rollo in their wake. She sipped her tea. 'Dearie me an' lackaday, dashin' an' a rushin' about, where'll it all end? Ah well, leastways now a body can sup 'er dan'elion tea in peace'n'quiet, afore it's time t'get lunch prepared!'

The four searchers stood at the edge of Redwall's pond. It was a pretty spot. Rushes and sedge sprouted thick in the shallows of its far edge, and an old, flat-bottomed punt lay moored at the east bank. At its southern end the ground was light and sandy, running from a soft mossy hillock into the sunwarmed shallows. Deeper out the water took on an emerald-green hue, and myriad small flying insects dipped to cause ripples in the stillness.

Gazing at the peaceful scene, Tansy raised a question which had been bothering her since she had first heard about the grayling.

149

'How do we *know* old Grimjaw is dead? Fermald never caught the fish and we've only her word that he died. Maybe Grimjaw was just too old to rise to the bait; perhaps he's still alive down there.'

It was a sobering thought. None of them fancied searching a dim pond where a big grayling might be lurking in the depths or hiding among the reeds to defend its territory against intruders.

Then Tansy came up with a quick solution. 'Hi, Glenner, got a moment to spare down here?' she called to the walltop.

Glenner was a young female otter, one of Skipper's crew. She was still on walltop patrol, keeping an eye out for gulls or vermin. Glad to be relieved of the monotonous task, she bounded readily down, calling, 'Good morrow, mates, anythin' I can do for ye?'

Flicking a pebble into the pond, Tansy watched the ripples spread. 'Glenner, d'you think there's a big old grayling in there?' she asked.

The otter thumped her tail thoughtfully on the bank. 'I dunno, could be. Skipper always told us when we were young never to disturb big ole fishes, they can be very dangerous an' bad-tempered. There's an ole otter poem we had t'learn as young 'uns.

'Frisk in the water if you wish,
But stay clear of the big ole fish,
'Specially those with the fin like a sail,
They're the rogues who'll take yer tail,
So stay in the shallows an' bright sunlight,
An' y'll live to sleep round the fire at night!'

Rollo drew patterns in the sand with his footpaw. 'Er, haha, is that what they say, really? Er, I don't suppose that you'd like to, er, maybe check the pond to see if there is actually a grimling, er, grayjaw, er, big fish living in there?'

Glenner's reply was cheery and prompt. 'Cost you a

good pan o' hotroot'n'watershrimp soup, mates. I ain't riskin' me pretty young rudder in that pond fer nothin', oh no!'

Tansy grabbed Glenner's paw and shook it vigorously. 'Done! One pan of soup for one pink pearl!'

The otter cocked her head on one side quizzically. 'Wot pink pearl? Y'never said ought about a pink pearl, matey.'

'The big pink pearl that's lying at the bottom of that pond, puddenhead!' said Piknim. 'You don't think we wanted you just to amuse yourself in the water looking for a fish, did you? If a big fish was all we wanted to know about, why, we could've tossed in a Dibbun to see if he got eaten, then we'd know there was a big fish in there!'

Chortling, Glenner shoved the mousemaid playfully. 'Go on with yer, missie, you wouldn't sling no liddle Dibbun in there. Right, stan' back, pals, if'n the fish eats me then give my soup to Skipper when he gets back from searchin' for yore Abbot!'

Glenner took a running dive, slipping into the pond without a single splash. They glimpsed a thin stream of bubbles rising from her chin, then she was gone, lost in the greeny depths. Tansy paced up and down the bank, wondering how anybeast could hold its breath for what seemed an eternity.

'Glenner should have been up by now,' she said. 'I wonder what she's doing down there? Hope she hasn't bumped into old Grimjaw . . .'

Like an arrow from a bow, Glenner shot from the pond in a rush of water, springing up onto the bank beside them. 'Whooh! There's two graylings down there, mates, I seen 'em!'

Rollo's glasses slipped from his nose. 'Two big fish?'

Glenner shook herself, spraying them with a cascade of droplets. 'Aye, two, though one's long dead. I swam down to the bottom an' didn't see no grayling, just some minnows, roach an' a gudgeon. Then I spotted 'er, up alongside some boulders, a big tidy-lookin' female grayling, she was guardin' the bones o' Grimjaw 'er mate. He must've been a big 'un, too, by the size o' 'is frame. Looked like he died of ole age an' the minnows nibbled 'is carcass clean.'

Tansy clapped her paws with excitement. 'The pearl, did you see the big pink pearl, Glenner?'

'No, miss, 'fraid I didn't see no pearl. Does that mean I don't get me pot o' soup?'

Rollo polished his glasses carefully. 'Sorry, not until we get the pink pearl.'

Glenner winked at them, banging the last droplets from her sturdy rudderlike tail. 'So be it, we'll 'ave to figger out a way t'keep the female grayling off my back, so I can search proper for yore pink pearl. Get me a good long staff. Ha! that punt pole will do. Now, let's get the punt over t'this bank where the shallows are clear, and stan' it up on its side. No big fish is goin' t'do Glenner out o' a pot o' hotroot'n'watershrimp soup made in Redwall's kitchen.'

Craklyn turned to Piknim, bewildered. 'What in the name of crab apples is that crazy otter up to?'

Tansy took them by the paws and headed for the punt. 'Don't ask silly questions. Whatever it is, I'm willing to give it a try. Come on, you two!'

21

There were two hilltops close to the northern inlet of Sampetra. Hardly a blade of grass stirred in the warm humid morning as Rasconza the fox and the rebel crews stood on top of one hill, facing Ublaz and his guard of Trident-rats and Monitors waiting on the other. The Emperor moved first, descending alone into the valley between both hills; Rasconza watched him a moment then followed suit. Ublaz sat down upon the grass, placing his only weapon, the silver dagger, on the ground in front of him. Rasconza unbuckled his belt with the ten daggers it held and slung the lot down, then he sat.

The mad-eyed Emperor smiled broadly. 'You carry a lot of blades, Rasconza.'

The corsair fox matched his smile, but avoided his eyes. 'Aye, an' I can use 'em, too, Ublaz!'

The Emperor placed his silver dagger on top of Rasconza's weaponry. 'Then take mine as a token of our friendship, for we did not come here today to talk of using knives, my friend.'

Rasconza flipped the dagger into the air and caught it deftly. 'Hah! A pretty toy, thankee. Oh, I'm fergettin' me manners, exchange of gifts, 'ere's somethin' fer you.'

A gauzy silken scarf landed wisplike in the pine marten's lap. He picked it up and admired it. 'Fine silk, hmm, green suits me, too. Does this gift signify anything? Is there a meaning behind it?'

Rasconza continued flipping the silver blade, watching it glitter in the sunlight.

'Oh, it signifies right enough, Ublaz. Wot you do is you puts it over yore face. That way you can see me, 'cos 'tis only thin silk, but I won't be lookin' into yore eyes. Aye, I've 'eard all about those glims o' yourn, an' I don't intend starin' into 'em an' losin' control o' my mind!'

Ublaz bound the scarf lightly across his eyes, chuckling. 'A wise move, fox, very wise indeed! I can see I'm going to enjoy business dealings with you. Now, what is it you want?'

This time Rasconza did not catch the dagger. It landed point down in the ground. 'The cap'ns are all dead,' he said. 'I meself slew Barranca, but you know that. So, I'm in charge of all the crews now an' I want peace. There's no profit in both sides killin' each other off. 'ere's my proposition. You appoint me Grand Cap'n of all the ships in 'arbour an' I'll serve yer.'

'Forgive my asking,' Ublaz interrupted, 'but how can you captain six ships at once?'

Rasconza shook his head. 'I don't want ter cap'n all six. *Bloodkeel*'s a good craft, she's my old ship, I'll take 'er. The other cap'ns I'll appoint from the crewbeasts, but I'll be the boss cap'n, and they'll take their orders from me when we're at sea. You'll control all on land. This is the way it'll work. I'll increase the tribute each ship 'as to pay, and we'll split it two ways, me'n'you, an' none the wiser. Of course you'll 'ave t'get off'n those timber stocks yore sittin' on, there ain't no more good wood on Sampetra an' the ship'll need wood fer repairs. Agreed?'

Ublaz spat on his paw and held it forth. 'Agreed!'

Rasconza also spat on his paw and clasped with the

pine marten. 'Haharr, you won't regret this day's work, matey!'

Behind the gauzy silk scarf the mad eyes glinted dangerously. 'I'm sure I won't . . . matey!'

Then, removing the scarf, Ublaz stood and hailed his guard. 'Nobeast will harm the crews, they can return to the harbour and use the taverns or board their ships as they please. You are not to fight with them; there is a truce. If you have any complaints against them, report to Rasconza, he is their leader. Disobey and you will answer to me. I am your Emperor, Ublaz. I have spoken!'

Late that evening the vermin crews roistered and sang in the harbour area of Sampetra. Only the fox Rasconza sat alone, brooding in the captain's cabin aboard *Bloodkeel*. Once he had been a mere bosun on this same vessel, now he was Captain in Chief of six ships. But a nagging thought had entered his mind as he went back over the day's events. It had all been too simple, Ublaz had agreed to his terms too readily . . . Why?

Ublaz sat upon his throne sipping wine, satisfied that he had defeated seven enemies in short time. Now he had only the fox to contend with. Easy game! The Emperor liked easy games, though he often cheated to win.

Martin and his friends had taken to the ditch, following Skipper as he tracked Lask Frildur and his company through Mossflower. The otter Chieftain halted and cast about looking for a sign, saying, 'Well, mates, ole Lask's learnin' a bit o' sense. See here, they've tried to cover their tracks, look, pawmarks. I reckon this is where they've climbed out o' the ditch an' prob'ly 'eaded west o'er yon field into the woods.'

Martin inspected the scratchmarks carefully. 'I think you're right, Skip. Once in the woods they'd find the river and follow it to the sea.'

With a leap and a bound, Clecky was out of the

ditch into the field. 'C'mon, chaps, after the scurvy bounders, wot!'

A slingstone whizzed out of nowhere, bouncing close to the hare's footpaw. He jumped back into the ditch with great alacrity. 'Ambush, chaps! Blinkin' nerve of the bottle-nosed blighters!'

The Warriormouse peered over the ditchtop, across the sunlit field, still sparkling with dew, to the shaded woodland fringe. There was no visible movement anywhere. 'As you said, Skip, the lizard is learning sense. He's left a rearguard behind to slow us up. They're in the woods somewhere, too well hidden for us to see.'

Gerul provided a swift solution to the problem. 'With yer permission, sir, I'll fly meself up high an' see if I can't spot the ould vermin.'

Before Martin could agree, the barn owl winged out over the field. As Gerul swooped low towards the trees he was struck by a heavy slingstone; he fell in a jumble of feathers. Immediately three gulls came screeching out of the tree cover and attacked Gerul as he lay dazed upon the ground.

Regardless of their own safety, Martin, Skipper and Clecky charged from the ditch, roaring.

'Redwaaaaaalllll!'

A Monitor and four searats loosed slingstones at them as they ran. The three friends separated, ducking and dodging, but still going forward. A well-hurled javelin from Skipper took one of the gulls out, then, with only his loaded sling, the otter Chieftain made a mad dash and flung himself upon the Monitor. Before the searats could come to the lizard's aid, Martin was among them with his sword. Clecky dropped his bow and arrows and, diving at the remaining two seagulls, he lashed out fiercely with his lethal long legs, protecting the fallen owl with his body.

The encounter was short and savage, with Martin and his friends emerging victorious, though one of the searats and a seagull escaped and fled off into the woodlands. But winning had its price. Gerul had been severely injured by the slingstone and the ravaging beaks of the gulls. Clecky made him comfortable whilst Martin attended to Skipper.

The otter had slain the carnivorous reptile with only a loaded sling and his natural strength. Skipper sat gasping, his back against a sycamore. Martin was horrified at the awful wounds inflicted by the Monitor's teeth and raking claws.

The otter winced as he grinned broadly, making a joke of the whole thing. 'Uuuuhh! I don't think I could manage t'fight another one of those rascals today, mate!'

Martin tore his cloak into strips, calling to Clecky, 'How is Gerul, is he all right?'

The barn owl flapped a wing limply. 'Arr, I'll live, sir, though me ould wing is as much use as feathers on a fish, so 'tis.'

Clecky was using the last of Gerul's sanicle on his friend's wounds. 'Be still, you boulder-beaked curmudgeon, here, put y'talon on this while I bandage it, you great feather-faced frump. Got y'self in a nice old mess, m'laddo, haven't you, wot!'

When the two casualties were cleaned up and bandaged, Martin looked at them despairingly. 'You two aren't fit to carry on. We'll have to get you back to Redwall and some proper nursing.'

Skipper struggled upright, glaring fiercely at his friend. 'Oh no you won't, matey. Yore job is to get the Abbot an' that liddle bankvole free. As fer me an' this bird, we can make our own way back t'the Abbey, can't we, matey?'

Gerul wobbled his way over to Skipper, and they stood supporting each other.

'Sure will y'look at the pair of us now, between us we make an owlotter, whatever that is, but don't you worry, sir, as me ould mother used t'say, the road may be long but it doesn't get any shorter by standin' gossipin', so we're off to Redwall now. Look after me friend Clecky an' treat him kindly, but don't turn yer back on him if there's food about, oh no, sir!'

The hare sniffed. 'Thank you for those few kind words, you feather-bottomed old fraud. See you back at the jolly old Abbey in a few days, wot!'

Martin could not suppress a smile as the two casualties staggered off across the field wing in paw, chattering animatedly as they hobbled along together.

'Ouch! I think I'm goin' to need great pots of soup an' lots of elderberry wine afore I'm right again, Gerul!'

'Isn't that a fact, sir, an' as for meself I think pasties an' puddens with a barrel or two of the good October Ale will put the sheen back upon me feathers, indeed, so they will!'

Clecky twitched his ears fondly, waving goodbye to his companion. 'Huh! D'y'know, I'd swear that chap's fakin'. Got himself wounded just so's he can fill his face at Redwall an' not share any of it with me. Typical of the blighter!'

Martin gave the hare's tunic a sharp tug. 'Remember what Gerul's old mother used to say, the road may be long, but it doesn't get any shorter by standing gossiping. Come on, let's get after Lask Frildur!'

22

Twilight was falling over the sea, and red sunrays cast a fiery path across the ebbing tide off the coast of Mossflower country. Aboard *Waveworm* the ferret Romsca leaned over the stern, scanning the darkening shore in company with her steersrat Bladetail.

'Where in the name o' gutrubbin's 'ave those seagulls got to?' she grumbled. 'I only told 'em to fly back an' see if Lask was on 'is way.'

Bladetail spat reflectively into the water. 'May'ap ole Lask kept them with 'im for some purpose.'

He turned and cast a glance towards the two prisoners huddled together on a heap of sailsheet amidships. 'Those Monitors are pesterin' yer liddle vole agin, Cap'n.'

Viola hid her face against the Abbot's robe, shaking with fear as a Monitor poked his evil head close to her, grinning and grinding his teeth, enjoying the volemaid's distress. 'Tazty vole, you will tazte nizzzze!'

Against her instincts, Romsca had found herself feeling protective towards Viola and the Abbot. She had spent the whole day keeping the lizards from tormenting the captives, and suddenly her temper rose. Whipping out her sword, she strode up on the unsuspecting Monitor and kicked him sprawling. Belabouring the reptile with the flat of her blade, Romsca snarled, 'Keep yer foul-smellin' snout away from the maid, scalescum!'

The Monitor scrambled upright, teeth bared, claws raised defiantly. 'I do az I pleaze, ferret. Lazk Frildur givez me my orderz!' He made as if to push Romsca out of the way, but the corsair moved with lightning speed, bulling the Monitor backward to the rail.

'Well, 'ere's an order from me, scalebrain,' she snarled. 'Die!' With a swift thrust she ran him through and tipped him overboard. Then she whirled on the other Monitors, pointing her sword. 'That goes fer the rest of you thick'eaded lizards! Stay away from the maid or y'll join yer mate there!'

Abbot Durral whispered softly to Viola, 'Romsca is not totally against us. We may have a friend.'

For a moment it looked as if the remaining Monitors were about to rush Romsca, but a sharp whistle from Bladetail brought the rest of the vermin crew on deck, fully armed. The corsair captain grinned invitingly at the lizards.

'Come on, yer beauties, want to try yer luck with us, do yer?' she baited them. 'I'll have yer guts fer garters an' yer tripes fer supper!'

'Ahoy, *Waveworm*, throw us a line! We're comin' aboard!'

Bladetail saw the group standing in the shallows. 'It's Lask Frildur an' the others at last!'

Shivering from the water, Lask pulled himself on board *Waveworm*. He glared at Romsca, demanding, 'Whatz going on, why is a Monitor dead in the waterz?'

The ferret turned her bladepoint towards the Monitor General. 'I slew 'im fer interferin' with the prisoners. I'm cap'n aboard this ship. You took yer time gettin' 'ere – wot kept yer?'

Lask pointed back to the shore. 'Creaturez from Redwall are after uz. I left five and the three gullz to hold them off. I do not know how many they are!'

Romsca snapped orders to her crew. 'Up anchor an' let 'er drift further offshore fer safety. See, Lask, I told yer those Redwallers were fighters.'

Grath Longfletch crouched low in her longboat, watching *Waveworm* from a distance. It was drifting from its original mooring, further out to sea. A long shout like a warcry rang out from the shore.

'Eulaliaaaaaa!'

In the falling light, Grath saw the steersrat Bladetail topple over the stern, pierced by an arrow from the shore. A stoat leapt up on the stern, whirling a slingshot to retaliate. Grath decided to help out. Grabbing her bow, she placed a shaft on the string and whipped it back.

Lask watched in surprise as an arrow seemed to grow out of the stoat's skull. Pandemonium broke out aboard *Waveworm* as the vermin staggered backward and fell to the deck. Lask Frildur dashed into his cabin and slammed the door, and the other Monitors ran for cover.

Slashing the air with her blade, Romsca roared out orders. 'Take 'er out deeper where arrers can't reach! Make some sail that'll move us along faster! Break out some boat'ooks an' longpikes in case they tries t'board us! Stir yer stumps!'

Abbot Durral acted then. Lifting Viola, he shuffled to the rail and threw her over the side, shouting, 'Swim, little one, make for the shore!'

A searat grabbed the Abbot; throwing a noosed rope over him he bound the old mouse's paws to his side, then he dragged him to the mast where he made the rope fast.

Romsca dashed to the rail, shouting, 'Get the maid out o' the water, look lively!'

A searat ran halfheartedly to the rail with a rope; he screamed and fell wounded by a green-feathered arrow, yelling, 'Longboat t'the port side 'eadin' this way!'

Grath Longfletch laid aside her weapon, racing towards the small figure floundering in the water as the outgoing tide carried it seaward. Gripping the little tiller tight the otter sent her craft skimming between the waves. Viola was pulled by the current; she swallowed seawater, scrabbling at *Waveworm*'s prow as she drifted in front of it, blinded by stinging salt water.

Grath was close enough to see now. It was either a mouse or a vole – no searat this. Risking everything on a desperate gamble, the otter lashed the tiller to her stern seat with the aft line. She saw the enormous prow of *Waveworm* looming up, but regardless of danger she grabbed the volemaid's apronback with both paws and pulled her clear of the advancing ship's bow.

Bump! Craaaack!

Waveworm caught the longboat, ramming it amidships and turning the small craft momentarily over on its side. Grath was in the sea, with Viola clinging to her. Striking away from the ship, she shouted. 'Take a good deep breath an' hold on t'me!'

Swimming as only a powerful grown otter can, Grath Longfletch dived and turned underwater, streaking away from *Waveworm* towards the shore. Viola bankvole closed both eyes and held her breath, dark water rushing past her as the otter sped them both out of danger. Then panic overtook Viola, the breath ran from her in a stream of bubbles and she began swallowing water.

The next thing she knew a paw was patting her back as Clecky spoke to her in a reassuring voice. 'Dearie me, missie, fancy tryin' to swallow all the sea in one go! C'mon, give it back, cough it all up now, you'll be fine!'

Between coughs and spurts of seawater Viola could see her rescuer introducing herself to Martin.

*   *   *

Waveworm was now well out of reach. Grath crouched in the lee of some rocks with Martin, Clecky and Viola.

The Warriormouse watched the corsair vessel, saying, 'Let's hope she's dropped anchor there, maybe tomorrow we'll be able to do something about Abbot Durral.'

Clecky left off patting Viola's back. 'I think we're on a loser at the moment, old chap, they're holdin' all the acorns in this little game, wot! Now if we had a ship . . .'

'Stay here, I'll see what's happened to my boat!' Grath said, and she was off, running down the beach and disappearing into the sea.

Clecky shrugged and raised an eyebrow at Martin. 'Odd sort o' gel that'n, fights like mad t'get ashore, then runs straight back into the bally water?'

23

At the edge of Redwall Abbey pond the punt had been hauled out of the water and dragged around to the sandy shallows. Glenner the otter explained her plan to the four friends.

'Y'know wot they always say about the simplest plans, mates? They're the best 'uns. We stand this punt up on its side first. Well, come on, lend a paw there. I can't do it alone!'

It was an old flat-bottomed craft and quite heavy. They stood paw deep, grunting and gasping as they tried to lift the punt clear of the water. Auma the badger Mother was out for a stroll around the grounds with three Dibbuns, Gurrbowl and Diggum the molebabes and the little squirrel Arven. They wandered across to the pond.

Auma watched the curious proceedings, then enquired, 'I don't know what you're up to, Rollo, but d'you need any help?'

Placing both paws on his back, the old Recorder straightened up. 'Ooh, my aching bones! We'd be extremely grateful if you'd help us to stand this punt on its side in the shallows.'

Little Arven rolled his smock sleeves up briskly. 'Stanna side, Rolly, we do it easy. Cummon, moles, we showem 'ow to lifta boat, us on'y likkle but we's horful strongly!'

As the three Dibbuns charged into the shallows, Auma scooped them neatly up in her huge paws and set them back on the bank. 'Keep an eye on these rogues, Tansy. Everybeast stand clear now!'

Then the big badger set the punt on its side with a single powerful heave. 'There, is that what you wanted? What do you expect to do with the boat in this position?'

Glenner picked up the long punting pole. 'There's one o' them pink pearls somewhere on the pond bottom, marm, but there's also a big ole female grayling. So I'm goin' to dive down there an' chase 'er into the shallows with this pole. The plan is to drop the punt upside down on 'er, so the fish'll be trapped, then I can search for the pearl without that big ole grayling botherin' me. You'll all need t'stand on the boat; yore weight will stop the fish escapin'. It should work.'

At the mention of a big fish, the Dibbuns became excited. They danced about on the bank squealing and shouting.

'Hurrhurr, oi'll swim down with ee an' chase ee gurt fisherbeast!'

'H'an' I bite its tail off. Chomp! Like dat wi' my big sharp teefs!'

'Burr aye, an' oi'll sit unner ee boat an' 'old ee gurt fishbeast 'ard an' toight, so ee don't 'urt you'm creeturs!'

Auma shook a warning paw at them. 'You'll stay with me and keep tight hold of my paws or I'll tan your tails and send you off to bed!'

All the helpers were huddled behind the boat. Auma poked her head around the side and called to Glenner, who was wading through the reeds at the pond's far edge, 'We're all ready here, down you go, Glenner. Be careful!'

The otter submerged into the crystal-clear water, holding the pole like a lance in front of her. The female grayling lurked in the boulders at the deep centre of the pond, unwilling to move away from the skeletal remains of her long-dead mate. Glenner tapped her gently on the head with the pole, but she refused to budge. However, a second tap brought the big fish's dorsal fin upright, and she became aggressive. Like a flash she charged, but the otter fended her off skilfully, tapping away sharply with the butt end of the pole, and bumping the grayling on her head, sides and tail until she ceased her attack and turned in retreat. Glenner was right after her, urging her along, shepherding her with the punting pole.

Auma peered around the side of the punt. 'Here she comes, get ready now, when I say push . . .'

Tansy took a quick peek; the big female grayling made a brave sight. Wriggling backwards into the shallows the great purply-sheened body bucked and quivered as it snapped and fought the teasing pole. The high, long-based dorsal fin stood clear of the water like a spined streamer; iridescent scales flashed in the sunlight, splashing water left and right.

'Now push!!!' Auma shouted.

The punt hit the water with a flat thwack, landing over the fish like a huge mouth closing. Caught up in the excitement of the moment, Rollo hitched up his habit and roared, 'Jump on top! Jump on top! Quick, everybeast on top!'

They scrambled on top of the upturned punt, their combined weight causing it to bed firmly into the sand of the shallows.

Sudden imprisonment made the big female fish go berserk. It leaped and bucked, whacking the bottom and sides of the punt furiously, throwing itself wildly in all directions.

Tansy clung to Rollo, Piknim clung to Craklyn, and all four then clung to the most solid beast around, Auma. The badger Mother had her paws full trying to keep hold of the Dibbuns, who chortled helplessly, wriggling and skipping across the bottom of the punt as if it were all a wonderful game. Under the grayling's onslaught the punt shuddered and quivered.

Tansy was amazed at the mad strength of a single fish. She stood swaying on the thrumming timbers, holding Arven's paw tightly, and said, 'If Glenner doesn't hurry up, the grayling's going to wreck this punt and send us all into the water!'

Auma eyed the upturned punt bottom doubtfully. 'It's a big powerful fish, right enough. These old timbers aren't going to last very long if it carries on the way it's going.'

'Ahoy, mates, let loose the ole fish!'

Glenner stood in the reedy shallows at the far side waving to them. En masse they leapt off and hurried up onto the bank. Auma went wading back in and lifted the punt slightly. With a whooshing rush of water the grayling shot out and was lost in a sandy swirl. She made straight for the safety of the boulders at the pond bottom, reunited with the frame of her dead partner.

Glittering wetly, the rose-coloured pearl caught the afternoon sunlight as Glenner tossed it high in the air, catching it deftly as it fell.

'Don't throw it about like that,' Rollo called sternly. 'It's not a plaything, Glenner. Bring it here this instant and don't drop it!'

The otter popped the pearl into her mouth. 'Wharr marr panna sowp?' she said around it.

Auma looked at Tansy and shrugged. 'What's the beast talking about?'

Glenner dropped the pearl from her mouth into Tansy's waiting paws. 'I said, where's my pan o' soup?'

Piknim pounded the otter's back happily. 'You'll get your pan of soup, you old water-walloper, well done!'

Arven picked up a small round pebble and gave it to Piknim. 'Me 'ave soop too!' he said.

'Where exactly did you find the pearl, Glenner?' asked Tansy.

Glenner sat down on the mossy bank, shaking her head sadly. 'You'll never believe it, matey, but it was that pearl wot killed ole Grimjaw. It was stuck in the bones where 'is throat once was.'

The hedgehog maid stared at the beautiful orb resting in her paw. 'So that was it. Fermald must have tossed this pearl into the pond and Grimjaw thought it was food and tried to swallow it, but the pearl lodged in his throat and choked him. I don't suppose that was what Fermald meant to do, but unwittingly she killed Grimjaw. Dearie me, she finally did defeat her old foe!'

Rollo sat down beside Tansy. 'Cheer up, missie, at least we've got the pearl. Don't look so unhappy, the greedy old fish slew himself, really.'

Tansy continued staring at the pearl, and said, 'It's not the fish I'm unhappy about, Rollo. I was just recalling the line of Fermald's poem which says, patience pays but once this time. This pearl is the one payment; we've got no piece of paper with clues to lead us on to the fourth pearl. What do we do next?'

Diggum the molebabe's reasoning was simple. 'Do now? Us'ns make ee gurt pot o' soop furr ee otter, marm!'

Rollo patted the little creature's velvety head. 'A capital idea, my friend; a good feed will help us all to think a little more clearly!'

Tansy was not convinced, however. She wandered glumly back across the tranquil lawns towards the Abbey. However, the irrepressible Piknim and Craklyn could not endure their companion's long face, and they danced around her, singing to lighten her mood.

'Pick me flowers for Redwall,
To grace the tables of Great Hall,
Go out upon the grassy ground,
Where flowers bloom all round.
Periwinkle primrose pimpernel,

Buttercup burnet and bluebell,
Arrowhead anemone asphodel,
Tansy's a flower as well!
Campion cowslip columbine,
Speedwell spurge and snowdrop fine,
Toadflax thrift and also thyme,
But pretty Tansy's mine!
Foxglove figwort feverfew,
Harebell hemlock hawkweed too,
Forget-me-nots with petals blue,
Sweet Tansy I'll pick you!'

Arven plucked a buttercup, and made Tansy bend so
he could place it behind her ear. Then the little squirrel
leapt onto her back and sang raucously the only part
of the song he could remember: 'Swee' Tansy I pick
yooooooooou!'

The hedgehog maid could not stay gloomy in such
company. She seized Arven and tickled him soundly.
'You little maggot, roaring down my poor ear like that,
you've deafened me!'

Arven shrieked with helpless laughter, trying to wrig-
gle free of the tickling paws. 'Yeeheehee, lemme go,
heeheeheehee. Tansy not tickle me yeeheehee!'

Tansy continued tickling, pretending Arven really had
deafened her. 'Eh, what's that? Speak up, sir, I can't
hear you?'

Trooping into Cavern Hole, they made themselves
comfortable. Friar Higgle strode in behind them, swinging a ladle, his face a picture of mock severity.

'Somebeast needin' a pot o' watershrimp'n''otroot
soup?' he said.

Glenner held up her paw hopefully. 'Aye, me, sir, I was
promised the soup by – '

The good Friar cut her short. 'Well, I don't know
nothin' about any promises, streamdog!'

Higgle watched Glenner's face fall mournfully and

smiled. A rap on the table from his ladle brought Teasel in. Pulling a serving trolley up to the table, she indicated the bubbling pot. 'A little bird tol' us you might be needin' this.'

The soup was so hot and spicy that only Glenner continued to refill her bowl; otters are known to be very partial to watershrimp and hotroot soup. The rest were well contented to cool their mouths with strawberry cordial and do full justice to a plum and apple crumble, supplemented by a large platter of redcurrant tarts which Teasel had baked for them.

Tansy brought the scallop shell case out and placed the third pearl in it, alongside the other two that had been found. Auma held the open shell up so that it caught the candlelight, and admired the three rosy orbs.

'The Tears of all Oceans,' mused Rollo, 'beautiful, are they not? But without the other three, they are quite useless. If we are to bargain for our Abbot and Viola all six are needed. Though I would give ten times that amount to have our friends back here safe.'

Auma closed the shell and fastened its clasp firmly. 'Aye, what price treasures when Redwallers are in danger? I dread to think of Martin and our friends out somewhere risking their lives against evil beasts. I wish there was something we could do to help them.'

Tansy placed the shell in its bag and fastened the bag to her apron strings. 'That's what's making me feel so bad, Auma. There are no more clues to the other three pearls. It would help them if we could find even the tiniest hint to set us on the trail again.'

Rollo settled himself wearily upon a wall-ledge. 'I think it's time to stop talking and start thinking.'

After the activity at the pond and the good food following, heads began to nod and eyelids started drooping in the warmth and quiet of Cavern Hole. First Rollo, followed by Auma and Glenner, then Tansy and the other two young maids Piknim and Craklyn. Little Arven would have drifted into sleep, but his head bumped the table as he leaned forward. Cramming tiny paws into his eyes he rubbed them until he was wide awake.

The two molebabes Diggum and Gurrbowl were snuggled down on a rush mat. Arven woke them and, smiling mischievously, he pushed and pulled the dozy pair up the stairs into Great Hall. Tweaking the molebabes' snouts none too gently, Arven roused them into full alertness. 'Cummon!' he whispered fiercely. 'Alla big 'uns sleepydozin', we got 'portant work!'

Gurrbowl blinked owlishly and sat on his fat little tail. 'Nothin' be as apportant as sleepen to a growen choild!'

Diggum, who had entered heartily into the conspiracy, pulled Gurrbowl upright, wagging a small digging claw at him. 'You'm nought but a gurt foozletop mole. Wot ee be wantin' us'ns t'do, zurr h'Arven?'

'We goin' a find the uvver free pearls f'Tansy!'

'Ho urr, gudd idea, whurr do ee think purrls be 'idden?'

'Gah! You a maggit, Gurrb'l, 'ow I knows where pearls be?'

'Burr, you'm doan't knoaw? Then whurr do us'ns start lukkin'?'

Arven thought about this for a moment, narrowing his eyes and whipping his bushy tail back and forth, then suddenly he brightened. 'Uppa stairs, where nobeast find us, tha's where!'

Giggling and pulling at one another's tunics, the three Dibbuns clambered up the dormitory steps, pushing and shoving to be first to the top. It was a good game, and what if a search did turn out to be a game? It was all good fun to the three Abbeybabes.

Tansy turned over, pulling her cape around her. Through the foggy haze of sleep's corridor, she recognized the heroic figure looming towards her. It could be none other than Martin the Warrior of ancient times. His smile radiated tranquillity; his voice was warm as a far-off bell on summer noontide.

'You are troubled, little one?'

The hedgehog maid sighed deeply in her sleep. 'I must find the next clue if I am to continue my search for the pearls, but I don't know where to begin looking.'

Martin's lips never appeared to move, though his voice echoed around Tansy's mind. 'Find the three babes and you will know . . .' The vision faded and Tansy slept peacefully on.

Craklyn was wakened by an odd sound.

'Shhlpp, shhlpp, shhlpp!'

The funny noise continued with monotonous regularity. Craklyn opened her eyes and sat up slowly.

Glenner withdrew her head from the soup pot, licking her whiskers and chin. 'Nought like 'otroot soup, matey, tastes just as good cold as it does warm. I'd eat it any time, night or day!'

Gradually the rest of the company awoke. Auma stretched mightily. 'Oooooh! What time is it? A fine bunch we are, lying about napping like a pile of Dibbuns!'

The word set a train of thought going in Tansy's mind. 'Dibbuns! Where are Diggum, Gurrbowl and Arven?'

She jumped up and began searching Cavern Hole.

Glenner licked the last soup drops from her chin as she watched Tansy. 'What's the panic? Dibbuns can't leave the Abbey, they're prob'ly playin' somewheres close by.'

The hedgehog maid checked under the table. 'I saw Martin the Ancient Warrior in my dreams. He told me to look for the three babes and I would know!'

Auma peered into an empty barrel standing in a corner. 'What would you know?' she said.

Tansy strode resolutely for the steps leading to Great Hall. 'Where the clue to the next pearl is, of course. Come on, we've got to find those Dibbuns!'

24

Rasconza called the two searats Baltur and Gancho to his ship, and the three of them leaned over the stern rail, speaking in low murmurs. The fox looked across the sunlit harbour, up to the palace of Ublaz. He knew the mad-eyed Emperor was probably having them watched.

Rasconza kept his face straight and his voice level. 'I don't like it, mates. Ublaz gave in too easy, that's not like 'im. I tell yer, that'n's a dangerous beast.'

Baltur glanced sideways at Rasconza. 'So, what're yer goin' t'do about it?'

'Well, I ain't 'angin' about in this 'arbour waitin' fer Ublaz t'make 'is move, so 'ere's me plan. I says we sail away from Sampetra tonight on the floodtide, an' once we're shut o' this place we don't come back!'

Gancho drummed a paw nervously on the rail. 'But Ublaz will see us if'n we all pulls anchor an' sails at once. It's too risky, 'e'll 'ave laid plans t'stop us!'

The fox shrugged. 'That's a chance we'll 'ave t'take, mates. The best bet is to let the crews know secretly, pass the word about quietlike. I'm appointin' both of you cap'ns, you'll get yer own ships. We'll wait until dark, then at my signal slip off, ship by ship. Are yer with me, mates?'

The two searats nodded, fired by their sudden promotions to captaincy. Baltur spoke for them both. 'We're with yer, Rasconza, give us our orders!'

Word passed between the wave vermin lounging around the taverns and harbour of Sampetra.

'Keep it under yer 'at, messmate, Rasconza sez we're sailin' tonight when it's dark.'

'Sailin' t'night? Wot, y'mean all of us?'

'Keep yer voice down, bucko, you just pass it on nice an' easy, everybeast t'be back aboard their ole ships by sunset!'

Gradually the whole quay area was rife with whispered messages being passed from one to another. In the late afternoon a grizzled searat with a patch on one eye and a rusty cutlass at his side stumped out of a tavern. He left the area as soon as he was sure nobeast was watching.

Two Monitors ushered the searat into the Emperor's throne room. Ublaz watched as the searat cast aside his disguise and picked up his trident.

'Tell me what you heard, are they planning to attack, or run?'

The Trident-rat stood rigid as the pine marten's eyes blazed into his brain. Then he told all he had heard.

Afternoon shadows were lengthening into the hour before twilight as Ublaz headed a powerful force of Monitors and Trident-rats to the jetty. Rasconza stood amidships on his vessel, in company with Baltur. The searat watched Ublaz approaching, and his paws began quivering.

'It's the Emperor, 'e knows wot we're up to!'

Rasconza smiled, showing no sign of alarm. He dug his claws sharply into Baltur's side. 'Shut yer gob, rat, an' stop flappin', I'll see t'this.'

The pine marten cut a handsome figure, clad in gold silks topped by a white turban set with a feather and greenstone jewel. He appeared to be unarmed. Ublaz smiled, greeting Rasconza pleasantly.

'So, how is my Chief Captain today? Everything ship-shape?'

Rasconza matched the Emperor's smile and manner immediately. 'Never better, yore mightiness, an' pray, wot brings yer to our 'umble ship on this fine day?'

Ublaz whipped out the green silken gauze the fox had given him. He winked at Rasconza before binding it lightly around his eyes. 'Hah! Nearly forgot my manners there. You've probably heard that I hypnotized a poisonous water serpent – I've got to be careful of these magic eyes of mine. Don't want to go putting any spells on my trusted Chief Captain, now do I?'

Rasconza felt a shudder pass through him. Instinctively his paw roamed to the silver dagger Ublaz had given him. 'Thank ye, Sire, but I'm sure y'never came all the way down 'ere to tell me that. Just wot do yer want?'

Ublaz stooped, looking at the stern of the vessel at water level. 'Nothing really, I merely thought it was about time I started making good my promises to you. I presume that now would be a good time to start overhauling our fleet. My carpenters will do the work. We'll start by replacing all your tillers and rudders, I've got fine stout timber to make new ones.'

Still smiling, but fuming inwardly, Rasconza was forced to stand helplessly by as Trident-rats and Monitors swarmed over his ship, removing the tiller and rudder, rendering the vessel useless.

When the other vessels had been similarly treated, Ublaz had six Trident-rats line up on the jetty in front of Rasconza. He pointed them out one by one.

'Galdra, Fentz, Orlug, Kerrat, Somgil and Criuth. These are your six new captains, all trustworthy creatures. Bow to your Chief!'

The six Trident-rats bowed respectfully to Rasconza.

The fox nodded formally to them, doing a quick mental calculation. 'Six, you say? But we only 'ave six ships,' he said.

Ublaz smiled winningly at his adversary. 'Ah yes, but you command them all. Soon they'll be good as new, and when we've replaced the tillers and rudders, we'll see about new masts for our fleet. I bid you good day, my Chief Captain!'

Ublaz removed the green gauze from his eyes and turned to go.

Baltur began arguing with Rasconza. 'I thought you made me an' Gancho cap'ns? Wot right does Mad Eyes 'ave puttin' 'is own cap'ns in our place?'

Ublaz wheeled about, fixing the searat with a piercing stare. 'You there, what is your name?'

Baltur appeared dumbfounded for a moment, unable to tear his eyes from the gaze of Ublaz. 'I'm called Baltur,' he said.

'And how long have you been a searat, Baltur?'

'Long as I can remember, Sire.'

'So, you like the sea, eh?'

'I likes it well enough, Sire.'

Ublaz chuckled, both eyes boring into the hapless vermin. 'Good, then perhaps you would like to try a swim now.'

The brief interview was at an end. Ublaz turned and strode away, followed by his army, several of whom were lugging the tillers and rudders of the ships with them. Behind him there was a splash as Baltur threw himself into the sea.

Rasconza watched two corsairs pull the spluttering Baltur up onto the jetty, and signalled to one of the new Trident-rat captains. 'You there, Orlug is it? Step aboard, mate, this'll be yore ship from now on, I'll show yer round.'

That evening, just after sunset, Sagitar entered the

Emperor's throne room and placed a sword down in front of Ublaz.

The pine marten glanced at the stained blade. 'What is this thing and why do you bring it here?'

Sagitar measured her words carefully. 'Mightiness, I was leading the evening harbour patrol when the fox Rasconza gave this to me and bade me bring it to you. He said to tell you that one of your new captains, Orlug, was given the sword by him, in honour of your appointing Orlug captain. But unfortunately Orlug was unused to wearing a sword, and he tripped and fell upon the blade, slaying himself. Rasconza says that you have no need to appoint another captain, he will be master of his own ship. Those were his words, Sire.'

Much to the astonishment of Sagitar, the Emperor burst into gales of hearty laughter. The Trident-rat stood at attention until her master's merriment subsided. Ublaz wiped his eyes on a sateen kerchief and took several deep breaths. 'Go back to the harbour, tell Rasconza I send him my compliments. Oh, and say also that there has been a little mishap on my part, not quite as serious as the loss of a captain. Unfortunately my clumsy Monitors dropped the tillers and rudders and they are all broken. Without them to use as patterns it will take considerably longer to make new ones, but I will tell my carpenters to do their best. Go now!'

Long after midnight Rasconza sat in his cabin, sharing a flask of seaweed grog with Baltur and Gancho. The fox had just finished telling them of his latest encounter with Sagitar, messenger of the Emperor.

Gancho hurled his beaker at the bulkhead and pounded the table. 'First 'e cripples our vessels, then 'e destroys all the rudders an' tillers. Ublaz's got us like fish in a barrel, rot 'is eyes!'

Rasconza poured a fresh beaker for the irate searat. 'No 'e ain't, I told ole Sagitar to take this message back to 'im. I've still got five of those new cap'ns safe with us 'ere, so I 'ope that we'll 'ave new tillers'n'rudders within five days. Five cap'ns an' five days; maybe they're all as clumsy as that rat Orlug. Who knows, somethin' awful might 'appen to each of 'em, one a day, an' we don't want that to 'appen, do we? 'Cos then I'd 'ave t'give you buckoes yer jobs back as ship's masters – you two, an' three others.'

Rasconza clinked beakers with Baltur and Gancho, their roaring laughter ringing out across the dark floodtide.

Rasconza was sure that he had won the next round in the murderous game.

25

Martin crouched with Clecky and Viola behind a small outcrop of rocks on the shoreline. It was the hour before dawn, still and calm. All activity aboard *Waveworm* seemed to have ceased; she rode smoothly at anchor, too far out to be reached by bowshot.

Clecky's keen eyes picked up movement further along the beach at the water's edge. 'I say, there's our otter chum, pullin' an' haulin' on her boat. It looks in jolly bad shape if y'ask me, wot!'

Martin turned to Viola, who was shivering fitfully after her ordeal in the sea. 'Stay here, little one. Clecky and I are going to help the otter to beach her boat. If any danger threatens while we're away, leave these rocks and hide in the woodlands, d'you understand?'

The volemaid's teeth were chattering so hard she could only nod.

Stooping low, Martin and Clecky hurried along the tideline, all the time keeping a weather eye on *Waveworm*. Grath Longfletch was glad of their help, and between them the three creatures hauled the longboat across the shore, back to the rock cover.

Grath surveyed the damage ruefully, saying, 'She's stoved in bad amidships, and there's not a lot I can do without the proper materials to fix her up. I've even lost my provisions in the sea.'

Clecky slumped down mournfully next to Viola. 'Starvin', wet, cold, tired, wot! I've been in worse places, but I'm blowed if I can remember where they were!'

Martin held up his paw for silence. 'Listen!'

Grath had heard the sounds too. She grabbed for her bow and arrows, which had mercifully survived the encounter with *Waveworm*. 'Somebeasts comin' downstream, get your heads down, mates!' Stealthily the otter peered landward, over the rocks into the breaking dawn.

Then she laughed aloud with relief. 'Haharr, it's Log a Log an' the Guosim!'

Swift as arrows six logboats were skimming downstream from the woodlands to the shore. When they caught sight of Grath, the shrews whooped gruffly, flinging themselves into the stream shallows and wading ashore with open paws.

Log a Log was first to pound his otter friend's back.

'Grath Longfletch, you ole waterdog!'

'Log a Log, you liddle streamwalloper!'

'Don't tell me you've wrecked that barnacle-crusted cockleshell *again*, Grath! Good job we happened along. Hi, Martin! Martin of Redwall!'

The Warriormouse chuckled joyfully as Guosim shrews crowded round, shaking his paws. 'Log a Log, old friend. Dabby, Curlo, Dimple, what a pleasure it is to see your faces again!'

Clecky pointed to himself and Viola. 'Pay no heed to us, chaps, we're only a couple o' butterflies hangin' about waitin' for summer, aren't we, m'dear!'

A fire was built on the sand behind the rocks, and Guosim cooks busied themselves, while shrewmaids outfitted Viola bankvole in one of their smocks. Curlo and Dabby got a repair gang together and began straight away fixing Grath's longboat.

Log a Log sat by the fire with Martin and Clecky,

discussing their position. When he heard about the ambush in the ditch, the shrew Chieftain looked thoughtful. 'We found a searat wandering lost upstream,' he said. 'My mates have got him under guard over there. I wonder if he can tell us where they're planning to take your Abbot? Ahoy, mates, bring that vermin over t'me!'

Bound and gagged, a dispirited searat was hauled up in front of the shrew Chieftain.

Martin recognized him instantly. 'That's the villain who escaped after ambushing us. We slew the rest of them, but this one got away.'

Grath Longfletch strode up. Borrowing a knife from one of the cooks, she cut the searat's gag and the rope that bound his paws. Then, notching a green-feathered shaft to her great bow, Grath nodded meaningly at the terrified searat.

'Get running!' she snarled.

The searat took one look at the grim-faced otter and her lethal weapon and fell down on all fours, pleading and sobbing. 'Yer gonna kill me, I know y'are. Mercy, I beg yer!'

Grath seized the creature roughly, hauling him upright. 'I'm givin' you a chance, scum, that's more'n you did for my family when you murdered 'em! I'm Grath Longfletch, last of the Holt of Lutra; remember it. Now run!'

Martin placed himself between Grath and the searat, saying, 'You can't kill him, friend, we need him to give us information. He's valuable to us.'

Grath's voice trembled as she replied, 'I like you, Martin of Redwall, you're a warrior born, but this searat is a coward and a murderer. I'm sworn to avenge my family, so step aside, Martin, I don't want to hurt you!'

'Then you'll 'ave to 'urt us both, matey!' Log a Log stood up alongside Martin and spoke gently to the otter. 'Grath, yore lettin' revenge rob you of yore senses. Put aside the bow an' shaft now, there's a goodbeast. Martin's right an' you know it, friend.'

Slowly Grath lowered her bow and shot the arrow into the sand between her footpaws. The searat gave a moan of relief. Grath smiled regretfully at the two creatures facing her. 'I'm sorry, Martin, you're right. Log a Log, you sound more like my father than any creature I've ever known. Forgive me.'

The Warriormouse patted Grath's paw. 'There's nothing to forgive, friend, I'd have done the same in your place. Now, how about some breakfast by the fire while we question this wave vermin and make our plans for the day?'

Viola and Clecky sat with the boat repair crew around their fire, watching a pot of pine resin bubbling. The volemaid sipped steaming vegetable and seafood soup from a scallop shell bowl and devoured hot shrewbread in a manner far removed from her former prissy self.

Curlo winked at her. 'Tastes good, don't it?' she said.

Viola nodded gratefully as the shrew refilled the shell for her. 'Almost as good as the taste of freedom. Oh! Poor Abbot Durral, I hope they haven't harmed him. He risked his life to help me escape from that horrible ship and those awful lizards. Do you think there's a chance that we can rescue him?'

Clecky bent his long ears towards the other fire, munching delicious shrewbread as he spoke. 'Never give up hope, m'gel, Martin an' ole Log a thing are prob'ly cookin' up a plan right now with that tough-lookin' otter.'

Day broke cloudy and grey with a calm sea and little or no breeze. Romsca placed a bowl of some doubtful steaming mess in front of the Abbot.

'Get that skilly down yer, Durral, no sense in starvin' t'death!'

The old mouse peered up at the corsair from where he sat tethered to the mast. The loss of his glasses affected his poor eyesight. 'Thank you, my child, and thank you also for the kindness you showed to the little volemaid.'

Romsca shook her head and laughed. 'I ain't yore child, ole mouse, an' you can't get around me. You shovel those vittles down an' pray t'the fates that yore mates come up with the Emperor's six pearls!'

Further discussion was cut short as Lask Frildur came hurrying out on deck. The ship had drifted sideways, allowing the Monitor General a disturbing view of the shore.

'Have you no eyez in your head, idiot?' he snarled nastily at Romsca. 'Look landwardz!'

Romsca was about to argue, but a quick glance to the shore gave the corsair great cause for concern. Small warlike creatures in considerable numbers, all wearing bright headbands and sashes with rapiers, stood boldly in plain view on the beach. Pulled up onto the sandy banks of the stream that flowed to the sea were six dugout treetrunk boats, equipped with paddles and single sails. Nearby on a clump of rocks were three more creatures, a strong-looking mouse with a great sword strapped to his back, a big otter and a lanky hare, both armed with bows and arrows. They were watching a group of the small creatures repairing a ship's longboat by the glow of several small fires.

Romsca shook her head in disbelief at the scene. 'Stripe me! Where'd that lot come from?'

Lask Frildur paced the deck, tail swishing and teeth bared. 'Who knowz? There are enough of them to take thiz vezzel, and they have boatz. We are no longer zafe anchored here!'

Kicking the bowl of food from the Abbot's paws, the lizard pulled him as close to the rail as the rope tether would allow. 'Who are thoze beaztz, mouze? Tell me!'

Durral squinted at the distant shore. 'Without my glasses it is difficult to say, though by the bright colours they wear I would guess they are Guosim shrews.'

Lask brought his face close to the old mouse. 'Warriorz?'

Tucking both paws into his long sleeves, the Abbot

turned sideways to avoid the Monitor General's foul breath. 'Yes, my son, the Guosim are renowned both on land and water as fierce warriors. Their fighting spirit knows no bounds.'

Lask pulled the Abbot roughly to him. 'Old fool, I am your enemy, not your zon!'

Gazing calmly into the glittering reptilian eyes, Durral said, 'I am an Abbot; nobeast is my enemy. Why do you not let me go free and sail from here in peace?'

Lask shook the frail mouse savagely. 'I cannot leave without my Emperor'z pearlz. When I have them then you can go free!'

Romsca interrupted impatiently. 'Lissen t'me, mouse, an' save yerself a lot o' grief. The only way yore leavin' this ship is in exchange fer those six pearls. Now who's got em?'

The Father Abbot of Redwall shook his head slowly. 'Pearls? Pearls? I know nothing of any pearls.'

Romsca faced Lask Frildur. 'Well, you 'eard 'im. He knows nothing. What are y'goin' to do? Take my word, Lask, wotever it is, you'd best do it quick. Look at that crowd on shore, they're gettin' ready to come out 'ere, an' I'll wager it's not to present us with six pearls. Make yer mind up, lizard: do we stan' an' fight, or cut an' run?'

The shrew Trimp put aside a length of caulking rope and patted the side of Grath's longboat. 'That's the best I can do for ye! She's seaworthy agin, but for 'ow long I don't know. Yore pretty rough on boats, matey!'

The otter braced the headrope across her shoulders and began pulling her craft down to the stream. 'My thanks to you, Guosim, I hope I can pay you back someday.'

Martin and Clecky helped her to launch the longboat at the head of the shrew flotilla. Log a Log put both paws to his mouth and gave a long ululating call, the battlecry of Guosim shrews.

'Logalogalogalogaloooooog!'

Grath hoisted her sail, while Martin and Clecky used the oars to propel the longboat, their three different warshouts joining the shrews paddling behind.

'Redwaaaaaall!'

'Eulaliaaaaaa!'

'Holt Lutraaaaaa!'

The little warfleet sped from the stream estuary into the waves. Each shrew, armed with slingshots and rapier, bent its back to the oars, spreading into a half-circle, with the longboat at its centre. Lashing the tiller dead ahead Grath made her way to the prow, notching a shaft to her bow.

She roared out across the sea to the figures on the deck of *Waveworm*, 'Release your prisoner or die!'

Lask Frildur cast a meaningful glance at Romsca. 'Sail!' he hissed.

Speed was of the essence. The corsair captain slashed at the anchor line with her sword, bellowing orders to her crew.

'Bring 'er about course west! Make sail, full sail!'

Waveworm turned on the swell as her steersrat brought the tiller hard round. Wetting a paw, Romsca held it aloft, frowning. 'We need the breeze, they're comin' up on us fast!'

Lask and his Monitors stood astern, long boathooks and pikes ready should the attackers try to board. The Monitor General looked nervously from the oncoming boats to Romsca. 'Where iz the wind, we need wind in the zailz!'

Grath Longfletch knew she was within range now. Drawing her bowstring tight, she aimed at Lask and let loose a shaft. Fortunately for the Monitor General the breeze arrived, at the very moment *Waveworm* hit a stretch of choppy water. The arrow struck the lizard standing to his left; the reptile gurgled, tugged at the shaft sticking from his chest and toppled overboard.

Romsca balanced in the prow, feeling the ship begin to

rise and fall. 'Haharr,' she cried. 'The breeze is freshenin',
we'll outsail em!'

Martin glanced up from his oar at Grath. 'They've got
the wind with them now!'

Grath tried another arrow, but it was whipped sideways in flight. 'Aye, but so have we, Martin!' she said.
Then she dashed amidships and went to work, tighten-
ing the lines in their cleats until the single square sail
billowed tautly.

Log a Log was yelling and ranting above the howling
gusts, 'Come on, Guosim, bend yer backs, pull! Pull those
oars, buckoes!'

The shrews strove bravely, battling with their heavy
logboats and small sails to keep up with Grath's craft.
Waves crashed over the sides of the shrewboats, sending
water cascading into them as the windforce built the
seas high.

Chopping the Abbot's tether rope clear of *Waveworm*'s
mast, Lask Frildur dragged the old mouse up to the stern
gallery. Securing the rope end to the rail, the lizard
pushed his prisoner over, leaving him dangling at the
after end above the waves.

'Let them fire arrowz now if they dare!' he rasped.

Grath Longfletch threw down her bow in disgust. Then
she suddenly flung herself flat in the prow as she heard
an ominous noise, calling, 'Belay, the mast is gone!'

Craaaaack!

The longboat's mast snapped like a twig, unable
to withstand further strain from the gale-tightened
sail. Martin found himself enveloped in canvas, being
dragged along the boat's bottom as the wind began
blowing the loose sail. Clecky was laid flat by the broken
mast spar. The Warriormouse struggled madly. Tearing
himself free, he whipped out his sword and severed the
mast ropes with a few swift slashes. Broken mast, sail
and cross spar went swishing out across the sea like a
runaway beast.

Grath cradled the unconscious hare's head in her paws, a look of despair on her face as she watched *Waveworm* pull away with the Abbot dangling high astern.

'They've beaten us, Martin. We'll never catch them now!'

The Warriormouse brushed seawater from his eyes as he watched the corsair vessel recede into the watery wastes. 'No, they haven't beaten me! Not yet they haven't!'

Log a Log gave orders. Lashed together prow to prow and stern to stern the small flotilla turned and headed for land.

Night had fallen; a beacon fire burned bright on the beach. Viola and four other shrews who had been left to guard the searat saw the crews come in to shore. Heads down, panting and gasping for breath, Log a Log and his Guosim shrews staggered up to the fire, followed by Martin and Grath carrying Clecky between them. Saturated by seawater and exhausted from their battle to reach dry land, everybeast flopped wearily around the fire area. Viola and the four shrews hurried about, serving hot vegetable broth and oatcakes as they went.

Late into the night Martin sat at the fire with Log a Log and Grath. The shrew Chieftain fed fresh wood to the flames, and glanced across to where the hare was now sleeping peacefully, wrapped up in old sailcloth.

'That one'll live to eat another day, I never knew a hare that couldn't rise to the sound o' a ladle in a cookpot. So, Martin, yore bound an' determined to follow the corsair ship.'

The Warriormouse watched the flames crackling around a pine log. 'That's right, Log a Log. If I have to follow them over the world's edge and it takes me all my life, I'll bring our Abbot back to Redwall Abbey. I swear it on my sword!'

26

Like a soft cloak of dark velvet, buttoned and studded with stars, the last night of spring lay soft over the ancient sandstone Abbey of Redwall. Lanterns and torches glimmered and flickered in the grounds like fireflies. Tansy hurried up from the pond to where Auma stood in the open doorway of the Abbey, calling, 'No sign of those Dibbuns yet?'

Pulling forth a large red spotted kerchief, the badger Mother dabbed at her tired eyes. 'Not a whisker. It's as if they disappeared into thin air. Here's Wullger, maybe he'll have some good news for us.'

The otter shook his head as he approached them. 'I've tried the gatebar meself, marm, 'tis too high an' far too 'eavy fer Dibbuns to lift. Besides, if they'd left the Abbey, who'd 'ave locked the gate after 'em? You *sure* those liddle rogues ain't inside anywheres?'

Tansy threw up her paws in despair. 'I've searched the Abbey three times, so have Piknim and Craklyn and lots of others. Trouble is, there's so many places three Dibbuns could hide. Ooh, that Arven, if I get my paws on him . . .'

Wullger gave a dry chuckle. 'Aye, that'n's the ringleader all right. No use gettin' yerself upset, missie, they'll show up soon as they're 'ungry enough. It's my guess they found somewheres snug an' fell asleep, all three of 'em, the rogues!'

Auma nodded her agreement with the gatekeeper. 'Wullger's right, Tansy. They're obviously someplace in the Abbey. After they've had a night's sleep, they'll turn up tomorrow for breakfast, you'll see.'

A look of horror registered on Tansy's face. 'Mother Auma, you're not going to bed, are you?'

The badger shook her head vehemently. 'What? Me going to bed while three of my little Dibbuns are missing? I should say not, missie! I haven't had a full night's sleep since Abbot Durral and Viola left. I'll sit on some sacks in the kitchens, dozing with one eye open, mayhap they'll creep in for a stolen snack. I'll be waiting for those villains if they do and I'll make them sorry for the upset they've caused around here, believe me I will!'

Wandering indoors, Tansy made her way to Great Hall. As she passed the tapestry she remembered the dream she'd had when Martin told her that the fourth clue was where the three babes were hidden. She shook her head worriedly. She was so anxious about the missing Dibbuns that she'd almost forgotten about the pearls. Piknim and Craklyn were still searching fruitlessly around the big room's darker corners.

Rollo was half dozing in the Abbot's chair. He sat up straight as Tansy entered, and asked, 'Still no sign of the rogues, eh?'

The hedgehog maid perched wearily on the arm of the chair. 'No. I've just searched around the pond again. What are we going to do, Rollo?'

The old Recorder's eyes twinkled slightly. 'The only thing we can do, Tansy. Stop thinking like responsible creatures and start thinking like naughty Dibbuns. Imagine you were Arven, Diggum or Gurrbowl, where would you hide if you didn't want anybeast to find you?'

Piknim and Craklyn strolled over to join the conversation.

'Down the cellars maybe?'

'No, little ones would be afraid down there in the dark.'

'What about up in the dormitories?'

'But that's the first place we looked, they weren't there.'

A sudden thought struck Tansy. 'I know we've already looked once in the attics above the dormitories, but perhaps we should take another trip up there. Hardly anybeast has been in the attics since Fermald passed away.'

Arven sat miserably with the two molebabes inside a cupboard in Fermald's attic. A lantern light glowed in the enclosed space. Gurrbowl yawned, fighting against sleep.

'Oi wants t'go daown, oi'm gurtly 'ungered an' toired, hurr!'

Arven had found Fermald's old fishing rod in the cupboard, and now he waggled it in the mole's direction. 'No no, can't go down, Gurrb'l, not now. Lookit us'ns, we all filfy an' dusty. Wait'll inna mornen, an' I catch tha' bigga fish out the pond an' we cook 'im an' eat 'im all up!'

Diggum inspected her dusty smock sadly. 'Bo urr, lackaday, ee badgermum'll 'ave summat t'say when 'er sees oi!'

Arven stuck out his stomach and pulled his little chin in as he did his impression of Auma. 'Jus' looka you, straight inna baff, you mucky maggits, great seasings! Where you 'ave been? Straight inna bed an' no suppers, tha' teaches you naughty Dibbins t'be more good inna foocher!'

The molebabes laughed at the tiny squirrel's antics. Then Gurrbowl did his imitation of Sister Cicely. 'You'm never knowed wurr you'm been, oi give ee gurt bowls o' warm nettil zoop, that'll make ee be'ave thoiselfs!'

Diggum held one paw to her stomach and the other to her mouth. 'Bwuuuurk! Turrible stuff ee warm nettil zoop be. Gruuurgh!'

Arven waved the fishing rod. 'When I big me gonna make Siss Cicely 'ave nettil soop ev'ry day for 'er lunch. Hah! Tha' soon make 'er be sicked!'

The three Abbeybabes' conversation tailed off, and they huddled together in the enclosed cupboard space. Soon their eyelids began drooping as sleep overtook them.

Lanterns glowed flickering and golden as Tansy and her two friends ascended the gloomy spiral staircase up to the attics. It was so hushed and still that they found themselves tip-pawing, speaking to each other in subdued whispers. Piknim stood in a pale moonshaft which shone down through the rock crystal window and gazed around into the dusty darkness. 'I'm not so sure the Dibbuns'd come up here, Tansy,' she said. 'It's almost as spooky as the cellars at night.'

The hedgehog maid began casting about with her lantern, peering into corners and recesses. 'Maybe you're right, but it's still worth one last good look. Dearie me, imagine living and sleeping up here all alone. How Fermald did that for all those seasons I'll never know.'

Craklyn emerged from a small side chamber off the main room. Holding a paw to her mouth for silence she beckoned them to her. A knowing smile lit up the squirrelmaid's face as she whispered, 'There's a big old wall cupboard in there. Follow me quietly now, I want you to have a listen and tell me what you hear!'

Tansy put her ear to the cupboard door and, exchanging knowing glances with her companions, she listened. 'Sounds like three Dibbuns snoring to me,' she said.

The door creaked as Piknim opened it to reveal the

three culprits: grimy, dust-covered and deep in sleep, whiskers twitching gently to each squeaky snore. Without further words Tansy and her two helpers picked the Abbeybabes up and carried them down to the sick bay.

Sister Cicely, clad in long nightcap and gown, pursed her lips severely at the sight.

'Bring them in and put them together in my bed. We'll deal with the villains in the morning!'

Two hours after dawn on the first morning of summer season it was already warm. Above the eastern horizon, a newgold sun began climbing to preside over a cloudless vault of powder-blue sky. Columns of steamy mist rose from the dense woodlands, rising to the upper air, accompanied by happy trills of sweet birdsong. Out on the flatlands kingcup and daisy opened delicate petals with silent grace, the first dry rustle of grasshoppers sounded around gorse and furze. It was a good day for anybeast to be alive. Well, almost anybeast.

Clean-smocked, red-eyed and still smelling of verbena soap, Arven, Diggum and Gurrbowl sat penitently on an upturned wheelbarrow in the orchard, their breakfast forgone after several bowls of Cicely's favourite cure-all, warm nettle soup. A sorrier trio of Dibbuns had not graced the Abbey in many a long day. Thoroughly chastened, they sat dangling their footpaws as Auma the badger Mother lectured them soundly, in front of an audience of old and young.

'You could have been suffocated in a closed cupboard with a lantern alight in there, d'you realize that? Everybeast in Redwall was searching for you from twilight until well after dark. But did you think of letting us know before you went off alone . . . No! The trouble, worry and upset you have caused to all is dreadful, it was very naughty of you! Arven, I'm certain you were the ringleader. Have you anything to say for yourself, sir?'

The tiny squirrel pawed soap and water from his ear. 'Wot's succafated?'

Diggum shook her head at the squirrel's ignorance. 'The wurd be fusticated!'

Gurrbowl interrupted her. 'Naw et bain't, ee wurd is custifated!'

Friar Higgle Stump waved his ladle at them threateningly. 'Suffocated, the word is, suffocated! An' it means that you liddle rogues would've died in yon cupboard 'ad it not been for miss Tansy an' 'er friends findin' you!'

Auma nodded her great head, agreeing with the Friar. 'Exactly, you're very lucky to be alive. Missus Teasel, will you take these three creatures off to the kitchens and find them some chores to keep them busy for the day?'

Teasel beckoned the wretched trio of Dibbuns to follow her. 'I cert'nly can, Auma, there's always lots o' greasy pots, messy dishes an' floors t'be scrubbed. Veggibles need peelin' too, I shouldn't wonder. Come on, Dibbuns, step lively now!'

They were led off, murmuring to each other.

'Yugh! Gurt greasy pots an' mucky ole floors. Boo urr!'

'Us'd been better off fusticated!'

'Me was nearly succafated with alla tha' nettil soop!'

When they were gone, Auma turned to the otter gatekeeper. 'Wullger, would you do me a favour? Take Furlo Stump with you; get hammer and spikes, and nail that attic cupboard shut. We don't want any more wandering Dibbuns hiding in there.'

Wullger was about to carry out Auma's bidding when Glenner called out from the northwest walltop, 'Two creatures approachin' the Abbey, looks like Skipper an' the owl, in need of 'elp the way they're staggerin' about!'

Auma was up and ambling swiftly for the main gate. 'Come on, Wullger, you too Sister Cicely! Tansy, will you and Rollo see to that cupboard, please?'

Rollo waved after the badger. 'Aye, you go and look after Skipper and Gerul. Come on, Tansy, and you, Piknim and Craklyn, I'm getting a bit old to be wielding a heavy hammer. It's bad enough having to climb all those stairs!'

Piknim held a wooden baton across the cupboard door. Craklyn positioned a spike between the baton end and the door frame, holding her head to one side, and said, 'Go easy with that hammer, Tansy, mind my paws!'

As she was about to strike, Tansy paused. 'Find the three babes and you will know . . .' All at once the words of Martin the Warrior came back to her. She lowered the hammer. 'Move that baton aside,' she said. 'Let's just check inside the cupboard before we board it up.'

The inside of the cupboard was empty, save for Fermald's fishing rod. Rollo held it up, testing the rod's balance, and nodded. 'This is a fine old fishing rod, if I'm not mistaken it looks like the one that belonged to Martin's grandsire, Matthias, he was a splendid angler I've heard say. Yes, wonderfully made, see the pawgrip, good stout yew, the rest is made from young crack-willow whipped and bound with waxed flax . . . What's the matter, Tansy?'

Tansy took the rod from her friend the Recorder and inspected the middle part carefully. 'Rollo, lend me your knife a moment,' she said.

Mystified, the old bankvole passed Tansy the small quill knife he used for resharpening feather quill pens. The hedgehog maid explained as she worked, 'The middle of this rod has been rebound. I noticed some of this flax looked newer than the rest, so I'll cut through it carefully and unwind it . . . Like this . . .'

Snipping through the binding she began reeling it off, her voice sounding more excited as she twirled the rod in her paws. 'Hahah! I had a feeling we would find something, and I was right! Look, there's a piece of paper underneath this binding!'

Thin parchment showed clearly. Piknim caught the flax, tugging it as Tansy twirled the rod swiftly, and the yellowed slip floated to the floor. As it landed, they could all see two words written large on the back: 'Well done.'

The four friends sat on the floor as Tansy turned the parchment over and began to read Fermald's clues to the fourth pearl.

27

Skipper and Gerul ate hungrily, slopping down elderberry and rosehip cordial between mouthfuls of leek
pastie and hazelnut cheese. Sister Cicely and Brother
Dormal the herbalist worked diligently, cleaning and
binding their dirt-encrusted wounds. The otter Chieftain
had told their story to the Redwallers who crowded into
the kitchen. Some of them shook their heads in disbelief
at the narrative.

'Great seasons, Skipper slew one o' those awful
lizards?'

'He ain't a Skipper of otters for nothin', that'n's
tough!'

'Look at that scar down Skip's side!'

Skipper chuckled and patted Gerul. 'You should've
seen me ole mate 'ere. He gave 'em what for!'

Gerul lowered his head, modestly picking crumbs from
his feathered chest. 'Ah, 'twas nothin', sir, as me ould
mother used t'say, leave yer enemies like a plate after
a good feed, well licked!'

Auma brought a pail of warm water infused with herbs
for the pair to bathe weary paws and talons in. 'Would
it do any good to raise a force and follow Martin?' she
asked. 'He and the hare may be in sore need of help if

they're still trying to rescue Viola and the Abbot. What d'you think, Skipper?'

The otter winced as Sister Cicely snipped away fur from a wound. 'I don't think Martin'd want Redwallers roamin' the country lookin' fer 'im, marm. I'll send a score of my otters – they'll make it down t'the sea followin' the streams.'

Brother Dormal inspected Gerul's damaged wing gingerly. 'I think your flying days may well be over, friend,' he said.

The owl was about to shrug, but thought better of it. 'Ah well, not t'worry, sir, flyin's not everythin', y'know. Sure I'll get about just grand on me stout talons, like me ould mother used t'say, walkin's good as wingin' whenever it's wet!'

Friar Higgle placed a platter of fruit tarts between Gerul and Skipper. 'At least it hasn't affected your appetite.'

Standing on a bench next to an old stone sink, three apron-clad Dibbuns scoured away at breakfast platters and pots. Arven glanced across to where Gerul and Skipper were being fussed over and fed. The little squirrel nudged his mole companions.

'Tchah! Looka them, they runned away an' cummed back all muckied up an' everybeasts be's nice to 'em, but wot 'appen to us'ns? We on'y went missin' a likkle time an' didden get filfy like tha'.'

The molebabe Diggum scrubbed away halfheartedly at a pot with a wedge of soft sandstone. 'Ee be roight, mate, we'm be scolded an' put t'work, hurr, but theybeasts be treated vurry noice, et bain't furr!'

Gurrbowl pulled an oatmeal-crusted bowl from the sink. 'Burr aye, may'ap if us'ns stayed away longer an' cummed back lots dustier, we'm be treated gudd an' get noice vittles.'

Arven clenched a chubby paw resolutely. 'Me make a plan! Nex' time us'ns be lotsa brave, runaway inna woodlan's, take big bagga foods an' weppins, we fight alla badbeasts. Hah! we come back very very muck filfy, mud splatty, yurk! Then they be much gladda t'see us!'

Tansy's voice echoed round the attic as she read Fermald the Ancient's message. It was very complicated, but the four intrepid searchers expected no less.

'My fourth tear I shed,
For the Abbey Redwall,
Laid where it never
Should hatch or fall.
Below the mouth of a mouse looking south,
All in a deserted dwelling.
So sit o'er the maidenhair, gaze up north,
And solve what my next words are telling.

Put a home with our Abbey Warrior,
North East South at the start,
Then to complete this riddle,
Add the last thing in "my heart".'

Tansy shook her head despairingly. 'Well, I've seen some riddles in my time, but this one's a beauty. It's about as clear as a swamp-covered frog. Still, we won't solve it sitting round here.' She jumped up and led the way down the spiral staircase. 'Let's have lunch and spend all afternoon and evening on the puzzle.'

By midday it was hot, and the grass was curling and dry, as if spring mists and rains were long gone. Friar Higgle had set up a buffet table in the orchard, and now he sat in the shade of a spreading damson tree with Auma and some Redwall elders. The Friar gazed up at the thick white masses of flowers crowding the boughs overhead and recited a season poem.

'When the damson tree's crowned white,
And wild pear blooms also,

I thank the season for this sight,
That lets good creatures know,
Summer is come to shed its gold,
Warm days grow long as holm oak flow'rs
The bees hum songs they learned of old,
To shorten night's long hours.
For spring is fled and summer's come,
Gather its blossoms and bring me some.'

Rollo nodded appreciatively as he nibbled busily at the edges of a raspberry and apple turnover. 'That's a nice poem, Higgle. I've never heard it before. Did you write it yourself?'

The Friar took a deep draught of his October Ale. 'Bless yer, no, Rollo, I couldn't write verses t'save me spikes! 'Twas Brother Dormal taught it t'me, he knows all about poems an' seasons an' growin' things, ole Dormal's a right clever 'un!'

Dormal lowered his eyes modestly, blinking away a white blossom that had fallen on his eyelid. 'It's nothin' really, the verses write themselves in my head.'

Rollo licked raspberry juice from his chin. 'But none knows more than you about growing things, right?'

Dormal was a shy old mouse; he shrugged lightly. 'I suppose so. I love the things that grow as much as I like to write poetry. Why d'you ask?'

'Because I would like to know if we have maidenhair growing anywhere within Redwall.'

'You mean spleenwort,' Dormal corrected.

The Recorder shook his head. 'No, I mean maidenhair!'

Dormal warmed to his favourite subject. 'The correct name is spleenwort, though it is also commonly known as maidenhair. It's a wall-growin' fern. Hmm, we do have some growin' wild somewheres, now let me think . . .'

Rollo was about to urge the old mouse to hurry his memory up, when Dormal nodded knowingly, and said, 'On the inside o' the south wall, slap bang in the middle, about halfway up. I culled some for Sister Cicely last autumn. But why d'you want to know about spleenwort, Rollo?'

Dormal found himself speaking to thin air. Rollo had left.

Tansy, Piknim and Craklyn sat on the upturned wheel-barrow, giggling as they tried to protect their lunch against Skipper and Gerul, whose injuries seemed to have increased their insatiable appetites. Winking both eyes at the three Abbeymaids, the owl allowed his talons to rove perilously close to their food.

'Ah now, what would three slender young beauties like yerselves want with stodgy hazelnut pudden, 'twill only make fatbeasts of ye, missies. My ould mother always used t'say, if yer not fat there's a slim chance some creature'll fall in love with ye, so she did, an' herself as thin as a beanpole an' greatly loved by all, so she was!'

Tansy pulled the pudding out of his reach. 'Tut tut, mister Gerul, your mother couldn't have loved you much, you great butterbarrel. Hahahaha!'

Skipper agreed with her, swiping a couple of black-berry muffins as he did so. 'That's right, missie. I don't know which is bigger, ole Gerul's eyes or his belly. Hohoho!'

'Hah! Look who's talking, old famine-tummy himself!' said Craklyn, then she neatly caught one of the muffins as it was halfway to the otter's mouth and tossed it to Piknim.

Gerul intercepted the muffin, and before Piknim could stop him he had crammed half of it into his beak. 'True words, miss, true words, I'd sooner keep Skipper in vittles for a day than a season, so I would!'

Rollo strode busily up and tapped his paws on the wheelbarrow. 'No time for fooling about, friends – I've just made an important discovery. Follow me and forget lunch!'

Before they could argue he had ushered them off in the direction of the south Abbey wall. Gerul watched them go, dividing the hazelnut pudding in two with a spoon. 'T'be sure, there's somethin' heroic about a vole who won't let vittles keep him from his duty. That'n will be voted Abbot one day, Skip, you mark me words. Rollo the Righteous they'll call him, so they will!'

Maidenhair spleenwort grew spiderlike from the cracks in the stonework of the high south wall. Fronds of different lengths spread in all directions, each stem covered in tiny spearhead-shaped leaflets ranging from pale to bright green. Upward of a dozen or more plants clung to the sandstone, forming a tracery almost from ground to ramparts.

'So sit o'er the maidenhair, gaze up north,' Tansy said, as she checked the poem parchment.

Piknim and Craklyn were already racing away towards the wallsteps. 'Last one to the steps is a crawly old caterpillar!'

Rollo stared over the top of his glasses at Tansy. 'I know I'm the crawly old caterpillar, but where are they going? Have I missed something?'

Tansy took the old Recorder's paw. 'The only way we can carry out Fermald's instructions is to sit on the battlements of this wall, over the maidenhair. Then we'll see what to make of this riddle. Come on, no hurry, we'll be crawly caterpillars together.'

28

Day broke hot and hazy over the isle of Sampetra as the murderous game between Ublaz and Rasconza took a new turn. The fox was asleep in his cabin when a sharp rat tat on the door awoke him. He sat up groggily, yawning and blinking.

'Quit that knockin' an' come in!'

The door swung open to reveal the mad-eyed pine marten. Rasconza leapt for his sword, which lay on a nearby table. Ublaz held both paws wide to show he was unarmed. 'Leave your blade, friend. I could have crept in here and slain you as you slept.'

Rasconza poured himself a beaker of seaweed grog, careful not to lock eyes with Ublaz. 'So, what gets you outta yore bunk this early?' he snarled.

The Emperor had dressed in brown silk that morning. He looked around at the stained benches and chairs, and chose to stand. 'I merely called to tell you that the first new rudder and tiller are ready. My workers toiled through the night to finish them. Even as we speak my creatures are fitting them to this vessel.'

Rasconza was nonplussed. He stood staring at his beaker. 'Well, I'll say this for ye, matey, y've got some nerve comin' down 'ere. Don't ferget, I could order the crews to attack. We still outnumber yore forces!'

Ublaz gestured elegantly towards the open door. 'I took the precaution of arriving silently. Your sentries are asleep and the other five crews snoring inside their cabins. A simple but effective operation, Rasconza. Oh, and one other thing. Stay away from your sword – you would have to *face* me if you were intent on slaying me. Then our eyes would meet. And if I can put a poisonous water snake under my spell, a simple fox would present no problem. It's your move, friend.'

Rasconza could hear the Trident-rats hammering the rudder pins home and fitting the tiller above decks. Smiling with a confidence he did not feel, the fox answered Ublaz, 'I still hold five of yore creatures, the captains, remember? One shout from me and they'll all be fishbait!'

The pine marten had painted his claws red to offset the brown silk. He breathed on them and buffed them on his flowing sleeve as he murmured, 'Shout away, fox, shout away. Do you think I gave you valuable fighters to captain these ships? Like Orlug, whom you slew, those five are worthless fools. Kill them if you want to.'

Rasconza scratched his matted tail with grimy claws, baffled. 'Well, what *do* y'want? You've got me cornered in 'ere; y'don't care about yer own creatures, and now yer fixin' me ship up with a new rudder an' tiller? You've prob'ly got a gang of yer best lizards waitin' outside to slay me, is that wot yer want?'

Ublaz leaned back against the cabin door, smiling. 'I've already said I don't want to slay you, Rasconza. Friendship and trust, that's what I want. Look, here's what I propose. Forget the rats I appointed as captains. Choose your own from among the crews, and I'll give the order for mine to stand down. Then I want you to pick out all those loyal to you and crew this ship up. If we are to rule Sampetra together you must prove yourself to me, Rasconza! I want you to captain this vessel, sail anywhere you please, but bring me back the finest cargo of plunder ever seen on a corsair ship. Prove you are my Captain in Chief!'

Rasconza's eyes lit up. 'You mean that? Fair enough, Ublaz, I'll pick me crew an' bring back plunder t'this isle that'll make yer eyes pop out!'

The Emperor grinned wryly. 'Oh, I don't think I'd like that to happen, but I'm glad you see things my way. You are a worthy partner, Rasconza. I like having cleverbeasts around me, there are too many fools in this world.'

When Ublaz had departed Rasconza called the crews together and gave them a highly falsified version of what had taken place between himself and the Emperor, giving them the impression that he had outsmarted Mad Eyes. The wave vermin cheered wildly, and began to break open kegs of grog. Then the fox banged his sword hilt on the jetty for silence, and continued his narrative.

'So I sez to ole Mad Eyes, get those rats o' yourn off our ships. I won't 'ave nobeast commandin' these vessels but our own. So, Baltur, Gancho, an' you Groojaw the stoat, an' you, Deddgutt the ferret, an' you Buckla the searat – yore my five new cap'ns now! Stan' up lively, the rest o' yer, I'm takin' my ship *Bloodkeel* on a plunderin' trip, an' I wants none but the best alongside o' me!'

Amid scenes of wild revelling on the sunlit jetty, Rasconza chose his crew for the voyage. They leapt aboard *Bloodkeel* yelling and roaring in anticipation of plunder and slaughter.

Guja, the former steersrat of Barranca's ship *Freebooter*, was made steersrat of *Bloodkeel* because there was none better for the job. The vermin laughed and cheered as he twiddled a tune on his melodeon, singing in a cracked baritone,

'Would yer plunder from yer mother?
Yes I would, yes I would,
For me mother always said I was no good.
I'm a searat bred an' born,

204

An' I'm sailin' in the morn,
Stan' aside, me lucky buckoes, let me go!

Cut me teeth upon a cutlass
Yes I did, yes I did,
An' me pore ole daddy ran away an' hid,
Sayin', "That's no child o' mine,
Let 'im sail across the brine,
Stan' aside now for the vermin, let 'im go!"

If there's plunder in the offin'
That's fer me, that's fer me,
An' I never charge, I'll kill you all fer free,
Give me lots o' lovely loot,
An' a cask o' grog ter boot,
Up the anchor, loose the sails an' let me go!'

Sinking majestically into the western horizon the sun
burned skies of blue and gold to a crimson hue. Ublaz
and Sagitar watched from an upper window as the hot
day drew to a close. *Bloodkeel* was a mere speck far out
to the southeast.

The Emperor poured two goblets of rich dark wine, and
pushed one in the direction of his chief Trident-rat.

'Now you may ask me,' he said.

'Ask you what, Sire?' replied Sagitar apprehensively.

The pine marten sipped his wine, still watching
Bloodkeel diminishing into the hazy distance of the
ocean. 'What is on your mind,' he said. 'Why did I
repair the fox's ship, why did I let him sail off with
a crew of his own choosing, why did I not crush the
wave vermin this morning when I had the chance?
These are the questions on your mind, am I correct?'

Nervously, Sagitar swallowed the wine in one gulp.
'Mightiness, you have read my mind!'

Ublaz refilled the goblets, narrowing his eyes to keep
Bloodkeel in his vision. 'You are only thinking what every
otherbeast on Sampetra is thinking at this moment, so I

will tell you. Rasconza is a born troublemaker, ambitious and deceitful. Like Barranca, he is popular with the corsair crews. This would make him dangerous in the long run, so I decided to dispense with him. First I let him choose a crew, knowing he would choose his closest allies. You see, there may be those among them who would also be future trouble to me, so I dispense with them also. But I do not want the other crews to know I am responsible for the slaying of Rasconza and his friends. I want them to think that their Emperor is benevolent to them – if they consider me their friend I will have their loyalty. So, there you have your answer.'

Sagitar paused, the goblet half lifted to her lips. 'But Sire, you have not slain Rasconza and his crew. They have sailed away alive, free to return to Sampetra when they will.'

Ublaz smiled, shaking his head at the Trident-rat's simplicity. 'Look out to sea, Sagitar. If you can still see Rasconza's ship, then take a last look at it. *Bloodkeel* has only one place to go, straight down! When my workers fitted the new tiller and rudder this morning they were carrying out my instructions. Below the waterline, they hewed the stern until the wood was thin, then they fitted the rudder. It has a special metal spike protruding from the back of it. Every time the steersrat moves the tiller, that spike gouges into the thinned stern below the waterline. By morning *Bloodkeel* will be where I have sent her with all aboard, deep down on the ocean bed!'

The goblet smashed upon the floor as it fell from Sagitar's nerveless paws. She stared with speechless horror at the smiling pine marten. Ublaz spread his paws wide.

'Now I have no enemies and I own the corsair fleet. Nobeast in all the seas and oceans is more powerful and wise than I!'

The mad-eyed Emperor had emerged as victor in his murderous game against the wave vermin. However, he had reckoned without the chain of events he had set off by slaying Lutra and his kin for six rose-tinted pearls.

29

On Mossflower shore, dawn arrived, bright and warm. Log a Log and his Guosim shrews had been busy most of the night, working on Grath's longboat to make it seaworthy again. The big otter viewed their work admiringly, pacing up and down as she inspected her new craft.

The shrew Chieftain pointed out the features his workers had accomplished. 'We used eight long willow boughs, still green. See, we've made a double outrigger of yore liddle boat by fittin' a shrew logboat to each side of 'er. My shrews put a longer keel on yore boat, too; you'll need it on the high seas. She's a good 'un now, matey!'

Grath had to agree; the new craft was ideal for seafaring. It rode in the stream, with a logboat fixed either side by the willow boughs, leaving enough space between the outriggers to enable it to be paddled by oars. Shrews were wading into the stream, stocking the logboats with provisions, which left more passenger space on the main vessel. Clecky joined them, a bowl of soup in one paw, a slice of oatcake in the other, and a large seaweed poultice bound to the bump he had received between his ears.

'Spiffin' idea, wot! I've always fancied m'self as a jolly

207

old nautical type, y'know. I say, d'you think we'll have enough grub along for the voyage? A chap could starve out there without plenty of fodder. I'll be captain, of course, natural air of command an' all that, born to lead my old pater always used t'say, wot?'

Martin placed a bowl of soup in front of the captive searat and sat down next to him. 'Here, that'll take the edge off your hunger,' he said. 'Now – what's your name?'

The rat grabbed the bowl gratefully. 'They calls me Bladeribb, sir.'

The Warriormouse tore off a hunk of shrewbread and gave it to the rat. 'No need to sir me, Bladeribb. Where d'you think the ship has gone?'

Lifting his lips from the bowl, Bladeribb nodded seaward.

'Due west fer Sampetra, I'd take me oath on it.'

Martin stared levelly at him. 'Then your oath better be good, because you're coming with us. How far away is this place you call Sampetra?'

'Some say 'tis beyond where the sun sinks in the west, too far for yore liddle boat t'sail, I'd say.'

Martin eyed the distant horizon as he strapped the sword to his back. 'You let me worry about that. Now, tell me all you know about Sampetra.'

By late morning they were ready to sail. Log a Log and the Guosim crowded around the bank as Martin, Grath and Clecky waded into the shallows, leading Bladeribb by a rope tied about his middle. Viola bankvole followed them, crying, 'I'm going with you to help free Abbot Durral!'

Martin had noted a change in Viola. She seemed more sensible and confident since her captivity; several times that morning she had requested to sail with them. Now, as before, Martin gave her his answer.

'Sorry, little one, it would be far too dangerous for you.

We'll bring the Abbot back, I promise you. Go back to Redwall now, there's a good creature. Log a Log and his shrews will see you get home safe.'

Water splashed as Viola stamped her footpaw in the shallows. 'Just because I'm not a grownup warrior you don't want me! It's not fair, I'm being treated like a silly little Dibbun!' She turned and flounced off across the shore towards the woodlands.

'Viola, we don't think you're a Dibbun,' Martin called after her. 'All of us know that you're a very brave young bankvole, but you're not old enough yet to find your way through the woods alone. Wait for Log a Log to take you home.'

Paws akimbo, Viola turned and glared at Martin. 'I know my own way back to the Abbey, thank you! I don't need a whole tribe of shrews to hold my paw. Goodbye!' With her apron strings streaming out in the breeze, she strode resolutely off.

Log a Log turned to Martin. 'She's a bold creature sure enough. But yore right, Martin, she's far too young to be travelling on her own. Jesat and Teno, follow the little maid and see her safely back to Redwall. Talkin' of which, I'm not lettin' you go without extra help, matey. There's two 'ere who'd be proud to sail with ye. Plogg, Welko!' Two stout shrews leapt forward and joined the party in the shallows.

Grath Longfletch looked them over approvingly, saying, 'Are you sure you can spare two strong beasts like these, Log a Log?'

Throwing a paw fondly about the shoulders of the two, Log a Log nodded at his otter friend. 'These are my two sons. They can eat, fight, sail and sing like no other shrews I know of. They've pestered me 'alf the night to let 'em sail with ye. Haharr, anythin' to avoid the iron-pawed discipline of their father, ain't that right, buckoes?'

Plogg nudged his father's ribs playfully. 'I'll bring ye back a nice walkin' stick, ole feller!'

He ducked a hefty swipe from his parent, who was grinning proudly. 'Gerroutofit, you tadpole, bring me back any walkin' sticks an' I'll break 'em o'er yore tail. Take care of each other an' our friends, you two, an' always remember yore the sons of a Guosim Chieftain. Don't do nothin' I wouldn't do, ye blood puddens!'

Welko stamped back ashore, his face serious. 'I ain't goin' on no ship that don't 'ave a name!'

Log a Log folded both paws across his fat stomach. 'Yore right, Welko. Ahoy, Grath, that's why yore vessel's 'ad so much bad luck, matey – she ain't got a name. Wot are ye goin' to call 'er? Dabby, bring some markin' dye to paint a name on.'

The big otter scratched her scarred head. 'Hmm, a name. I've never given it much thought . . .'

'Freebeast!'

They all turned to look at Martin. He pointed at the vessel, and said, 'We're all freebeasts and we're on a mission to free a good old beast, the Abbot of Redwall. So let her name be *Freebeast!*'

As the tide began to swell a short ceremony was carried out in the mouth of the river. Every creature present was issued with a beaker of shrewbeer. Log a Log was lifted aboard the craft bearing two beakers, one in each paw. Standing in the prow he recited a Guosim boat-naming poem.

'Whether she sails on river or sea,
May the wind be always behind her,
May she always be welcomed by friends like me,
May the foebeast never find her.
Let her crew hold the lives of each other dear,
And avoid every sharp rock or reef,
Good seasons and fates now listen and hear,
Keep this gallant *Freebeast* from all grief!'

Amid rousing cheers Log a Log poured one beaker over the prow and drank the other in a single swallow, along with everyone else. Martin and his friends tossed their weapons aboard and hauled themselves over the side. Grath took the tiller as Plogg and Welko hoisted the sail upon its new ashpole mast. Martin and Clecky stood for'ard, punting deep either side with the oars. *Freebeast* skimmed out of the river and into the open sea, her sail billowing bravely as she caught the wind and bucked head on into the first rollers. Clecky shipped his oar as Martin did. Standing upright, the five crew members of *Freebeast* held their weapons aloft and roared their warcries across the sunflecked waters to the Guosim on the shore.

'Redwaaaaall! Eulaliaaa! Holt Lutraaaa! Logalogalog-alog!'

Seabirds wheeled overhead in the bright summer day. Framed against the cloudless blue above, the sun beat down on the strange three-hulled vessel as it ploughed the waves. On into the unknown deeps of the wild ocean, questing for Durral the Father Abbot of Redwall Abbey. The voyage had begun!

30

Sitting on the south walltop alongside her friends, Tansy looked upward to the north. 'Well, what do you see?' she said to Rollo.

Gazing in the same direction, the old Recorder answered, 'I see the south face of the Abbey building as you do. Anybeast see anything different?'

Piknim and Craklyn began giggling, a sure sign that they were on to something. Rollo glared sternly over the top of his glasses at the Abbeymaids.

'Well, I'm glad some creatures find the situation amusing. No doubt you are about to tell us something, when you are quite finished with your fit of the giggles.'

Struggling to regain control of themselves, the pair responded, 'Teeheehee! Er hrmph! Don't you think we should be paying more attention to the next words of the poem, sir?'

'Teehee! Craklyn says we look like four fledglings waiting to be fed. Heeheehee! Sitting on top of a wall with our heads up.'

Tansy stifled a smile at the thought. Rollo unrolled the thin parchment rather huffily, spreading it on the walltop.

'Ahem! Just as I was about to do,' he said. 'Now let me see.

'Put a home with our Abbey Warrior,
North East South at the start,
Then to complete this riddle,
Add the last thing in "my heart".'

Nodding to each other, Piknim and Craklyn gave the answer.
'Another name for a home?'
'A house!'
'Who is our Abbey Warrior?'
'Martin!'
'Put them together and name me a little bird . . .'
'House martin!'
Tansy was about to speak when Rollo jumped in ahead of her. 'North East South start N E S. The last thing in my heart is the letter T. Put them together and we have nest! We're looking for a house martin's nest!'
Not to be outdone, Tansy swiftly added her contribution.

'Below the mouth of a mouse looking south,
All in a deserted dwelling.
So sit o'er the maidenhair, gaze up north,
And solve what my next words are telling.

'Look, a small attic window, and see carved in the stone above it, I'll wager that's the head of a mouse. See!'
Four pairs of eyes peered keenly up at the highest window on the north side of the Abbey. Sure enough, the arched apex of the stone was decorated with a carved head.
Rollo polished his spectacles hard, blinking, and said, 'Yes, it is a creature of some sort, but it's too high up to tell what it is. The only way to be sure is to go up there . . .'

Tansy tugged at the old Recorder's sleeve to gain his attention. She pointed to the spot where Piknim and Craklyn had been sitting a moment before. 'They've already gone. Come on, old friend, let's follow.'

She assisted the old bankvole down the wallsteps.

'I wonder what the last one up there is this time?' he muttered, shaking his head. 'A tottering tadpole or a boggled beetle?'

The hedgehog maid smiled as they crossed the lawn. 'I'd better not tell you, or you'd have Mother Auma send 'em to bed with no supper.'

The high window in question was the one in Fermald's attic. It was filled by a large chunk of translucent rock crystal. Tansy reached it by standing on the back of Fermald's armchair. Craklyn climbed up to help her, whilst Rollo and Piknim held on to the battered old chair, steadying it.

The hedgehog maid gave a cry of delight as she felt the lump of crystal move beneath her paw. 'Haha! It's not even cemented in. Mind your paws, Craklyn – look out below!'

She pulled it loose; the crystal sent up a cloud of dust as it thudded onto the cushioned armchair seat. Craklyn crawled into the window space and poked her head out to look around.

Piknim danced up and down with impatience. 'Can you see the house martin's nest, is the pearl there?'

Only when Tansy and the squirrelmaid were safe back on the attic floor did Craklyn make her report. 'Phew! I felt awfully dizzy looking out of the window. D'you realize how high up we are? But I could see the nest – it's on a narrow stone parapet, wedged in a corner.'

Rollo was obviously trying to keep calm as he asked the vital question. 'Hmm, did you see the . . . er, pearl?'

Craklyn perched on the chair arm, looking at her friends' expectant faces, framed in the sunlit shaft from the window. 'I saw the nest, a typical house martin dwelling, almost like a round ball with a small hole for an entrance. But I don't think any birds have used it for some seasons. It looked empty.'

Tansy nodded thoughtfully.

'Exactly as the rhyme says. "Below the mouth of a mouse looking south, all in a deserted dwelling." The nest is the deserted dwelling. But the thing that really mystifies me is, how did a very old squirrel like Fermald manage to get the pearl into the nest?'

Piknim clapped a paw to her mouth, but could not stop the giggle that bubbled forth. 'Teeheehee! Ask mister Rollo, he's pretty ancient. Heehee – he should know!'

Quite unexpectedly, the old Recorder smiled and made a slight bow to the mousemaid. 'Thank you, Piknim, nice to see you showing some respect for your elders. As a matter of fact the question puzzled me for a while. However, I think I know how Fermald managed to place the pearl in that house martin's nest.'

It was the three Abbeymaids' turn to look surprised. Rollo seated himself in the armchair and explained in three words. 'Fermald's fishing rod!'

Tansy clapped her paws in delight. 'Of course! I'll go and get it!'

Craklyn lay in the window space, leaning outward, while Tansy and Piknim held tight to her footpaws as she fished for the nest. It was a lot simpler than they thought. With a triple-barbed hook attached to the line the nest was easily snagged. Craklyn reeled it up carefully, as Rollo paced the floor chatting away to himself, highly pleased with his own wisdom.

'Quite basic, really. Fermald hooked the nest, reeled it up here, placed the pearl in it and lowered it back into position again. Hah! You can't beat an old head on old shoulders!'

Craklyn swung the nest inside, and Tansy caught it skilfully. Seasons ago a clever little house martin had formed the circular structure of grass, leaves and mud, leaving a round opening. She had probably used it several times to rear her eggchicks.

Rollo grinned broadly at the three eager faces as he upended the nest and shook it.

'Just as the rhyme says. "My fourth tear I shed, for the Abbey Redwall, laid where it never should hatch or fall." Behold, here is our fourth pearl, young maids!'

But only an acorn shell fell out onto the attic floorboards.

In complete silence Tansy took the nest from Rollo. The hedgehog maid rummaged inside it with her paw, then she shook it and held it up to the light, her face a picture of disappointment. 'There's no pearl! It's gone!'

Piknim and Craklyn were both shocked. They too inspected the empty nest, but no amount of looking could conjure up a pearl that was not there. All four friends slumped on the attic floor totally dejected.

Tansy picked up the acorn shell and looked closely at it. 'This is an empty shell – it's been cracked and stuck together again. See!' She split the shell and drew forth the scrap of parchment which had been rolled up inside. 'Here's the clue to our fifth pearl, though I don't intend opening or reading it until we find the fourth pearl. Agreed?'

Rollo spoke for himself and the other two maids. 'Agreed, it would not seem right. We must discover each pearl in the order that Fermald intended us to. Come on, cheer up, friends, we'll discuss our next move after dinner.'

Auma sat with Gerul and Skipper at the table in Great Hall. Late evening sunlight streamed through the stained glass windows onto a table that did full justice to the culinary skills of Redwall cooks. Neither beast had let injury blunt his appetite. With no great interest in the elderberry tart or the small beaker of plum cordial before her, the badger Mother turned to Skipper, saying, 'No news of Martin and Clecky yet?'

The brawny otter looked up from his summer salad, took a draught of October Ale and wiped his mouth on the back of a paw. 'I'm afraid not, marm, though I expect the otter patrol I sent out to be back with some information before dawn tomorrow. Who knows, may'ap they'll bring Martin an' Clecky with 'em, the Abbot an' Viola too with any luck.'

Auma sniffed hard, blinked back a tear and sighed. 'Poor Durral and Viola. I hope they're not still in the clutches of that foul lizard thing and those scurvy searats.'

Gerul demolished a wedge of celery and mushroom turnover with all the ease of a seasoned trencherbeast. 'Ah now, don't be a worryin' yerself over things y'can't control, marm. Sure, as me ould mother always used t'say, ten seasons from now y'll be wonderin' wot you were bothered about today, if yer still around t'bother. Will y'look at ould Rollo an' those young maids over there, they've got faces on them like frazzled frogs, so they have. Hi there, Tansy! Bring y'friends over here an' join the Redwall worriers.'

When the four friends had joined Auma, Skipper and Gerul, the owl applied himself back to a chunk of heavy fruit cake. 'There now, aren't we the grand ould miserable tablemates, what are you lot lookin' so down in the whiskers about?'

Tansy explained in detail about the house martin's nest. Gerul listened carefully as he helped himself to Auma's tart. 'Hmm, so there was no pearl in the nest, eh? Well, wot d'yer suppose happened, did it fall out, have y'searched the grounds below the nest?'

Rollo picked at a slice of apple pie. 'Oh yes, we went over the ground below with a fine-tooth comb. There was no sign of anything resembling a pearl.'

Gerul picked crumbs from his chest as he talked.

'So, where in the name o' faith d'ye think the pearl went?'

Rollo pushed away his apple pie and shrugged. 'How should I know?'

The owl blinked his enormous eyes. 'Tchah! Me ould mother wouldn't be too pleased with you, Rollo. A beast of yore long seasons an' wisdom not bein' able to see wot's starin' ye in the whiskers. If the pearl never fell, then sure it was taken by somebeast or other, that's clear enough!'

The Recorder of Redwall Abbey stared indignantly at Gerul. 'Oh indeed? Somebeast took it, eh! From over halfway up the Abbey wall in a nest on a tiny ledge? Pray be good enough to tell me, sir, what sort of creature was it?'

Gerul finished his crumb-picking ablutions and hopped down to the floor, chuckling at the angry Recorder. 'Ah, sure, yer gettin' y'whiskers in a tizz over nothin' at all. I hate leavin' a luvly table o' vittles like this, but if y'll be kind enough t'follow me good self I'll try t'help yer!'

The four friends followed Gerul up to Fermald's attic. He waddled around the abandoned martin's nest, touching it now and again with a hefty talon as he enquired, 'An' this is exactly as y'found it, just like it is now?'

'Just as we found it,' Tansy answered.

Gerul looked from one to the other. 'An' of course you all had yer eyes shut tight, did ye not?'

Piknim was running out of patience. 'Silly owl, we had our eyes wide open,' she said, stamping her paw down.

From amid the dried grass and mud of the nest Gerul picked a small greyish-black feather. 'So, you had yer eyes open an' never saw this, hah! Me ould mother would've given yez the length o' her beak, so she would!'

Tansy twirled the feather in her paw, mystified. 'What is it, Gerul?'

The owl hopped up onto the armchair and blinked at

Tansy. 'Faith, don't y'know, missie? 'tis the neck feather of a jackdaw, the greatest robber ever to have an ould set of wings. Yore pearl was stolen by a jackdaw. They'll have anythin' shiny, the thievin' blackguards, they'd have the eyes out o' yer head if you weren't watchin' 'em, so me mother used t'say!'

Rollo plopped into the armchair glumly. 'You mean to tell us that the fourth pearl was stolen by a jackdaw? It could be anywhere in Mossflower, or even beyond by now. How are we ever going to find it?'

Gerul leapt to the floor and started waddling off back to the remains of dinner in Great Hall.

'Easy. I'll show ye after breakfast tomorrer!' he said.

Wullger the otter gatekeeper poked his head round the door of Great Hall and called to Auma, 'Visitors t'see yer, marm, you too Skip!'

Led by Log a Log and half a score of burly otters, the Guosim shrews piled into the hall. Despite his still-healing wounds, Skipper dashed to meet them.

'Ahoy, Rangapaw, you timed that nicely, dinner ain't over yet. Log a Log, y'old son of a shrew, how are ye, matey!'

Greetings were exchanged as helpers ran to put out extra food for the newcomers. Log a Log and Rangapaw joined Auma and the otter Chieftain at the big table. Skipper poured October Ale for them, giving them a moment to slake their thirst.

Rangapaw was a large sleek otter. She stood almost a head taller than Skipper, her father. Mopping off a tankard of ale, she gave Skipper a friendly buffet across the back which nearly knocked him from his seat. He winked fondly at her.

'Now then, y'great waterhound, stop knockin' yore ole daddy about an' make yore report.'

The big otter poured herself more October Ale. 'Well, we travelled as fast as we could when word came from

Log a Log that it was our mates the Redwallers in trouble, but we arrived too late. Ole Log a Log can tell you the rest; we met him on the shore.'

The Guosim Chieftain went on to explain how Lask Frildur and Romsca had sailed off with the Abbot and Martin had taken up pursuit of them with his small band. He told of Grath Longfletch rescuing Viola, then looked about, saying, 'Is the volemaid not back yet? She should have arrived more'n a day ago.'

Auma looked shocked. 'Back here? No. Surely Martin didn't let the little maid travel alone?'

Log a Log shook his head. 'Of course not, marm. She had an escort of two stout shrews. Hey, Jesat and Teno, what say you?'

Jesat and Teno stood forward. 'We saw her right to the gates, marm. She thanked us politely, but insisted on going in by herself.'

Rangapaw quaffed her second tankard of ale and stood up. 'Pack some o' those vittles for me an' the crew; we'll go straight away an' search for the liddle maid.'

When the otters had departed Log a Log patted Auma's paw reassuringly. 'Ahoy now, don't fret y'self, marm. They'll find her; and Martin an' his crew won't rest until they bring yore Abbot back 'ome. I know it, an' you would too if'n you'd seen the iron in his eyes when he set sail after those wavescum. Hah! That's one warrior they won't shake off, I'd take me affidavit on that!'

'That may be so,' said Rollo. 'But we must not slow down our search for the pearls; if we find the ransom, we may be able to save some bloodshed.'

A moment later Sister Cicely stormed in and banged the table with a medicine spoon. 'I'll wager nobeast has seen those three Dibbuns! They're not in the dormitory, I've searched all around the Abbey . . .'

Tansy interrupted the irate Sister. 'D'you mean Arven, Diggum and Gurrbowl?'

Cicely brandished the medicine spoon fiercely. 'Who

else! Oooh, just let me get my paws on that little wretch Arven, he's the ringleader, the other two babes would follow him anywhere. I'll dose him purple with nettle soup when I get him! I'll bath him until his ears are bright red, I'll . . . I'll . . .'

Auma interrupted the Sister sternly. 'You'll leave them to me, Cicely. After all, they are only Dibbuns. No doubt they'll be hiding somewhere, like last time. I say let us wait until they get hungry enough to come out, then we'll see what they have to say for themselves.'

At that moment the three Dibbuns in question were wandering deep in Mossflower Wood. Wullger had left the Abbey main gate ajar when he admitted the otters and Guosim shrews, and the three Abbeybabes had seized their chance. Armed with sticks and a blanket, which they intended to make into a tent, they set off. They also had a big fruitcake, a bag of candied chestnuts and a flask of strawberry cordial purloined from the kitchens.

Arven smiled to himself as he muttered to his willing companions, 'Thissa time we get lotsa mucky and dusted, catcher some o' those blizzards an' smack 'em wiv our big sticks. Then they be gladder to see us, I betcher!'

Diggum waved her stick about savagely. 'Bo urr, us'ns be orful turrible h'aminals.'

Gurrbowl agreed wholeheartedly. 'Yurr, an us won't mightn't cumm back till we be growed up. Hurr hurr, we'm shout at 'em all an' purrem up t'bed early!'

The soft folds of velvet summer night descended over the woodlands, silencing birdsong as the three tiny figures were swallowed up in still-warm darkness.

31

Dawn broke hot and warm over a sheltered inlet on the northwest coast of Sampetra. The ebbing tide had thrown up some flotsam from the vessel *Bloodkeel*. Still intact, the rudder and tiller lay among the shells and seaweed festooning the tideline. Lashed to it by a heaving line were Rasconza the fox and his steersrat Guja. Pounded and battered by the seas, they coughed up salt water as they extricated themselves from the ropes, tiller and rudder that had kept them alive for almost two days on the ocean. The pair dragged themselves painfully over the shore, into the shadow of a rock overhang at the foot of a hill. There they found fresh water.

Greedily the two corsairs lapped at the tiny rivulet of cold, crystal-clear liquid which threaded thinly and dripped from the mossy underside of their shelter. Rasconza picked salt rime from his eye corners, gazing beyond the cove, out to where the deep ocean glimmered and shimmered in early morn.

The fox's voice was rasping and painful, bitter and vengeful. 'A full crew, matey, an' we're the only two left alive t'tell the tale!'

Guja had scraped some of the damp moss off with his dagger. He chewed it until there was no more moisture or nourishment left, then spat it out viciously. 'Aye, Cap'n, all our shipmates, either drowned or eaten by the big fishes, every beastjack o' them slain by Mad Eyes' treachery!'

Rasconza unbuckled the saturated belt which held his daggers, and laid the weapons out one by one on the grass. Selecting his favourite blade, he began honing it on a piece of rock. 'Mark my words, Guja, the worst day's work Ublaz ever did was to leave me alive. Though he don't know it, his dyin' day is near!'

As Chief Trident-rat, it was Sagitar's duty to report to her Emperor morning and night. As she entered the pine marten's throne room, Sagitar could see that Ublaz was in a foul mood. He slumped on his throne staring at the lifeless form of Grall, his messenger gull. The great black-backed bird had died of exhaustion bringing news back to its master.

Ublaz touched the limp wing feathers contemptuously with his footpaw. 'Hah! Grall was the only one of my gulls to make it back, and now look at him – useless bundle of birdflesh!'

In the silence that followed, Sagitar shuffled nervously. Feeling it her duty to make some comment, she enquired meekly, 'Did the bird bring good news of your pearls, Sire?'

Ublaz rose and, stepping over the dead gull, he stared out of the wide chamber window at the ocean beyond. 'Lask Frildur and Romsca are sailing back to Sampetra. They didn't get the pearls. Instead they're bringing the Father Abbot of Redwall Abbey as a hostage – the Tears of all Oceans are to be his ransom. What d'you think of that?'

Sagitar's voice was apprehensive as she answered, 'Well, at least you have something to bargain with, Sire . . .'

Ublaz whirled upon her, his eyes blazing angrily.

'Bargain? I am Ublaz, Emperor of Seas and Oceans, I *take*! Twice my creatures have failed me. Twice! If I had gone after the pearls myself in the first place I would have them now, set in my new crown! There will be no more bargaining or playing of games. When that ship drops anchor here, we will sail again back to the land of Mossflower and Redwall Abbey. All of my ships and every creature on this island. That way there will be none left behind to seize power and plot behind my back. I will lead everybeast, Monitors, Trident-rats and corsairs, against Redwall. I will smash it stone from stone and rip those pearls from the wreckage. The ruins of that Abbey will remain as a marker to the deadbeasts that lie beneath them – the ones who tried to defy the might of Ublaz!'

Romsca ushered Abbot Durral into her cabin. With a few swift slashes of her sword she released him from his rope shackles. The corsair ferret sat Durral upon her bunk, issuing him with a beaker of seaweed grog and some hard ship's biscuit.

The old mouse sipped at the fiery liquid, squinting without his eyeglasses as he stared curiously at Romsca.

'Why are you helping me like this, my child?'

Romsca sheathed her cutlass blade firmly. 'I ain't yore child, I keep tellin' yer, an' I ain't doin' this to 'elp you, 'tis more fer my benefit you be kept alive. We're sailin' into bad cold weather, you wouldn't last a day out on deck. Sit tight in 'ere an' keep the door locked, d'ye hear?'

Abbot Durral smiled warmly at the wild-looking corsair. 'You are a good creature, Romsca. What a pity you chose the life of a corsair.'

Romsca stood with one paw on the doorlatch. 'It ain't none o' yore business wot I chose ter be,' she said harshly, "tis a long hard story 'ow I come t'be

wot I am. Any'ow, I likes bein' a corsair an' I ain't
ashamed o' my life. Now you stay put, ole Durral, an'
don't open this door to none but me. I don't trust that
Lask Frildur no more, he's got a crazy look in 'is eyes
of late.'

Slamming the cabin door, Romsca went aft. The
weather was cold and the seas a slate grey. She faced
for'ard and peered anxiously; the wind was dropping,
a deep fogbank was looming up, and ice was beginning to form on the rigging. Turning, she looked aft,
scanning the waters in the ship's wake. Somewhere
out along the eastern horizon Romsca thought she
saw a small dark dot. She blinked and looked again,
but she had lost the location of the dot owing to
the ship's movement on the oily waveless swell. A
slithering sound behind Romsca caused her to turn
swiftly, paw on swordhilt. Lask Frildur was standing there watching her. Though he looked cold and
seasick there was a crafty glimmer in the Monitor
General's eyes.

'Where have you hidden the Abbotmouze, Romzca?'
he hissed.

Romsca drew her cutlass and circled until the lizard
was backed to the stern rail. She pointed the blade at him.
'Never you mind about the Abbot, I'm takin' charge o'
him. Keep yore distance, Lask; or I swear I'll spit yer on
this blade!'

Lask flicked his tongue at the corsair ferret. 'Lzzzt!
Food iz running low, weather iz growing colder, you
have got uz lozt again.'

Romsca stared contemptuously at the Monitor. 'Vittles
is as short fer me'n'my crew as they are fer you an' yore
lizards. As fer the weather – well, it'll get colder afore
we're out o' these waters, an' if you think I've got ye
lost then yore welcome to navigate fer yerself. Other
than that, you stay out o' my way an' don't start any
trouble that y'can't finish.'

Lask stayed leaning on the rail, shivering, but still smiling slyly. 'When I ztart trouble, Romzca, you will be the firzt to know!'

The longboat with the outriggers either side of it bobbed and swayed as Welko the shrew slid down from the masthead. Grath helped him to the narrow deck.

'Well, was it the corsair ship you saw to the west?' she asked.

Welko drew his cloak against the cold. 'I'm not sure. I thought I saw a sail, then I lost sight of it. There could be fog ahead, mayhap she's sailed into it.'

Clecky was seated aft, guarding a small cooking fire he had made on a bed of sand surrounded by slate. The lanky hare had taken to being very nautical. 'Ahoy there, me heartychaps, grub – er, vittles are about ready,' he called out to everyone. 'I say, Plogg old cove, nip over into the larboard shrewboat an' dig out a few apples, will you, there's a good ol' barnacle, wot?'

The two shrewboats that served as outriggers to the longboat were loaded with supplies; Martin had made space in the starboard one for Bladeribb, their searat captive. The searat stared sullenly at Plogg as the latter climbed across to the far logboat. The shrew rummaged through the ration packs before calling back to Clecky, 'There's not many apples left!'

Grath glared across at Bladeribb. 'Have you been sneakin' across at night an' stealin' apples?'

Martin patted Grath's broad back. 'No, he's been right there all along, I've kept my eye on him. Clecky, you haven't been pinching the odd half-dozen apples, have you?'

The hare's ears stood up with indignation. 'Er, d'you mind belayin' that statement, ol' seamouse, I haven't touched a single apple. Hmph! Bally cheek of some crewbeasts. Take a proper look over there, I'm sure you'll find heaps of jolly ol' apples rollin' about somewheres, wot!'

Plogg began turning the packs over and checking them. Suddenly he gave a shout of alarm as he rolled back a crumpled canvas cover. Drawing his sword, Martin leapt aboard the logboat, only to find Plogg wrestling with a kicking, screaming Viola bankvole.

Martin caught her sharply by the ear. 'What in the name of thunder are you doing here, miss? I told you to go back to the Abbey. You could have been drowned or injured or . . . or . . . How did you manage to stow away on this logboat, and what happened to Jesak and Teno?'

Viola wriggled free of the warrior's grasp and skipped nimbly over to the longboat, where she hid behind Clecky, shouting, 'I gave them the slip and doubled back and stole aboard while you were all drinking and naming the boat. I wasn't drowned or injured, see! Told you I was going to help rescue Father Abbot, didn't I! Well, what're you going t'do now? You can't turn back or throw me overboard!'

Grath Longfletch grinned and winked at the volemaid. 'Yore right there, young 'un. My, yore a peppery one an' no mistake. Looks like we're stuck with you.'

Clecky looked over his shoulder, viewing the stow-away sternly. 'You're lucky we aren't searats or those corsair bods, m'gel, or we'd have chucked you overboard to the fishes just t'save feedin' you, wot!'

Martin shook his head in despair as he gazed at the defiant volemaid. 'Think of the distress you've caused Mother Auma and all your friends back at the Abbey. They probably think you're still a prisoner aboard that ship with the Abbot. If you'd gone back to Redwall as I told you, it would have saved a load of worry for everybeast who cares what happens to you, miss!'

The sudden realization of what she had done caused tears to flood down Viola's cheeks, and she hung her head in shame.

Martin could not bear to see a young creature so unhappy. He patted the volemaid's head gently. 'There,

there, now, don't cry. Your motives were good and I know you were only trying to help. Welcome aboard, Viola. Come on, smile, and we'll try to make the best of it.'

They dined on toasted cheese and hot shrewbread, half an apple apiece and some oat and barley cordial. Martin carried a plateful across to Bladeribb; the searat was quite comfortable, wrapped in a cloak and a blanket.

The warrior once again questioned his captive. 'Could that have been the vessel *Waveworm* that Welko sighted earlier? Are we on the right course?'

The searat grabbed his plate of food, nodding. 'Aye, that'll be 'er. You'll be sailin' into wintry seas now, cold an' dangerous, fog an' ice. If'n we gets through it you'll prob'ly sight 'er agin in the good weather. She'll be 'eaded due west towards the settin' sun, like I told yer.'

Martin caught the searat's paw as he was about to eat. 'Play me false just once, Bladeribb, and I'll slay you. Is that clear? Steer us true if you want to stay alive.'

The searat shrugged. 'I'm bound t'die sooner or later, if not by your paw, then it'll either be Lask Frildur or Ublaz Mad Eyes for allowin' meself t'be taken captive.'

32

Viola got on famously with Plogg and Welko, the sons of Log a Log. As night began setting over the deep, the small crew wrapped an old sailcloth around them and sat in a circle with Clecky's little fire at the centre to keep out the intensifying cold.

The lanky hare sang a song to keep their spirits up.

'Of all the creatures in the land,
The sea or in the air,
Not one of 'em is half so grand,
Or noble as a hare.
A hare can jump, a hare can run,
He don't live down a hole,
In fact a hare's a lot more fun,
Than almost any mole.
A hare's courageous and so brave,
Good-mannered and quite courtly,
Sometimes he's serious and grave,
But never fat, just portly.
He never puts a footpaw wrong,
His disposition's sunny,
With ears so elegant and long,
Not stubby like a bunny.

So sing his praises everywhere,
This creature bold, with charm to spare,
The one thing better than a hare,
Is two hares, that's a pair!'

Clecky helped himself to a piece of toasted cheese. 'I'd take a bow, but I don't want to rock the jolly old boat, wot?'

Grath nodded in mock admiration. 'Yore far too modest for words, matey.'

The hare nodded agreement as he gobbled the cheese down. 'Hmm, shy an' retirin' too, though it's more a bally virtue than a fault to a chap like me, y'know.'

Grath snatched the last piece of cheese before Clecky could lay paw to it. 'Well said, matey, yore just the shy retirin' type we've been lookin' for to keep first watch. Wake me in an hour's time.'

The little craft with its outriggers sailed through the night towards the fogbank with Clecky's mutterings echoing faintly across the still waters.

'Hmph! Good job I'm polite an' withdrawn too, not like these otter types, brash common wallahs. Still, what can one expect of a creature with funny little ears an' a tail like a bally plank.'

The night was pitch black and wreathed in thick damp fog when Grath shook Martin to take third watch. 'Come on, matey, time for yore watch. Here's a beaker of oat'n'barley water I heated up on the fire. Wake Plogg for his watch when you've done yores.'

Martin thanked the otter and moved up into the bow of the longboat. Crouching, he snuggled into his cloak, sipping gratefully at the hot drink as he kept watch. However, it was only the damp bitter cold that kept him awake. All that was visible, even to the keenest eye, was a solid wall of whitish grey fog. How long he crouched there Martin did not know. Strange shapes loomed up out of the mists, only to vaporize and vanish. Martin knew they were all from his imagination; one after another the spectres appeared before his wearying eyes, dragons, great fish, corsair galleys, at one point he actually thought he saw Redwall Abbey. Shaking himself and rubbing his eyes, he tried hard to stay awake and keep a sense of normality in a world of wraithlike apparitions, swirling and roiling like patterns in watery milk. He watched as a towering mountain of ice loomed large directly in front of the longboat. Another trick his mind was playing on him, he thought, blinking furiously . . . Or was it?

Crrrrunch!

Suddenly the Warriormouse was wrenched to his senses by the danger.

'All paws for'ard!' Martin yelled.

Freezing icy seawater poured into the longboat; it sizzled and hissed as it drowned Clecky's small fire. Grath grabbed Viola as she dived towards the bow to join Clecky and the two shrews. There was a tearing, rending noise followed by an agonized scream, which was cut short in a whoosh of water. Grath scrambled back along the cracking planks of the disintegrating longboat to investigate. She was immediately back, yelling, 'Overboard, everybeast abandon the boat!'

Leaping over the side into the freezing water, they were amazed to find that it was no more than a thin stream. They found themselves standing paw-deep on top of solid ice. Only Grath could explain the phenomenon.

'Where I come from on the far north coast, we heard tales of this from seals and sea otters. This is a floating mountain of ice, I think they called it an iceberg. From what I can see, our craft ran into a deep crack in the shallow edge of this iceberg. It crushed both the shrewboat outriggers – we jumped overboard as it struck the longboat. Bladeribb the searat didn't stand a chance.'

Viola shuddered at the thought of the searat's fate. 'Crushed to death by an ice mountain. What a dreadful way to die.'

Grath put aside her bow and quiver, nodding grimly. 'Don't feel sorrow for that 'un, missie, his passin' was quick an' easy. Not like the innocent creatures he slew for no reason. Right, wot's the next move, Martin?'

The Warriormouse adjusted the sword belt across his shoulders. 'We'd best go and see if we can salvage anything from the wreckage. Plogg and Welko, you stay here with Viola, it should be light soon. Grath, Clecky, come with me.'

The hare jumped from the ledge onto the watercovered ice shelf. Immediately he slipped, falling flat on his tail. 'Tchah! I say, you chaps, this's all a bit much, no boat, no grub, no fire and now a blinkin' wet behind, wot!'

Grath slid across the ice, using her tail as a rudder. Reaching the edge, she called out happily, 'Ahoy, there's the logboat with the supplies in it! Come an' lend a paw, mate!'

The shrew craft was floating just a short distance from where they stood, practically undamaged. Having the longest reach of the three, Clecky took Martin's sword and, while they held him teetering on the edge of the ice floe, he leaned out and jabbed at the logboat, using the sword like a harpoon. There was a soft thunk as the sharp steel tip bit into wood. The hare drew the narrow craft slowly and carefully in, then Grath leaned out and grabbed the stern firmly.

'Got it! What a stroke of luck. This logboat must have snapped off and shot backwards into the sea instead of being crushed. Here, Martin, hold on to my tail while I pull her up onto the ice.'

With a mighty heave the powerful otter lifted the stern clear of the water and slid the logboat up onto the ice. Martin sharpened a broken spar into a pointed stake, then dug a hole in the ice with his swordpoint. Clecky held the stake steady as Grath drove it tightly into the hole. They made the logboat fast to the stake by its headrope, then climbed aboard to take stock of the supplies.

Gradually the greyish fog changed to soft white with the advent of dawn. The silence was total; even the voices of the small crew sounded muffled and subdued by the heavy, all-pervading mist curtain. Using a canvas sail, the friends had rigged a tent from for'ard to aft on the logboat. Now, relatively snug, they sat watching Clecky. The hare had gathered wood from the wreckage, splitting it to find the driest pieces. Using a flint, he struck a spark against Martin's sword blade onto a heap of splinters and torn sacking scraps from the supply wrappings.

A faint glow, accompanied by a wisp of smoke, had the hungry hare chortling happily. 'Ohohoho, I say, pals, never mind the dangers an' flippin' perils besettin' us, who's for a good hot scoff, wot wot?'

Everybeast in the crew contributed their cooking skills, to make what for cold and famished creatures was an epic feast. Martin and Viola chopped carrots, mushrooms and any vegetables they could find among the packs, Clecky and Grath boiled water in an iron pot, adding herbs, dried watershrimp and hotroot. Plogg and Welko toasted shrewbread and warmed some damson wine.

Soon they were tucking into tasty bowls of soup, followed by hot shrewbread spread with cherry preserve and small beakers of damson wine, warm from the fire.

Welko patted his stomach. 'Eat up, mates, there's nought like good vittles to keep yore spirits high!'

'Aye, make the best of it,' Plogg responded, a little gloomily, 'there's little enough left. Over half our supplies were lost along with that searat in the other logboat. Dunno where the next good meal's comin' from.'

Viola leaned across and dabbed some cherry preserve onto the pessimistic shrew's nose. 'Thank you for those few cheery words, sir, you little fat misery! Aren't you glad t'be alive?'

Welko tugged his brother's ear heartily. 'C'mon, smile, you sulky liddle toad, smile!'

Plogg pulled a long face, at which Martin burst out

laughing. 'If only your father could see you now. I vote, as captain of this craft, that if Plogg doesn't start smiling and singing straight away, we toss him into the water and let him turn into an ice lump!'

There was a loud cry of agreement. Grath seized the shrew by his belt, winking at Clecky. 'Good idea. I ain't sittin' in the same boat as a shrew with a gob on 'im like a flattened ferret!'

Immediately Plogg grinned from ear to ear and broke into song.

'Oh, I'm 'appy as the day is long,
I'm cheery, merry, bright,
From early morn I sings me song,
Until last thing at night.
Chop off me paws, slice off me tail,
An' my pore neck start wringin',
You'll never 'ear me cry or wail,
Because I'll still be singin'!
Ooooo, flugga dugga dugga chugchugchug,
With a smile like a duck upon me mug!'

Plogg's song was greeted by laughter and cheers, merriment that would have soon ceased had the friends known that keen dark eyes, scores of them, were watching through the mists as heavy damp forms slid wet and silent towards the little logboat lying on the broad watery ice ledge.

33

Powder-blue and cloudless, the morning hung hot and still over Redwall Abbey. Dewdrops evaporating from leaf and grass left orchard and lawn a soft summer green; trilling birdsong resounded from Mossflower Wood beyond the ancient sandstone walls. Summer was blossoming into long hot days and still-warm evenings.

Hogwife Teasel sat at breakfast between Auma and Tansy. She rapped the table impatiently with her ladle, glancing from one to the other as she remonstrated with them.

'Sittin' 'ere a frettin' ain't doin' you a smidge o' good. I tell you, Auma, those three Dibbuns will show up when they've a mind to, and those others will soon find Viola; we can be sure of that. An' as for you, missie Tansy, great seasons, just lookit yoreself, a mopin' an' a floppin' about like a fish on a bank, what 'elp is that to anybeast?

'Now you lissen t'me, friends, this Abbey'll be searched from attic to orchard today an' those three babes will be found and that's an end to it! Now I needs somebeast t'lend a paw sortin' through the fruit an' veggies from the spring crop. Seein' as I don't 'ave Abbot Durral to 'elp me, I'll need you, Mother Auma.

'Tansy, take yore liddle friends an' old Rollo and get

searchin' – lands sakes, we may need those pearls to get our Abbot back! Leave the Dibbun searchin' to Brother Dormal, Skipper an' Sister Cicely – they've got every Abbeybeast organized for a day-long Dibbun hunt.'

The badger pushed away her half-empty platter and gave a huge sigh. Smiling, she patted Teasel's workworn paw. 'Right! Lead me to those fruit and vegetables. Tansy, you heard our good hogwife, back to your search, miss!'

Piknim, Craklyn and Rollo were trying to pry Gerul loose from the breakfast table. The greedy owl was hurriedly stuffing the last of a batch of bilberry scones into his beak and washing them down with cold mint tea.

'Arr now, don't be rushin' me, y'dreadful creatures, or I'll get indigestions in me ould stummick an' I won't be able to think.'

Tansy folded the scones into a serviette and gave them to him. 'Here, faminebeak, take these with you. Who ever heard of an owl thinking with his stomach?'

Gerul hopped ahead of them to the attics, still protesting. 'Any sensible owl thinks with his stummick, shows how much you know, miss spike'ead. Me ould mother always used t'say t'me that my head was so full of nonsense that I'd have t'think with me stummick an' that way if I fell on me head I wouldn't hurt me brain. So y'see I've got to have plenty o' packin' round me stummick to protect it in case I need t'do some serious thinkin'.'

When they reached Fermald's attic, Gerul took the house martin's empty nest and placed a glittering fragment of crystal in it.

'Here now, Craklyn, yore young'n'spry, attach this nest to the fishin' rod and place it back down on that ledge where y'found it.'

As the squirrelmaid carried out Gerul's instructions, Rollo realized what the owl's plan was.

'Oh, I see. Now we wait for the jackdaw to return

236

and steal the piece of crystal, then we follow it. Good idea!'

Gerul perched on the armchair and unwrapped his scones. 'Aye, I'm not just feathers an' a beak, y'know, us owls are supposed t'be very wise. Now, Tansy, you take Piknim an' Craklyn, stay below on the south walltop an' watch the nest from there. When y'see the ould jackdaw, you'll have to move sharp-like t'keep up with 'im, 'cos y'don't want to lose the bird, do yer? Now hurry along, young misses. Me an' Rollo will watch from up here.'

About mid-morning Friar Higgle Stump came waddling along the walltop with a laden sack upon his back. He stopped by the three Abbeymaids and nodded to them. 'Good day t'you, misses, ain't you joinin' the search for those missin' Dibbuns?'

Still staring up at the nest on the high ledge of the Abbey building, Piknim shook her head. 'Oh, g'day, Friar, no, we're not searching.'

Higgle set the heavy sack down. 'Hmm, I see. So what *are* you doin', pray tell – watchin' our Abbey t'see if it grows any taller?'

Without taking her eyes from the nest, Tansy replied, 'No, we're just watching that house martin's nest, Friar.'

Higgle nodded understandingly. 'Oh, I see. Good hobby, nest-watchin'. Per'aps you'd like to shell these chestnuts, they're good'n'dry enough for shellin' right now.'

Craklyn looked at the Friar, taking her eyes from the nest momentarily. 'Tch! Do we have to?' she said.

Higgle nodded, smiling affably at the squirrelmaid. 'Aye, 'fraid y'do, miss, that's if y'want strawberry flan an' meadowcream for lunch, no work no food, can't 'ave idle paws around Redwall an' chestnuts don't shell themselves, y'know.'

Automatically the three friends began shelling nuts, still gazing upward at the nest as they talked.

"Tain't fair, we're already doing one job, watching the nest.'

'Hmm, now we're doing two jobs, watching and shelling.'

'Maybe if we waggled our tails a bit we could sweep the walltop, then we'd be doing three jobs.'

'Aye, and who knows, if we started singing a song together that'd keep those down below happy, and that'd be four jobs we'd be doing.'

'But just think, if Sister Cicely saw us, watching the nest, shelling nuts, sweeping the walltop with our tails and singing, you know what would happen, don't you?'

'Yes, she'd think there was something dreadfully wrong with us and she'd put us to bed in sick bay and feed us warm nettle broth.'

'Groooogh! Let's just stick to two jobs.'

Rising to its noontide zenith, the high summer sun shone down on the three Abbeymaids sitting on the walltop.

The same sun also shone on three tiny Dibbuns trundling far in the depths of Mossflower. Not surprisingly, they had stayed awake half the night, wrapping themselves in the blanket they intended making into a tent. They had kept up their courage by eating all their supplies three hours before dawn. Now they staggered on, pawsore and weary, completely lost and dispirited. Arven, the leader, was the only one of the trio who had been outside in the woods before. The other two followed him, complaining.

'Yurr, h'Arven, do ee knows whurr you'm a takin' us'ns?'

'Course a knows, we goin' to de Abbey, it not far now.'

'Gurr, you'm said that when ee dawn breaked. We'm still wan'erin' round tho', oi'm a thinken us'ns be losted.'

Arven took a swipe at a tall nettle with his stick. 'Losted? Don' be silly, I don't get losted. But I orful 'ungry, you'm scoffed all our cake, Diggum greedytummy.'

Gurrbowl sat down, curling into a ball on the woodland floor. 'Hoooaw! Oi be turrible sleepery.'

Diggum joined him, covering her snout with her apron. 'An' oi too, may'ap ee likkle rest do's oi gudd.'

Arven sat down by the two molebabes, brandishing his stick. 'Aaah, you two be's on'y h'infants. I stay 'wake an' keep guards.'

A short time later all three were curled on the ground, snoring uproariously in the windless sunwarmed woodlands. Without knowing, Arven had led them north and in a curve to the west, and now they were not far from the main path leading to Redwall. Somewhere nearby a songthrush trilled melodiously, his music mingling with that of a descending skylark out on the open flatlands, where grasshoppers chirruped endlessly in a dry chorus. But none of this disturbed the deep slumbers of the exhausted Dibbuns. They slept on, snouts twitching and paws quivering occasionally as they dreamt small dreams.

34

Gerul had placed the crystal so that it could be seen through the nest opening. Late noon sunlight glinted off the fragment, sending out pale green and soft golden facets of twinkling light. Scruvo the jackdaw saw it immediately. Ever on the alert for bright objects, the bird had been ranging far and wide after taking a midday repast of grubs and woodlice from a rotting log he had found in a woodland clearing. Scruvo wheeled in mid-air, his needlesharp eyes watching the iridescence of the crystal shard as he performed a neat loop in his flight west. Soaring gracefully downwards, he spread dark-feathered wings wide and stuck his talons forward, beating the air back as he landed on the ledge. He cocked his head to one side, squinting with one eye at the treasure. Bright, shiny, twinkling. He hopped towards it and gave a harsh cry of delight.

'Tchak! Keeyaaa!'

He struck the crystal with his beakpoint as if attacking a living thing. It did not move or fight back, so he struck it several more times to assure himself it was harmless. Quite satisfied, the jackdaw did a curious hopskip shuffle, his victory dance, then he plucked the piece of crystal from the nest and flung himself from the ledge. Down he spiralled crazily, like a dark torn scrap of cloth buffeted by breezes, then, levelling out, he winged strongly upward and shot off southeast into Mossflower.

Leaping to their paws, the three Abbeymaids scampered down the wallstairs, stumbling in their haste, calling, 'It's the jackdaw, there it goes!'

Gerul and Rollo descended the stairs as fast as they could, making haste out to the lawn. They arrived in time to see the three friends slipping out of Redwall by the small south wicker gate in the outer wall.

The owl looked sadly at his damaged wing. 'Faith, 'tisn't the walkin' I mind, but I do wish I could fly agin.'

Rollo shaded his eyes with both paws, peering up into the blue. 'I fear they'll have lost that jackdaw by now; it would be far too difficult to follow a bird through woodlands.'

The old Recorder's fears proved true. Tansy and her friends were far too small to keep track of a high-flying jackdaw, but they were not about to admit defeat. Craklyn went scooting up a nearby sycamore with all the agility of a young squirrelmaid. Piknim and Tansy almost lost sight of her, until she emerged swaying among the topmost branches. She watched awhile, then pointed eagerly before scrambling down. Back on the ground, breathless and dishevelled, she shouted, 'Circling south, the jackdaw's taking a round sweep southward!'

Tansy grinned and clapped her paws. 'Of course, it's headed to old Ninian's church! Come on!'

As they dashed by the southwest corner of the Abbey, the maids bumped into Gerul and Rollo, who had exited Redwall by its main gate.

Rollo was agog for information. 'Did you see the bird? Which way did it go?'

Tansy nodded. 'To the old church, I think!'

Dust rose in a small column as the three Abbeymaids

hurtled off down the path, Rollo and Gerul following them at a more sedate pace.

The old Recorder explained to the owl about the ancient building. 'Nobeast really knows when Ninian's was built, or who built it. Every once in a while creatures will try to settle there, but it's so damp and decaying they leave after a short time. It would be an ideal dwelling for scavengers like jackdaws.'

Gerul hobbled along the dusty path as swiftly as he could, leaving Rollo behind. 'Sure, if there's more'n one jackdaw t'deal with, those young maids will be in trouble,' he shouted as he went. 'Those are bad'n'dangerous birds if'n they're disturbed. I'll try t'catch up with them.'

Twilight's first shadows were stealing gently over the woodlands when a long javelin sank deep into the ground next to the sleeping Dibbuns. Arven was wakened by a huge dark shape which swept him up into its powerful paws.

'Yeeeek! It'sa blizzards, they got me, 'eeeeelp!' he yelled.

Still befuddled by slumber, Diggum and Gurrbowl found themselves hefted upward in similar fashion.

'Hoo urr, let oi go, zurr, we'm nought but babes!'

'Ee blizzards goin' to eat uz all oop, oh woe!' the molebabes cried out.

Chuckling deeply, Rangapaw, daughter of Skipper, held the kicking, struggling Arven firmly. 'Belay there, you liddle maggots, we ain't goin' to eat ye! Quit wrigglin' or you'll fall on yore 'ead!'

Diggum scrambled up onto the shoulder of the otter who was holding her. Grabbing his whiskers, she stared into her rescuer's eyes, and said, 'Yurr, you'm bain't no blizzard, you'm a h'otter!'

Rangapaw tucked Arven firmly into her side as she retrieved her javelin. 'Hoho, matey, lucky fer you we are. Now wot are you three rogues doin' a wanderin' off from yore Abbey? Can't y'see 'tis close on nightfall? And we're supposed to be searching for a volemaid, not blizzard-hunters.'

Arven popped out of his captor's grasp. Landing nimbly on the ground, he folded his paws across his small fat stomach and murmured darkly, 'Us was 'untin' for blizzards who took Farver h'Abbot an' Voler, us was gonna catcherem an' get all mucky an' scratchered an' bringem back to the h'Abbey an' not get shouted at.'

The big otter shook with silent laughter at the three Dibbuns. She could understand their predicament, having had many similar adventures when she was small. 'You did well, mates,' she said, 'we saw a great crowd o' them blizzards, just a short time ago. They was runnin' fer their cowardly lives 'cos they knew three warriors like you was abroad trackin' 'em. Ain't that right, mates?'

The otter crew caught her broad wink and nodded solemnly.

'Ho aye, runnin' scared stiff they was!'

'Harr, I wouldn't 'ave liked to be one o' them if'n you three'd caught up with 'em!'

'Save us from those bloodthirsty Dibbuns, they was cryin' – I 'eard 'em wid me own two ears!'

Arven scowled ferociously, picking up his stick and shaking it. 'Cummon, you c'n 'elp us, we soon catchem!'

Rangapaw swept the tiny squirrel up onto her shoulder. 'Nah, leave 'em, mate, they ain't worth it. We got to get you roughnecks back to Redwall. Ahoy, Rushcutter, break out some supplies so these warriors can eat on the way back.'

Gurrbowl prodded the otter in question.

'Hurr aye, an' 'urry ee up, oi be gurtly 'ungered!'

Back at the Abbey, Higgle Stump checked the contents of his ovens for the third time that evening. 'What'll I do, Teasel? Serve the meal or empty these ovens an' let the vittles cool before they get spoiled?'

Goodwife Teasel continued ladling cooked gooseberry and rhubarb into a bowl. She was making a crumble. 'Can't serve food if'n they're all still out searchin'. Wait'll I finish this, then I'll go an' find Mother Auma, see wot she wants us t'do with all this good fare.'

Auma was sitting on the Abbey doorstep with Skipper, scratching her muzzle worriedly. 'We should have started searching for those little ones last night,' she said. 'Sister Cicely wanted to and I stopped her, leave them I said, they'll come out of hiding when they're hungry enough. Now look, we've searched all day long, everybeast in the Abbey, and still not a trace of them. It's all my fault, Skipper – and there's poor Viola too, out there in the woods alone – lost or captured, or worse . . .'

The tough otter laid a gentle paw on his friend's shoulder. 'Don't you go blamin' yoreself, marm. I'd 'ave said the same, knowin' those three liddle snips. Hearken, wot's that?'

Bong boom, boomabong!

Furlo Stump's shouts rang out from the belltower between the peals of Redwall's twin bells. 'Otter crew comin' down the path with three Dibbuns, I see 'em clear. Open the gates, Wullger!'

The big badger Mother of Redwall swept away a tear with her apron corner as she hurried to the main gate. 'Praise the fates! They're safe! But what of Viola?'

Sister Cicely caught up with her. 'There's no sign, but at least these three are alive, seasons be thanked. Outside the Abbey walls, if you please, wandering all over Mossflower without a care in the world, I'll be bound. Well, just wait until I have a word with those three. I'll wager it was that little ragtag Arven who kept them out in those woods!'

*　　*　　*

A single bell tolled four times, calling all Redwallers to the meal in Great Hall. Owing to the addition of Log a Log and his Guosim shrews, who had stayed to help with the search, and Rangapaw's otter crew, extra tables had been laid.

Auma approached Rangapaw anxiously. 'Was there no sign of our little volemaid?' she asked. 'I can't bear to think of her lost and alone out in those dark woods.'

'Sorry, marm,' replied Rangapaw, 'but rest assured. As soon as we've dealt with these three little ones we'll resume our search.'

Sister Cicely and several of the other Abbey elders were of the opinion that the three Dibbuns should be sent straight to bed after a good dressing down for all the trouble they had caused. However, it was not to be. Skipper's daughter Rangapaw defended the babes stoutly, winning Auma and many others to her side. The otter went into comical detail relating the attitude of Arven and the two moles, and soon had everybeast nodding and smiling. Finally, she seated the trio among her otters.

'Mates, I can't think of no better tribute t'these three warriors who saved this ole Abbey from bein' overrun by blizzards, than bein' made official members of my otter crew. We need brave beasts like Arven, Diggum an' Gurrbowl t'protect us in our ole age, when they're growed an' we're staggerin' about all grey-furred.'

Before Sister Cicely could protest, Log a Log stood up, saying, 'I second that! No sense in breakin' their spirits by shoutin' at 'em an' sendin' them off t'bed with no vittles. They're three good 'uns, what d'you say, Skip?'

The otter Chieftain stroked his whiskers thoughtfully. 'Well, if y'put it thatways, matey, wot c'n I say? We could've all been slayed or taken prisoner by blizzards, wotever they be, but fer these three. I'll say this, though, if'n they're to be otter crew then they got to abide by our laws . . .'

Here Rangapaw turned to the three Dibbuns and stopped them stuffing their faces with strawberry junket for a moment. 'D'you three take an oath by fur, fire'n'water that you don't go wanderin' off agin, unless it's with my permission? Also, d'ye swear that you'll act like proper otter crew warriors, obeyin' the orders of yore elders, never tellin' fibs, bein' good to allbeasts, an' growin' up well mannered? D'you take the oath?'

Diggum stood up on her chair, waving a spoon. 'Ho aye, zurr, us'ns take ee oats!'

There was general cheering and laughter as the three Dibbuns stood nobly, paws on stomachs, because they were not sure where their hearts were located. Even Sister Cicely managed a smile.

Rangapaw called her scouts together and spoke gravely to Auma before silently slipping away to resume the search for Viola. 'Don't you fret, marm. We won't rest night or day until we've searched every tree, nook and hollow of Mossflower woods and found the little maid.'

The merriment ceased abruptly when the Abbey door banged open wide and Wullger the gatekeeper staggered in, holding up Tansy and Craklyn. They made it to the front of the main table then collapsed on the floor, breathless and sobbing.

Wullger looked pleadingly at Auma. 'I can't get no sense outta them, marm, but I think somethin' terrible's 'appened down at ole Ninian's church!'

Auma was around the table surprisingly quickly for one of her long seasons and great girth. The big badger bathed the Abbeymaids' tearstained faces with cold water from a bowl. Skipper and Log a Log kept back the press of anxious Redwallers who had left their seats to crowd around the two exhausted creatures.

Goodwife Teasel assisted, bathing Tansy's brow and calming her until she had recovered enough to speak coherently. Teasel leaned close to the hedgehog maid, stroking her cheek, and said, 'Easy now, liddle 'un, take your time, yore among friends.'

Tansy's voice was racked by sobs, and great tears coursed down her face as she explained breathlessly, 'Ran all the way here . . . Attacked by jackdaws . . . Ninian's . . . Rollo hiding . . . in ditch . . . Gerul said get help . . . Piknim . . . Piknim . . . *Oh, no* . . . Oh, Piknim!'

Auma was nursing Craklyn; she heard what Tansy said as if from afar. The badger clasped the squirrelmaid's face between her paws and asked, 'Is this true?'

Craklyn nodded, her head falling forward in exhaustion. The badger Mother looked at her paws, bloodstained from the deep scratches on the squirrelmaid's face.

Log a Log drew his rapier, his paws trembling with rage as he turned to Skipper. 'Fetch back yore daughter an' her crew. Guosim, arm yoreselves, we've got business to attend to double quick. Come on!'

35

The Emperor Ublaz Mad Eyes rose in a thunderous mood. He had been awakened by timid tapping on his bedchamber door.

'If you must knock, then knock! Don't stand around there all day tipping and tapping. Get in here!'

Chief Trident-rat Sagitar gingerly stepped into the bedchamber. A shaft of early morning sunlight cut across the rumpled silk sheets onto the face of the pine marten. Ublaz shaded his eyes with a paw, blinking irately at the hapless rat.

'What is it now? Speak up!'

Sagitar took a deep breath before launching into her report. 'Sire, one of your Monitors was washed up on the tideline this morning at dawn. He was lashed to a rudder and tiller, slain. This was stuffed in his mouth, Sire.'

Ublaz snatched the damp scrap of sailcloth from the rat's nerveless paws, unrolled it swiftly and sat staring at the message written in the blood of the Monitor.

'Death to Mad Eyes from Rasconza and the Wave Brethren!'

Flinging the sailcloth from him, he ran to the window

and glared out at the hot tropic seas, peaceful and quiet in the early morn. 'That makes four altogether in two days, all Monitors! Tell me, have the wavescum returned to the taverns?'

Sagitar shook her head decisively. 'No, Sire, nor have they sought to board their ships; the whole harbour area lies deserted. The corsairs and searats have taken to the hills . . .'

Ublaz pushed the Trident-rat aside with a snarl. 'I know that, blockhead. They have food, supplies and arms that they took with them.'

'Could we not hunt them down, Sire?' Sagitar suggested helpfully.

Ublaz whirled on her, his temper rising. 'No, we could not. They are only waiting for me to leave this palace unguarded and they will be in here immediately! Go away, marshal all your Trident-rats and the remainder of my Monitors, place guards around the whole area and keep me informed of any movements out there. Leave me now, I must think.'

Buckla the searat captain, Guja the steersrat and Groojaw the stoat captain had captured another Monitor. They had the lizard bound and gagged; he tottered ahead of them as they prodded him forward with stolen tridents.

Rasconza sat roasting a lobster over the embers of a campfire at the northwestern inlet of Sampetra. He nodded affably at the trio as they hurled the lizard to the sand.

'Haharr, another prisoner, eh, mates? Wot's 'appenin' down at our Great Emperor's palace?'

Buckla squatted in the shade of a rock, away from the sun's fierce heat, and took a draught from a jug of seaweed grog. 'Aaaah, that's better, ain't gettin' much cooler, is it? Ole Mad Eyes is forted up in 'is palace, afraid t'move out. We delivered the last Monitor like y'said, floated 'im in all pretty like. Sagitar took yore message up ter Ublaz. We caught this'n guardin' the ships on the jetty.'

Rasconza prodded the glaring lizard with his sword-point. 'Don't you fret, matey, you won't 'ave to suffer such rough company as us much longer. We'll deliver yer back to ole Ublaz by nightfall, one way or another, eh, mates?'

The corsairs and searats lying about the camp laughed uproariously at their leader's crude jest.

'Do we deliver 'im back in a bit, or bit by bit? Hawhawhaw!'

Groojaw was not interested in the banter. 'When do we take back our ships?' he said, scowling at Rasconza.

The fox smiled craftily. 'When we're good'n ready, mate; that's wot Ublaz is expectin' us t'do, raid the jetty to get back our vessels. Hah! Ole Mad Eyes'd 'ave a plan laid to stop that, never fear. No, the palace is more important than the ships to us right now. We'll keep Ublaz 'emmed in there until he's ready to parley . . .'

Guja looked quizzically at Rasconza. 'Then wot?'

The fox drew his favourite dagger and licked the blade slowly. 'Then we plays 'im false an' kills 'im. Pine martens ain't the only ones good at treachery, y'know.'

Groojaw was still not happy. 'But we need ships. What about our vessels?' he said.

Rasconza thought about this for a moment, then he stood and walked to the hilltop overlooking the cove. He pointed down at the vessel that had been scuttled there.

'Yer want a ship, Groojaw, see, there's Barranca's ole craft the *Freebooter*, she's only been scuttled. I'll wager a goodbeast like yerself with a decent crew could seal 'er up, bale 'er out an' drag 'er ashore at low tide. Once the ole *Freebooter* is seaworthy agin there ain't a faster craft in all the seas.'

Groojaw took a crew down to the cove. When he had gone, Rasconza lay back and cracked the shell from his roasted lobster. 'There, that should keep Groojaw 'appy. Besides, we could do with 'avin' a ship afloat that Ublaz don't know about, it'll come in useful.'

As night fell Ublaz himself went down to the escarpment to view the body of the Monitor that had been dumped there by Rasconza's crew. Surrounded by an armed guard of Monitors and Trident-rats, the pine marten paid little attention to the dead lizard. He was more interested in the sailcloth that had been thrust into its mouth. Retrieving it, he stood to one side and read Rasconza's scrawl.

'We will talk together tomorrow. Ignore this and I will burn you out. Hoist a green flag if you agree to meet me, mid-noon in middle of island. Rasconza.'

Ublaz motioned Sagitar away from the rest, then he walked her out of earshot along the escarpment before whispering to her, 'Bring six good archers to my throne room before midnight. Let nobeast see them and speak of this to none.'

Ublaz smiled to himself as he strode back to his palace. He was once more back in the game. The fox would soon know he could not outsmart an Emperor.

Waveworm had been free of the fog and ice for more than two days. She ploughed on westward as the weather grew more clement. The sun shone, although the wind was still cold and the seas were rough. Abbot Durral sat in the cabin of Romsca the ferret captain. He gnawed hard ship's biscuit and sipped at a beaker of none-too-clear water. Durral's mind was anywhere but aboard a corsair vessel; mentally he was back at his beloved Abbey, picturing himself pottering about in the orchard with his friend Rollo, or helping Teasel and Higgle with the baking. The old mouse wrinkled his nose, sniffing, and imagined laying a tray of hot scones, fresh from the oven, on a window ledge to cool. Smiling, he had a vision of several mischievous Dibbuns loitering near the scene, to see if they could liberate the odd scone. Durral actually wagged a paw, warning them off. Little rascals!

He was jerked back to reality by the sounds of steel upon steel and roars of conflict as paws stamped around the deck outside. Matters had finally reached a head; the fighting had begun. Either Romsca had attacked Lask Frildur or vice versa.

Pushing a table in front of the cabin door, Durral sought about for any other furniture that might block the entrance. Meanwhile the sounds of battle grew outside on deck, accompanied by the occasional scream and splash as somebeast went over the side. Pulling the grimy blanket from Romsca's bunk, the Abbot huddled in a corner. He wrapped himself tightly and sat miserably in the dim cabin, hoping that Romsca would triumph over the hated Monitor General. The sounds of fighting seemed to go on endlessly as day drew gradually to a close.

Durral closed his mind to everything, even thoughts of his own life or death. Eventually he fell into a doze, his mind lulled into slumber by the vision of a mousemaid singing sweetly to him.

'High o'er the hills, far o'er the seas,
Fly with the small birds, follow the breeze,
Go with your heart, where would you roam,
Back to the rose-coloured stones you call home.
Where faded summers will echo again,
Brown autumn trees, or the spring's gentle rain.
Shadows are falling 'cross woodlands you know,
Rest, weary one, in the warm firelight glow.'

It was fully dark when Abbot Durral came gradually awake. Creaking ship's timbers and the endless wash of waves against the vessel's sides were the only sounds he could hear. The din of conflict had ceased altogether. Holding the musty blanket around him, the old mouse groped his way cautiously across the cabin floor. With no light to guide him and the absence of his eyeglasses denying him clear sight, Durral fumbled his way forward until a table leg came into contact with his paw. At least the cabin door was still securely blocked, he thought. He sat with his back against the table, not knowing what to do next, longing for contact with some other living creature, providing that it was a friend.

Dawn came gradually, cloaked by grey skies and soft drizzling rain. It was warmer, though humid. Faint gloomy light began pervading the cabin from a small dirty window, too high for Durral to reach. A sound caused him to become alert – somebeast was scratching at the cabin door from outside. Not knowing whether it would be friend or foe, but fearing the worst, Durral crept back to his corner and sat waiting, watching the door. The scratching gave way to a thumping noise, faint at first, but growing heavier. The Abbot of Redwall sat filled with apprehension as the door began to shake under the blows, then suddenly there was a sharp, splintering crack and a cutlass blade thrust its way through the rifted wood. Durral watched fearfully as the blade was withdrawn, only to slash through again a moment later. Shrinking down into his blanket, he watched, horrified, as the blade hacked and sliced at the quivering timber, splintering the door in its onslaught.

The old mouse could stand it no longer. 'Who's there, who is it?' he cried out.

Krrrakkk!

An entire panel burst and the huge reptilian head of Lask Frildur was thrust through the broken aperture.

36

From the shelter of the little canvas tent on the ice floe, Viola was first to see the intruders. She gave a shriek of alarm and instantly the sword was in Martin's paw. Shoving the canvas awning away from him, he came upright ready to do battle.

Clecky, who had clapped a paw across Viola's mouth, stared about in astonishment at the mass of creatures surrounding the logboat. 'Great seasons of salad, where'd this mob of nautical nightmares come from, wot?'

Snub-nosed, stiff-whiskered and dark-eyed, the huge beasts crowded around, staring curiously at the little logboat and its occupants. Martin raised the sword threateningly to warn them off.

Grath Longfletch moved cautiously to the warrior's side, murmuring, 'Put up that sword, Martin, they're the sealfolk. Don't make any sudden moves or they'll bull us into the sea and drown us.'

Martin lowered his blade, keeping his eyes fixed on the sealfolk. 'What do we do next?' he whispered to Grath.

The otter relinquished her bow and arrows to show she was unarmed. 'Leave this to me. Sealfolk used to visit the holt of my kin. They don't speak our language, but I can understand them a bit.'

Grath climbed from the logboat and approached the foremost seal. He was a great bull, dark grey in colour and mottled with heavy spots. The big beast watched Grath impassively, head held majestically high, round black eyes unblinking.

Grath crouched upon the ice, taking care not to raise her head higher than the lead bull. Holding her paws out level, she clapped them gently together several times and said, 'Feryooday, Haaaawm!'

Immediately the seals around began making a sort of coughing barking sound, in surprise that Grath could speak their language.

As the big leader bull silenced them with a haughty glare, Martin joined Grath and murmured to her, 'What did you say to the big fellow?'

'I gave him a greeting, feryooday, just like saying good morning, then I called him Hawm, but long, like this – Haaaawm. It means great leader or king; the longer you sound it, the greater your respect. Sshh! He's going to say somethin'.'

The seal looked regally down his wide flattish nose at them. 'Thessez m'hoil, ommin Haaaaaaaawm floooooe!' He moved his head about in a wide circle as if indicating the iceberg where they were standing.

Grath held up her chin and closed both eyes as she answered, 'Haaaaaaaaaaaawm floe yaaanh!'

It seemed to satisfy the leader. He raised a massive flipper and slapped it loud and wetly once upon his sleek chest.

Grath explained, 'I can't unnerstand it all, but best as I c'n make out he said, this is my island, I am king of this ice floe. All I could think of to answer was to tell him he was a mighty king and this surely was his floe.'

'Do you know how to say not mine?' Martin asked Grath swiftly.

Grath thought for a moment. 'Er, you just say ommino, I think.'

Martin stepped forward, aware of the vast number of seals watching him. He spread his paws and brought them together, clapping softly as he had seen Grath do. Then he slapped one paw hard on his chest as the seal king had done.

'Haaaaaaaaawm Martin! Ommino floe. Ommino!' Martin said.

This seemed to amuse the king greatly. He pointed a powerful flipper at Martin and said, 'Ommino! Omminooooo!'

The seals fell about, rolling on the ice, slapping their flippers loudly and emitting great barking merriment.

The great bull seal towered above Martin. Raising his flipper high, he brought it down gently on the mouse warrior's head and patted him. 'Haaaaaaaawm Ma'tan Haaaaaaaaawm!' he rumbled.

This caused even greater jollity among the sealfolk; they shook their heads and blinked rapidly as they honked with laughter.

Clecky climbed out of the logboat to join Martin and Grath. 'I say, good thing these wallahs have a sense o' humour, wot!' The hare slithered boldly over the watery ice to face the king. Straightening his long ears, Clecky brought them together several times as if clapping. Pursing his lips comically he mimicked a seal. 'Haaaaaaaaaaaaaaaaawm old chap Haaaaaaaaaaaaawm. Howzat!'

This time the hilarity was unbridled. Even the king rolled his gargantuan bulk over and over, tears streaming from his round dark eyes as he held both flippers to his sides, shaking helplessly with laughter. This drove the hare on to further efforts. Lying stomach down and holding himself up with his front paws, Clecky looked majestically down his nose, bobbed his stubby tail about and let one ear flap down hard across his brow. Then, in a perfect imitation of the seal king, he called out, 'Haaaaaaaaawm Clecky, that's me chaps, Haaaaawm Clecky!'

Some of the seals were laughing so hard they fell off the iceberg into the sea.

Martin pulled Clecky upright. 'You'd better pack it in now, we don't want to be held responsible for any of these creatures laughing themselves to death, especially the great Hawm there, he looks fit to burst.'

It took quite a while for the laughter to subside, but it had worked wonders. Some of the little seal pups slid out of the pack and nuzzled up against Clecky. The king pointed a flipper at Grath and looked questioningly at the other seals as he barked out a single word, 'Waaylumm!'

There was a moment's silence, then every seal began waving a flipper towards the otter and echoing the word, 'Waaylumm! Waaylumm!'

Grath was mystified. She looked at Martin and shrugged. 'I dunno wot they mean.'

Further discussion was cut short as the friends found themselves lifted up bodily by the seals and tossed back into the logboat. Knowing the sealfolk meant them no harm, they sat in silence, watching the procedure. With a mighty smack from his flipper, the king broke the stake holding the headline of the logboat. Other seals came flapping up with cables made from thick rubbery seaweed. These they proceeded to attach to the vessel from stem to stern until the little craft was festooned with woven seaweed ropes. Half a dozen stout young seals slid the logboat off into the water.

Viola looked over the side. All the seaweed fastenings were held in the jaws of at least three seals to a cable; the king alone held the headrope in his teeth.

He let out a sharp bark. 'Gittarra!'

The logboat's crew fell over backward as the craft sped off into the fog, sending up a great bow wave. Plogg and Welko scrambled up to the for'ard bowsprit. They watched fascinated as the sleek forms of the seal pack sped their boat through the seas at a breathtaking rate of knots.

Clecky settled back, winking at Viola. 'Just the ticket, m'gel. Beats sailin' an' rowin', wot? Absolutely top hole, hope these chaps know where they're jolly well goin'!'

Grath blinked spray from her eyes as they shot out free of the clinging fogbanks. 'Oh, they seem t'know where they're bound, all right. Harr! 'tis good t'see clear day an' sunlight again, though!'

Martin agreed wholeheartedly. 'It certainly is, friend. Well, at least we're out of trouble with icebergs and I'm sure the sealfolk mean us no harm. Only problem is, they don't know where we want to go and we don't know where they're taking us.'

Clecky began rummaging about in the remainder of their supplies. 'Well, wherever we're jolly well goin', I ain't travellin' on a bally empty tummy. Let's see what the tuck situation is, wot!'

'Yeeeek, look, look!' Viola was pointing out to sea. All eyes followed her paw.

Martin could not believe his eyes.

'Wh . . . What are they?'

Grath had seen them once before in her lifetime. She took a deep breath. 'On the far north coast where I was reared we saw those sea creatures once. It was spring an' they swam almost up to the beach. My mother said they were called whales an' no creature in all the seas is as big as 'em. They blow water out o' their heads, straight up like a big fountain. Their tails are like the spread o' two large oaks. See!'

They stared, stunned by the size of the creatures. One of the whales raised a mighty fluke and slammed it down on the face of the ocean, causing an enormous white explosion of water.

Martin watched the leviathans of the deep as they sported and played, each one like a black island rearing from the main. 'Great seasons! I could imagine old Rollo

258

laughing at me if I told him I had seen fishes as big as Redwall Abbey!'

Plogg and Welko were inclined to agree. 'Hah! The Guosim'd say we'd been asleep an' seen the whales in our dreams, or they might say we'd eaten too much of Clecky's cooking.'

The hare looked up, his face smudged from blowing on the ashes of the fire to get it rekindled again. 'Oh, they would, would they? Base ingratitude! I've a jolly good mind to let you chaps get the scoff ready for that! I say, how about askin' old Hawmface to steer over that way, so's we can catch one of those whale type chaps. I wonder what they'd taste like cooked up. Hmmm, y'd need a blinkin' big pan . . . Yagh!'

The hare shook himself as the rest of the crew shot water at him with their paws. He twisted his ears to wring them out. 'Yah boo rotters, y've gone an' put me flippin' fire out!'

Towards evening the weather started to become mild and warm, though they were still feeling the breeze, owing to the fact that the tireless sealfolk never once slackened their breakneck pace. The logboat hissed through the water, bouncing across the waves like a runaway arrow.

Then Martin became worried. 'See, the sun is setting in the west, over that way. We're being taken northward!'

Clecky had finally managed a small fire. He passed them each a slice of toasted shrewbread and some warm oat and barley cordial. 'Nothing we c'n do about it at the moment, old lad. They're obviously takin' us someplace, though. Let's wait until we get there an' figure out our next move from where we land, wot?'

Grath stared out across the uncharted seas. 'Aye, like as not the fates'll send us where they want.'

On the western horizon the sun dipped beneath the sea like a crimson fireball, shooting rays of scarlet, pink and gold onto the underbellies of purple and cream cloudbanks. Viola snuggled down in the stern, nibbling a crust of shrewbread and thinking how different it all was from sitting in Great Hall and dining off the sumptuous fare commonplace to Redwall Abbey, far from the lonely sound of waves upon open sea.

37

A full summer moon shone down on the path to Ninian's, casting pale flickering shadows upon three grim-faced creatures pounding through the woods purposefully at the head of a mixed band of shrews and otters, each one armed with either sling, javelin, rapier or bow and arrows. Bravely Skipper kept pace with Log a Log and Rangapaw, bearing his injuries stoically. From between the trees they glimpsed the half-ruined spire of the ancient building.

Log a Log gritted his teeth, clasping his shrew rapier tight. 'Soon be there now!' he said.

'Friend, is that you?'

Momentarily they halted and looked around. Again the voice sounded out into the night. 'I'm in the ditch, friends. Help me!'

Throwing themselves flat at the pathside, Skipper and his burly daughter delved through nettles and reeds that grew up the bank.

'Got 'im. Git the other paw. Up y'come, Rollo sir!'

His face smeared with mud and his garments rent and torn, the old Recorder was hauled swiftly up onto the path, where he sat gasping out his story.

'We were attacked, or I should say the young maids

were. It was jackdaws, a whole colony of the wicked birds. Gerul heard them screaming when we arrived at Ninian's; they were inside. Gerul told me to stay outside and charged in – there were awful sounds, screaming and cawing. Next thing I knew, Tansy and Craklyn were flung out through the door by Gerul, and he shouted for them to bring help from Redwall. So they could travel fast they lowered me into the ditch, telling me to hide and keep out of harm's way. I don't know what happened after that, until I heard one of you speak as you ran by.'

Log a Log saw that Skipper was breathless and his wounds were bothering him; the shrew Chieftain sat the otter down on the path next to Rollo. 'Stay here and guard him, Skip, you'll only slow us up. We've got enough here to do the job, me'n this big 'un of yores.'

The Skipper of Otters nodded, he understood. 'If'n our friends are hurt, then give those birds blood'n'vinegar. Go on, mate, git goin'!'

Without a backward glance they charged through the rotting doorframe of Ninian's. Jackdaws scattered everywhere as they tried to escape from the warriors who teemed in roaring the Abbey battle call.

'Redwaaaaaaallll!'

Scruvo their thieving leader and another of his band had Gerul on the floor, tearing savagely at him with their wicked beaks. Rangapaw hit Scruvo across the head with her otter javelin, the force of the blow shattering the weapon's haft and slaying Scruvo instantly. The other jackdaw gurgled its life out at the thrusting point of Log a Log's rapier. Other birds had fallen to the deadly nemesis of otters and shrews, though some of them fled, winging off into the night, never again to be seen in Mossflower.

Skipper and Rollo hobbled up to the gate in front of Ninian's. Log a Log and several other shrews were binding Gerul with strips from their tunics and ditch mud mixed with herbs to staunch his dreadful injuries. Skipper hastened to his friend's side. He stared down at the owl's homely face. 'Is he alive?'

Log a Log shrugged, totally at a loss. 'Aye, mate, there's still life in this owl, though why that should be I don't know – the bird's taken enough to kill any three of us! I counted four jackdaws in there that he'd slain. I've seen some tough 'uns in my seasons, but none like yore mate Gerul!'

A heart-rending cry, like that of a dying beast, escaped Rollo's lips. Rangapaw strode slowly out of Ninian's carrying a forlorn little bundle in her hefty paws. Log a Log held Rollo back as he tried to intercept the big otter. The old Recorder's body was racked by sobs.

'No! No! Not Piknim my little friend! Say she lives. Please!'

Tears rolled openly down the sturdy face of Rangapaw. She clasped the limp form to her as if nursing a babe. 'Pore young maid, she'll always live in the memories of 'er mates.'

As Rangapaw walked off towards Redwall with her sad burden, Rollo tore free of Log a Log's grasp. Straightening himself up, he wiped his eyes upon his habit sleeves and turned to the other Chieftain. 'Skipper, will you help me to do something?' he said.

The otter grasped Rollo's frail old paw. 'Anythin', matey, just ask!'

Rollo pointed to the doorway. 'Go in there and find a large pink pearl. It will probably be in the nest of the leader of those birds.'

Skipper was not long gone. As he emerged, everyone held their breath. He opened his paw to reveal the fourth pearl nestling in his palm. He handed it to Rollo, who clasped it tightly.

'Now, I want you to put flame to this place and burn it down!'

Skipper's voice registered his incredulity at the proposal. 'Burn it down?'

But there was no hesitation in Rollo's determined mood. 'Aye, burn it down until it is just a heap of rubble and bad memories. This has become a place of evil. I have read in the Abbey Records that on two occasions the enemies of Redwall used this place as a refuge. The first was Cluny the Scourge in the time of Matthias the Warrior, then there was Slagar the Cruel in the time of Mattimeo, when I was but a Dibbun. Now it has been used a third time as a den of thieves and murderers. Burn it!'

Dawn the next morning was gentle and bright; a silence seemed to lie over Mossflower country, even the birds remaining mute. Goodwife Teasel and the badger Mother Auma stood together on the ramparts of the outer wall facing south. From where the path curved they could see a dark column of smoke rising above the tops of the woodland trees.

Auma nodded towards it. 'Skipper and his crew are still down there, seeing that it burns to the ground and the fire doesn't spread. Will you pack some food for them, Teasel? I'll take it down myself.'

The hogwife patted her friend's paw. 'Aye, I'll pack plenty, knowin' wot good appetites yon otters 'ave. Though at the moment I detests to look at vittles or prepare 'em. Friar 'iggle, bless 'im, he sent me off from the kitchens an' stayed to fix brekkist fer anybeast as wants some, but none came.'

The hogwife threw her flowery apron up over her face and wept. 'The pore liddle maid, to end up like that, an' she were so young too. I ain't no warrior, marm, but I 'opes those wicked birds got all they deserved off Log a Log an' Skipper's big gel!'

Auma stroked her friend's headspikes soothingly. 'There, there, don't take on so, those birds paid dear for their evil ways. Log a Log told me all about it last night: 'twill be many a long season before we hear the call of a jackdaw in our land again, I promise you.'

The grief at Piknim's death was so great in Redwall Abbey that Auma had to assume the mantle of Abbess and request that none came to the burying, because it would be far too upsetting for young and old. Accordingly at mid-noon she and Rangapaw laid the young mousemaid to rest themselves. They chose a shady spot in the orchard, to one side beneath a great sweetchestnut tree, where they held a simple ceremony. Small gifts of remembrance from every Redwaller were placed in the grave. When the task was done both Abbey bells tolled slowly, their clappers muted with velvet to soften the tone.

Craklyn, Tansy and Rollo stood at an upper window overlooking the orchard, despite the protest of Sister Cicely regarding their condition. The otter Glenner supported Craklyn as she stood at the window and sang. Her sweet voice, which had sounded out in harmony with Piknim many times before, was now alone. It echoed beautifully off the outer walls until it seemed to fill the entire Abbey and its grounds.

'Fare you well upon your journey,
To the bright lands far away,
Where beside the peaceful rivers,
You may linger any day.
In the forests warm at noontide,
See the flowers bloom in the glades,
Meet the friends who've gone before you,
To the calm of quiet shades.
There you'll wait, O my beloved,
Never knowing want or care,
And when I have seen my seasons,
We will walk together there.'

Glenner and Sister Cicely walked the three friends back

265

to the room they were sharing at the infirmary. There they lay upon their beds, all with their own deep personal thoughts. Teatime passed and still they had not stirred. Tansy lay on top of her counterpane, fully dressed, watching the sunlight lengthening afternoon shadows through the window.

The door creaked open and Friar Higgle Stump crept in bearing a tray laden with slices of nutbread, a hot mushroom and leek pastie in gravy, a bowl of fresh fruit salad and a flagon of his brother Furlo's best dandelion and burdock cordial. He wiggled his nose at them.

'Good afternoon, friends. I couldn't bear the thought of you up 'ere bein' fed warm nettle broth; that shouldn't 'appen to anybeast. So I brought up a little summat to tickle yore appetites.'

He placed the tray down, but they did not even look at it. The Friar shook his head sadly. 'Dearie me, now if miss Piknim were about she'd 'ave beat you all to it an' gobbled everythin' up.'

Craklyn sat up shaking her head. 'No she wouldn't. Piknim would have shared it with us 'cos we're her friends . . . I mean, we were her friends.'

Rollo sat up also, arching his eyebrows indignantly. 'Were? You mean we're not *still* Piknim's friends?'

Then Tansy sat up, glaring at Rollo. 'Craklyn never meant that. We'll always be Piknim's friends, her dearest and best most treasured friends, so there!'

A smile played around Friar Higgle's face. 'I knows 'ow you can be such good friends with Piknim that nobeast'd believe it!'

Craklyn and Tansy spoke in unison. 'How?'

The Friar perched upon the window sill, his face serious. 'Just carry on like yore doin' now an' don't eat no more, you'll soon be reunited with yore friend by starvin' t'death!'

He winked broadly at Rollo, knowing the Recorder would recognize the wisdom in his words. Rollo did. He sat up, filled himself a beaker and chose a thick slice of nutbread, then, eating and drinking, he began to speak.

'I vote we carry on searching for the Tears of all Oceans. Now, you maids keep silent, just eat and listen to me. Eat!'

The old Recorder's voice was sharp and commanding; neither Tansy or Craklyn had ever heard him speak like that. Seating themselves close to the tray, they began eating.

Rollo tossed the fourth pearl in the air and caught it.

'See this thing? Piknim gave her life for it. Between us we vowed to find those six pearls because they may be needed to ransom our Abbot back from the enemy. I don't know about you two, but Rollo bankvole never breaks his word. I intend to find the other two pearls. Tchah! I'll wager Piknim would have had a very low opinion of us had she seen us a moment ago. Moping and moaning with no thought of carrying on the very quest that she died for. Is that the act of friends?'

Tansy slammed her paw down on the tray so hard that she broke the bread platter. 'We'll find those pearls together, all three of us!'

Craklyn whirled her bushy tail fiercely. 'Aye, and when we do we'll stuff 'em down the throats of those scum who kidnapped our friends, one by one!'

Friar Higgle crept smiling from the infirmary, murmuring, 'Very nice talk for young Abbeymaids, charmin'. Enjoy yore tea.'

38

Tansy split the acorn shell that held the scrap of parchment. Unfolding it, she read aloud,

'There is a warrior,
Where is a sword?
Peace did he bring,
The fighting Lord.
Shed for him is my fifth tear.
Find it in the title here,
Written in but a single word,
An eye is an eye, until it is heard.'

Tansy paused, shaking her head in despair. 'Written separate to the rhyme is a pile of numbers which don't seem to make any sense at all. Listen to this: Lines. One of one. Eight of two. One of three. Three of four. One of five. Six of six. Two of seven. Four of eight.'

She tossed the scrap of parchment to Craklyn. 'There you are, friend, sort that little lot out!'

Chewing slowly on a wedge of pastie, the squirrelmaid narrowed her eyes, glaring a challenge at Tansy. 'Do you think I can't?'

Rollo peered over the tops of his glasses at her. 'We have great faith in you.'

Craklyn took a great swig of her dandelion and burdock cordial. 'Then you're both a pair of dimwits, 'cos I haven't the faintest clue what it all means!'

The three friends sat staring at one another for a moment, then broke out into spontaneous laughter.

Rollo dug his spoon into the fresh fruit salad. 'If we're a pair of dimwits then that makes you a blockhead, so between the three of us we'll solve it. Hahaha!'

The Skipper of Otters was on his way upstairs to the infirmary when he met Sister Cicely coming down. Waving his rudderlike tail politely at her, he said, 'Good noon t'ye, marm. I was just on me way up t'see Gerul. How is he today? Prob'ly still sleepin' his injuries off, I wager.'

The good Sister glared frostily at the husky otter. 'Hmph!' she replied.

Ever the gentlebeast, Skipper nodded courteously at the Sister. 'Humff, marm? I s'pose there's a wealth o' meanin' in the word, but it don't tell me nought about ole Gerul. The pore bird was so badly wounded he was at death's doorstep last night. Pray tell wot's his condition today, marm?'

Cicely was in no end of a huff. 'That . . . that . . . *owl*! He rose not an hour ago, refused all treatment and hurled a pot of my best warm nettle soup from the infirmary window! You want to know his condition, go and find out for yourself, sir – he's down in the kitchens, surrounded by otters, shrews and Dibbuns, cooking and eating everything in sight.' Brushing Skipper aside, Sister Cicely flounced downstairs.

Friar Higgle and Hogwife Teasel had dismissed the kitchen roster for the day, leaving the place open to anybeast wanting to drop by and prepare something. Gerul and his friends had taken Higgle and Teasel at their word, and now chaos reigned in Redwall Abbey kitchens.

Gerul and Arven were demolishing a huge fruit cake between them, whilst issuing orders to Rangapaw, Diggum and some shrews.

'Ah now, don't be stingy, throw in a few more pawfuls of those luvly candied chestnuts. An' y'need far more meadowcream than that if yore t'make a decent sweet owl junket. As me ould mother used t'say, plenty more's better'n plenty less if yore cookin' fer more'n a few. Ain't that right, Arven me liddle mate?'

The squirrelbabe was sure it was. Waving a ladle at the cooks, he issued orders like one born to command. 'Gerra more chessnuts anna big buckit of cream, a hooj big 'un. An' frow some strawbees in, Arven like strawbees!' Then he turned to his owl friend with a serious frown. 'Yore muvver musta been good an' clever.'

Gerul dipped his talon in a pot of plum jam and sucked on it. 'Ah, sure she was so clever she used to ask herself questions, so she did, it's no good knowin' wot y'know if you can't ask yer own advice, she always said. Log a Log, how's that shrew concoction comin' along?'

The shrew Chieftain looked up irately from a steaming pan he was stirring. 'The vegetables are doin' nicely, but every time we get the pastry rolled out those moles keep pinchin' it. Gerroutofit, rogues!' He threw a wet dishcloth at Gurrbowl and several other young moles who were shuffling off with his latest batch of pastry.

Foremole blinked quizzically at them over the top of a special deeper'n ever pie he was creating. 'Hurr, wot do ee wanten all um pastry furr, Gadgee?'

The molebabe Gadgee poked his snout out from under a floppy layer of pastry he was carrying. 'Furr maken 'unnymoles, zurr!'

Skipper joined the little moles as they kneaded dough on a countertop, busy as bees and covered in flour. 'Ahoy, mates, wot's an 'unnymole?' he asked.

Gurrbowl crossed his digging claws on his stomach, tut tutting at the otter's ignorance. 'Chut chut, zurr! You'm doan't knoaw wot ee 'unnymole is? Lukk an' oi'll show ee, you'm pay 'tenshun naow!'

The molebabe rolled out a small patch of pastry, spread it thick with honey and placed on it a strawberry and a raspberry. Wrapping the pastry carefully over the fruit he coated the lot with a mixture of honey and damson juice. It looked nothing like a honeyed mole, but the molebabes thought it did. Gurrbowl licked his digging claws proudly and added his "unnymole' to several others on a tray, ready to go in the oven. He wrinkled his nose proudly at Skipper.

'Hurr, that'n be 'ow t'make 'unnymoles, zurr!'

Skipper winked broadly at the molebabe. 'Thanks, matey, I'll remember that, should come in useful!' Then, opening a cupboard, he took out a bag of dried watershrimp.

Glenner sidled up with an expectant gleam in her eye. 'Shrimp'n'hotroot soup, Skip?'

The otter Chieftain showed his white teeth in a mock-villainous grin. 'Aye, matey, you go get the 'otroot, oh, an' some onions. Ahoy, Rangapaw, where do they 'ide the mushrooms in this galley? An' leeks too, we'll need lots o' leeks, aye, an' white turnips.'

Gerul meanwhile had finished the last of the fruit cake, and now he and Arven set about making another, even bigger one.

'Cummon now, ye young rip, a tankard of October Ale, flour an' honey, what's next?' asked the owl.

Arven counted off the ingredients on his paws. 'Plums, damsins, 'azelnuts, chessnuts, blackb'rries, er, er . . .'

Gerul limped off to the pantry chunnering to himself. 'Sure we'll toss in a bit of everythin', as me ould mother used t'say, if y've got everythin' in a cake then yer sure t'have left nothin' out providin' it's all in!'

Sister Cicely had brought Auma down to the kitchens. She pointed a paw of condemnation at the shambles.

'Just look at that. Did ever you see such a mess in your life?'

The badger Mother wandered over to where the molebabes had left their tray of honeymoles to cool, and popped one in her mouth. 'Mm, very tasty! Cicely, let them have their fun – have we not had enough sadness and misery in Redwall for one day? This bit of disturbance is easily cleared up, but it helps them to recover their spirits, especially the young ones. I look on this not as mourning the death of Piknim, but celebrating the happy life she led. Come now, Sister, leave them to their enjoyment.'

Tansy, Craklyn and Rollo had deserted the confines of the infirmary. The early evening was soft and balmy, and it was far nicer out in the fresh air than lying about indoors and being fussed over by Sister Cicely. They sat on the gatehouse steps, staring at the rhyme and puzzle that went with it, but the clue to the fifth pearl remained a mystery to them.

'Perhaps if we concentrate on the rhyme it may help.'

Craklyn shook her head at Tansy's suggestion. 'No, I'm sure the key is in these figures. Once we know what they refer to I have a feeling the rest will be easy.'

Rollo polished his glasses and scrutinized the figures closely. 'Hmm, I've a feeling you're right, miss. Let's concentrate all our attention on these figures for the moment. Lines. One of one. Eight of two. One of three. We'll take that bit first.'

All three gazed at the parchment scrap, cudgelling their brains for inspiration.

Wullger the otter gatehouse-keeper was in the process of cleaning out his small domain. He opened the gate-house door wide and began sweeping about with a heather-topped broom. So pleasant was the aroma of the heather that he took his own good time, brushing diligently in every corner and singing a song as he went about his chore.

'There was an otter by a stream,
Come ringle dum o lady,
Who fell asleep and had a dream,
All on the bank so shady.
He dreamt the stream was made of wine,
It flowed along so merry,
And when he drank it tasted fine,
Like plum and elderberry.
And all the banks were made of cake,
Come ringle ding my dearie,
As nice as any cook could bake,
That otter felt quite cheery.
He drank and ate with right good will,
Till wakened by his daughter.
She said, "I hope you've had your fill,
Of mud and cold streamwater!"
Come ringle doo fol doodle day,
Come wisebeast or come witty,
A fool who dreams to dine that way,
Must waken to self-pity.'

The three friends on the wallsteps outside heard Wullger's song clearly; they shook their heads and chuckled. As Wullger emerged sweeping dust in front of him, Craklyn called down, 'That's a good ditty, I've never heard it before.'

The old otter smiled up at the squirrelmaid. 'I'm glad you liked it, missie, 'tis a song that's been passed down through my family. If you like I'll teach ye the lines . . .'

Tansy leapt up, yelling, 'The lines, it's the lines!'

Wullger stared in amazement at the three creatures dancing paw in paw on the wallsteps as they chanted together, 'The lines, the lines, it's the lines!'

He shrugged and went indoors to continue his cleaning. 'Maybe when yore not so busy dancin' an' chantin' I'll learn ye the song.'

Tansy scanned the poem's first line.

'There is a warrior, that's line one, so one of one must mean the first word or the first letter of the line. What d'you think, Rollo – the first word or the first letter?'

The Recorder was quite definite which it was. 'It has to be the letter, one of one. Because the second clue states eight of two, but there's only four words in the second line, so we're looking for enough letters to make a word.'

Tansy read out the lines, Craklyn counted the letters and Rollo scraped each letter upon the sandstone step with his quill knife.

'There is a warrior. One of line one. Letter T.
Where is a sword. Eight of line two. Letter A.
Peace did he bring. One of line three. Letter P.
The fighting Lord. Three of line four. Letter E.
Shed for him is my fifth tear. One of line five.
    Letter S.
Find it in the title here. Six of line six. Letter T.
Written in but a single word. Two of line seven.
    Letter R.
An eye is an eye, until it is heard. Four of line eight.
    Letter Y.'

The friends sat but for a brief moment, looking at the word Rollo had scratched upon the step. Then Craklyn and Tansy dashed off towards the Abbey, with Rollo hobbling behind as they yelled, '*The tapestry!*'

39

Sagitar did as she was bidden. Late night lay still and heavy from the day's tropical heat when she arrived at the Emperor's throne room. Six Trident-rats accompanied her, each one armed with a bow and quiver of shafts. Ublaz awaited them, clad regally in an umber robe bordered with silver filigree work and wearing a turban of dark green with silver fringes.

At the centre of the room a small wood log stood on its end. Ublaz directed the archers, one to each corner of the vast room, one by the window and one by the door. Moving himself and Sagitar out of the line of fire, he instructed the archers.

'I have raised my paw, thus. When I drop it you will shoot at the log. I want to see six arrows sticking from the log. Arm your bows and await my signal.'

There was a swift rattle of wood as the rats set shafts to their bowstrings. Ublaz saw they were ready; he dropped his paw.

Sssssssthunk!

Six arrows thudded into the log before it fell, propped up by two of the shafts. The Emperor's mad eyes creased into a smile. 'Excellent! Sagitar will show you your positions. Be watchful and stay well hidden. Tomorrow you will see me meeting with the fox Rasconza. As I move towards him I will hold up my paw in greeting. When I let it drop I will also fall flat to the ground. That is your signal to shoot the arrows. I need not tell you that all six shafts must find their mark, or none of you will be alive to see the sunset. Finish the task properly and you will all be well rewarded. Go now!'

Bowing low, the archers followed Sagitar out.

Down in the small cellar chamber Ublaz donned his crown with its six vacant pearl spaces still empty. He held the torch level, watching as the coral snake slithered sinuously out of its water trough, glimmering gold in the torchlight. Gliding effortlessly across the floor, it reared dangerously in front of him, mouth open and fangs bared, beady eyes focused on him as he started to sway and chant in dirgelike tones.

'Golden guardian of my wealth,
Hear me now, be still,
Deathly fang and coiling stealth,
Bend unto my will.'

The snake hissed, its dark flickering tongue vibrating as it drew back to strike. The eyes of Ublaz grew wider as he kept up his steady chant, swaying, swaying. Then the snake began to move in unison with Ublaz, weaving smoothly to and fro as he swayed.

Gradually the pine marten exercised his power over the serpent; it sank down into bunched coils, both eyes filming over, the venomous mouth relaxed and closed. Ublaz stroked the snake's head once, then turned and departed the room. The two guards on the door could hear his voice echoing back down the stairway as he made his way back to the throne room.

'None can stand against Ublaz, my eyes conquer all, my will is stronger than that of any living thing. I rule, others obey!'

* * *

Midday sun burned like a great blazing eye upon the shallow valley in the centre of Sampetra. On the ridge of a rolling hill searats and corsairs crowded, watching the lone figure of Rasconza standing bold and unarmed, awaiting the arrival of his adversary.

Atop the opposite hill a regiment of Trident-rats were marshalled. Ublaz left his position at their centre and made his way down towards the fox. Wisely, Rasconza kept his eyes averted slightly to one side as the pine marten approached. Less than a dozen paces from Rasconza, Ublaz threw up his paw and called out in a voice laden with false cheer, 'Ah, Rasconza, there you are, friend. Greetings!'

Now Ublaz was less than four paces away; he fell to the ground.

Silence. Looking up, he saw Rasconza, eyes still averted, chuckling.

'You got to watch yore step round 'ere, matey,' said the fox, "tis dangerous ground. Only last night six rats tripped an' fell on their arrows, but they could be pardoned fer bein' clumsy, 'cos it was still dark.'

Ublaz leapt up and was dashing back towards his regiment as Rasconza waved to the sea vermin and roared, '*Charge!*'

They poured down from the hill, cheering and shouting as they brandished a fearsome assortment of weaponry.

Surrounded by his Trident-rats, Ublaz fled back to the palace in shameless disorder. Robbed of his surprise plan, the pine marten was seething with rage. He broke clear and dashed ahead of his regiment's panicked retreat. Far speedier than any of the Trident-rats, Ublaz raced on with one thought uppermost in his mind. Had Rasconza secretly sent a force round in a wide sweep, to gain control of the palace? He had left it with only Sagitar and the remaining Monitors to guard it.

The first wild rush of the Wave Brethren subsided to a steady lope as, still yelling bloodcurdling cries, they continued in Ublaz's wake. Rasconza jogged along in their midst, a villainous smile fixed on his wily face as he called out to Groojaw and Buckla.

'Haharr, lookit 'em go, like frightened chicks with an eagle on their tails. Run, Mad Eyes, run, y'swab!'

The steersrat Guja, who had not been privy to his leader's plans, looked questioningly over at the fox. 'But Cap'n, why aren't we chargin' faster? We could've beaten 'em in an open battle with our numbers!'

Rasconza winked craftily and chuckled. 'Aye, may'ap we would, matey, but it would've been a great slaughter an' who knows 'ow many of us would've fallen to those long tridents. My way's better, Guja; now we'll 'ave the mighty Emperor just where we want 'im, outsmarted an' isolated!'

Ublaz was astounded to find his palace unharmed. Monitors held open the gates as he hurtled in ahead of his pawsore followers. Straight through to the throne room he hastened, to find Sagitar and a Monitor called Flaggard surveying the harbour from the window. The pine marten slowed, regulating his breath, allowing himself a brief smile of relief.

'So, the seascum did not attempt any attack here. How foolish of Rasconza, he might have taken this place in my absence.'

Sagitar pointed down to the deserted jetty. 'Sire, after you had left a small force of them sailed in to the jetty aboard the vessel *Freebooter*. They have made it seaworthy again. They towed away all the ships that were docked there, from right under our noses. Lord, they laughed at us and waved their swords in the air. It was as if they knew that we could not desert the palace and go outside to do battle with them.'

Ublaz dismissed the Monitor with a nod, then poured wine for Sagitar. His mind was forming a plan even as the wine gurgled into the two goblets. Sagitar looked slightly bemused that her master was not angry. He gazed at the empty harbour and nodded.

'The fox has won a battle, but I will win the war. Come!'

Rasconza and his vermin stood on the rocks, a safe distance away from the rear of the palace. Guja the steersrat perched on top of a rocky outcrop, his keen eyes watching the high back wall of the building.

Then Rasconza addressed his captains and their crews.

'Ole Mad Eyes is trapped like a rat in 'is own cage now, buckoes, he ain't got nowheres t'go. We got the ships, so we rule the seas. We got the island too. Looks like we're in charge as long as Ublaz is bottled up in there. Any signs o' movement, Guja?'

Shielding his eyes, the steersrat peered towards the wall. 'Nah! . . . Wait! Aye, there 'e is, ole Mad Eyes 'isself, an' the rat Sagitar too if'n I ain't mistaken. Hah! Sagitar's got a bow an' arrow. Look out, she's about to shoot!'

Rasconza flicked his favourite dagger high, catching it as it spun downward. 'Hoho! They kin fire shafts all day, we're well out o' range!'

The arrow cut the air in a high arc, dipping to hit the ground far short of the Wave Brethren.

Rasconza nudged a couple of rats. 'They ain't shootin' to slay nobeast, that's some kind o' message. Go an' fetch it, mates, we'll see wot Ublaz has t'say.'

Rasconza read aloud the message written on a parchment attached to the arrow.

'The five ships you have are useless without rudders and tillers. I still hold the timber stock needed to repair them. At dawn tomorrow I will meet you where this arrow fell to earth. I will come alone, unarmed, ready to reach an agreement. My compliments to your skill as a leader and an adversary.

I do not wish any further enmity to you; we will make peace and rule together.

Ublaz'

Rasconza tied a red silken kerchief to a speartop and waved it back and forth, signalling agreement to the meeting. As he did so, he said to his captains, 'So, wants to talk peace, does 'e? Haharr, I'd trust that 'un like I'd trust you lot with a keg o' grog. But never fear, buckoes, I knows wot Mad Eyes is up to, an' I'm ready!'

Ublaz tied his green silk kerchief to Sagitar's bow and waved heartily in reply as he gave instructions to his Chief Trident-rat.

'This time there will be no mistakes. You have your orders.'

Sagitar averted her eyes from the mad hypnotic stare. 'Sire, your orders will be carried out.'

The pine marten continued waving the kerchief, his voice laden with menace.

'Fail me this time and your trident shall be fixed to the jetty, Sagitar. With your head mounted upon it!'

40

It took quite some time for the Abbot to muster up his courage and uncover his eyes. Lowering the blanket slowly, he peeped out at the head of Lask Frildur protruding through the smashed panel of the cabin door. Durral sat fascinated with horror, staring at the big lizard's head, until gradually the truth dawned upon him. There was no foul-smelling breath, the mouth was loosely open and the reptilian eyes were glazed over, half closed. Then the old mouse heard the drip drip onto the floor from a hideous slash beneath the scaly chin, right across the neck . . .

The Monitor General was dead!

Durral began to shake all over, his frail body quivering with relief. Slowly he rose and ventured towards the door.

'Hello, is anybeast out there?' he called.

A low, hoarse voice answered. 'Ahoy, mouse, 'tis yer old messmate Romsca. Open the door!'

Fearfully, the Abbot shifted the table that had been wedging the door. Trying not to look at the slain monster he unbarred the shutter, pulling inward. Hampered by the weight of the Monitor the door sagged open; Durral hurried past the dead lizard, out onto the open deck.

Romsca sat with her back to the mast, a cutlass clutched loosely in her paws. With an effort she lifted her head and smiled weakly at the Abbot. 'You ain't goin' t'start callin' me yore child, are yer?'

Durral shook his head numbly, trying to ignore the scene of carnage around him. Deadbeasts were draped everywhere on the silent ship as it ploughed the watery wastes – from the masts, over the rails and on the deck, from stem to stern. *Waveworm* resembled a floating slaughter house. Romsca's head fell forward and the cutlass slipped from her grasp, her voice half chuckle, half gurgle.

'Pretty, ain't it? There's only you'n'me left, Durral.'

Hurrying to the corsair's side, the Abbot cradled her head, using the blanket he had brought with him as a pillow.

'Friend, you're hurt!' he cried.

Romsca's head lolled against Durral's stained habit. 'Aye, that's the truth, bucko, but I fixed ole Lask good'n'proper, didn't I! Aaahhh! Don't move me, there's only this mast holdin' my back t'gether . . .'

Durral tried to glance over the ferret's shoulder at her back. She winced and shook her head slightly. 'Don't look, you don't wanna see wot that lizard's claws'n'fangs did ter me, mate. Now lissen careful, 'cos there ain't much time. Let go of me easy like, an' make yer way t'the tiller. She's still 'eaded due west, so take a stern line an' lash 'er steady. Go on, Father Abbot, do like I say!'

Making Romsca as comfortable as possible, the old mouse eased himself away from her and scurried aft. Taking the stern rope he tied it to one side of the gallery rail, looped it several times round the tiller and tied the other end to the opposite rail, lashing the ship on course, due west. Then he went on a tour of the vessel. Stumbling over a slain Monitor and two searats he found glowing embers in the brazier in Lask's cabin. He added wood, lamp oil and sea coal and soon had a fire rekindled.

First he put on some water to heat, then hunted around until he found an old canvas and some blankets. It was still drizzling lightly when he returned to Romsca; she had dozed off. Durral made a lean-to with the canvas and covered the corsair ferret with blankets to keep her warm, then he resumed his search of the ship.

Noon found the sky darkening. Bruised purple clouds hung over the oily foamless swell of billows, and now the drizzle had turned to steady rain. It was still warm, though, and steam rose from Durral's fur as he bustled out to Romsca with food and drink.

The corsair opened her eyes feebly. 'Yore a good creature, but an ole fool. Take care o' yerself. I ain't worth it, my string's played out.'

Durral cradled Romsca's head as he ladled soup into her mouth. 'I'm afraid it's only dried fish and ship's biscuit with some water, but 'tis the best I could do, friend. You saved my life, and you were good to Viola too. Without you we would both have fallen victim to those lizards long ago. Drink up, now.'

Romsca turned her mouth away from the ladle. 'Water, just give us a drop of water, matey. I'm parched.'

The Abbot carefully guided a beaker to her mouth. Romsca sipped the liquid and winked faintly at him. 'You 'earken t'me, Durrall, y'could never sail this tub back ter Mossflower, but she's bound due west, and with luck y'll landfall at the isle of Sampetra. I've got mates there, tell 'em yore my pal. 'Tis yer only chance, may'ap they'll 'elp you.'

Durral stroked the corsair's tattooed paw. 'Now, now, my child, none of that talk. You'll live to see your friends again, I'll make sure of it.'

Romsca smiled, her voice growing fainter as she replied, 'I 'opes y'make it back to Redwall Abbey some-day, it looked like a nice place t'be. Hmph, you won't be bothered with types like me then, corsairs an' searats an' all manner o' wavescum . . .'

She shuddered, and Durral drew the blanket up to her chin. 'Hush, now, and rest, my child.'

As Romsca's eyes closed, she murmured drowsily, 'My child. I like that. Thank ye, my Father.'

Her head lolled forward onto the Father Abbot of Redwall's paws for the last time.

Durral sat nursing the dead corsair until it grew dark, heedless of the rain that soaked him as *Waveworm* sailed silently westward on the drifting swell with its lone cargo. One old mouse.

BOOK THREE

When Tears Are Shed

41

Viola was wakened by the sounds of low voices nearby. It was Martin and Grath talking together. The logboat was almost stationary, bobbing in the warming dawn. Seaweed hawsers trailed limply along the boat's sides, and the sealfolk were nowhere to be seen.

Martin stood in the prow, staring up at a mountain that reared out of the ocean. 'Well, it's big enough,' he said, 'but it doesn't look like we can land anywhere. Why did the sealfolk slide off and leave us here, I wonder? It's nought but a mountain thrusting up out of the water.'

Grath was as puzzled as the mouse warrior. 'Maybe there's somethin' or somebeast here they wanted us t'see. Let's use these broken struts as oars an' paddle o'er there.'

Plogg poked his head from under the canvas awning. 'Gwaw! I'm stiff as a board. Where are we?'

Welko thrust his head up alongside that of his brother, grinning. 'Nice'n'warm, though,' he said, 'looks like it's goin' t'be sunny. I'm starvin' – is that ole cooky awake yet?'

A long paw reached out and cuffed the shrew's ear. 'Ole cooky indeed, you graceless, scruff-furred wretch. I, sir, am Cleckstarr Lepus Montisle, of the far northern

Montisles doncha know, an' furthermore, young feller m'lad, I don't well appreciate foul young blots like y'self snorin' down my delicate ears all night. As for breakfast, 'fraid you'll have to whistle for it. Clean out o' grub, we are, wot!'

Viola shook her head in disgust. 'Well, there's a fine thing, those seals sliding off without so much as a by your leave, and us without a bite of food, floating around goodness knows where, with nothing to show for it but a hulking great mountain shoving itself out of the water!'

Grath could not help smiling at the complaining volemaid. 'Well tut tut, missie, grab a cob o' wood an' start paddlin'. We won't *talk* ourselves outta this fix, that's for sure.'

The rock was massive: smooth-sided, high and impregnable, and there was no discernible opening in it. They paddled most of the day, skirting the stone monolith, searching for a place to land, but the quest seemed fruitless. Sometime around mid-afternoon they stopped to rest, sweltering under a hot sun.

Clecky gazed longingly at the clear blue sea. 'Looks wonderful, don't it? I say, chaps, if I don't get something soon to wet my jolly old lips I might try a drink o' that.'

'I wouldn't recommend it, seawater can be nasty stuff!'

Clecky nearly fell overboard with shock. A young female otter had slid gracefully into the logboat and was sitting beside him.

'Who the flippin' 'eck are you, miss, an' where's y'manners? Jolly well near scared two seasons' growth out of me ears, poppin' up like that! Kindly don't do it again, bad form, wot!'

The little ottermaid smiled prettily, twitching her nose at them. 'Beg y'pudden, sir, but what are you? You're not an otter.'

'Hmph, I should say not, m'gel. I'm a hare, actually. Name's Clecky.'

'Pleased t'meetcher, mister Clecky. I'm Winniegold of the holt of Wallyum Rudderwake. I 'spect the Hawm and his sealfolk brought you here to see us.'

Clecky twitched his ears rather irately. 'Tchah! Well, if he did he never said anythin' to us about it, blinkin' feller should say where he's takin' a chap, instead of all this haaaawmin' an' haaaaarin', wot wot!'

'Excuse me,' Martin interrupted, 'but if you two could break off this pleasant conversation long enough, perhaps you, miss, could show us to the holt of your father Wallyum Rudderwake.'

Realization suddenly struck Plogg. 'The seals were sayin' Waaylumm! Maybe that's 'cos they couldn't say Wallyum properly!'

Clecky absentmindedly cuffed Plogg's ear. 'Huh, I know that. Seal language, speak it perfectly, old chap, perfectly. I think friend Martin's right though, missie. You'd better take us to your dear old pater, wot!'

Winniegold directed them to take the logboat further round the side of the rock. A cable made from twined seaweed and kelp hung from a niche carved into the rock; it trailed away into the sea like a great thick serpent. The little ottermaid unhooked the cable and, passing it to Grath, she explained its purpose.

'Look down into the water, what d'you see?'

Grath stared downward into the clear depths. 'There's a hole like some sort o' tunnel in the mountain, right near the surface here. The cable goes into it!'

Winniegold lowered her voice as if revealing a secret. 'If we wait the sea will lower itself and the tunnel will appear in front of us. My father says it is the trough between every nineteenth and twentieth wave that washes against the east side of our mountain; suddenly the sea level will sink and expose the cave mouth. If we all lie flat in your boat and heave on the cable we can pull ourselves through to the inner island.'

Viola leaned over the boat's edge, gazing at the great hole in the rock fearfully. 'But it's underwater,' she cried, 'we'll all be drowned! I'm scared!'

Winniegold giggled at the timid volemaid. 'Silly, there's no need t'be feared, you'll see. I haven't been countin' the waves, but I think it's best we all lie down.'

Without warning a wave lapped high, sending the boat up on its crest, then it dropped sharply. There was a swoosh as if some gigantic monster had exhaled and they were looking straight into the mouth of the tunnel, wide and dark and dripping seawater, directly in front of them.

'Get down, mates, lie flat!' Winniegold yelled.

She gave a mighty heave on the cable and the logboat shot into the opening, like a tiny fish into the mouth of a whale. They were surrounded by an eerie blue light shimmering from the tunnel walls. The logboat rose, stopping no more than a pawslength from the shell-encrusted tunnel ceiling. As Winniegold tugged on the cable their vessel shot forward, and the entire logboat crew seized hold of the thick kelp and seaweed hawser and, lying flat on their backs, began pulling. The little craft sped along inside the tunnel. Limpets, barnacles, shells and hanging fronds almost scraped the prow of the boat, and great crabs scuttled about in the bluish light above their faces. The transition from sudden bright tropical sunlight to aquamarine dimness caused golden sunbursts upon their vision whenever they blinked. It was the oddest of experiences.

Suddenly it was bright, hot daylight again. Still holding the cable they stood up slowly and gazed awestruck at the scene surrounding them. Where the cable ended it was made fast to a treestump on the banks of a broad stream. Fields stretched about the entire area, ending in trees, which gave way to dense vegetation and shrubbery climbing the mountain's inner slopes.

Martin turned full circle, staring up at the high circular rockrim. 'It's like some kind of a massive crater, as if the mountain had had the heart taken out of it. We're in a big basin!'

Cupping both paws to her mouth, Winniegold cried out, setting echoes bouncing and ringing from the surrounding heights: 'Rudddaaaawaaaaaaake!'

Otters came bounding from everywhere, dashing across the fields, tumbling down the banks and popping from the stream's surface. They crowded around the logboat, staring silently at the newcomers. Everybeast, male and female, even the babes, was fully armed; slings, clubs and javelins were much in evidence. Then a murmur ran through the ranks and they parted.

A magnificent male otter, fully a head taller than the rest, strode purposefully forward. His fur was dark, almost sable, and he was forbiddingly muscled through his sleek neck and broad shoulders. Grath stared curiously at the big bow he carried, a shaft set ready upon its bowstring. Over his shoulder she could see a quiverful of red-feathered arrows. He glanced down from the top of the bank, noting that she also carried a bow and arrows, then he nodded and stood to one side.

From behind the big otter another appeared, old and grey, but radiating a presence of wisdom and calm. The old otter carried an oak staff and was garbed in a long, homespun tunic of light brown colour. His voice was deep and warm.

'Do you come to Ruddaring in peace? Are you friends?'

Martin realized who the patriarchal-looking beast was. Leaving the boat he waded ashore and, bowing low, placed his sword on the ground in front of the old otter.

'Peace be upon you, Wallyum Rudderwake, and all of your holt. I am Martin the Warrior of Redwall Abbey. The Hawm of sealfolk delivered us to your island. We are friends.'

Wallyum's grizzled features creased into a gentle

smile. He nodded to Grath. 'Which holt come you from?'

Grath inclined her head to one side, allowing her rudder to rise and tip beneath her chin in a courtly old-fashioned gesture.

'I am Grath Longfletch of Holt Lutra, sire.'

Wallyum appeared extremely gratified by Grath's politeness. 'Well said, maiden. It is a long time since I saw such courtesy in an otter – would that half of my holt had your good manners! You and your friends look as if food would do you no harm. Come, I always find conversation far more pleasant over a good meal. Inbar, will you carry our friend Grath's bow and arrows for her?'

Wallyum's huge, dark-furred son leapt forward willingly, missing the smile that passed between his father and Martin.

The old otter picked up the Warriormouse's sword. 'I will carry this for you. 'Tis a blade that I have only once seen the like of, the sword of a great warrior, ancient and beautiful.'

Helped by numerous otters, the friends set out along the streambank to Holt Rudderwake.

42

The holt was a sprawling comfortable cave in the mountainside, next to where the streamsource bubbled from the rocks. Thick woven rushmats and rockslabs for tables were the only furniture; a fire was kept under an oven made of baked clay and stone.

The otters were partial to great soups and stews of seaweed and shellfish. Also much in favour, owing to the tropical and fertile nature of their island, were magnificent fruit salads. As they ate, Martin related their story to Wallyum and his wife, a great fat old grandma otter called Dorumee, who seemed always to be surrounded by grandbabes climbing over her and swinging on her apron strings. Wallyum listened carefully to Martin's narrative, as did several of the holt elders.

Clecky was the centre of attention with the rest of the otters. His ever-present appetite for staggering amounts of food astounded them. The hare declined shellfish, but did justice to everything else.

'Can't abide the old edible molluscs, wot!' he announced. 'Cockles'n'mussels an' all that bring me out in an itchy paw rash, chaps, sorry. Oh, I say, you fellers, this big ball tastes rather splendid!'

The otters hooted with laughter.

"Tain't a ball, mate, that's a melon. Yore not supposed to eat the seeds, though.'

'Oh, I dunno, taste pretty good t'me. 'Scuse me, old chap, d'you mind not hoggin' that seaweed soup? Nice salty taste, sort o' contrasts jolly well with these peach thingees. Owch! My word, y'could use these stones to chuck from your slings, great lumpy things, er, you there, otterchap, have the decency to unstone that big peach for a feller, will you, that's the style!'

Inbar was admiring Grath's bow and arrows. 'Nice string, well twined. I don't know which has the stronger pull, your bow or mine. Our arrows are the same length, too.'

Grath closed one eye, sighting down the shaft of one of Inbar's red-feathered arrows. 'Mmm, good'n'straight – they'd fly true!'

The normally taciturn otter tested an arrowpoint on his paw. 'That's my full name – Inbar Trueflight. I'll show you where I usually practise, maybe we can loose off a few shafts together?'

Grath agreed, a hint of challenge in her smile. 'I'd like to do that, Inbar. We'll match each other arrow for arrow after we've eaten.'

Wallyum's wife Dorumee was speaking to Martin, whilst her husband took the little otters off to watch Clecky. The babes had never seen a hare before.

'Our Holt of Rudderwake's lived on this isle I don't know 'ow long. It goes right back into the mists of time. There's some say that it were four otter families who escaped from a corsair vessel an' found their way to this place purely by accident. Anyway, Martin, our ancestors made Ruddaring Isle their own. They fought a great battle with the lizards that used t'live 'ere. Wot lizards they didn't slay were driven off to another isle 'way west o' here, may'ap 'tis that Sampetra place you talk of. That was more seasons ago than a score of otters could count. Ruddaring Isle is our 'ome now. Searats an' corsairs passin' in their ships don't even know this is an island, to them 'tis just a mountain pokin' up out o' the ocean with no place to land upon. Nobeast knows we're livin' 'ere, 'cepting the seals an' you an' yore friends, Martin. Swear if ever you leave 'ere not to tell a livin' creature of our isle.'

The Warriormouse patted Dorumee's paw. 'I swear it will be so. I'd hate to think of me or my crew being the cause of ever bringing unwelcome visitors here to your beautiful home.'

Viola, Plogg and Welko were trying to learn an otter dance. They found it very difficult, not having the balance that an otter's rudderlike tail affords. Winniegold and her chums were whirling and wheeling about, balancing first on one footpaw, then hopping onto the other with a skilful tailspin between each leap.

A deep-voiced old otterwife battered two drums with her tail as she sang for the dancers.

'Ho comb yore whiskers, brush that tail,
Place a flow'r behind yore ear,
Wash those paws in my ole pail,
We're off a dancin', dear! Oooooooh!
Paws up high, rudder on the deck,
Pace up to yore partner, check!
Rudder in the air, paws on the ground,
Whirl that otter round an' round!
Vittles onna table, drink's there too,
Hear the music playin',
Smile at me I'll dance with you,
- Every otter's sayin'! Oooooooh!
Shuffle back an' clap both paws,
I'll clap mine an' you clap yours!
Turn away now back to back,
Slap those tails down whackwhackwhack!'

Giggling and laughing, they fell to the floor exhausted.

Clecky looked up from a wild grape trifle, shaking his head. 'Do y'self a mischief, prancin' about like that after eatin'. Don't you chaps know any good slow ballads t'settle the jolly old digestion?'

He was immediately beset by several young otters. 'Sing for us, mister Clecky! Oh, please do, sir!'

Finishing his trifle in two great gulps the hare was up on his paws, ready to sing, but denying it strenuously. 'Oh, have a heart, you young rips! I haven't twiddled the old vocal chords in an absolute age, doncha know!'

'Now leave our friend alone if he don't wish to sing,' Old Wallyum remonstrated.

The hare took the centre of the floor as if he had not heard Wallyum's remark. 'Oh well, if you insist, I'll just do one. A very bad salad, er ahem, I mean sad ballad. Right, here goes, chaps . . .'

Drooping his whiskers and quivering his ears in a most pathetic manner, he clasped both paws and stared soulfully at his audience.

'This is the story of Corkal hare,
Which is most terribly tragic, horribly sad an' pretty
    awfully fearfuuuuuuuuul!
So pray give attention, list' to my song an' don't fall
    asleep,
Although 'tis not too cheerfuuuuuuuuuuuul!
Poor Corkal fell foul of an evil fox
Who was mean an' horribly cruuuuuuuuuel!
An' foolishly he challenged him,
Next mornin' at dawn to a duuuuuuuuuuuuuel!'

Here Clecky paused and glared at Plogg and Welko. 'Either of you rogues spit another melon seed at me an' I'll kick y'little fat tails halfway up yonder mountain. Ahem, beg pardon for the untimely interruption, chaps, now where was I? Oh, yes.

'Both creatures chose as their weapons,
To hurl at each other, salaaaaaaaaaaaad!
Good job they never chose soup or else,
I might never have wrote this ballaaaaaaaaaad!
So the very next mornin' as dawn did break,
All bright'n'hot'n'warm an' sunneeeeeeeeeeee!
Which considerin' it was the dead o' winter,
Our hero did not find too funneeeeeeeeeeee!'

Clecky jumped and clapped a paw to his tail, glaring at
Plogg and Welko, who were sitting looking the pictures
of innocence. 'Just one more melon seed, you rotters, just
one more . . .'

He continued his elongated recitation.

'There in the field the two creatures met,
Each beast with salad ladeeeeeeeeeeeeeen!
A terrible sight not fit for the eyes,
Of any tender young maideeeeeeeeeeeeen!
An' the lettuce an' the carrots an' the onions they all
    flew like lightniiiiiiiiiin'!
An' they fought'n'they ate, an' they ate'n'they
    fought,
The scene was pretty frightniiiiiiiin'!'

Clecky twitched his nose as a melon seed bounced off
it. He narrowed his eyes and pointed vehemently at the
two shrews. 'Right, that's it! Soon as I'm finished this
heartrendin' ditty you two are *for* it!'

He finished the song at top speed as if it were a fast jig:

'But now my friends I've reached the end of my
    most sad renditiiion,
At the end of the epic battle royal this was the sad
    positiiiion,
Neither the fox nor the hare had won, they were
    both in bad conditiiiiiion,
Sufferin' from fierce indigestion because, they'd ate
    all the ammunitiiiiiiion!'

With a bound he was away after the two shrews, who shot off like sardines with a shark on their tails. The audience fell about laughing helplessly.

Dorumee held her tubby sides, shaking with mirth. 'Ohohohohooohooh! That'll teach 'em t'spit melon pips at 'im!'

Viola and Winniegold were chuckling so hard that tears coursed down their cheeks as they confessed. 'Heeehee, it wasn't heehee Plogg or hahaha Welko spittin' those pips . . . Hoohoohooh! It was us. Heehahaheehohoho!'

Wallyum Rudderwake and his otters were excellent hosts to the first land visitors they had ever received. Entertainment, singing, eating, drinking and dancing went on far into the night, only stopping because everybeast was totally exhausted. Interspersed with the weary logboat crew, otters slept where they fell, everywhere about the cave. Babes, youngsters and parents lay draped over rocks or curled on rush mats in a tangle of paws and tails.

Wallyum sat in the light of the oven fire. He and Martin were the only two left awake. The otter patriarch stared piercingly at the Warriormouse until eventually Martin felt he had to speak and break the silence.

'Tell me, Wallyum, how did you come to know the sealfolk?'

The otter shifted his gaze to the fire and shrugged. 'We have always known them. My father and his father before him treated the seals – bulls, wives and pups – for injuries and ailments. So it has fallen to my lot now. I am their Healer. Hawm and his followers have great respect for the Holt of Rudderwake; they would do anything for us. Lucky 'twas that you had an otter in your crew, or they might never have brought you to my island.'

That seemed as much information as Wallyum was willing to impart. Silence fell on the two creatures as they sat together in the soft tropic night, staring into the ash-shrouded embers burning low beneath the oven.

Martin felt slightly uneasy in the presence of Wallyum. From the corner of his eye he noted the otter had transferred his gaze from the fire. Hairs on the back of the Warriormouse's neck began to prickle. He turned suddenly and locked eyes with Wallyum's piercing stare. 'Friend, is there something you are hiding from me?'

Rising slowly, Wallyum beckoned Martin to follow him. 'Let us walk together in the moonlight,' he said.

In the limited view of sky surrounded by the high mountainous crater, a summer moon hung like a pale gold coin, shedding its light on the two figures strolling through lush grasses towards the streambank. Wallyum Rudderwake spoke when they were out of hearing from the cave.

'Hearken to me, Martin of Redwall, I have things to tell you, things that I could tell to no otherbeast, lest they think I am growing feeble in the brain. Would it surprise you to know that I already knew your face, that I had seen you long before you came to this island?'

The Warriormouse sat down on the streambank. 'It would surprise me greatly. Tell me more, Wallyum.'

Leaning on Martin's shoulder, the old otter lowered himself to sit upon the bank. He tossed a twig into the stream and watched the water bear it away to the seas.

'Three moons ago I had a dream. That was when you appeared in my mind – but was it you, or one who looked just like you? It was a mouse, a warrior like yourself. When you arrived at my island today, I knew then, it was you! You were not wearing armour like the mouse in my dream, but your face was the same as his and the sword you carried was the same wonderful blade. I knew this for certain when I picked up that sword to carry it for you. I could feel it in the hilt and the blade.'

Martin nodded, understanding beginning to dawn on him. Wallyum had been visited in his dream by the first Martin of long ago. 'Did the mouse speak words to you, friend? Was there a message?'

In the darkness, the otter's eyes opened wide with surprise. 'Yes, he did! I felt a great calm come over me. His voice sounded like a distant bell, echoing, warm. These are the very words he spoke. My name is Martin of Redwall. You are a goodbeast, Wallyum Rudderwake – help my friends to defeat evil and bring happiness back to our Abbey. Do this thing for me and the name of Holt Rudderwake will be remembered on the stones of Great Hall.'

The old otter grasped Martin's paw firmly. 'Tell me what to do, Martin of Redwall, and I will help you!'

43

Auma the badger Mother sat at supper flanked by Skipper and Foremole, the three of them highly amused as Arven and the Dibbuns served the meal. Further up the table Sister Cicely sniffed, 'Those babes should have been abed hours back!'

Skipper glanced down the table. 'Trim me sails, wot's the matter with the Sister? She looks as if she's swallered some of 'er own nettle soup.'

Auma directed the otter's attention to Diggum and Gurrbowl trundling a laden trolley towards them. 'Pay no heed to Cicely. She's got a knot in her tail because her patients have deserted the infirmary and she's got nobeast to boss around. Will you look at these babes, how nice of them to serve us supper!'

Diggum clambered up onto the table, her tiny face creased in a serious frown as she set about tying table napkins around the necks of Auma, Skipper and Foremole.

'Yurr, you'm keep'n these on, et'll save ee splashin' zoop all over ee. Doan't ee take em off, or boi 'okey oi'll send ee all oop t'bed wi'out no zupper. Hurr!'

Gurrbowl ladled out hotroot soup for all three, which Auma attempted to refuse, saying, 'No thank you, sir, it

301

looks a bit too spicy for me. I'll just have salad and a little nutbread, please.'

The molebabe glared at the big badger Mother. 'Yoo'll 'ave wot oi gives ee, marm, an' sup et all, 'tis gudd for ee. Cummon, finish et oop an' ee'll grow gurt'n'strong loik oi, bain't that roight, Skip?'

The Skipper of Otters nodded vigorously. 'Oh, 'tis right enough, matey. I'll see she eats it all, you go'n'attend to the others. Sister Cicely looks famished, serve 'er.'

The Dibbuns ambled off, pushing their serving trolley.

Arven was trying to feed a mousebabe, arguing furiously with him. 'Likkle maggit, eatta up all dese scones or grayshuss me I tell badgermum to baff you inna baff wiv lotsa soap uppa nose, ho yes!'

The rebellious mousebabe flung a scone at Arven. 'No! I h'ain't got 'nuff teeths to eat 'em, um like rocks, you maked d'scones, you eat 'em!'

It was at that point that the door slammed wide as Craklyn and Tansy rushed into Great Hall, shouting, 'The tapestry! The tapestry! The secret's in the tapestry!'

Immediately the diners deserted their seats to crowd round the Abbeymaids.

Foremole held up a huge digging claw, calling over the ensuing din, 'Yurr, missie, wot be in ee tarpesty?'

Rollo came panting in and fought his way to the front of the huddle. 'The fifth pearl, of course,' he said, 'at least that's what the clues say.'

Arven wriggled his way through and stood facing the tapestry. 'Well, wherra purl, Tansy pansy?'

Tansy tweaked the little squirrel's bushy tail. 'We'll tell you when we find it, nosy!'

Auma's huge voice boomed around the hall. 'Stand back, everybeast back, please! Make room for Rollo and those maids to do their job. Move yourselves, please!'

Reluctantly the Redwallers shuffled back a pace. Auma

302

joined Rollo. 'I don't like intruding, but perhaps we can all help. How did you know the pearl is in the tapestry?'

Rollo unfolded the parchment scrap and, spreading it on the floor, he demonstrated how they had solved the puzzle of the poem lines and letters to make up the word tapestry.

'That's as much as we know at present, but we're convinced the fifth Tear of all Oceans is hidden somewhere in this tapestry.'

All eyes were on the mighty needlework hanging from the wall.

It depicted Martin the Warrior in the bottom right hand corner, armoured and leaning both paws on his swordhilt. The warrior had a reckless smile upon his handsome features, and all around him was a woodland scene showing vermin, some lying slain, others fleeing in all directions from the Hero of Redwall.

Auma read the rhyme aloud:

'There is a warrior,
Where is a sword?
Peace did he bring,
The fighting Lord.
Shed for him is my fifth tear,
Find it in the title here,
Written in but a single word,
An eye is an eye, until it is heard.'

Foremole scratched his dark-furred head. 'Hurr, 'tis a gurt puzzlement, if'n ee purler be 'idden in um tarpesty oi doan't see et. 'ow do ee foind the h'objeck?'

Craklyn picked up the parchment and strode back and forth in front of the tapestry. 'Here's how, we dismantle the poem bit by bit, eliminating the pieces we don't need until we find the vital line. Right . . . There is a warrior.' She pointed at the figure of Martin, continuing, 'Where is a sword?'

Foremole indicated the blade that Martin leaned on. 'Thurr! Wot do et say nex', missie?'

'Peace did he bring.'

Tansy pondered for a moment. 'Doesn't sound like a clue. Carry on, Craklyn.'

'The fighting Lord.'

'No, that's not much help. What's next?'

'Shed for him is my fifth tear.'

'That means Fermald gave the fifth pearl to Martin,' Rollo interrupted. 'Continue.'

'Find it in the title here.'

Skipper thumped his tail thoughtfully. 'Title, wot title?'

Arven snorted impatiently. Marching up to the tapestry, he gestured. 'There, that'sa tykle, there!'

Embroidered on the bottom border of the work, right beneath the figure of the mouse, was a word. 'Martin.'

Craklyn could not conceal her excitement. 'Aye, that's it, listen to the next line. Written in but a single word. A single word, and that's it. Martin!'

A buzz of conversation arose from the onlookers; everybeast seemed to be speculating and arguing with each other.

Skipper was forced to roar over the hubbub to restore order.

'Quiet now, silence! Stow the gab an' let these maids git on with it. Oh, sorry, Rollo sir, an' you too. Wot d'you think?'

Rollo polished his spectacles carefully. 'I think we should hear the last line. Craklyn?'

The squirrelmaid read out the poem's final line: 'An eye is an eye, until it is heard.'

The silence which had fallen over Great Hall deepened. Everybeast stood looking at the tapestry, mentally repeating the line.

Gerul limped forward from the table, where he had sat through it all, staunchly chomping away at every morsel in sight. He waved a slice of heavy fruit cake at Craklyn and Tansy. 'Sure aren't none of yer lissenin'? As me ould mother used t'say, 'tis as plain as the paw behind yer back in a fog.'

Tansy folded her paws resignedly. 'Oh, that's a great help. I thought you were going to tell us all something intelligent for a moment there!'

The owl pecked a few crumbs from his wing feathers. 'Faith, an' so I am, missie. Will ye think of the line for a moment. An eye is an eye, until it is heard. Does it not tell you anythin'?'

Tansy shook her head. 'Not a thing!'

Gerul pointed at one of his eyes. 'What pray is this?'

Tansy's reply was swift. 'An eye, it's your eye!'

The owl chuckled. 'Ah, the brains of the young are surely marvellous. Now tell me, what's this?' He pointed at Tansy's right eye.

The hedgehog maid gave a long sigh of impatience. 'It's an eye, my eye! What are you getting at?'

Gerul went to a nearby table and took up a knife. 'Me ould mother always used t'say, if y'can't see with yore own two eyes what's in front of them, then y'better off closin' 'em an' goin' t'sleep, 'tis far more restful!'

As he was speaking, the owl was scratching something on the floorstones with his knifepoint. He pointed at it. 'Now, what would y'say that was?'

Tansy studied it for a moment. 'It looks like the letter I to me . . .'

Gerul smiled. He had made his point. 'Right, you just said it, the letter I, at least that's wot I heard y'say. See, I point to me eye, that's the eye y'can see, but you just said I, that's the I y'can hear!'

Arven was first to the tapestry. He ran his paw quickly over the name Martin embroidered on the hem and, thrusting his other paw behind the hem, he ripped something away from behind the dot of the letter I in the warrior's name.

'It d'purl!' he yelled.

The fifth pearl fell to the floor, bounced twice on the stones and rolled a little way, coming to a halt in front of Auma. The badger picked up the pretty rose-coloured orb. It glowed softly in the lamplight as she presented it to Tansy, saying, 'I believe Gerul deserves a vote of thanks for his help.'

Shamefaced, Tansy shook the owl's talon gently. 'Gerul, friend, forgive me for getting so snippy with you.'

The friendly bird blinked his great eyes. 'Ah sure, cut us an ould slice of fruit cake an' yer forgiven!'

Craklyn swept the half-cake that was left from the table. 'You deserve it all, and I'd bake your mother one twice this size if she were here!'

Arven had been gradually sidling away until he was at the foot of the stairs. Suddenly Tansy caught sight of him and shouted, 'The sixth clue! Arven, bring it here this instant!'

The squirrelbabe did a little dance, wobbling his head comically. 'Tansy pansy toogle doo! I foun' it, d'paper's mine!'

Waving the scrap of parchment, which had been stitch-tacked lightly behind the tapestry to hold the pearl, Arven fled upstairs giggling.

Rollo threw up his paws. 'You two run and catch him. I'm too old for this sort of game. Well, go on, last one to catch Arven is a something or other, shall we say a baggy-bottomed beetle?'

But Tansy and Craklyn were not listening. They were dashing headlong for the stairs to catch the squirrelbabe.

Arven stood on a dormitory window sill, hidden by the drape of the curtain. He wriggled in anticipation as the door slowly creaked open. Tansy popped her head in. 'Aaaaarven, are you theeeere?' she called in a singsong tone.

A small giggle sounded as Tansy and Craklyn tip-pawed into the dormitory. Craklyn pointed silently to the moving curtain as it wriggled and flapped against the sill. Tansy smiled, and called out in the same singsong voice, 'Aaaarven, you're hiding on the window siiiiiill!'

A small giggly reply came from behind the curtain. 'Teeheehee! Nooohooo, Arven not heeeeeeyer!'

Craklyn whipped the curtain aside, revealing the squirrelbabe grinning mischievously, the crumpled scrap of parchment held tight to his small fat stomach.

Tansy injected a note of serious authority into her demand. 'Give me that paper, sir, immediately!'

'Kyeeheehee! No, it mine, I foun' it!'

Craklyn launched herself at Arven, but he was too quick. Grabbing the curtain he swung outward, let go and somersaulted onto a bed. Tansy jumped upon Arven, and immediately he stuffed the parchment into his mouth and shut it tight.

Tansy shook him. 'Open your mouth at once, we need that parchment!'

Arven shook his head, attempting to speak. 'Nmff, ut mahn!'

Craklyn leapt to her friend's assistance. 'Right, you've asked for this, you little maggot!'

Grabbing both Arven's footpaws, the squirrelmaid tickled furiously.

'Yahahahahoohoostoppiiiiit!'

Triumphantly, Tansy held up the damp scrap of parchment. 'Got it!'

Craklyn stopped tickling, only to find Arven's footpaws thrust in her face.

'More tickles, want more tickles pleez!' he squealed.

Later that night the three friends sat in Great Hall taking a late supper together. In front of them lay the scallop shell, open to reveal five rose-coloured pearls and one remaining space in the soft red cloth that lined the shell case. Rollo nibbled celery and cheese turnover briefly before rubbing his paws together.

'Well, let's see the final clues. I trust the parchment was not damaged too much by that little savage stuffing it in his mouth.'

Tansy spread the parchment carefully on the tabletop. 'No, it's still quite legible. I dried it off in the kitchen ovens, but treat it carefully, it's a mite crispy.'

The friends read the lines slowly together.

'My sixth and last tear I give unto you,
When Redwallers lie abed,
At midnight see, in full moon view,
The purple arrowhead.
Travel east, six rods from the tip,
To the rose that blooms ever fair,
See if you can find the right hip,
Turn west and you're halfway there.'

Rollo pushed away the remains of his supper, cupped his head in both paws and leaned on the table dejectedly. 'Huh! And we thought the last *five* clues were difficult?'

Craklyn stared miserably at the oak-grained pattern of the tabletop. 'Right! I don't think poor Piknim would've sorted any real information from that rhyme, and she was far brighter than I am.'

Tansy yawned and stood up, stretching. 'I agree with both of you, but enough is enough for one night. I'm off to join all the other Redwallers who are lying abed.'

The last thing Tansy heard before dropping off to sleep was the voice of Martin speaking to her.

'The Abbess will find it for Piknim on the same ground where the fifth was found.'

44

Ublaz stood on top of the mighty piles of timber heaped against the back walls of his palace, and peered over the walltop at the rocks where Rasconza had agreed to meet him at dawn. There was still an hour to go before daybreak, but the pine marten was leaving nothing to chance this time. With his superb vision, he could make out tiny moving shapes on the low hill in the distance. Searats and corsairs were beginning to mass on the hilltop. Ublaz checked that his remaining threescore Monitors were waiting, armed with long lances, in the courtyard behind him. To the left and right, behind the hill where the Wave Brethren waited, two fire arrows flared briefly in the dark skies.

The Emperor's eyes glittered with fiendish delight. The trap was laid. During the night, Sagitar had secretly left the palace at the head of the entire army of Trident-rats and, at her Emperor's bidding, she had split the force and hidden them well among the hills. When he arrived, Rasconza would be walking into a well-laid trap. The massed Trident-rats would sweep down behind his wavescum and ambush them from the rear. From there they would be driven against the back outer palace wall, where Monitors could thrust down into their ranks with long spears, followed by flaming bales of dried wood and grass.

A jubilant lark arose to greet daybreak, chirruping happily as she ascended the upper air, sunrays from the east making her wings almost transparent against the still blue skies. She was unaware of what was taking place on the ground below. Rasconza was of the opinion that only a fool would go unarmed to any meeting with Ublaz, and the wily fox had slid a keen-edged dagger inside his tunic. Grinning wolfishly at his captains, he strolled down from the hilltop with them.

'Sink me ship'n'drown me crew, would he? Well, today's the day the Emperor o' Sampetra gits toppled off 'is throne an' fed to the fishes. Wait 'ere until I give the signal, buckoes, 'tis supper in the palace fer the Wave Brethren tonight. Right, I'm off! I 'ates ter keep anybeast waitin' t'be slain!'

The corsair fox strode jauntily to the meeting place, where Ublaz's arrow had fallen on the previous day.

Ublaz issued final orders to four Monitors standing nearby. They were holding a long, heavy rope with thick knots at short intervals along its length.

'Lower me down gently and leave the rope hanging over the wall. I will return fast, so be ready. When I grab the rope haul me up with all speed. Do you understand?'

'Yarr, Mightinezz!'

Moments later Ublaz was lowered to the ground outside the palace and, alone and unarmed, he marched forward to where Rasconza awaited him.

Both beasts halted within three paces of each other. Since the pine marten had dispensed with wearing a transparent silk scarf across his eyes, Rasconza was careful to keep his gaze averted in the presence of his enemy. Rasconza was the first to break the silence.

'So then, yore 'ighness, I unnerstand yer want peace. Well now, that's a bit of a turnaround fer the Ruler of

Sampetra an' Terror of all the Seas, ain't it? Still, I s'pose it makes sense, since all y've 'ad to deal with afore was fools an' lizards.'

Ublaz sneered at the swaggering corsair. 'You may think you're a clever fox, but you made a big mistake the day you tried to pit wits against me. Watch!'

Ublaz raised his paws high and spread them, roaring at the top of his voice, 'Attaaaaack!'

Rasconza picked a small flower and sniffed it appreciatively. 'Save yer breath, Mad Eyes. I'm the only one who'll do the attackin' this day. Take a look at yonder 'ill, wot d'yer see?'

An uneasy feeling began to stir within Ublaz. Something was wrong.

A figure, garbed in a long cloak and hood, stepped forward from the Wave Brethren crowded on the hill crest. Now it was Rasconza's turn to shout.

'Unsheet yerself fer the mighty Ublaz, matey!'

It was Sagitar. Immediately she showed herself, tridents began to bristle among the vermin horde. Rasconza's paw began slowly moving towards the dagger hidden in his tunic.

'Yore Trident-rats 'ave changed sides,' he gloated. 'They've got a new leader. Me! Sagitar says to tell you 'er 'ead ain't decoratin' no trident on the jetty. Yore finished, Ublaz!'

Then, whipping out his dagger, Rasconza pounced.

But Ublaz was fast; he sprang to one side and, dealing the fox a smart blow on the back of his neck, he knocked the corsair flat on his face. Then he landed a swift kick to the fox's side, driving the wind out of him.

Unarmed and seeing the massed creatures pour from the hilltop towards him, Ublaz took to his heels and ran. Rasconza was tough; he leapt up and gave chase after his foe. With his paws pounding the earth like pistons, Ublaz dashed for the wall; a quick glance over his shoulder confirmed his fears. Rasconza was coming after him and the fox could run like the wind. He was quickly closing the gap between them.

Many seasons of soft living had slowed the pine marten. He was running flat out, but the fox was leaner and tougher; even half winded he was twice the runner Ublaz would ever be. Increasing his pace, Rasconza raced along, dagger in paw.

Ublaz made it to the wall with Rasconza only a short distance behind him. Grabbing the knotted rope, Mad Eyes bellowed hoarsely, 'Pull! Pull me up!'

The four Monitors hauled with all their might, and Ublaz shot upward. Rasconza leapt, striking out savagely with his blade.

Ublaz screeched in agony as the dagger pierced his footpaw, then he was seized by scaly claws and pulled over the wall to safety. Limping and hopping about on one footpaw, he yelled, 'Defend the walls, hurry!'

The front ranks of Wave Brethren attempting to scale the walls were met by vicious thrusts from the Monitors' lances. Sitting on the woodpile, Ublaz nursed his paw, staunching the blood with his cloak hem. He beckoned the largest Monitor over.

'Zurgat, you must keep them at bay. If they breach the wall you and your Monitors are deadbeasts.'

The big lizard slithered her tongue in and out, nodding. 'Yarr, Lord. Zearatz and corzairs have no pity on Monitorz. They will not enter here while we guard theze wallz.'

Ublaz patted her scaly hide as he lied encouragingly. 'We *will* defeat them. Lask Frildur is due back within the next day or so, with his Monitors and a full vermin crew that I can bring under my will. We'll soon chase that rabble into the sea.'

By nightfall the Wave Brethren had retreated from the walls and set up camps a short distance away, Rasconza's plan being to lay siege to the palace. Searats and corsairs, sharing a healthy fear of the great flesh-eating lizards, were only too willing to go along with the fox's scheme. Better to harass and starve Ublaz and his Monitors out than face them head on in battle.

Inside the palace, Ublaz stood at his throne room window, staring out to sea as he tried to gather his thoughts. At least the wavescum had only one ship seaworthy; the rest were without rudders and tillers, and two were without proper masts. He did not have to worry about an attack from the sea, as long as he could hold on to the timber needed for repairs. Below him the jetty lay deserted; it presented no problem at present.

Suddenly, the Emperor's keen eyes picked up a dark object to the east. He watched it getting closer, realization dawning on him. *Waveworm*! It was Lask Frildur and the Monitors, with Romsca and her crew, bringing back the Abbot of Redwall as hostage. Unknowingly Ublaz had been telling the truth to Zurgat when he had spoken to her earlier.

His mad eyes lit up as he formulated a plan. *Waveworm* would soon be at the jetty. He would go and meet the ship and, once he had Lask, Romsca, and the rest back inside his palace, he could defeat Rasconza's rabble.

Gritting his teeth, Ublaz stared at the approaching vessel. He had fought against odds before and won. The pine marten convinced himself that his present troubles were due to the treachery and stupidity of others. This time he alone would control events. He, Ruler of all Oceans and Lord of Sampetra, the Emperor Ublaz! If he trusted only himself and no otherbeast, victory over his enemies was a certainty!

Abbot Durral was sick and exhausted. He had spent long days clearing the ship of dead lizard and vermin carcasses, consigning each one to the depths of the sea in silence. Weakened by lack of food, ill with loneliness and despair, the old mouse crouched in a darkened cabin.

Shivering and semi-conscious, the lone passenger aboard a vessel taking him he knew not where, he did not even feel the keel grinding onto seawashed sand and gravel as *Waveworm* ran unchecked, missing the jetty and nosing to a halt on the shores of Sampetra.

Swathed in a dark silken cloak, Ublaz slid out of the main gates like a furtive cloud shadow, stealing by deserted taverns across the waterfront. He could not understand why *Waveworm* had not berthed properly alongside the jetty. It lay in the shallows, with neither anchor nor picket line to hold it. Ublaz waded out, hoping to catch the crew asleep at their posts.

The first thing Ublaz noticed as he climbed aboard *Waveworm* was the total absence of noise, not even the snoring of crewbeasts. Making his way to the for'ard cabins he found one with the door hanging crazily by a hinge, its centre panel shattered and bloodstained. It was empty. Dashing through the accommodation the pine marten flung open doors, staring around in disbelief. Empty, all empty!

Making his way aft the first thing he noticed was the tiller, lashed in position. Then he saw the dark stains on rail and deck planking, which told their own grim tale. Death had visited the *Waveworm*.

In a stern cabin he found a fire brazier and, stretching his paws inside, Ublaz felt a slight warmth. Within the last day or so, somebeast had managed to get a small fire going there. He checked a pan nearby, wrinkling his nose at the cold, rancid water.

Then a thin, cracked voice called from the shadow of a bunk. 'We'll need more blackberries if we're to make a pie that big, Friar Higgle. Where's Teasel? She'll know where to get some . . .'

Stealing silently across to the bunk, Ublaz lifted aside the tattered blanket. The Emperor of Sampetra found himself looking at the prone, shivering figure of Redwall's Father Abbot.

45

The logboat that had once been part of the craft *Freebeast* was in as good a shape as skilled paws could make it. Provisioned fully by the good otters of Ruddaring Island, it was ready to face the seas again. Martin and his crew once more lay flat, pulling themselves on the thick hawser through the fantastic grotto-like tunnel, with its shell-crusted ceiling and luminous blue light. When the vital wave arrived, they gave a final heave. Hot sunlit daylight streamed in from outside as the tunnel mouth yawned wide. Like a cork, the logboat bobbed out onto the open main. Wallyum Rudderwake, his sturdy son Inbar and several other otters had followed, and now they hung lightly on the boat's sides.

The otter leader had a wooden whistle slung about his neck. He shook seawater from it and blew the whistle several times.

'What'n the name o' goodness is he blowin' that thing for?' Clecky whispered to Martin. 'I can't hear a bally sound from it, chap's got a broken whistle I'd say, wot?'

'Maybe you can't hear the whistle, but the sealfolk can,' Martin explained to the bemused hare. 'Wallyum told me they would stay in these waters roundabout until he had spoken with them about us.'

Clecky chose a large, ripe peach from the supplies. Juice dribbled down his chin as he chomped into it. 'Funny business if y'ask me, old scout. Tunnels through mountains, whistles y'can't hear an' whatnot . . .'

Grath nudged him sharply. 'Well we never asked you, so be quiet and wait!'

Wallyum sounded the whistle again. This time a dark, rounded head broke the waves a short distance south. The seal barked once, dived and was gone. The friends sat in the logboat waiting; the otters occasionally swimming away to circle round slowly.

It was over an hour before anything happened. Suddenly, the waters around the logboat broke with a great whoosh, and sealfolk appeared everywhere, smacking their flippers and rolling about between the waves. Hawm, the massive king bull seal, broke the surface directly in front of the otter leader.

'Feryooday, Waaaaaaaaylumm!'

The Chieftain of Holt Rudderwake clapped his paws together. 'Manyahooday, Haaaaaaaaaaaaaawm!'

'My father is saying that he hopes the king lives long,' Inbar murmured to Grath.

Then Hawm and Wallyum went into a long animated discussion. Martin watched them carefully, though he understood almost nothing of what they were saying. However, now and again he heard his own name mentioned as Ma'tan and he figured that the word 'Sarmpat' meant Sampetra. The logboat crew sat patiently until the discussion was over, then Wallyum held out a paw to his son.

'Help me aboard the boat, I would speak with our friend Martin.' Inbar vaulted aboard the logboat and with Grath's help lifted the old otter clear of the water and swung him inboard.

The mouse warrior listened intently as Wallyum counselled him. 'Hawm says that he knows the isle of Sampetra. It is southwest of here. Nobeast reads the ocean, its tides and currents, like the king of the sealfolk; he will get you there with all speed. But he says that it is a place of great danger and he will not risk the lives of his tribe by staying there long. Once at that island you are alone with your crew; be on your guard at all times because it is a place of great evil. Tread carefully and may fates and fortunes aid you and your five companions, Martin of Redwall.'

'With your permission, I would make Martin's companions six, father.'

Wallyum clasped his son's paw. 'I know you would, Inbar Trueflight – ever since the boat arrived at our island and you set eyes upon another. You have been a good son and Ruddaring is a tiny rock in the ocean. It will be a good thing for you to see the world outside, knowing that you may return to your home if it is not to your liking. Go, my son, and may all your seasons be filled with happiness!'

Inbar nodded his head vigorously, shaking off a teardrop into the sea. He clasped his father's paw tightly. 'Thank you, sir. May the holt not need another leader for seasons untold. Would you wait here while I go back for my bow and arrows? I left them on the riverbank.'

Grath patted the weapons lying alongside her. 'I have them here, Inbar. Your father was not the only beast who could see that you wanted to come with us.'

Wallyum smiled, nodding fondly at Grath Longfletch. 'Take good care of each other,' he said.

Then the old otter slid into the water to join the other otters who had swum through the tunnel. He held up a paw to the seal king. 'Gittawooom, nugorra omminsawll. Gittarra, Haaaaaaaaawm!'

The seal king barked sharply, his voice echoing from the mountain. 'Feryoon Waaaaaylumm. Gittarra!'

Leaping to the logboat's trailing cables, the sealfolk

sent a huge bow wave spraying high as they sped off southwest.

Viola tugged at Inbar's paw. 'What did they say?' she asked.

The big otter smiled down at the volemaid. 'My father said, "Go with the waves, let none harm you, Ruler of Waters, go with all speed, great king." Then Hawm replied, "Stay well, Wallyum," then he told his seals "Gittarra", which means, go with all speed, or, literally, cut the waves.'

Clecky, who was already selecting from the provisions for the midday meal, sniffed. 'I knew that! Huh, seal lingo, speak it like a jolly old seal I do, y'can't fool the great Haaaaaaawm Clecky, y'know!'

Grath turned, looking back at the island. 'From 'ere y'd think it was just some straight-sided rock stickin' up out of the sea, nobeast'd ever guess wot it looks like inside.'

Inbar looked up from the chunk of beeswax he was rubbing upon his bowstring to protect it. 'Aye, that's what has always kept the island safe for the otters of Holt Rudderwake. Tell me, this place, Redwall Abbey – what's it like to live there?'

Grath borrowed the beeswax from him and began working on her bow. 'I couldn't say, mate, never been there, though I'd like to.'

Viola interrupted the two otters, not attempting to hide the note of pride in her voice. 'I was born and bred in the Abbey of Redwall. It's the most wonderful place you could wish to be. I'll tell you all about it.'

Martin perched in the for'ard peak of the speeding logboat as it skimmed the sunlit waves, a fine seaspray causing him to blink as he gazed down at the Hawm of sealfolk. Shining like dark mottled glass, the great bull's sleek form cut the waters a pawslength beneath the surface, towing the boat with his seals, as easily as a feather upon the breeze. Touching the hilt of the sword slung across his shoulders, the Warriormouse stared at the horizon, watching for the first glimpse of Sampetra and wondering what fate and fortune awaited them at the perilous isle of the mad-eyed Emperor Ublaz.

46

Arven was stealing the hazelnut cream pie from beneath Tansy's nose. The young hedgehog maid knew he was, but she could not be bothered trying to stop him. Pulling dreadful fierce faces, the squirrelbabe puffed his cheeks in and out as he helped himself to her beaker of rosehip tea, then, climbing up on the table, he performed a somersault and landed right in front of her face.

'Tansy pansy toogle doo. Boo!'

Glum-faced and pensive, Tansy lifted him down to the floor. 'Oh, toogle doo yourself, you little nuisance, go and play outside with the other Dibbuns. Go on, be off with you!'

Arven waggled his bushy tail sternly at her. 'Shuddent talk t'Arven like dat, me a h'otter wurrier now. Kyah! You not funny any more, Arven goin' a play!'

Hopping and skipping, he bounded from Great Hall, out into the warm late afternoon orchard, to see what mischief he could create with his Dibbun comrades. Tansy watched him go, then turned back to the table, leaning moodily, chin in paws.

'My, my, what a long face! You look as if you've just had a good dose of my warm nettle soup! What ails you, miss?'

Tansy made no reply, merely shrugging at Sister Cicely's enquiry. But Cicely was not one to give up easily. She persisted with her interrogation of the hogmaid.

'You suffered no permanent damage at Ninian's and your friends Craklyn and Rollo seem to be in good health. Come on, Tansy, this is not like you. What's the matter?'

Tansy pushed away her plate and beaker. 'Do you know where to find the purple arrowhead, Sister, or the rose that blooms ever fair, or the right hip for that matter? Because if you do I'd be pleased if you'd tell me, but otherwise I wish you'd please leave me alone. I mean no disrespect, Sister, but I've got such a lot of thinking to do.'

Sister Cicely sniffed rather frostily. 'As you wish, Tansy, but I hope you solve your problem and it brightens up your disposition a bit.'

Tansy rose dispiritedly from the table and wandered off towards the gatehouse. Even before she reached it, Craklyn's voice could be heard repeating the sixth rhyme aloud.

'My sixth and last tear I give unto you,
When Redwallers lie abed,
At midnight see, in full moon view,
The purple arrowhead.
Travel east, six rods from the tip,
To the rose that blooms ever fair,
See if you can find the right hip,
Turn west and you're halfway there.'

The gatehouse door was wide open, and Tansy walked in. Dust motes floated everywhere in the sunrays streaming through window and doorframe. Rollo sat poring over old copies of Abbey Records.

Craklyn lay sprawled in the armchair. She looked up at Tansy, and said, 'It's no use, Rollo has searched and rummaged through all the back records and we haven't come up with a single clue.'

The old Recorder slammed a volume shut in a cloud of dust. 'Atchoo! Oh, 'scuse me. Craklyn's right, though, I've been hard at it since dawn and there's not a single mention of purple arrowheads anywhere in the records. Great seasons, Wullger's going to have a fit when he sees the mess we've made in here – he cleaned the gatehouse out only last evening. Well, misses, it looks like we're really stuck this time. If only we had one clue, just one tiny thing to help us! Time is running out – goodness knows where the Abbot is now, with Martin gone after him. And Viola still not found – she may have been seized again by rogues and vermin. We may well need those pearls for ransom. We must be ready. Remember what we said, we must find those pearls for Piknim.'

Suddenly Tansy recalled the previous night. 'Before I fell asleep last night I thought I heard the voice of Martin the Warrior. He said to me, the Abbess will find it for Piknim on the same ground where the fifth was found. At least I think that's what he said. I can't recall anything else because at that point I must've fallen asleep.'

Craklyn hurled an armchair cushion at her friend. 'You great puddenhead, Martin spoke to you last night and you've only just thought to mention it now?'

Tansy caught the cushion and threw it back. 'Well, that's because I only recalled it now! Tell that bushtailed buffoon, will you, Rollo!'

The old Recorder took the cushion as Craklyn aimed it for another throw. He stared at them both over his glasses, and said, 'Now, now, young maids, no fighting please. Tansy's right, Craklyn, the remembrance of our dreams is often triggered by somebeast saying a certain phrase. For instance, a moment ago I said that we must find those pearls for Piknim. Martin mentioned the words find it for Piknim, and that's what caused Tansy to remember. Though it does sound rather odd, the Abbess will find it for Piknim. Which Abbess? Redwall only has

322

an Abbot, fates and fortunes rest favourably upon him wherever he is now. We don't have an Abbess.'

'But we do have a clue at last,' said Tansy, who had brightened up considerably. 'On the same ground where the fifth was found. We found the fifth pearl in Great Hall. Come on!'

Friar Higgle and Auma were carrying things out to the shore of the Abbey pond. Halfway across Great Hall, laden with firewood and sweet herbs, they stopped at the sight of the three friends standing in the middle of the large chamber, looking about.

'Hi there, what are you searching for, more clues?' Auma called.

Craklyn explained about Tansy's dream to the badger Mother, and Auma found herself looking around, at the ceiling, walls and floor. 'We must never ignore anything Martin tells us,' she said, 'but what are you hoping to find here?'

Rollo held up the scrap of parchment for her to see. 'A purple arrowhead, that's what it says here.'

Friar Higgle took the parchment. 'Let me see that. Aye, yore right, a purple arrow'ead, but you got to look for it when Redwallers lie abed, at midnight by the light o' the full moon. So till then you may's well do somethin' useful, 'elp us to set up supper on the pond edge. Lucky fer you there is a full moon t'night. Supper's allus good fun on a summer night by the pond when 'tis moonlit.'

Gurrbowl, Diggum and Arven were in the kitchens, loading up a procession of Redwallers with food to take out to the pond's edge. Diggum made sure Tansy was well laden.

'Yurr, marm, ee be a gurt strongbeast, you'm be taken this cheese an' yon breads, cummon, 'old out ee paws!'

'I can't!' Tansy protested vigorously. 'I'm already carrying a meadowcream trifle, a pear flan and a stack of mint wafers, any more and I'll drop something.'

The molebabe stared severely at Tansy and balanced

a loaf on her head. 'Thurr, doan't run now an' coom straight back yurr, oi've lots more for ee t'carry, hurr aye!'

Tansy hid a smile from the bossy molebabe. 'A slavedriver, that's what you are, Diggum.'

Arven prodded her none too gently. 'Keep a movin' y'likkle maggit, you 'oldin' up d'line!'

Tansy tottered, trying to keep her load balanced. 'Yowch! You fiendish infant, what's that you're prodding me with?'

Arven waggled the implement under her nose threateningly. 'It my whip, now keepa goin' or y'get more prodders!'

Hurriedly Tansy unloaded her burdens onto a table and made a grab at Arven's whip. 'That's Fermald's old fishing rod. The *rod*!'

Rollo let go of a heavy cheese he was rolling; it trundled off alone across the kitchen floor. 'What rod?'

Tansy showed it to him proudly. 'This rod, Fermald's old favourite. Think of the rhyme, travel east, six rods from the tip. When we do have to travel east I'll wager this is the rod we measure off with!'

The Recorder of Redwall chased off after his cheese, calling, 'Well done, miss, it looks like things are coming together a bit!'

Firelight and full moon reflected in the waters of Redwall Abbey pond. Every creature sat upon the sandy bank, leaving the food untouched until Auma had finished speaking.

'Friends, Redwallers all, let us not forget in the midst of this summer night's festivities, the names of our good Father Abbot Durral and young Viola bankvole. May the season protect them from harm wherever they may be this hour. Let us also keep in mind our Abbey Warrior, Martin. He and Clecky, with the sons of Log a Log and the otter Grath are probably out on the great waters, searching for Abbot Durral to bring him back safely home to our Abbey; and Rangapaw and her brave crew are ranging in the woods, still hunting for poor Viola. Let us wish them success in their endeavours. Strong hearts and true companions!'

Every voice echoed Auma's last words, 'Strong hearts and true companions.'

Arven flung a piece of fruit cake in the pond. 'Anna likkle supper for d'big fish who live down der!'

A silvery flash followed by a faint splash told them that the female grayling had taken the squirrelbabe's offering. The Redwallers took this as a good omen, and cheered.

Gerul sat with Skipper, Foremole and Higgle. The greedy owl grabbed the remainder of the fruit cake Arven had broken to feed the fish, saying, 'Ah, now, don't be givin' any more vittles to that scaly divvil, 'twill only make it fat an' lazy. Here, Skipper, would y'pass a pore bird some o' that woodland pudden, it might do me broken wing a power o' good, so it might. Foremole, pour the October Ale, will yer, before we all die o' the drought!'

Higgle laughed at the irrepressible owl as he set his talons on a chestnut and mushroom flan. 'Hoho! Is there anythin' *I* can do for ye, sir, may'aps you'd like me to wipe yore beak in between bites?'

Gerul widened his great eyes at the Friar. 'Ah sure there's no need fer that kind o' talk, me good feller, but seein' as y'sittin' there doin' nothin', why not gerrout that hogtwanger thing o' yores an' play us a tune? As me ould mother used t'say, y'can play dead, play sick or play yer friends false, but y'better playin' a tune if y'can carry one.'

Higgle produced the curious instrument and began tuning it on his headspikes. 'I'll play if you sing. D'you know "Trees o' the Wood"?'

Clearing his beak with a draught of October Ale, Gerul nodded. ''Tis an ould ditty Clecky an' meself sang together as a trio.'

Craklyn grinned. 'The two of you must have sounded amazing as a trio. You start, sir, and I'll take the alternate line. Ready, one, two . . .'

The hogtwanger struck up and the pair sang with a will.

'Abroad I strolled in the forest one day,
I walked till me paws were sore weary,
I heard an ould mistle thrush close by me say,
"O here's to the woodland so cheery!
There's ash and beech and rowan and oak,
Weepin' willow with leaves trailin' down O,
Many rowans I've known full o' berries when
    grown,
And laburnum that wears a gold crown O.
So of all the trees growin' here in the wood,
Tell me which is the finest and best, sir,
I'll find that one ere springtime is gone,
And I'll surely build me a nice nest there.
There's cedar and elm and hornbeam and
    yew,
Sycamore buckthorn and alder so fine,
Sweet chestnut and fir and shrub elder where,
Grow dark berries on which I can dine.
Aye I'll find a stout tree for to make a safe
    nest,
Just like a good-livin' bird should,
Then me chicks will all fly and just like I,
Seek a tree for themselves in the wood!"'

There was great applause, for 'Trees o' the Wood' is a fast and difficult song, but neither the owl nor the squirrelmaid missed a note.

Then Higgle played whilst the Dibbuns got up and did a Beedance. Huge roars of laughter greeted the Abbeybabes as they buzzed about, whirring their paws and jabbing the air with stubby tails.

Sister Cicely retired early to her bed in the infirmary,

and this gave Brother Dormal the opportunity of doing his tongue-twister.

'If Sister Cicely serves some soup,
She'll surely see some sup it,
Sip that soup if you're sick,
Swig it swift sure and slick,
Should it set stiff'n'slimy, then suck it.
If Cicely suspects that such soup has been scorned,
She'll slip slyly and even the score,
So if Sister persists, woe to him who resists,
Cicely's certain to serve him some more.'

Auma held a huge paw across her mouth as she shook with laughter. Teasel upbraided Dormal playfully. 'Tut tut, Brother, 'tis just as well the good Sister went t'bed early. Let's 'ope the young 'uns don't learn yore rhyme, or they'll be recitin' it in Cicely's presence, if'n I knows Dibbuns.'

Dormal fiddled with the rope girdle of his habit, slightly chastened. 'But 'tis all in good fun, I mean the Sister no real disrespect. Besides, any Redwaller who thinks they can get their tongue around my twister will have to think again if they try!'

The perfect summer night continued happily. Wullger the otter was giving his hopskip jig when Tansy and Craklyn noticed old Rollo dozing off. They nudged him. 'Come on, Rollo, this is no time for napping, we've got work to do in Great Hall. Let's slip away quietly, shall we?'

Noiselessly the three friends padded into the Abbey's vast main chamber. It was deserted and so silent they felt obliged to converse in whispers. Whilst Rollo set flint to tinder lighting a lantern, Tansy and Craklyn gazed around. Dark shadowy niches and recesses gave way to patches of soft multicoloured light where the moon beamed through long stained glass windows. Looking up towards the high polished ceiling beams gave both Abbeymaids a feeling of insignificance in the massive hall.

Rollo had the lantern lit; in its golden glow he spread the parchment on an empty dining table. 'Now, where to begin? Have you got Fermald's fishing rod, Tansy?'

The hedgehog maid went to the tapestry, and from behind it she produced the rod. 'I put it there this afternoon – Martin's been keeping it safe for me. Read the rhyme again, Craklyn.'

The squirrelmaid did not need to read, she knew the rhyme off by heart because she had repeated it so often.

'"My sixth and last tear I give unto you" . . . by that I take it Fermald means us three, the searchers. Then, "When Redwallers lie abed". Well, in normal circumstances they'd all be in their beds now, save for the fact they're holding a moonlight feast outside. See, these next two lines, here's where the puzzle really starts. "At midnight see, in full moon view, the purple arrowhead."'

Lantern light glinted off Rollo's spectacles as he shook his head. 'There it is again, that confounded purple arrowhead. But where do we find it?'

Tansy had a sensible suggestion. 'Let's split up. I'll take one end of the hall, Craklyn, you take the other. Rollo, you can search the centre, here.'

Step by step Tansy combed the far end of Great Hall, around sandstone columns, inspecting every stick of furniture, feeling wall hangings and peering behind them, even scrambling onto low window ledges to check the sills thoroughly. Her search proved fruitless. Then the moon went behind a cloud. Tansy could see the small golden pool made by Rollo's lantern in the dimness, and she made her way towards it. The old Recorder was inspecting the east wall, unaware that the hedgehog maid was behind him. He was at the edge of a passage leading off the hall when Tansy's voice cut the silence shrilly.

'Rollo, stop where you are, don't move!'

The Recorder froze, wondering if he was in any danger. Behind him he heard Tansy calling out, 'Craklyn, come and see this!'

Leaving off her search, the squirrelmaid came scurrying up, not knowing what to expect. Tansy was pointing to the back of Rollo's robe, just below the old bankvole's neck.

'What d'you think of that?'

Craklyn gasped in surprise. Beaming faintly luminescent purple, a perfectly shaped arrowhead was formed on the Recorder's back.

Rollo could stand the suspense no longer. He turned around to face them, and demanded, 'What is it? What's all the excitement about?'

Tansy was still pointing. 'Look at the front of your robe, it's *there* now!'

Rollo stared down at the purple arrowhead of light. 'Hah! So 'tis, it must reflect on this wall when I'm not standing here, like this . . .'

He moved a pace to one side, leaving the spectral thing shining softly upon the wall. Adjusting his spectacles, Rollo stared upward to the apex of two curves at the top of a long narrow side window on the west wall, high above the tapestry.

'I thought so, it's the moonlight coming through that window, see, where it is pointed at the top like an arrowhead. The glass is reddish during the day, but in the moonlight it appears purple.'

Craklyn giggled; the whole thing struck her as rather funny. 'And you couldn't see the arrowhead because it was on your back!'

Tansy had Fermald's fishing rod ready. 'Travel east six rods from the tip, that's what the rhyme tells us. We're at the east wall, the only way we can go further east is down this passage!'

Rollo stared down the darkened passageway. 'This

only goes off to the cellars, but let us see how far six rodlengths will take us.'

He held the lantern high whilst Tansy and Craklyn measured off six lengths of the fishing rod at the same height on the wall as the arrowhead. At the end of six lengths there was a wall decoration carved in relief standing out from the stone: a single rose on a long stem rising up from the floor.

Craklyn ran her paw over it. 'There it is, pals, the rose that blooms ever fair, summer or winter. It doesn't matter what the season, this rose still stands halfway down the passage, carved from stone, blooming eternally. It'll never shrivel or lose a single petal.'

Rollo stifled a yawn. Despite the excitement he was starting to feel drowsy. 'Yes, very poetic, missie, extremely touching. Now will you be kind enough to get on with the next clue. When you've seen as many seasons as I have you'll understand the value of a bed!'

Craklyn repeated the last two lines of the rhyme. '"See if you can find the right hip, turn west and you're halfway there."'

Tansy seemed to be performing some kind of awkward dance step.

Rollo held up the lantern and peered at her curiously. 'What in the name of fur and feathers d'you think you're up to?' he said.

The hedgehog maid continued with her strange manoeuvre. 'Well, I've found my right hip and now I'm turning west, why?'

The old Recorder slid down the wall into a sitting position. 'Oh, nothing, you continue with your dance. Craklyn and I will concentrate on the carving. See, halfway up the stem is a leaf either side, and beneath each leaf is carved a rosehip . . .'

Tansy stopped her quaint movements. 'Rosehips?'

Rollo nodded. 'Aye, rosehips, you know, those round things the size of a plum, tapered at one end. You'd usually see them after the roses have bloomed and faded, we make rosehip syrup from them!'

Craklyn grasped the rosehip on the right side of the stem. 'Shall I turn it to the west and see what happens?' she asked breathlessly.

Rollo smiled wearily. 'Please do, miss!'

Craklyn turned the rosehip. It budged slightly, but nothing else happened. She turned to Tansy. 'What d'you think I should do now?'

The hedgehog maid bounded forward. 'Keep turning as hard as you can, and I'll give it a good shove!'

As Craklyn struggled to turn the stone protrusion a bit more, Tansy hurled herself at the wall. Her body struck the stone, and a portion of it began moving inward. She pushed harder; this time it made a grating noise and opened completely.

The three friends found themselves staring into a small dark room. Picking up the lantern from the floor, Craklyn entered; Tansy and Rollo followed her in. They moved together towards the room's single piece of furniture, a small angler's stool made from canvas and strips of wood. On the seat of the stool, the lantern light revealed a tiny box made from yew wood.

Rollo picked it up and opened it.

47

It was still dark, humid and windless. The Hawm of the sealfolk gave a quick flick of his head and tossed the rope he had been pulling back into the logboat. Martin and his crew had been standing ready for hours, since the first glimpse of Sampetra loomed upon the night horizon.

Clecky leapt overboard into the shallows. 'So this is the place, eh,' he said, his voice booming from the high hills surrounding them. 'Jolly good work, you sealchaps!'

Martin was alongside him swiftly, his paw clamping tight over the hare's mouth. 'Keep your voice down! No need to advertise our arrival!'

Inbar Trueflight held a brief conversation with the seal king before joining Grath and Martin on the sandy beach of a small cove where they had landed. 'The Hawm can no longer help us now. He is worried about the young ones of his tribe being in these waters; they are leaving.'

Martin bowed, clapping his paws gently at the seal king. 'Gittarra, Haaaaaaawm! Manyahooday!'

Blinking his dark round eyes, the seal king snuffled gently. 'Manyahooday, Haaaaaaaaawm Ma'tan!'

There was a quick flurry of water and the sealfolk disappeared into the nightdarkened seas.

Standing on the hilltop overlooking the cove, Martin issued instructions to his crew.

'There's still a few hours left until dawn; we'd better take a look around. I think we've landed on the east side of this island, so we'll meet back here at noon. Inbar, Grath, you take Viola with you, travel northwest and see what you can find. Clecky, Plogg, Welko, come with me, we'll travel southwest. I've no need to tell you all to be careful, travel silent and stay low. Make your way back here by following the coastline. That way we'll have covered most of the island between us. Any questions?'

'Ahem, er, what time's food at, old scout?'

Martin shook his head in bewilderment at the irrepressible hare. 'Clecky, stop thinking of how to keep your stomach full and give a little thought to keeping your skin in one piece.'

The hare saluted smartly, dipping both ears. 'Forget jolly old tum, keep skin in one piece. Gotcha, sah!'

They split off into two groups and set off across the island.

Ublaz Mad Eyes was worried. His hopes of getting reinforcements on *Waveworm*'s return were dashed. All his force consisted of now was less than threescore Monitors, since random sniping from the Wave Brethren had accounted for several lizards who had been slain by arrows and spears. The time for talking was gone – there would be no further communication with Rasconza, no more double-dealing. It was war to the finish, and now Ublaz was under siege, a virtual prisoner in his own palace.

Ublaz strode across his throne room to the corner where he had chained the Abbot and watched him. Durral tugged feebly at the manacled chain that hung from a ring in the wall. He was lying on a bed of rushes, a bowl of water and a piece of dried fish nearby. Still delirious, the old mouse rambled on, half conscious and unaware of both his surroundings and the pine marten who stood over him.

'Wullger, will you help me and Brother Dormal? All this fruit has to be gathered in before winter, and it's frosty already, I can feel the cold. Let go of my footpaw, little one, we must harvest all that good fruit from our orchard before it perishes.' He continued tugging at the chain that held his footpaw.

Ublaz turned callously away, and went to lean on the window sill.

'Less than threescore lizards and a crazy old mouse,' he muttered to himself, 'one ship and not a searat under my command. Oh, Rasconza, fox, give me time to think and I will dance upon your grave!'

Striding regally over to a burnished metal mirror plate set in the wall, Ublaz stared at his reflection. The strange eyes narrowed and widened alternately as his voice rose shrilly.

'I am Lord of the Oceans, Emperor of Sampetra, I, Ublaz! If I had the Tears of all Oceans now, they would be set in my crown, all six of them, wondrous rose-coloured pearls! I would don my green silk mantle, or maybe the black one with gold trim. Then I would walk out among those tavern rats, those wavescum! I would stare at them, snare them with my gaze! Then they would bow to me, salute me, because they would know who I am. Ublaz!'

The Emperor's current Monitor General, Zurgat, entered the throne room.

'Mightinezz, they are gathering for another attack on the wallz. Do we uze the balez of fire to throw down on them?'

Ublaz paced up and down in front of the impassive lizard. 'Attacking again, eh? No, don't use the fire bales yet. Throw stones down on them, and tell your Monitors to use their long spears.'

Zurgat flickered her long dark tongue in and out, her eyes straying to the shackled Abbot. 'We cannot hold them off for ever with zpearz and ztonez, Lord, there are too many of them.'

Ublaz grabbed the Abbot's water bowl and flung it at Zurgat. 'You'll hold them off as long as I say you will!' he shouted, his voice hoarse with rage. 'Insolent reptile, without my palace walls to keep you and your lizards safe you would all be fishbait by now. Get out. Out!'

Camped in the foothills at the edge of the sunny plain, Rasconza was completely at ease. A sail canvas afforded him shade, fruit abounded on the island, and fish, like the birds of the air, were plentiful. He sat with his captains, watching the latest assault on the palace rear walls.

Deddgutt the ferret captain dipped his breaker in a cask of seaweed grog, which had been plundered from the deserted taverns lining the harbour. He filled a second beaker for Rasconza. 'Wet yer whistle with that, matey, 'tis goin' t'be a long 'ot day.'

Sipping the grog, Rasconza winked roguishly at his captains. 'Well, we got all the time we like, ain't we, mates?'

Buckla flung away a half-eaten fish, chuckling wickedly. 'Aye, an' we don't 'ave nowheres special t'go, do we? Haharrharr!'

Groojaw the stoat captain pointed a rusty cutlass at the high walls in front of them. 'Noplace 'ceptin' the palace. Wouldn't ye think ole Mad Eyes'd come out an' welcome us? 'Tain't good manners to h'ignore the guests when ye've got company. Hohoho!' ·

Laughing heartily, the Wave Brethren commanders watched their fighters harassing the hard-pushed Monitors. Searats and corsairs would strike suddenly, raining arrows, spears and slingstones on the lizards. When the Monitors grouped at that point to retaliate, the wavescum would drop back, regroup and attack in a different place. Relying only on their long spears and rock rubble to tip down on the foebeast, the great lizards were hard pressed.

Guja the steersrat and a score of others stayed in the middle distance, well out of rock and spear range, and constantly sniped with arrows at the frustrated Monitors. The traitor Sagitar and her Trident-rats kept watch from the low hills to the south side of the walls. They scouted the palace from a vantage point, reporting any undue movement or fresh tactic back to the captains.

Rasconza was a good and wily leader; his strategy was working well. Idly he turned to Deddgutt. 'They've 'ad enough fer now, mate,' he said, indicating the group who were attacking the wall. 'Call 'em off. I'll send another gang at 'em tonight, that'll keep those lizards up on their paws an' stop 'em gettin' any sleep. Once we've taken that back wall they'll retreat inside the palace. That's when the battle will get fierce an' bloody, but they'll be well worn down by then.'

Deddgutt saluted and trotted off to carry out the instruction.

Baltur and Gancho drew close to Rasconza's side. 'Can we 'ave first crack at the timber piled be'ind the wall, Cap'n? That wood is worth its weight in gold!'

The fox threw his paws about their shoulders. 'Harr, don't you fret, messmates, there'll be timber enough fer everybeast. Sagitar sez there's enough wood piled back o' that wall to build three ships.'

Baltur's eyes shone longingly. 'Never mind buildin' three ships, we'll 'ave enough timber to repair our own vessels, then we'll be a proper fleet agin. Corsairs an' searats, with their own island an' their own fleet!'

Rasconza laughed, hugging both beasts tight. 'Haharrharr! I tole yer t'stick with me, mates . . . Ahoy, wot's that? Who's messin' about back there?'

Clecky had stolen up on the camp from behind. Lying on the slope of a sandy dune, he had heard all that went on between the fox and his captains. But the loose sand

336

had shifted and, unable to stop himself, the hare had rolled down the slope and landed against the back of the canvas awning with a bump.

Immediately he heard Rasconza calling, Clecky decided it was not a good place to be. Thinking quickly, the long-legged hare lashed out several times with his strong footpaws, knocking the canvas sunshade down on top of the corsairs. Then he scrambled upright, dug in his paws and took off east, with shouts ringing in his ears as Rasconza and his captains threw aside the fallen awning.

'Ahoy, mates, 'tis a big rabbit – get 'im!'

Clecky paused indignantly on the hilltop for a fleeting moment. 'Big rabbit? Cheeky blighter, must need his bally eyes seein' to, big rabbit indeed. Hah! If you weren't a fox I'd say y'were a frog's uncle, sir, wot?'

An arrow hissed into the sand close by. Clecky took off.

Groojaw and six others gave chase, panting to each other as they toiled uphill.

'I never knew there was rabbits 'ereabouts?'

'Me neither, mate. Look at 'im go, 'e kin run all right!'

'I 'opes that rabbit's got plenty o' family an' friends, rabbits is good eatin', I'm partial t'roasted rabbit!'

Clecky was not especially bothered by the pursuers, who were slow and clumsy. He led them a merry dance over plain and hill, knowing that he was leading them away from Martin, Plogg and Welko, who had circled down to the harbour area.

Puffing and panting, the exhausted Wave Brethren pressed on doggedly after the strange beast. Groojaw held his aching side. 'Ahoy, mates, 'old up, where's the lop-eared swab gone?'

Completely out of breath, they halted, looking about them.

Clecky popped up a short distance away. 'I say,

mind who you call a lop-eared swab, you carrot-nosed bilgeswiller. Come on, chaps, keep up, no laggin' behind, wot!'

A searat flung his sword, hoping to stick Clecky. It fell on empty ground, and the hare had vanished again. He emerged a moment later, off to the left of the hunting party.

'You there, baggybelly, I'll bet your dear old mum'n'dad wouldn't be too proud of you, chuckin' your sword about like that!' He disappeared once more.

Groojaw wiped his slavering mouth. 'Where in the name o' blood'n'plunder 'as that rabbit gone?'

Clecky materialized, this time to their right, and pointed an ear sternly at Groojaw. 'I say, watch your language, sir, there might be maidens or young 'uns of a tender disposition in the area. Too much grog an' not enough healthy exercise an' clean livin', that's your problem. Right, come on, chaps, off we jolly well go again!'

Pawsore and panting, but thoroughly enraged, they chased after their elusive quarry. At one point Clecky appeared right in the middle of the group, running along with them. He tapped a searat on the back and issued instructions to him.

'You're running all wrong, old lad, more thrust on the backpaw and don't flail the tail about so much, keep it well tucked in. That's the style, well done, wot, two points to this feller!'

Dropping to the back of the group, he clipped another searat smartly across both ears. 'Come on, laddie buck, keep up, no slackin' now. Hup two three, hup two three, hup, hup, hup, that's the ticket!'

Vanishing, appearing, dodging, ducking and weaving, Clecky peppered the fuming Wave Brethren with alternate insults and advice as he led them where he pleased.

48

High noon sun beat down on the weathered planks of the jetty. The harbour of Sampetra lay silent and shimmering under a blue tropical sky. Flanked by Plogg and Welko with their shrew rapiers drawn, Martin unslung his sword and hurried across the strand to where the ship bobbed calmly on a lazily swelling tide. Checking left and right and turning often to stare back at the palace upon the escarpment, the three friends made their way into the shallows.

'This is the ship,' said the Warriormouse, keeping his voice low. 'I remember its name, *Waveworm*. Either the Abbot is aboard here or somewhere on this island, probably in that big building up on the rock. Stay here and keep watch, I'm going aboard to take a look around.'

Gripping the sword blade between his teeth, Martin began hauling himself paw over paw up a headrope hanging from the for'ard peak. Waist-deep in warm shallow seawater, the shrews waited. Plogg held up a paw to his ear, leaning inland.

'Listen, can you hear anything?'

Welko waded closer inshore, cocking his head. 'Aye, sounds like shouting or fighting, I think maybe 'tis comin' from somewheres round that big buildin' up there.'

Faintly the noise of warfare drifted on the still air. Plogg looked at Welko and shrugged. 'Hmm, somebeast's havin' a tussle, that's plain.'

'Hi, you two, come aboard, the ship's empty!'

Martin threw an extra ropeline over the side so the brothers could board more quickly. Sheathing their rapiers, they clambered onto the *Waveworm*.

Plogg pointed over to the palace. 'Seems to be a bit o' trouble over that way, Martin.'

The Warriormouse studied the palace a moment, then leapt into sudden action. 'Aye, and there's a bit o' trouble headed this way! Grab some of them long poles there, you two, we're about to steal a ship and sail off. Hurry, there's no time to lose!'

Ublaz had watched Martin and the two shrews from his throne room window, puzzled by the appearance of strangebeasts upon his island, but not for long. When he saw them climb aboard *Waveworm*, the Emperor quickly summoned four Monitors. Ublaz had been keeping *Waveworm* as a standby, in the event that he had to leave the island in a hurry. Now, in danger of losing his vessel, he dashed down to the main door with the four lizards scurrying in his wake. They were just out of the door when the mouse who carried a great sword happened to look up and see them.

With Martin punting his long pole hard on the for'ard starboard and the shrews doing the same on the portside at *Waveworm*'s after end, the ship began swinging round to face seaward. Martin joined his friends at the stern end, noting that the tiller was lashed, holding the vessel to head straight out. Between the three of them they poled furiously, watching the land slip away as she caught the gentle swell.

'Well done, mates,' Martin gasped. 'See if you can loose some sail to catch the breeze further out. Good job I looked up and noticed those creatures, or they'd have boarded and taken us by surprise.'

Ublaz dashed along the jetty. Shaking with rage he stood wordlessly, watching *Waveworm* coast by, safely out of his reach. At that moment the pine marten would have given anything for a bow and arrows. He glared at the mouse, a strange-looking creature, stern and solid, and obviously a warrior by the splendid blade he carried. Silently the mouse stared back at him, not the least bit afraid of the mad-eyed Emperor. The four Monitors stood watching dumbly as canvas billowed out and the sails caught the breeze.

Then something happened to the pine marten which had never occurred in all his seasons. He found that his hypnotic power had no effect on the mouse. Piercingly, wildly, he glared at the stranger, but the warrior never budged a fraction, just remained leaning coolly over the rail, staring back, matching Ublaz eye to eye until his adversary was forced to look away. However, Martin kept watching the receding figure of his enemy, knowing that this was the beast he would have to reckon with.

Evening shades were falling fast over the small cove on the east of Sampetra. Grath and Inbar were resting on the grassy slope when Viola came and shook them. 'There's a ship coming this way. Look!'

Welko waved to them from the forepeak of *Waveworm*. 'Ahoy, mateys, d'you like our new ship? No more logboats fer us!'

Grath took the heaving line which Plogg threw to her and made it fast to a rock. Martin and the shrews waded ashore, Martin calling to Inbar, 'Is Clecky back yet? We lost touch with him over the other side of the island – he probably found something to eat.'

'Don't you worry about mister Clecky,' Viola giggled, 'he can take care of himself.'

There were still plenty of provisions left in the logboat,

so as night fell Viola and the two shrews lit a fire whilst Martin and Inbar began preparing a meal. Immediately a vegetable stew began to simmer, a jovial voice hailed them from the darkness.

'What ho, the jolly old camp! Rovin' fighter returnin' with tales of derring do, high adventure an' all that nonsense, wot!'

The friends burst out laughing, and Viola called back, 'I had an idea you'd arrive as soon as supper was ready, you great furry foodbag. Where've you been?'

Clecky ventured into the firelight, pulling behind him a searat tied up with his own belt. 'Evenin', chaps. I say, that smells rather nice. By the by, I don't suppose you've met this vile felon, captive o' mine, says his name's Gowja. Say hello to the nice creatures, Gowja.'

The searat, who sported an enormous lump on his head, stood glaring at them. Clecky pushed him so he fell into a sitting position.

'Old Gowja's the strong silent type, doncha know. Come on, you jolly old sulker, no hard feelin's, wot? Say hello to the chaps, don't sit there like a lovelorn limpet, speak up!'

Martin ladled stew into a deep shell and passed it to Clecky. 'Leave him for the moment. Let's have supper in peace. Later on he can talk. There's a lot of information we need about this island, the big building I saw today, and what both sides are fighting about. I'm sure Gowja can tell us that.'

Baring his yellowed teeth, the searat spat on the ground. 'I ain't talkin' to nobeast an' you can't make me!'

With startling speed, Grath leapt over the fire, and landed in a crouch facing Gowja, and fixed him, eye to eye. Her voice was dangerous, like the growl of thunder on a far horizon.

'Keep lookin' at me, scum, an' don't dare blink! I am Grath Longfletch of Holt Lutra, the only one of my

342

tribe left alive after yore kind visited my home. When I've eaten me vittles you'll talk t'me, in fact I'll wager you'll make a babblin' brook seem dumb by the time I'm finished with you!'

Wide-eyed with fright, Gowja whined fearfully to Martin, 'I'll talk to yer, I'll tell everythin' you needs t'know, but keep this otter away from me, I beg yer, please!'

The searat winced as Clecky patted the bump on his head. 'That's the ticket, me heartie, we'll even let y'sing us an 'orrible pirate ditty if you behave nicely, wot!'

While they ate supper, Inbar told Martin of what Grath, Viola and himself had discovered that day.

'We ranged as far as the northwest coast an' found a steep cove, much bigger'n this one. Six vessels were berthed there, big ships, each one about the size of the craft you captured, Martin. There were about five or six vermin guarding them – we figured that there must be lots more on this isle to crew the ships, though.'

Clecky tore off a hunk of barleybread from a big flat loaf. 'Oh, I found those blighters, there's a great crowd of 'em, pastin' the blue blazes out o' a pack of those lizard types who seem t'be defendin' the back walls of the palace. I overheard 'em sayin' it belongs to a chap called Mad Eyes. Anyhow, the jolly old vermin want the palace, and the timber stacked behind the back wall, to repair their ships, but Mad Eyes isn't too keen on lettin' 'em have either – the blighter's keepin' tight hold o' both, like a squirrelbabe holdin' on to a candied chestnut.'

Martin contributed his intelligence to the hare's. 'Aye, I've seen that palace from the front; there's a harbour with a jetty there. Saw Mad Eyes too, in fact we saw each other. I'm pretty certain that he's holding Abbot Durral prisoner in that palace. I'll get all the information I can out of the searat and then we'll have a better idea of a rescue plan.'

Whilst Martin questioned the prisoner, his friends sat

around the fire in the still tropic night. Viola lay on her back, gazing up at the velvety vault of dark skies, scattered with countless stars and a half-moon. The volemaid marvelled at the sight of random comets, trailing fiery tails across the wide infinity in brief glory.

Inbar and Grath moved away from the roisterous snores of Clecky and the two shrews. The son of Wallyum watched *Waveworm* tilt into a slight list as the ebbing tide allowed her keel to rest in the shallows, and said, 'Never have I seen such hatred on any face as I saw when you faced that searat this evening, Grath.'

The powerful otter glanced sideways at her friend. 'And I never told you my story. When I was huntin' alone I formed the whole of my tale into a poem, because I don't ever want to forget, nor want the otter people to. Would you like to hear it?'

Inbar nodded. 'I'd be honoured if you'd say it for me.'

Grath's voice rose and fell, sometimes quivering, often ringing like a brazen bell, as she recited the verses. The words burned themselves into Inbar's memory.

'Sad winds sweep the shores,
Near a place called Holt Lutra,
Where first I saw daylight the day I was born,
And the lone seabirds call,
O'er the grave of them all,
Whilst my tears mingle into the seas as I mourn.
For those Tears of all Oceans,
Six pearls like pink rosebuds,
Once plucked from the waters beneath the
    deep main,
Oh my father and mother,
Dear sisters and brothers,
In the grey light of dawn all my family were slain.
They sailed in by nightdark,
Those cold heartless vermin,

Their pity as scant as the midwinter's breath,
Then laughing and jeering,
As slashing and spearing,
My kinfolk were slaughtered by wavescum to death.
But their greatest mistake was,
They left Lutra's daughter,
I swore then an oath that the seasons would show,
My green arrows flying,
And sea vermin dying,
Cursing with their last breath the swift song of
my bow.
So vengeance will drive me,
As long as my paw's strong,
To sharpen a shaft and my bowstring to stretch.
The price vermin paid,
For six pearls from a raid,
Is that death bears the same name as I, Grath
Longfletch.'

Inbar Trueflight turned slowly to look at his companion. 'That is a tragic an' terrible tale, Grath. I see now how close to death that searat came when you spoke to him.'

Grath plucked an arrow from her quiver and sighted down its shaft, testing it for straightness. 'Since I laid my family to rest an' went rovin', many corsairs an' searats have fallen to these arrows o' mine.'

Her friend shook his huge head in wonderment. 'I've never known killin' or war. Ruddaring Isle is a place touched only by good order an' peace. You've seen my archery skills, I'm a deadshot with bow an' arrow, but never did I aim at a livin' thing.'

Ramming the arrow back into its quiver, Grath stood upright. 'I was the same till the wavescum came to our holt on the far north shore, but I've learned different, mate. Any creature holdin' out the paw of peace to searats or corsairs will get it chopped off by a sword.

That's the lesson I've been taught, an' you'll learn the same soon, so get used to it. I'm goin' t'sleep now.'

Turning on her footpaw she stalked off to her place by the fire. Inbar remained seated, staring at his wide, powerful paws. His father had told him that the outside world was a different place; he was not sure he was going to like the difference.

Clecky opened one eye. In the soft dawn light he found himself staring at a brightly hued beetle perched upon his nose. With a twitch and a puff of breath from the side of his mouth, he dislodged the insect, blinking disdainfully at it as it trundled off through the sand and grass.

'Cheeky-faced object, go an' perch on some otherbeast's hooter! No blinkin' respect, that's the trouble with beetles ... I say, do I smell brekkers? Jolly good show, you chaps!'

Plogg, Welko and Viola had been up and about since the crack of dawn. They had rekindled the fire and made a meal. Clecky sat up, waggling his ears in anticipation as Viola served him.

'Hot shrewcakes, honey, fruit salad and melon juice,' she said. 'We thought you deserved a break from cooking. Anyhow, you always cook too much so that you can have three helpings.'

. Grath was sitting between Martin and Inbar having breakfast. Suddenly she jumped up, looking left and right, reaching for her bow.

'Where's the searat? He must've escaped.'

Welko allayed her fears quickly. 'Ole Gowja's safe, marm, don't you fret. Me'n Plogg couldn't stand lookin' at 'is ugly mis'rable mug, so we took 'im down aboard the ship an' secured 'im all snug'n'tight with a fetter an' chain stapled to the mainmast, even gave 'im vittles too.'

Martin smiled and winked at the shrew. 'Well done, 'tis poetic justice really. I'll wager that was the same chain they used to keep the Abbot prisoner on the voyage.'

After breakfast Martin called them all to a council of war. Drawing on the sandy ground with his swordpoint, he illustrated a plan he had formed.

'Right, here *we* are, and here's the palace which is under attack. Now, I'm certain Abbot Durral is somewhere in that building and it's our job to free him and get away from this island, so here's what I propose. If we're to get into the palace we must create a diversion so we're not overrun by lizards or whatever beasts are up there. Listen carefully, you all have a vital part to play in this scheme, and it's highly dangerous and we run a great risk of losing our lives. Anybeast who feels they cannot take part in my plan speak now, I'll understand.'

Viola answered for them all.

'We came here to free our Father Abbot and take him home to Redwall. If our enemies were ten times the number they are now we would never back down, never! Tell us your plan, Martin sir, everybeast here is with you to the death!'

Tropical morning sunlight beat down on the cove where *Waveworm* lay, east of Sampetra. Martin's great sword slashed paths and patterns in the earth as his crew sat listening to the daring idea unfold. Stirred by the excitement of it all, Plogg drew his short rapier, glaring resolutely towards the west coast of the island.

'Aye, 'tis perilous, that's sure. But if I live through this 'un, it'll make a great tale to tell around the fire on a winter's night to me grandshrews in the seasons t'come, matey!'

49

Rollo emptied the contents of the little yew box out onto the seat of the angler's stool; Craklyn held the lantern close so they could see clearly in the darkened chamber. Dry and crisp, light as thistledown after its long sojourn in the box, the dried carcass of a bee lay on the stool.

Tansy stared at it, her voice shrill with disappointment. 'A dead bee, is that all?'

The old Recorder peered into the box, blew into it and poked a claw about inside. 'Well, there's nothing else in here, but I expected something like this. Tell me the end of the poem again, Craklyn.'

The squirrelmaid thought for a moment then recalled the lines. '"See if you can find the right hip, turn west and you're halfway there."'

Picking up the dead bee, Rollo seated himself on the stool. 'Halfway there! I knew it. Fermald the Ancient isn't giving up the last pearl so lightly to us. This pitiful dead thing is only half the clue. We've solved the first part by getting this far, and an old dead bee is the second part. When we've found what it means the last pearl will be ours.'

Tansy almost danced with irritation. 'But there's nothing with it, no parchment or poem, nothing except a silly

348

old thing that was once a bee, though goodness knows how many seasons ago!'

As they walked back into Great Hall, Craklyn had an idea. 'Maybe it's something beginning with the letter B?'

Rollo gazed around the moonshadowed hall and yawned. 'How about bed, that begins with B. I'm tired.'

Tansy took the dead insect from him. 'Oh, that's brilliant, sir,' she said, her voice echoing angrily. 'Brilliant begins with B too, and breakfast and bath and badger and . . . and . . .'

Craklyn took hold of Tansy's paw gently. 'And bad-tempered beast. Rollo's right, it's late and we're all tired. Come on, pal, time you were in bed. We'll see if we can sort this thing out tomorrow.'

Shamefacedly, Tansy passed the dead bee back to Rollo. 'I'm sorry, sir, it's not your fault we only found a bee. Forgive me!'

The old Recorder leaned heavily against her, chuckling. 'I'm not bothered by bees, but ready to do battle with blankets, my friend. Carry me upstairs!'

Tansy shook him off playfully. 'You're getting far too old to go upstairs, we'll have to get Furlo Stump to make you a little barrel bed down here!'

With surprising agility for one of his seasons, Rollo hitched up his robe and scampered off up the stairs, cackling, 'Too old, am I? Well, last one up is a frazzled frog, heeheehee!'

Three hours after dawn the next morning birdsong echoed from the Abbey's inner walls, white clouds flecked a cheery blue sky and the treetops of Mossflower Wood rippled in a light fragrant breeze. Tansy was still asleep in her bed when she was set upon and attacked by Dibbuns.

'Cummon, missie, waykee h'up, gurt pudden'ead, still asleepen, hurr!'

Struggling awake, she tried to fight back, but Arven buffeted her soundly with a pillow.

'Tansy pansy toogle doo! Sleep alla day an' y'get no brekfiss!'

Kicking off two molebabes who were tickling her footpaws, the hedgehog maid succeeded in capturing Arven and rolling him in a blanket. 'Leave me alone, you little maggot, I was up very late last night and I need my sleep, now go on, be off with you!'

Diggum waved her digging claws under Tansy's nose. 'Hurr, ee must git out o' ee bed roight naow, or Froir 'iggle says ee give'n yurr brekfiss to ee gurt owlyburd, so thurr!'

Tansy leapt out, dashing water from a basin onto her face and wiping it with a towel. 'No breakfast of mine is going to be scoffed by Gerul the Glutton! Out of my way, I need food!'

Chuckling and giggling uproariously, the Dibbuns pursued her downstairs, to where Rollo and Craklyn sat, halfway through their morning meal. Craklyn indicated a seat. 'Over here, Tansy, there's oatbread, raspberry preserve, strawberry cordial too, I know that's your favourite breakfast.'

Tansy sat down between her friends, panting. 'The Dibbuns said Friar Higgle was going to give my breakfast to Gerul, so I got down as fast as I could.'

Arven vaulted onto the tabletop, pointing at Craklyn. 'She tol' us t'say dat, Friar never said noffink!'

Craklyn ducked as Tansy's wooden spoon narrowly missed her. 'Well, we had to get you out of bed somehow, or you'd have snored until supper!'

Tansy spread raspberry preserve on a warm oatcake. 'Well, Rollo, any more news of our dead bee? It didn't get up and fly off during the night, did it?'

The bankvole polished his glasses on the tablecloth. 'Very droll indeed, young maid. We were about to take it to one who might help us, Brother Dormal. Nobeast in Redwall has a knowledge of plants and insects like the good Brother.'

Gulping down her drink and spreading another oat-cake with preserve, Tansy quitted the table. 'Good idea! Come on – what're we waiting for?'

Dormal was out in the orchard with Gerul, explaining the finer points of a redcurrant hedge to the owl as the three friends walked up.

Rollo held out the dead bee on the flat of his paw. 'Dormal, old friend, what do you make of this . . . Oh dear!'

A vagrant breeze caught the featherlike beehusk and swept it up into the air. Craklyn cried out, 'Stop that bee, it shouldn't be flying, it's dead!'

They watched it being swept up almost above the height of a well-grown apple tree. Tansy dashed about on the ground, with her paws outstretched, ready to catch the bee if the wind dropped. 'If it gets lost we'll never find the sixth pearl,' she cried. 'Oh please, somebeast, do something!'

Gerul flapped his wings experimentally, did an awk-ward hopskipping run and leapt into the air, flapping. He hovered for seconds, swaying on the breeze, then spread his awesome wings and soared upwards, flapping them slowly. Below, they watched open-mouthed as the owl swept round in a great wheeling arc and expertly picked the bee out of mid-air with his beak. In a trice he was back on the grass, depositing the bee in Tansy's outstretched paw.

She smiled and shook her head. 'You feathery old fraud, your wings were supposed to be far too badly injured for you ever to fly again!'

Plucking a redcurrant from the hedge, Gerul chewed thoughtfully. 'Yore right, missie, you ain't wrong, sure an' I thought the same thing meself till just a moment ago. I didn't know I could still fly, then I saw you all so upset over losin' yer bee, and I was in the air flyin' before I could stop meself, so I was!'

Brother Dormal scratched his nose to hide a smile. 'No

doubt your old mother would have had something to say about it all, had she been here, of course.'

Gerul crammed several more redcurrants into his beak. 'Yer right, sir Brother, so she would. I remember when I was a chick fresh out o' the egg, my ould mother used t'say, you'll never fly till yer try, an if yer never try you'll never fly, so try'n'fly an' y'll find out why, it's good to try an' nice t'fly!'

Tansy shook Gerul's taloned claw energetically. 'And never a truer word was spoken! Well done, sir!'

Brother Dormal listened as they told him how they had come to find the bee. He inspected the body closely, and said, 'Hmm, 'tis just a long-dead bee, friends. How am I supposed to help you?'

Craklyn curtsied prettily, playing up to the good Brother by flattering him. 'It was me, Brother. I said, let's go and ask Brother Dormal, of all Redwallers his knowledge of plants and insects is the greatest by far. Brother Dormal is a clever and educated creature, I said.'

Dormal smiled, pleased but slightly embarrassed by the compliment. 'Ahem, thank you, young maid. Hmmm, let me think, perhaps while I'm mulling the problem over, you could stop that owl bolting all my redcurrants, or he'll make himself too heavy to fly again.'

Gerul was shooed from the orchard complaining loudly. 'Ah, faith'n'seasons, 'tis a bitter day when a pore bird tries to help friends an' they reward him by starvin' the wretched creature. An' after me wearin' me ould wings t'the bone catchin' dead bees for ye, shame on y'all. Sure I'll take meself off to the kitchens an' tell me good mate ma Teasel about it, no doubt she'll toss me a few ould candied chestnuts t'keep beak an' feathers together. Oh, 'tis a hard cruel Abbey I'm livin' in!' He ambled off doing small practice flights, followed by the three friends' laughter.

Dormal took a piece of blackberry creeper vine, wound

352

the dead bee in it so that it would not blow away again, and gave it to Craklyn.

'My thoughts on this are very simple. Everything in its place, and a place for everything. For instance, if I had a dead fish I would immediately think of the pond; a cracked egg, the nest; an empty acorn cup, the oak tree. Any object originates from somewhere, so if you present me with a dead bee, straight away one word springs to mind. Hive!'

Rollo slapped a paw hard against his own forehead. 'Of course, the hive! You make things seem so simple with your straightforward logic, Dormal. How can we ever thank you?'

The good Brother smiled shyly. 'Oh, I have a feeling you won't be thanking me yet, at least not until I have discovered which beehive your pearl is hidden in. After all, I am the Abbey beekeeper, an unofficial title which I share with our cellarhog Furlo Stump. Actually I think our friends the beefolk like Furlo the best, he has a way with them. Let's go and ask him.'

50

Furlo Stump and Foremole were in the winecellars, their tabletop a barrelhead and their seats small kegs. The sturdy cellar-keeper was always glad of company.

'Come ye in, friends, we'd be be'olden fer yore advice!'

Tansy glanced at the array of food on the barrelhead table. 'They say fair exchange is no robbery, sir, and we've come for your advice on a matter of importance.'

Foremole moved the kegs apart and placed a plank between them, making a seat for all to sit upon. 'Yurr, mates, bain't nuthin' so apportant as vittles, you 'uns 'elp us'ns furst.'

Dormal sat willingly, eyeing the food. 'Certainly, what do you want us to do?'

Furlo brought out extra plates, beakers and knives. 'We're a tastin' cheeses against drinks to go with 'em. Now, 'ere's dandelion an' burdock cordial, October Ale, strawberry fizz, elderberry wine, mint tea an' plum'n'damson cup. The cheeses are t'be matched with 'em, there's the big yellow with chestnut an' celery, a white wi' hazelnuts in it, that pale gold with chives'n'apple an' the soft cream with almonds. Any'ow there's a few others that y'know, so take a nibble an' a sip o' anythin' suits yore fancy an' give us an opinion.'

They all set about the delightful task with a will.

'Ooh! The soft cream and almond tastes lovely with strawberry fizz!'

'Hurr, thurr bain't nuthin' loik 'tober Ale an' ee gurt yeller 'un wi' chessnutters'n'cel'ry, boi 'okey thurr bain't!'

'Yes, I'm inclined to agree with you, Foremole, but this one over here, the fawn-coloured one with carrot and acorn in it, now that really goes well with mint tea. Try it.'

'I like the plum'n'damson cup with chive and apple cheese. What's that one you've got, Tansy?'

'It's a sort of solid reddy one with radish and onion in it; it tastes marvellous with a sip of dandelion and burdock cordial.'

The tasting went on at length. Ever the Recorder, Rollo had been jotting down notes on a length of bark parchment as he sipped and nibbled, taking heed of their opinions with his own choice.

When they were finished, Rollo gave the parchment to Furlo. 'I've written it all down here, friend, which cheeses are matched with each drink by popular agreement.'

Furlo Stump accepted the list gratefully. 'Thankee all, now when there's a feast I only 'ave to glance at Teasel an' my brother 'iggle's menu, an' I knows which drinks to serve. You don't know 'ow much of an 'elp this'll be to us.'

Foremole nodded his velvety head in agreement. 'Burr aye, zurrs'n'missies, 'twill save a lot o' rushen abowt oop an' daown ee stairs on our ole paws, hurr hurr!'

Furlo cleared his barreltop table. 'Now, wot service can I render you goodbeasts in return?'

Sitting in respectful silence they watched the stout hedgehog move the dead bee this way and that, peering closely at it. He made small tutting noises as he turned the object back and forth on the tabletop, shaking his head.

'This ain't one of our bees,' he said, 'we 'ave good ole honeybees at Redwall, they don't carry as much fuzz on 'em as this feller.'

Brother Dormal nodded in agreement. 'Aye, that's what I thought, Furlo. Perhaps it's a redtailed bumblebee, what d'you think?'

Furlo picked the bee up and brought it close to his eyes. 'Redtailed bumblebee, eh? Well, you could be fergiven for thinkin' that, Brother, but this'n ain't no redtail, though it looks like one. I only ever seen a few o' these in my seasons. This is a mason bee, quite a rare insect in these parts.'

Craklyn looked at the carcass questioningly. 'A mason bee, what sort of hive does that live in?'

Furlo warmed to his subject. 'Mason bees don't 'ave a hive, missie, they're solitary creatures. They'll burrow into the side of a wall, 'twixt the gaps in stones where the mortar's gone soft. Sometimes they'll do it in solid sand, like the dry side of a riverbank, though walls is mainly their favourite place. The male an' female roots out a single space, and there they leave one egg with honey an' nectar t'feed the young when it 'atches. They seal the nest with mud an' go off to build the next one.'

Rollo threw up his paws in despair. 'So we're not looking for a hive, just a crack in a wall! This is a big Abbey with lots of stonework, it could be anywhere!'

Furlo took off his work apron and patted Rollo's paw. 'Don't look so down'earted, sir. There's six of us altogether, and me'n Foremole will 'elp you look, 'tis the least we could do.'

Gerul came hopping in, picking crumbs from his feathers. 'Good day to ye, the ould Friar Higgle sez that there's some food testin' t'be done down here, so I thought I'd be brave an' volunteer me services, so I did!'

Foremole waved a digging claw at the drinks and cheeses. 'Hurr, zurr, we'm already dunn et, but thurr's ee vittles if'n ee'd loik to try.'

The owl's eyes widened with pleasure. 'Ah well, 'twill be a terrible task but I'll do me best. You goodbeasts be off about yer business now. I'll give ye the results of me labours at supper tonight, so I will.'

Grinning and winking at one another, they quit the cellars.

Tansy stood at the centre of the Abbey lawn with the search party, her eyes roving about to and fro. 'Where to begin, anybeast got a helpful suggestion?' she asked.

Foremole came up with a scheme immediately. 'Ho aye, miss, you come'n wi' Furlo an' oi, us'ns search ee walls. Miss Craklyn, ee go with Rollo an' Dormal, you 'uns lukk round ee Abbey buildin'. That ways both parties do 'ave one young set o' eyes to 'elp.'

It was a good suggestion. The two parties went off to their allotted places and began searching.

Afternoon shades were lengthening towards evening when Rollo sat down against the east Abbey wall and polished his spectacles wearily. 'My old eyes are dizzy from looking. Searching for a mason bee nest may sound simple, but it's definitely not!'

Tansy and her party were halfway round the west wall, having just passed the gatehouse, working towards the south wall, and they were becoming equally dispirited. Sitting on the steps by the gatehouse, they took a brief rest. The hedgehog maid glanced up to see Sister Cicely approaching with a stern face, and said, 'Oh dear, here comes trouble. I wonder what the Sister wants?'

Folding her paws into her habit sleeves, Cicely pursed her lips and tapped her footpaw, the picture of righteous anxiety. 'It's those three Dibbuns again, missing! Take my word, 'tis not the seasons greying my fur or ageing my bones, it's that villain Arven and those two molebabes who follow him anywhere!'

Tansy tried hard to keep her patience with the pernickety mouse. 'I'm sure they've not gone far, Sister,' she reassured Cicely firmly. 'We're very busy here with a most important task, but if we see them I'll let you know right away.'

Cicely stood for a moment, gnawing her bottom lip, then she turned abruptly and swept off, muttering, 'If I find them in the usual state, smocks torn, filthy and dirty, scratched and bruised, they'd better watch out!'

Furlo pulled a face at Tansy and winked. 'That 'un's a good ole mouse in lots o' ways, but 'er temper don't improve with age. I wouldn't like to be those Dibbuns when she finds 'em, miss.'

Tansy watched Sister Cicely flounce into the Abbey. 'I agree with you, sir. Sometimes I think her main purpose in life is chasing after Arven and the molebabes, though half the time they're not missing, just playing somewhere. Matter of fact I know where they are right now, though I didn't tell the Sister because she'd only send 'em off t'bed early.'

Foremole chuckled, his small round eyes twinkling. 'Whurr do ee liddle rarscals be, missie?'

Tansy nodded in the direction of the east wall corner. 'Over there behind the bushes. They've been hiding there all afternoon, I can see the bushes shaking from here. Come on, let's take a walk across and see what they're up to.'

Arven, Diggum and Gurrbowl were prancing about in a den they had built among the bushes. They squeaked in dismay as Furlo Stump's strong spiked head poked through into their lair.

The kindly hedgehog grinned at the Abbeybabes. 'Now then, y'liddle maggots, what're you doin' in 'ere?'

Arven held a tiny paw to his lips and whispered furtively, 'Us 'idin' from Sissy Sissly an' dancin' bees dances, don' you tell 'er or she choppa tails off us!'

Tansy and Foremole joined the Dibbuns, and they all sat down together in the cool green shade. Tansy narrowed her eyes at Arven fiercely, but he knew she was only joking.

'Tansy pansy, we do's a bees dance for you,' he said.

Trying hard not to burst out laughing, the searchers watched the three Dibbuns go into their dance, whirring their paws and weaving circles about each other, stopping now and then to stab the air with their tails as they made bee noises.

'Fzz bzz bizzy buzz, fzz bzz fzzz buzz!'

Gurrbowl and Diggum buzzed on either side of Arven, who had appointed himself chief bee. They held the bushes aside and he danced his way in between them, fuzzing and buzzing comically. Then they let the bushes fall back into place and buzzed aloud as they poked at the air with stubby tails, awaiting his emergence. Suddenly Arven leapt from the bushes, all three buzzed once and bowed, and the dance was over.

Their audience applauded, and Furlo stroked Arven's head approvingly. 'Well done, mate, I thought you was real bees for a moment there. I like the way you flew back out o' yore hive.'

Arven looked pityingly at the cellar-keeper. 'Tha' notta n'ive, we norra bees wot live inna n'ive, us bees tha' live inna wall an' dig likkle 'oles.'

Furlo gave Tansy and Foremole a quick glance, and began questioning the Dibbuns.

'Bees wot live in a wall? Don't be silly, bees don't live in walls, they'd need 'ammers an' chisels to make nests!'

Arven shook a small grubby paw under Furlo's nose. 'Hah! Grayshuss me, you a bigga sillybeast, you know noffink. Us'ns know bees live inna wall, don't we, Diggums?'

The molebabe nodded her head solemnly. 'Ho yuss, zurr, they'm our frien's, ee beez give'n h'Arven a prezzink for umself, ho aye!'

Arven shot a warning glance at the molemaid. 'Garr, Diggums, you promise a say noffink to nobeast!'

Tansy leaned close to Furlo and whispered, 'Did you hear that? Diggum said that a wall bee gave Arven a present, a gift! Leave this to me, sir, I'll get the truth out of him.'

Arven waggled his tail in Tansy's face. 'Tansy pansy toogle doo, worra you been telled about whisperin', grayshuss an' dearie, bad bad manner it is!'

The hedgehog maid caught him firmly by the paw. 'Come here, my little maggot, and tell me, what is this gift the bee gave to you?'

Arven clapped both paws over his ears, closed his mouth firmly and screwed his eyes tight shut, just to let his inquisitors know that he was going to be stubbornly silent.

Foremole winked at Tansy and tried his mole logic on Gurrbowl. 'You'm loik deeper'n ever pie, zurr?'

The molebabe beamed broadly. 'Oi serpinkly doo, gurt bowls o' et oi can h'eat, zurr!'

Foremole took the little fellow's paw. 'Hurr, you'm a growen choild, oi 'spec y'can. Show us'ns ee 'ole in wall whurr bee lives, an' oi'll give ee a deeper'n ever pie bigger'n thoiself!'

With an apologetic glance at Arven, Gurrbowl took them through the bushes to the southeast wall angle and pointed to a joint between the huge red sandstone blocks, only two courses up from the ground, where the mortar had crumbled. 'Thurr be whurr our friend ee bee lives, zurr,' he said.

Furlo picked up a twig and pushed it gently into the crack. Buzzing irately, a dusty rust and brown striped wall bee emerged. Furlo blew gently upon its tail and it zipped off into the air like a pebble from a sling. Furlo probed the crack delicately with his twig, pulling forth a torn and dusty scrap of parchment. He gave it to Tansy.

Spreading the tiny fragment carefully, she read aloud,

'Your search is done, the sixth pearl found,
Perfect, rose-hued, pink and round,
Back home now in a scallop shell,
Which I hid well and good,
Tears of all Oceans, truth to tell,
Lie stained by death and blood.'

Tansy looked at Furlo. 'What do you make of that?' she said.

Tapping the wall crack with his twig, the wise hedge-hog explained. 'I c'n guess wot 'appened 'ere. The wall bee came across this 'ere 'ole by accident, so she thought she'd jus' clean it out an' use it 'erself. But first she 'ad t' get rid o' that ole pearl. An' I bet the Dibbuns were playin' 'ere jus' then, an' the bee pushed the pearl straight into Arven's paws. Be I right, Gurrbowl?'

The molebabe nodded emphatically. 'Ho aye, zurr, ee'm buzzybee gave et to h'Arven!'

Rollo, Craklyn and Brother Dormal were called from their search of the Abbey building, and everything was explained to them. Furlo, who was a great favourite with the Dibbuns, meanwhile continued the task of making Arven talk.

'Now then, me liddle mate, you kin take those paws out'n yore ears an' listen to wot I've got t'say.'

The squirrelbabe kept his ears well plugged, but opened one eye. 'A not lissenin' an' me not talkin', an' me can't see ya!'

The friendly cellar-keeper merely smiled. 'Fair enough, ole pal, you stay like that, I'll jus' chat to Diggum an' Gurrbowl 'ere about the feast in my cellars. Right, you two liddle snips, this evenin' I'll let yer stay up late. We'll play 'ide'n'seek 'midst the barrels, I'll rig up a seesaw, an' I'll roll you round an' round in a big empty barrel. Whilst we're doin' that down in my winecellars, I've no doubt miss Tansy an' 'er friends will make a fine feast an' bring it down to us. We'll 'ave a great party an' I'll supply the drinks, strawberry fizz, dandelion an' burdock an' gooseberry cup.'

Arven unplugged his ears and opened both eyes straight away. 'Worra bout Arven, me come a party too?'

Rollo polished his glasses brusquely. 'Certainly not! Any Dibbun who hides things from his friends and carries on in such a badly behaved manner deserves only one thing. Early bed and warm nettle soup!'

The squirrelbabe shot into the bushes and was out again in a flash. Dropping the pearl into Tansy's paws, he dashed about hugging and kissing everybeast.

'I norra bad Dibbun, see! Me a good frien', Arven like alla you!'

51

Grath Longfletch tapped her tail impatiently on the ground as she scanned the cove at midday. 'Great seasons o' slaughter, here we are all ready to go an' that long lollopin' hare's gone missin'. Where's 'e got to?'

'Ahoy there, you hearties, all aboard! I'm all kitted out an' ready to jolly well go an' do battle, wot!'

Viola had to sit down laughing at the sight of Clecky perched nobly on *Waveworm*'s prow.

The hare had done a thorough search of the vessel to outfit and arm himself. He had rigged himself out in a pair of baggy red pantaloons and a tawdry cream tunic fringed with blue silk ruffles. Both his long ears flopped under the weight of massive brass rings.

He carried a long piked boathook and a javelin, and into a gaudy green waistsash he had thrust a short axe, three curved daggers and a fearsome scimitar.

'All aboard the good ship *Wavethingy*, me buckoes, come on! Time an' tide wait for nobeast, doncha know!'

Martin turned to Grath. 'Have you got everything you need?' he asked.

The otter patted a pouch at her belt. 'Tinder, flint, canvas, flask o' lamp oil. That's all I'll need beside my bow and arrows. Two hours before sunset, then!'

363

Martin and Inbar clasped her paws. 'Good luck and good hunting, and fates go with you!'

Grath held tightly to Inbar's paw a moment longer. 'Remember wot I told you, matey, show no quarter to 'em. If they ever found yore father's island they'd slay yore kin an' laugh while they were slaughterin'. Keep that in mind, Inbar Trueflight!' Then, releasing her friend's paw, Grath took off southwest at a fast trot.

Martin and his friends boarded and got *Waveworm* under sail, skirting the coast northward to where the corsair ships lay.

The six wave vermin who had been left to guard the disabled fleet were ashore. Well supplied with grog and food, they lounged about on the sand near the shallows, gambling with shells for trinkets. They cheated and swilled grog, throwing the shells in the air, wagering on how many would land upside down.

'My dagger sez six on their backs, Crabsear!'

'Taken. I'll wager me bracelet agin yore blade, Kuja!'

The shells fell onto the sand; Kuja the corsair stoat crowed triumphantly at the searat Crabsear. 'Only five upside down, gimme the bracelet, I win!'

'No ye don't, 'tis six, the dagger's mine, mate!'

'Five I say, you turned that'n upside down yerself, cheat!'

'Cheat is it, yer slime-tongued eel, I'll give ye the dagger all right, straight in yore stinkin' neck!'

They were about to leap on each other when Clecky appeared, wading through the shallows around the cove's edge.

'Ahoy there, you unspeakable rabble, surrender your ships or I'll frazzle y'gizzards with me frogslicer, or whatever it is you chaps say to each other, wot!'

Exchanging wicked smiles, the six guards rose slowly, drawing their blades as they advanced on the lone hare.

'Well, stripe me, buckoes. Who in the name o' barnacles is this 'ere popinjay?'

Whipping out his scimitar, Clecky bounded forward to meet them, slaying the speaker with a single swipe of his enormous blade. 'Stripe you? Certainly, sir, anything to oblige. Next?'

They rushed him, failing to see Martin bearing down the hill at their backs with his sword ready for action.

Around the other side of the cove, Inbar heard the cries and mounted the rail, reaching for his bow. Plogg put a restraining paw on the otter.

'Best stay 'ere, friend, Martin an' Clecky'll be back shortly. There ain't no warrior in all Mossflower like Martin.'

Inbar allowed himself to be pulled down to the deck. 'But what about Clecky?' he said. 'There were six guards on those ships, I counted 'em myself!'

Plogg leaned back against the rail. 'Only six? Clecky could 'ave taken them 'imself! Don't be fooled by that'n's silly talk an' comical manner. As my ole dad always sez, hares are dangerous an' perilous beasts.'

The shrew's estimate was correct; it was but a short time until the two waded back around the cove, Clecky chatting animatedly.

'That vermin *was* cheatin', y'know, saw him m'self, he tipped a seashell wrong side up with his footpaw. What a rotter! I'd hate to have that'n sittin' alongside me at supper, he'd swipe all the salad whilst I had me back turned!'

Martin washed his swordblade in the water and wiped it dry on his sleeve before sheathing it. 'Hah! When did you ever turn your back on a salad bowl? Any creature trying to steal food from you would starve to death.'

When they had both climbed back aboard, Martin gave Welko and Viola their instructions.

'Throw all the canvas, spare wood and lamp oil into the hold of each ship – the grog too, that's pretty flammable stuff. You've got flints and tinder enough to do the job. Wait until you see the signal. We'll pick you up as soon as we can get back here – one of you watch for our ship from the covetop. Good luck!'

Waveworm sailed onward, still hugging the coastline. Welko and Viola stayed with the corsair vessels, waving to their friends until they were out of sight.

Grath Longfletch had gained the highest point overlooking the palace of Ublaz. Two Trident-rats lay limp close by; they had been standing sentry there when the vengeful otter visited them, silent as a leaf on the wind. Kindling a small smokeless fire in a hole she had dug, Grath sat binding oil-soaked canvas strips to four arrowheads. She had seen the exact targets where her shafts would do their work best.

Ublaz Mad Eyes peered over the wall at the Wave Brethren's encampment. He did not like what he saw.

'Zurgat,' he rapped out, 'get the fire bales ready for tonight. I have a strong feeling they'll mount a major attack on us once it's dark. Rasconza's vermin haven't bothered sending anybeast at us for hours. Look at them – lounging about over there doing nothing.'

Zurgat turned her slow reptilian gaze upon the far encampment. 'You are right, Lord, they are zaving themzelvez for the battle tonight. Fire balez will burzt upon them in the darknezz.'

Keeping his head low, the pine marten strode the length of the woodpile stacked against the wall, stopping at each of the four large firebales to inspect them. They were heaps of splintered dry wood and dead reeds, wound about with sailcloth and withered grass, liberally doused with vegetable oil.

Ublaz chanced another peek at the enemy camp before turning to the Monitor and saying, 'When I give the order, and only then. Have your lizards lift the bales clear of my woodpile to the walltop, light them and drop them over onto the vermin. That field is as dry as tinder, the flames will race across it and engulf Rasconza's camp. If it does sufficient damage, wait again for my command.

We should be able to charge around the ashes and finish them off in the confusion that will follow. But await my orders, Zurgat.'

The Monitor bowed after her Emperor's retreating figure. 'Mightinezz, I wait your commandz!'

She called sibilantly to the other reptiles guarding the walls. 'Victory will bring uz lotz of meat . . . Roazted by the firez!'

Dark forked tongues slithered in and out as the lizards hissed wildly.

Leaning over the rail of *Waveworm*, Martin watched the sun start to dip towards the western horizon.

Inbar checked the tension of his bowstring, and said, 'Grath should be starting an uproar about now.'

A green-flighted arrow stretched its length on Grath Longfletch's bowstring; the supple yew arched back as her powerful paw pulled against the beeswaxed string. Dipping the arrowhead into the fire, she watched it burst into flame. Sighting swiftly as she brought up the bow, Grath gave an extra heave against the yew and fired.

Zzzzzzzzzsssssssssttt!

Like a burning comet the shaft sped upwards, bending in a long arc, down to the palace courtyard. It struck the first firebale, which went up with a dull whump into a blazing mass.

As soon as the first arrow was in the air Grath had another one zipping viciously from her bowstring, followed by another and yet another. The fiery messengers sped off to find their targets.

A Monitor pointed with his spear, hissing, 'The firebalez, the f—' and fell, clutching the green-flighted arrow which had slain him.

Now Grath was moving, changing position. Some arrows she sent to slay Monitors, others to lay Wave Brethren low. The pandemonium she caused was instantaneous. Ublaz came roaring into the courtyard, lashing about with a spearhaft at the terrified lizards. 'Pull those bales away, tip them over the wall, save my timber!' he yelled.

The tremendous woodpile, having lain in tropical dryness for long seasons, was going up like a bonfire. Panic-stricken lizards leapt away from the inferno and cowered back against the palace, their fearful eyes glittering in the firelight. Ublaz dashed to and fro like a madbeast, unable to get near his precious timber because of the pulsating heat of the flames.

'Do something! Fetch water! Pull away the bits that aren't burning! Get wet sailcloths and beat at the flames!'

He rushed about belabouring the dull-witted Monitors until his spearhaft broke on their thick-scaled hides.

Rasconza ducked behind his canvas awning, grabbing Buckla and Deddgutt as they passed. 'Send some o' those Trident-rats, see if they can find the swab who's firin' those green arrows afore any more crewbeasts are killed!'

Baltur and Gancho wriggled up through the sand, keeping their heads low. Gancho pointed miserably at the blaze crackling high above the rear palace wall. 'Lookit that, will yer, there goes our chance to repair the fleet!'

Rasconza did not seem unduly worried. 'Never fear, mates, as long as we got one ship that kin sail we can always bring wood to Sampetra. Pretty soon that wall's goin' to collapse under the 'eat o' that blaze. Then we'll march in there an' drag Mad Eyes out. Muster the rest o' the Brethren an' tell 'em to stand ready.'

Plogg jumped onto the jetty and secured *Waveworm* by a stern line. Martin had drifted her in backwards, so that they could cut and run at a moment's notice. Night was falling fast, the palace up on the escarpment silhouetted by the fire that raged behind it. Clecky noted that the harbour area was still deserted and silent.

Plogg watched his three friends climb down onto the jetty. 'Let me go with you, Martin, I'm good with a shrew rapier.'

Martin pointed sternly to the ship. 'Sorry, but you know your orders. Now back aboard and have her ready to take off like an arrow the moment you see us coming back.'

Crestfallen but obedient, the young Guosim shrew did as he was told.

Before Martin, Clecky and Inbar were halfway across the harbour area, Grath popped out from behind a tavern and joined them.

'All goin' accordin' to plan, mates,' she said, nodding at the fireglow, 'that little lot's keepin' 'em busy at the moment. Now for the palace!'

They raced to the double wooden door at the top of a winding hill. Clecky sized it up before commenting, 'How's a chap supposed to get inside? Looks like we're stumped!'

Martin located the centre jamb and thrust his sword through it. 'Lend a paw here, Inbar, it's only a wooden bar across these doors holding them shut. When I give the word, lift the sword up hard.'

The big otter gently ushered Martin aside and gripped the sword handle in both paws. 'Not enough room for both of us to hold this handle, let me try.' Bracing himself squarely on the stones, Inbar bent slightly; the long muscles on his sleek back stood out as he swept the swordblade up. There was a clunk from the other side and, as Inbar pushed the doors, they creaked and opened inward.

Clecky nodded in admiration. 'Good idea that, I was about to suggest it m'self, wot!'

As they passed through the portals into the silent palace, Grath murmured in Clecky's brass-ringed ear,

'Remember, we're searching for an Abbot, not a dining room!'

Ublaz finally saw that the timber was hopelessly lost. As he peered through the flames, he also noticed a sagging dip in the walltop. Soon the rear wall would start to crumble, its mortar turned to dust and its stones cracked and burst by the constant searing heat of the blaze. There was only one option left now.

'Retreat into the palace,' he called to his Monitors. 'The vermin will charge once the wall falls. Retreat and we'll hold out there.'

52

In his fevered dreams, Abbot Durral was helping to carry a table out into the orchard at Redwall Abbey. He imagined it was autumn and a harvest feast would be laid out under the trees. The old mouse rambled on deliriously.

'Lift higher, Sister Cicely, we'll never get it out over the doorstep. What a heavy table this is! Where's everybeast gone?'

A voice came through his fogged mind. 'Father Abbot, 'tis your friend Martin!'

Feebly, Durral squinted one eye open. 'Ah, Martin, but which Martin are you?'

With tears in his eyes, Martin cradled his old friend's head. 'Durral, it's me, Martin!'

Opening both eyes briefly, the Abbot smiled. 'Yes, my son, but are you the Martin from the tapestry or my Martin who lives at Redwall? I can't tell, you see.'

The Warriormouse realized how ill the old fellow was. 'I'm your friend Martin who lives at Redwall with all our Brothers and Sisters. I've come to help you, Father Abbot.'

Durral lifted a wizened paw and stroked Martin's face.

'I knew you would. This table is so heavy and Cicely is too small to lift it. Will you help us, please?'

Then Grath called urgently from the doorway she was guarding. 'Hurry and get him out o' here, mate, somebeast's comin'!'

Viola was first to spot the glow lighting the night sky from the southwest. 'There goes the signal, burn the ships!' she yelled to Welko.

The shrew already had a fire lit in a brazier aboard Barranca's former vessel, *Freebooter*. Holding five torches ready, he shouted back to Viola who was descending from the hilltop. 'Hurry up, miss, get aboard *Freebooter* with me!'

The bankvole did as she was bidden, though slightly mystified by the odd procedure. 'We shouldn't be hanging about aboard this craft,' she said. 'You've got to set fire to it. What are you up to, Welko?'

The Guosim shrew indicated the other ships. 'Those're the ones I'm goin' to burn, miss, they're ole tubs, just like *Waveworm*. But this *Freebooter*, now this's wot I call a real ship. Look at the lines o' her, the beam, draught, sails. This craft's a real flyer, nothin' in all the seas could catch the spray of 'er wake when she's in full sail, I'll wager. We'll burn the other five an' wait fer them aboard this'un. Grath knows about ships, she'll agree with me.'

Viola thrust the five torches into the brazier. 'I suppose you know best. Come on, we'll go to the last vessel in line and make our way back here, setting fire to each ship as we go.'

Inside the palace Martin rushed to the throne room door to help Grath. Backed by a score of Monitors, Ublaz was coming up the stairs. The pine marten had not expected anybeast to be inside his palace. On seeing Martin at the stairhead, waiting with drawn sword, Ublaz did a swift about turn. Pushing his way through the Monitors on the staircase, he cried, 'It's only a mouse and an otter, slay them! Charge!'

The Warriormouse knew that to conquer the palace he must first deal with its ruler. Hurling himself down the stairs he roared, 'Redwaaaaaaaalllllll!'

But Ublaz was gone and Martin found himself surrounded by lizards. With battle light blazing in his eyes and a warcry on his lips, the Warriormouse swung his mighty blade on the crowded staircase. Monitors crowded upon him, pushed forward by the momentum of those behind; teeth bared, tongues flickering, hissing viciously as they sought to bring their long spears into play. The fabled blade of Redwall whirled into them, hacking, scything and slashing through spearhafts.

Grath stood quivering at the stairhead. 'Martin, come back, I can't get a clear shot with my arrows while yore down there. Fight yore way back!'

Clecky sailed past her and went bounding down to Martin's aid.

'Eulaliaaaaaaa!'

In a flash he was back to back with the Warriormouse, and they fought their way upward together. The hare's huge scimitar matched Martin's sword, blow for blow, as they struck at scaly flesh, ripping claws, snapping teeth and baleful reptilian heads. When they came within reach, Grath and Inbar hauled them up by the backs of their tunics. Martin's eyes were glazed over with a red mist of battle fury. Inbar broke the spell by shouting into his face, 'Go and take care of your Father Abbot!'

From somewhere behind the Monitors, Ublaz could be heard bawling hoarsely, 'Charge! Rip them to bits! Charge!'

Long spears bristling, the Monitors pressed up the stairs. Grath Longfletch already had a green-plumed arrow on her bowstring. She glanced coolly at Inbar Trueflight. 'Let's see 'ow good y'are with those red-feathered shafts o' yores, mate. Ready?'

Though Inbar was frightened of the big lizards scrambling up the stairs towards them, he found himself suddenly pouring shaft after shaft into their ranks. He roared at the top of his lungs to match his companion's warshout, and their cries mingled: 'Ruddariiiiing! Holt Lutraaaaaaa!'

Clecky held up the chain that was holding the Abbot fettered to the wall. 'Confounded manacle, and we haven't even got a blinkin' key to release the poor old buffer!'

Martin, still quivering for action and in the grip of a berserk rage, gritted his teeth savagely. 'Keep your paws wide and hold that chain tighter!'

Sssshraaaakkk!

The great sword flashed once through the air, its momentum causing the steel to whine like a tornado through ice.

Clecky stared at the severed chain hanging from his paws. 'Great seasons o' fur'n'famine! You don't dally about when you swing that blade, old scout! Well done that warrior!'

Rasconza had massed his vermin at the foot of a low hill. Weapons bristled around him like a field of corn.

'Come on, buckoes,' he cried, 'let's put Mad Eyes' lights out!'

A panicked screech rang out from Gancho on the hilltop. 'Fire! Fire at the cove! Some dirty scum's settin' light to our fleet! Fire!'

Like a wave, the vermin turned and swept up the hill. They jabbered and clamoured, pointing to the blazing red glow that lit up the night sky over the northwest inlet.

'Gancho's right, 'tis fire!'

'Aye, an' it could only be the ships!'

'Right, mate, there ain't nothin' else that big to set up a light like that! 'Tis our fleet right enough!'

Rasconza hurried uphill, his heart sinking within him

at the sight. Struggling to keep calm, he tried reassuring his crews. 'No, no, 'tis only the grass, mates. I'll wager ole Crabsear an' the others 'ave gone t'sleep full o' grog an' their campfire's gone an' spread a bit. 'Tis only the grass, I tell yer!'

With drawn cutlass, Baltur faced the fox challengingly. 'Wot d'yer take us for? We ain't stupid, mate, an 'alf blind toad could see that's our ships afire o'er there!'

Buckla backed him up aggressively. 'Aye, an' without ships we ain't corsairs or searats no more. You carry on believin' yer own lies, fox, we're goin' t'save our fleet. Who's with us?'

A mighty roar of agreement went up. Before Rasconza had a chance to say another word the whole horde was off, whooping and yelling behind Baltur, Gancho and Buckla, heading overland for the northwest cove. Rasconza's voice was lost in the din as he called after them, 'Come back, y'fools, can't yer see, we've got Mad Eyes cornered! Settin' that fire was only a trick to draw us away from the palace! Come with me, we'll make the villain pay for those ships with 'is blood!'

Finding his pleas fell upon deaf ears, Rasconza turned, to find himself standing alone, except for Sagitar. He glared at her. 'Why didn't yer tell me Ublaz was plannin' this? Yore a cap'n of Trident-rats, you shoulda known.'

Seeing the vengeful expression on Rasconza's face, Sagitar backed off, shaking her head. 'I knew nought of any such plan, believe me!'

Rasconza drew his dagger, advancing angrily. 'You lie. I never shoulda trusted one o' Mad Eyes' Trident-rats. Yore a traitor an' a turncoat, Sagitar, I knows yore kind. You'd betray me the same way you did Ublaz!'

Sagitar brought up her trident, hefting it with menace. 'Keep away from me, fox, there's none more skilled with a trident than I am. I'll spit ye like a fish in a barrel!'

Rasconza turned as if to walk away. Then, spinning round with frightening suddenness, he hurled his knife.

Sagitar stared in shock at the handle of the dagger that seemed to grow from her middle. She fell to the ground.

Rasconza stood over her, chuckling. 'Haharr, you might be skilled with yon trident, but nobeast can sling a blade like me. I never miss!'

Sagitar's lips moved. Rasconza leaned down to her. 'Wot's that y'say?'

Still gripping her trident, Sagitar thrust it upward with a final effort. Gasping, she spoke her last words to the fox lying alongside her. 'I said, I never throw my weapon away. I always keep hold of it!'

But it was too late for Rasconza to hear her.

Martin tore down a velvet wall hanging and wrapped the Abbot in it. The old mouse appeared to be sleeping contentedly since the appearance of his Abbey Warrior.

Despite the rantings and shouting of Ublaz, the Monitors had retreated around the curve of the staircase, out of arrow range. Inbar found he could scarce contain himself from trembling all over now that the action had ceased. Grath patted his shoulder. 'You did well, mate, we thinned their ranks a bit.'

The big otter looked at his shaking paws. 'I'm no good at this sort o' thing. I was frightened.'

Grath was already creeping downstairs to retrieve some arrows. She turned to her huge honest friend with a grin. 'You were frightened? Matey, 'ow d'ye think I felt when I saw those flesh-eatin' monsters chargin' us? I couldn't keep me teeth from chatterin' to each other an' me paws felt like jelly. We 'ad a good right t'be frightened, I can tell yer!'

Clecky and Martin joined them at the stairhead for a council of war. The hare was not overly optimistic.

'Righto, here's the picture, chaps. These stairs are the only way up or down, and we've got to get the jolly old

Abbot out o' this palace an' aboard the *Wavethingy*. Any suggestions?'

Grath passed a bunch of arrows to Inbar. 'We don't know 'ow many more of those lizards are waitin' downstairs, an' the pine marten's still commandin' 'em. I can't see 'im lettin' us out o' this place alive.'

With a swift wrench, Martin pulled down another velvet wall hanging. 'There's one way. If we can get at Ublaz and slay him, I don't think those lizards will have any heart left to fight. There's enough of these velvet wall trappings to make a rope. If I take Clecky with me, we could reach the ground from that window, come back into the palace and attack them from behind. Grath and Inbar could charge down the stairs at them and we'd have 'em both ways. It's a risky plan, I know, we're outnumbered ten to one, but with the element of surprise on our side we could escape from here.'

Inbar had a suggestion to make. 'Can we not all escape by the window, Martin?'

The Warriormouse shook his head. 'Too steep, rocky and dangerous. Besides, there's the Abbot. I still haven't figured how we're going to get him out.'

Inbar glanced over to where Durral was lying wrapped in velvet. 'I'm the strongest here, leave him to me. We'll carry out your original plan, Martin. When I attack with Grath I'll sling the old mouse in that velvet hanging across my back.'

Clecky began knotting the wall hangings together. 'Righty ho, crew, let's get movin', wot!'

Aboard the *Freebooter*, Viola and Welko had pushed off. Once away from the five burning ships, they dropped anchor in a safe position. Viola made a quick search of the vessel, and emerged from the galley to announce, 'Well, there's plenty of supplies aboard.'

Welko silenced her with a wave of his paw. 'Quiet, miss, lissen, can y'hear anythin'?'

Yelling madly, the searats and corsairs breasted the covetop and came pouring downhill towards the inlet. They stood in the shallows, their cries dying away into silence, faces registering horror in the ruddy glow of the firelight. Ships' timbers crackled and bellied, sails and rigging sent off black ash smuts like dark bats, to flit about on the breeze. Cascades of sparks and burning pitch shot skyward into the night. The entire scene was mirrored like a fiery portrait in the still-dark waters of the cove.

Gancho bellowed like a wounded beast, 'Waaaaaah! They're burnin', our ships're burnin', mates!' Throwing himself down in the shallows, he kicked and beat the water, bawling aloud like a babe in a tantrum.

Buckla stepped out of the firelight as far as he could and peered into the blackness until his eyes became accustomed to it. 'Haharr, mates, see! There's Barranca's ole craft, the Freebooter, sittin' out there as fancy as y'please with not a mark on 'er!' Pulling off his seaboots and tossing aside sword and belt, he plunged deeper into the water, shouting, 'Let's swim out to 'er! Firstbeast to clap a paw aboard o' Freebooter 'as the right to call 'isself cap'n!'

Ridding themselves of all encumbrances, searats and corsairs flung themselves into the water and began striking out for the ship which was riding at anchor on the swell.

Viola looked fearfully at Welko as they both crouched together behind the stern rail.

'What are we going to do now?' she said.

53

Ublaz had armed himself with a long curved sabre. He stood in the palace entrance hall, brandishing it at the forty or so Monitors left from his command. Zurgat came hurrying in from the rear courtyard.

'Mightinezz, Razconza and hiz vermin are gone! The rear wall haz collapzed, but nobeazt iz out there!'

Ublaz breathed a silent sigh of relief, then began berating the Monitors who kept trying to edge away from the stairs. 'You see, the wavescum probably perished in the flames trying to scale the rear wall. When we have cleared out those intruders from my throne room, the palace will once again be mine. Zurgat, you will head the charge upstairs – leave none alive. Now go!'

Zurgat saluted with her long spear and, bulling through the ranks of her subordinates, she mounted the stairs. 'Follow me, we will zlay – '

A red- and a green-flighted arrow struck her simultaneously.

'Ruddariiiiing! Holt Lutraaaaaa!'

The otter archers appeared around the stairwell, Grath slightly in front of Inbar, shielding her friend and the burden he carried. Both of them rained shafts of death at the Monitors.

Ublaz was turning to look for a safer place to command from, when he saw Martin and Clecky come thundering through the main doors. There were Monitors blocking his way to the rear door; dodging swiftly to a downward flight of stairs, he sped towards the cellars.

With his scimitar in one paw and a javelin in the other, Clecky pushed Martin towards the cellar stairs. 'You get after him, I'll help out here. I say, you chaps . . . Eulaliaaaaaaaa!'

The perilous hare flung himself at the back ranks of Monitors, flailing his weapons like a windmill in a gale. Attacked at front and rear the lizards fought back savagely. Regardless of wounds, Clecky battled valiantly forward, through spears, teeth and claws, striving to cut a path to his friends on the staircase. A spear tore his ear, and he vanquished its owner with a curving downward stroke of the scimitar.

'Fall back, the foebeast! Cleckstarr Lepus Montisle to the fray! A Montisle am I, 'tis death to stand before me! Particularly in line for dinner, wot! Forward the whites!'

Snatching a lighted walltorch from its bracket, Martin bounded down the cellar stairs. He raced along a short corridor and on to another downward flight of steps. The Warriormouse paused at the bottom and held up his torch. He was in an oblong chamber with a door at its far end. Martin could tell the door was ajar by the shaft of light that streamed out into the chamber. Taking a firm grip on his swordhilt, he moved cautiously up to the door and swung it open slowly. It revealed the eeriest sight he had ever witnessed.

Wearing a crown upon his head, the mad-eyed Emperor was crouching in front of a snake. He was murmuring a singsong chant as both he and the reptile swayed from side to side, their eyes locked in a frenzied stare. The small room shimmered in the golden torchlight. Everything was bathed in a radiance of gold, from the crown and the coils of the reptile, to the walls which swam in weaving patterns, cast by a large stone tank of water at the back of the room. Martin watched in fascination as the snake's eyes filmed over and its head stopped moving, the serpentine body lost its threatening stiffness and it subsided to the floor. Ublaz touched the poisonous reptile's head, stroking it softly as he spoke without turning to look at his pursuer.

'A coral snake is the most deadly killer in the seas. See how my power can render it harmless. Nobeast alive can perform such magic; only I, Ublaz, Emperor of Sampetra, Ruler of all Monitors and wavescum. They call me Mad Eyes, but never to my face. What do they call you?'

Martin stared at Ublaz's back draped in a flowing cloak of gold. 'I am Martin, the Warrior of Redwall Abbey!' he said.

'Ah yes, I should have known. You have come to free your Abbot. Did you bring my six pearls, the Tears of all Oceans?'

The Warriormouse's voice rang hard as the steel he held. 'I brought only my sword!'

The Emperor's voice took on a cajoling tone. 'Swords are dangerous things to bargain with, Martin. Death is the only payment they exact. What if I told you that I am willing to let you and your friends walk free from here?'

'I would say that you are lying and you would try to have us slain before we got to our ship.'

Whilst Martin spoke, Ublaz was slowly drawing the sabre from his waistsash. The movement was hidden by his flowing cloak. He tensed himself to spring as he continued talking. 'I was not always an Emperor. Once I was a corsair, the most feared swordsbeast of the high seas. I ruled with my blade.'

Martin's quick eye caught the shifting of the pine marten's cloak. Silently he stepped sideways and took up the warrior's stance. Ublaz made his move then, roaring as he whirled about and lunged with the sabre, 'Mine is the last name you'll hear. Ublaaaaaaaz!'

Clang! Clash!

Martin parried the thrust and brought his blade into play. Back and forth they dodged and skipped, slashing, riposting and countering, steel singing against steel to provide music for the dance of death. Warrior and Emperor, blade for blade, backing, weaving, their swordpoints seeking and questing, whirling in the flickering gold light. The pine marten rushed his opponent; gripping the sabre with both paws he battered the Warriormouse into a crouch. With a swift sweep of his sword, Martin sliced across his adversary's footpaw, then, bringing the blade up in a flashing arc, he fenced Ublaz into a corner.

The Emperor bulled his way out, inflicting a gash in Martin's side. They locked blades in the centre of the room, pushing sword hilt to sabre guard as each strove wildly to gain the upper paw. Panting and gasping, eye to eye, the combatants swayed, grasping for any hold their footpaws could find that might serve as a lever.

Then without warning Ublaz dropped his head to one side and bit savagely into the side of Martin's neck. With a mighty roar of pain the Warrior lashed out; his paw, locked tight around the sword handle, punched Ublaz solidly in the eye.

The pine marten's mouth fell open, coloured lights exploding on his vision as he staggered backward.

And trod upon the sleeping snake!

Faster than any eye could follow, the venomous reptile struck, burying its fangs in the leg of Ublaz.

Martin stood watching, his chest heaving as he sucked in air hungrily, a paw clamped to his wounded neck. Ublaz's sabre clattered to the floor. He was swaying, his head drooping to one side, squinting as his vision blurred. He stared dazedly at the coral snake, as it slithered across the room in a golden fluid movement;

back into its tank it slipped with hardly a ripple. The Emperor took a few unsteady backward paces until he reached the wall, then leaning against it he slid down into a sitting position.

Stretching forth his sword, Martin picked the crown from Ublaz's head with his bladetip. The thick, garnet-studded circlet slid down the hilt; Martin looked down at Ublaz, who was staring back at him in disbelief, his lips moving.

'Nobeast was mightier than me . . . Emperor . . . I was . . . Emp . . .'

Martin looped the crown onto his belt and squatted facing the dying pine marten. 'So, yours wasn't the last name I heard, but here's the last name you'll ever hear. I say it for a friend whose kin you had murdered for a half-dozen pearls.'

Martin brought his face closer to Ublaz and roared aloud, 'Holt Lutraaaaaaa!'

54

Clecky had succeeded in fighting his way through the ranks of Monitors to the stairway. He passed Grath his javelin and gave Inbar the short axe he had thrust into his sash. The two otters shouldered their bows, and Clecky and Grath placed themselves either side of Inbar, who still had the Abbot bundled upon his back.

Battling madly, they were halfway to the main entrance when Martin came charging from the cellar stairs to join them, shouting, 'Mad Eyes is dead! I have slain Ublaz!'

There was an immediate lull in the fighting as the Monitors lowered their spears and stared dully at one another.

Martin got behind Inbar to protect the Abbot. 'Come on, back to the ship, quick!' he yelled.

Plogg peered through the darkness at the huddle of creatures clattering along the jetty towards him. He drew his rapier, calling, 'Who goes there?'

Clecky could not resist. 'Just a one-eared hare, a wounded warrior, a sleepin' Abbot and a couple o' plank-tailed waterdogs. Yowch! I say, watch it!'

Grath smiled as she waggled the javelin tip. 'Sorry, mate, I slipped.'

Plogg helped haul the Abbot aboard. He was still sleeping, wrapped snugly in the velvet wall hanging. The shrew glanced up towards the palace, saying, 'There's about a score o' lizards millin' round up there, looks as if they're wonderin' what t'do.'

Martin pulled Clecky over the stern rail then severed the ropelines holding *Waveworm* to the jetty. 'We're not waiting to find out what they're going t'do. Make sail and let's get away from this place!'

Viola and Welko dashed back and forth on the deck of *Freebooter*. With a pair of oars they had found the two of them were smacking every head or paw that showed over the rails. There was a moment's respite. Quivering with fear and exhaustion the volemaid leaned wearily against the rail.

'Oh dear! Oh goodness me! We can't keep this up much longer. Good job they've given up for awhile. Yeeeek!'

Welko ran at her, swinging his oar. He brought it down, whooshing within a hairsbreadth of Viola, to crash upon the head of an evil-looking ferret gripping a cutlass between his gapped teeth.

'Don't turn yer back on the rail, miss, that'n near 'ad you,' he said. He stared out into the flamelit darkness. The burning ships were beginning to hiss and sizzle as they sank lower into the shallows. Welko shook his head in despair at what he saw.

'They've put some o' that burnin' timber out an' they're lashin' t'gether a couple o' rafts. We're in real trouble if Martin an' the others don't show up soon!'

On the shoreline, Buckla touched the top of his head tenderly. 'I'll keel'aul that perishin' volemaid for beltin' me with that oar. Make those lashin's tight, mates. Haharr, let's see 'em try ter stop us this time. Gancho, are the rafts ready?'

Gancho locked off a vine rope with two half-turns and a double hitch. 'Ready as they'll ever be, bucko. Come on, we kin paddle with our paws, 'tis no more'n ten shiplengths out to *Freebooter.*'

Corsairs and searats piled aboard the two rafts until they were low in the water. Baltur licked the edge of his cutlass meaningfully. 'Yaharr, keep the shrew alive, I wanna liddle fun with 'im afore the fishes get wot's left!'

The vermin on the rafts' edges began paddling with anything available: paws, spear blades and scraps of drift-wood. Both rafts were making fair progress until about halfway. Suddenly the nightdarkened waters exploded beneath them.

'Nuggoramaaa harrawoooom gurroochorrr! Harm not our friends. Go from here.'

The great bull seal Hawm and a pack of adult male and female seals had smashed the rafts to matchwood in seconds. Huge wet tails and strong flippers made loud thwacking noises as they rendered each vermin senseless with a single smack. Searats and corsairs flew out of the water and through the air to hit the sand, as the powerful mammals flung them ashore with mighty flicks of their sleek heads. Welko and Viola leaned over the rail of *Freebooter* laughing gleefully at the sight.

'Ooh! King Hawm gave that searat such a crack, did you see him?'

'Aye, lookit that ferret, 'e did a somersault in the air afore 'e landed onshore. Go on, mates, give it to 'em!'

'Oh yes, please, belt that slimy stoat good an' hard for me!'

King Hawm swam up to the side of the ship, then, clapping a flipper against his broad chest, he smiled and bowed.

Welko and Viola clapped their paws together joyfully, calling aloud, 'Haaaaaawm! Haaaaaaaawm!'

The king pointed his flipper at *Waveworm* rounding the cove. 'Ma'tan! Ma'tan!'

Dawn found a happy party taking breakfast on the

foredeck of *Freebooter*. Grath patted the rail, saying, 'Y'did well t'save this 'un, mate, she's a beauty. Martin, wot about ole *Waveworm* there?'

Wordlessly Martin thrust a torch into the breakfast fire. He leapt the gap between both ships, landed neatly on *Waveworm*'s deck and drew his sword. The searat Gowja screamed in terror as the blade whizzed past his head, severing the chain that tethered him to the mainmast. Martin hauled him to the side and booted him overboard.

'I give you your life,' he said. 'Swim for the shore, rat!'

The Warriormouse set fire to the sails before pitching the torch into the hold. Leaping back aboard *Freebooter*, he severed the ropes holding *Waveworm* to its side. A loud wail of despair arose from the vermin nursing their injuries on the beach. Grath reached for her bow, but Martin stopped her.

'Let them be, friend. They are marooned here for life, with no ships, no wood or trees growing. They could not even build a toy boat.'

Viola was sitting next to the Abbot. He was awake now, sipping hot soup, still wrapped in the velvet wall hanging. The volemaid wiped Durral's chin with the tattered hem of her apron.

'They've got better than they deserve,' she said. 'Fruit, fish and running water. Let them learn to farm the earth, like we do at Redwall. I'd say they were lucky to be alive, wouldn't you, Father?'

Durral sat up straight and smiled at Viola. 'I'd say *we* were lucky to be alive, young 'un!'

Clecky sniffed, helping himself to a fourth bowl of soup. 'Indeed? Well, I'd say it's jolly lucky for all here present with two ears! I lost one doin' battle with the lizard thingees. I say, d'you suppose a chap's ear'd grow again if he ate enough, wot?'

Viola checked the hare's ear stump, shaking her head.

'No, but if you like I could make you quite a nice ear with some of this red velvet backed with canvas. You've got enough ear left for it to fit over.'

Clecky snatched a chunk of shrewbread from under Plogg's nose. 'I say, what a spiffin' wheeze, but that red velvet, it'd look a bit odd on parade, a chap with a red velvet ear, wot?'

Martin stifled a smile. 'It's not like you to be so picky, friend. How about if Viola makes it like a decoration, a sort of bravery badge?'

Clecky's single ear stood straight up next to the wad of bandage wound round his stump.

'Top hole! I could dine out on somethin' like that for seasons t'come, wot!' He imitated a female hare's voice. 'Oh, mister Montisle, I do like your ear, so picturesque! . . . Ahem, thank ye, marm, 'tis an old war wound. Pass me the salad and I'll tell you how I jolly well came about it. There was I, surrounded by five hundred monstrous reptiles, armed only with a good breakfast under me belt . . .'

The crew of *Freebooter* dissolved into laughter.

'Haaaaaawm Ma'tan, feryooday!'

They looked up to see the seal king waddle aboard. He turned to Inbar and held a lengthy conversation, then stood by, head held high and both eyes closed, nobly, as befits a real seal king.

Inbar explained what he had said. 'The king said it is not the way of friends to desert each other, so he decided to return and help out. He is pleased your Abbot is safe and well, and he and his sealfolk would be honoured to tow your ship to Ruddaring.'

Martin shrugged, slightly puzzled. 'But we are going to Redwall.'

Grath twanged her bowstring and shuffled her tail awkwardly. 'Er, Inbar's only told the king so far, but, er, y'see, me'n'Inbar, we're goin' back to Ruddaring t'live there. Sorry fer not lettin' y'know sooner, Martin.'

The Warriormouse seized both otters' paws in delight. 'This is the most excellent news! May your seasons be long together with all the happiness that fortune sends you both!'

Congratulations were given all round to Grath and Inbar. In his strange seal language, the Hawm barked out the good news to his sealfolk, who somersaulted in the water, flapping and clapping their flippers in celebration.

Then Martin asked Inbar to translate a message to the Hawm. 'Tell his majesty we will be pleased for him and his seals to accompany our ship to Ruddaring straight away!'

Inbar passed on Martin's information, conversing awhile with the Hawm before turning back to the Warriormouse, who was holding a short conference with the Abbot.

'Martin,' Inbar said, 'our friend the Hawm says that he will be honoured to conduct your ship to within sight of Mossflower country when you leave Ruddaring. He knows secret routes and fast currents that can have you back home in half the time it would take any landbeast to navigate that distance.'

Hawm bowed regally, slapping the deck hard with an enormous flipper and gesturing at the seas in a wide arc, to confirm the truth of Inbar's words. Martin and the Abbot approached him, Inbar translating Martin's words as he proclaimed: 'Haaaaawm! Truly you are king of all sealfolk! Please accept this gift from the Father Abbot of Redwall Abbey.'

Unlooping the crown of Ublaz from his belt, Martin passed it to Durral, who with quiet dignity placed it upon the Hawm's head. The king clambered up onto the forepeak wearing the heavy gold ring that had once graced the head of the tyrannical Ublaz. There was a moment's silence, then the crew joined voices with the sealfolk massed about the ship.

'Haaaaaaawm! Manyahooday, Haaaaaaaaaawm!'

Wearing his new crown like a true king, Hawm did a sleek dive from forepeak to sea. He vanished beneath the waves, to emerge in a rush of water balancing the crown upon his nose, much to the amusement of everybeast present.

Lines were thrown out amidships and for'ard. Then, with a single slash of his sword, Martin severed the anchor cable as Clecky stood by shouting, 'I rename this vessel *Seaking*, may her cookin' fires be always lit an' the whole jolly crew well fed! Set a course for Ruddaring an' then head down for home, me beauties!'

Plogg and Welko had found an old attack drum in the hold. They beat on it with ladles and broke out into a Guosim voyaging song.

'Let the birds fly high before us,
An' our wake trail straight behind,
When yore heart is yearnin' for it,
Home is not too hard to find.
May our way be bright an' sunny,
Back to where the campfires burn,
There our friends an' families waitin',
For the warriors to return.
Are the old ones happily livin',
An' the young ones tall an' grown?
We will soon see smilin' faces,
Of all those we've always known.
Far we've travelled, long we've wandered,
Morn till night an' dusk to dawn,
But there's no place we'll rest easy,
Save the land where we were born.'

Martin leaned over the stern rail with Viola and the Abbot, watching the tropical island of Sampetra fade into the distance. Its inhabitants – the strange lizards, searats and corsairs – were marooned, left to fight and scheme among themselves, whilst their dead Emperor,

Ublaz Mad Eyes, lay stripped of his crown in a dark cellar with a poisonous snake to guard his eternal sleep. Plumes of black smoke still smudged the azure blue sky from behind the palace and from the north cove.

Tears flowed openly down Viola's face as she listened to the shrews' song. Abbot Durral gave her his wide sleeve to dry her eyes.

'Hush, little maid, think of the autumn harvest in Redwall Abbey. You'll be there with your friends to help gather it.'

The volemaid wiped her face and smiled. 'I'll never leave there again as long as I live, Father!'

55

Summer trailed off in glory as the season turned to
autumn. Misted mornings gave way to mild days, short-
ened by scarlet sunsets and nights lit by harvest moons.
Trees wore brown-gold leafy finery, promising the earth
a fine crisp carpet of russet, which would whisper wistful
messages as it shifted on the gentle breeze. It was the
time when Tansy was visited in her dreams by Martin
the Warrior of old. Dawn light filtered softly across
the dormitory as she awoke with his message clear in
her mind.

'Haste to the shore, look to the main,
Be not beset by fears,
Wait faithfully for a Sea King there,
And take with you six tears.'

No creature within the Abbey walls was more eager
or determined to carry out the Warrior's bidding than
Tansy. In the space of three days she had organized
everything and made the journey.

Auma had given Tansy permission to take a small
party with her and erect a marquee on the beach. However, the badger Mother had insisted that Skipper and
his otter crew, including Rangapaw and her searchers,

392

in company with Log a Log and the Guosim shrews, accompany the little expedition as bodyguards. Log a Log led them to the place where *Waveworm* had left Mossflower's shore, and a camp was set up. Tansy took with her Craklyn, Rollo, Gerul and Friar Higgle, and much against the badger Mother's better judgement, but after great persuasion by the hedgehog maid, Arven, Diggum and Gurrbowl. The Dibbuns were thrilled by their first visit to the seaside and promptly got into all kinds of mischief.

Rollo sat atop a rocky outcrop close to the tent, with Tansy and Craklyn at his side. Their eyes ached with two days of staring out to sea. The old Recorder polished his spectacles, drowsy in the noontide warmth.

'Are you sure that's what Martin said in your dream, miss, wait faithfully for a Sea King there?' he asked. 'What's a Sea King?'

Tansy held the six pearls in their scallop shell case on her lap. 'I haven't a clue. Sounds pretty fearsome, though, doesn't it? What d'you think this Sea King'll look like, Craklyn?'

'Well, my guess is that it's some kind of fearsome monster, just like those lizards who came with the searats. The Sea King probably has Abbot Durral and Viola with him, that's why Martin told you to take the pearls along, to ransom them both back from the Sea King.'

Tansy's eyes strayed to a rockpool where the Dibbuns were playing. 'Hmm, that makes sense, I never thought of it like that. Arven! Come here, you little maggot, and show me what you've got there!'

The little squirrel and the two molebabes carried a wooden shrew soup bowl carefully, water slopping over its edges. Approaching the rock where the friends were seated, Arven peered villainously up at them, holding the bowl up.

'Whooo, Tansy pansy, we gorra likkle spider wot

swims inna water, an' he gonna jump up an' bite you noses off!'

Rollo peered down at the tiniest crab he had ever seen, no bigger than a little apple pip. It scrambled sideways underwater, holding up two claws that were almost invisible to the naked eye.

The Recorder looked severely over his glasses at the giggling trio. 'That's no spider, it's a baby crab, and somewhere in that pool it has a mother and father as big as I am – no, bigger! If you don't put their baby straight back into the pool they'll be out here in a moment and have you three for dinner!'

'Gurr, ee do say, zurr? Purrum back ee likkle crabspoider, h'Arven, quick loik, oi bain't gettin h'etted up by that'n's mum'n'daddy!' They fled squealing to empty the bowl back into the pool.

Tansy returned her gaze to the horizon of endlessly shifting sea. She stared westward, and pondered, 'I wonder what happened to Martin and the others? I hope the Sea King hasn't harmed them. Maybe we'll be able to use the pearls and strike a bargain that'll get them all returned to us.'

Gerul wandered over, munching on a hot shrewcake. 'Sure an' I know how t'get me ould mate Clecky back here, just keep good vittles cookin'! That great gut-tub'd smell 'em from a hundred leagues off, so he would!'

'Aye, an' those two sons o' mine,' Log a Log called over from the cooking fire, 'they'd foller their noses down t'the gates o' Dark Forest if'n they thought they'd find a free feed there!'

Skipper looked up from some hotroot soup he was stirring. 'Let's 'ope none of our friends 'as found their way to Dark Forest gates,' he said.

A respectful silence fell over allbeasts who had heard the otter Chieftain's words.

Night fell over the encampment. Skipper gathered the snoring Dibbuns up from the remnants of supper and their broken sandcastles, carried them into the marquee and deposited them gently on a heap of dry rushes. Smiling fondly, he watched the Abbeybabes snuggle down, still asleep, but giggling and snuffling as they settled. Rollo was deep in slumber and Craklyn was sitting with the shrew and otter crews, singing ballads and ditties. Skipper hauled himself up onto the rock, where Tansy was still seated, watching westward over the night-time seas.

'Ahoy, miss, ruinin' yer eyesight ain't goin' t'get no Sea King 'ere a moment sooner than he's due to arrive, believe me.'

Tansy rubbed the back of the scallop shell case with her paw. 'I know, Skip, but I feel as if it's my responsibility, somehow. I'd hate to think of the Abbot and Viola arriving here by night, in the clutches of a foebeast, with not a friendly face to greet them. It wouldn't be right, would it?'

The otter Chieftain nodded. 'I know wot y'mean, young 'un, but you go off'n get yore rest now. I'll watch awhile then post some others later. If anythin' gets sighted I'll wake yer meself.'

Thanking the kindly otter, Tansy went into the marquee and lay down alongside the three Dibbuns. Outside she could hear the restless waves breaking on the shore. Flickering firelight shadows against the tent wall reflected the creatures sitting around the fire outside. She fell asleep to the sound of Craklyn joining the shrews and otters in an old woodland ballad.

'Shrum, shrum, double die dum,
Rivers may flow but the streams they do run,
Kissing the willows that droop sad and low,
Through sunlight and shadow as onward they go.
Shrum, shrum, fie upon thee,
Ye rivers an' streams that flow down to the sea,
I sit by your banks through the long weary day,

To mourn for my true love who you bore away.
Shrum, shrum, cruel is fate,
How long must I linger by water and wait,
You babble round rock and you swirl around stone,
And share your dark secrets with none but
    your own.
Shrum, shrum, tears may fall,
I'm bound for the place where the lone seabirds call,
I'll build me a boat and sail down to the sea,
There I'll search for the heart that is dearest to me.
Shrum, shrum, shrummmmmmmmmm!'

In her dreams Tansy was again visited by the ancient
spirit of Martin. This time he had only one thing to say.
'The Abbess will know what to do with the pearls!'

Morning light found a breezeless day, with heavy mist
wreathing the shoreline. Everybeast was up bright and
early to help with the day's chores. Tansy and Craklyn
took the Dibbuns along the tideline, gathering driftwood
for the fire.

It was a strange, subdued sort of day, even the
Abbeybabes seemed quieter than usual. Tansy and
Craklyn kept an eye on the little ones as they looped
a rope around the bundle they had gathered. Only the
gentle lap of waves against the sand broke the silence
where they stood, hemmed in by mist shrouds.

Suddenly Tansy felt an odd compulsion stir within her.
She turned to face seaward, staring into the mist. Craklyn
and the Dibbuns turned with her. Arven sounded rather
fearful as he tugged her tunic hem.

'Tansy, worra matter, sumfink out there . . .'

A great shining dark monster, dripping water and
wearing a gold crown upon its head, came shuffling
out of the sea, dragging in its jaws a thick rope. Casting
aside the rope the beast threw back its massively sleek
head and roared.

'Haaaaaaaawm!'

As Craklyn and the three Dibbuns clung to her, Tansy could hear herself shouting aloud, 'Help! The Sea King! Help! Help!'

Then the beach was alive with dark shining creatures of all sizes, from fully grown to little ones, all roaring as they flung ropes in the air.

'Haaaaaaaaaawm! Haaaaaaaaaaawm!'

Armed with javelin and rapier, Skipper and Log a Log came bounding through the mist. However, they skidded to a stunned halt when a dark mountainous object rode through the fog on a wave and ground to a halt, ploughed deep into the tideline sands.

Two figures slid expertly down ropes onto the beach.

'Sorry we couldn't find no walkin' sticks for ye, old feller!'

Throwing his paws around his two sons, Log a Log swept them clear of the ground, hugging them fiercely. 'Haharrharr! You scraggy-'eaded rips, sneak up on yore ole daddy like that, would ye? Yer barnacle-whiskered pups, welcome back! You musta smelled breakfast a cookin'!'

The *Seaking* had come home to Mossflower country!

56

An hour later bright rising sun had burned off the dawn mists and everybeast was aboard the big ship as it bobbed on the incoming tide. Martin, Viola and Abbot Durral held on to the paws of Tansy, Rollo, Craklyn and Higgle as if they would never let go again.

'Rollo, old friend, how good to see your face!'

'Father Abbot, you're really back! And Viola too; we thought you were lost in the woods!'

'Friar Higgle, I'll wager you missed me in the kitchens?'

'Missed you? Good job Teasel ain't here, or she'd be throwin' her apron o'er her face an' cryin' buckets. Oh, Durral, my friend, sometimes I doubted I'd ever see ye again!'

'Tansy, Craklyn, is it really you? Give me a kiss, friends!'

'Friends, that's what we are, Viola, for ever friends!'

'Martin, it does my old heart good to see our Redwall Warrior returned safe and well! How are you, friend?'

'All the better for having the honour to shake the paw of a great and wise Recorder, Rollo. You've grown younger in my absence.'

'Martin, Martin, all seagulls gone'd inna water, swimmed away?'

The Warriormouse untangled Arven from his footpaws and lifted him onto his shoulder. 'They're not seagulls, they're called seals. Gone, you say?'

Clecky and Gerul looked over the ship's side. Arven had spoken truly, there was not a sign of sealfolk or their Hawm anywhere.

The hare munched a chunk of warm shrewbread reflectively, and said, 'Without so much as a farewell or a toodle-oo! Still, I s'pose there's only me would've understood them, seein' as I'm the only one jolly well up on their lingo, wot. Very odd, though, very odd indeed!'

Gerul attempted to disguise snorted laughter as a cough. 'I'm thinkin' 'tis no odder than yoreself with a red velvet ear, me ould mate. I don't know wot me ould mother'd've said if'n she'd seen a lug like that!'

The hare straightened his red velvet ear and posed heroically. 'Rather good, doncha think, wot! Distinctive, stylish, yet with that touch of roguish dash about it. Wish I had two, really!'

Martin turned to stare seaward, shaking his head sadly. 'I wish the Hawm and his sealfolk had stayed longer. They were proper friends, good and true. Still, I suppose they had their reasons for leaving as they did. What are you staring at, Skip?'

'Yer neck, matey, that's a rare ole scar you've got there!'

The Warriormouse ran his paw across the wound. 'Aye, but you should see the other feller. I'll tell you all about it when we get back to Redwall.'

Plogg and Welko told their father about Grath, how she had found Inbar and gone to live at Ruddaring with him. Welko clapped his father's back and said, 'But Grath said that she'd never ferget 'er friend the Guosim Chieftain Log a Log. Ahoy there, are you cryin', dad?'

Log a Log did not attempt to wipe away the tears which rolled down his face. 'Of course I am, ye great buffer, that otter was like a daughter t'me, the one I never 'ad. I'm glad she's 'appy, though I'll miss 'er.'

Plogg pulled an object from his belt and placed it in Log a Log's paws. 'Grath said t'give you this to remember 'er by.'

It was a green-feathered arrow.

The Abbot stood on the forepeak with Tansy, Rollo and Craklyn.

'Did you solve your riddle?' he asked.

Rollo nodded. 'Indeed we did, all six of them. Six riddles to lead us to six perfect pearls. They were to be your ransom.'

'Ah,' cried the Abbot, 'now all is clear.' He folded his paws into his habit sleeves. 'Good! Who holds them at this moment?'

Tansy produced the scallop shell case and opened it to reveal the six rose-coloured pearls, each one lying in its niche. 'Here they are, Father. Martin tells me that they belonged to the family of Grath Longfletch. How can I return them?'

Abbot Durral stared at Tansy a long time, then he said, 'I have been told the pearls now belong to you!'

Tansy looked at the rose-coloured orbs. 'But what about Rollo and Craklyn? They helped me to find them.'

The Abbot of Redwall's voice was clear and firm. 'Yet still they belong to you, who found the remains of that corsair which led to the first clue. The Warrior of our dreams told me they were yours. Now think carefully, young one, what are you going to do with them?'

A silence fell over the whole ship, and every eye turned upon Tansy holding the pearls. She stared at them, her mind racing back to that first day in the woods and the corsair's skeleton, over the many hours spent searching painstakingly to gain each one, the puzzles, riddles, joys, frustrations and sorrows of the entire quest. Now it had all come down to this, a half-dozen round objects encased in a scallop shell. Her voice rang out, clear and certain.

'These pearls are said to be rare, precious and beautiful, yet when I look at them now I see only bloodshed, greed and death. There are many creatures lying dead because of them, from the family of Grath down to countless searats and corsairs. But one touched our own lives deeply, a young Abbeymaid who was friend to us all. Piknim was slain because of these six pearls. Truly they are called the Tears of all Oceans. We have no need for things such as these at Redwall Abbey, life is a far more precious and beautiful thing. I give back to the oceans these six tears, so that they will never cause grief or sorrow to any living creature!'

Tansy climbed to the bowsprit of *Seaking*, which had turned on the tide and now was moored to the shore, facing the open seas. Scooping the pearls from their case she flung them high and wide. Like six rose-tinted raindrops they flashed briefly in the sunlight, then they hit the waves and were lost to sight for ever. Tansy let the scallop shell drop from her paws. It fell with a gentle splash and sank under the keel. Slowly the hedgehog maid descended to the deck, where she apologized to Rollo and Craklyn.

'After all the days and nights we spent searching together, see what I've done! I am sorry, my friends.'

Craklyn grinned ruefully. 'Fermald the Ancient would be furious if she were here now. Just think, with one sweep of your paw you hid the pearls far better than she did with all her clues and scheming!'

Rollo nodded his head admiringly. 'Indeed, you certainly don't mess about when you've made up your mind to do something, miss. What do you say, Father Abbot?'

The good Father Abbot had quite a bit to say.

'From the time our ship left Sampetra to sail back here,

I have had the same dream over and over. Martin our Abbey spirit kept on telling me this message.

'"She who holds the pearls, the Abbess of Redwall will be,
She who holds on to the pearls, cannot rule in place of thee,
Only an Abbess whose heart sees truth, may give pearls unto the sea."'

Abbot Durral took Tansy's paw. 'Many times Martin repeated those words to me in my dreams. I was puzzled as to their meaning until today. Abbess Tansy!'

The enormity of what Durral had said caused Tansy to move away from the Abbot in bewilderment. She stood alone on the forepeak, scarcely noticing the sea, sparkling as wavelets caught mid-morning sunlight. Total silence reigned aboard the vessel.

Martin stole silently up alongside her. Drawing the great sword of Redwall, he laid it on the rail in front of her, and said, 'I am yours to command, Mother Abbess. What is your wish?'

Tansy picked up the sword. She had not realized it was so heavy. She presented it back to Martin, then, a smile hovering on her face as the depth of the honour conferred upon her sunk in, she turned to face the assembly. Trying hard to keep her paws and voice from trembling, she addressed them all.

'Er, listen, what I'd like to say is, er . . . Oh, let's go home and have a great feast to celebrate our friends' safe return!'

A resounding cheer split the air and everybeast crowded round to congratulate Tansy.

'I say, old thing, you'll make a jolly good Abbess if y'keep chuckin' out orders like that, wot!'

'Ah, 'tis right, an' as me ould mother used t'say, may yer shadow never grow less, an' it won't if y'keep it well fed!'

'Well done, young missie. Oops! I mean Mother Abbess, but when nobeast's listening I'll still call you Tansy and I hope you'll still call me Craklyn, your old pal!'

'Tansy pansy, worra h'Abbess mean? Ole Rollo call you muvver, heehee, you norra muvver, they hooj an' big like m'Auma!'

Wellwishers continued to flock round and shake Tansy's paw. She was very touched by Rollo's simple words.

'If I had been choosing an Abbess, my choice would have been the same as Durral's. This is the best thing to happen to our Abbey in all of my seasons. Rule well, young Mother!'

Epilogue

Extract from the writings of Craklyn, Recorder of Redwall Abbey.

The harvest is in, let winter come, we are safe, happy and well supplied within these great walls. Our Mother Abbess wisely delayed homecoming celebrations until the fruits of autumn were safely stowed in our cellars and larders. Then we had a feast which lasted seven days and nights!

Redwall fare excelled itself; even the young ones will talk about that feast when they are old and grizzled. How could we go wrong with goodwife Teasel and two Friars to run the kitchens, Friar Higgle and old Friar Durral, happy to be doing what he always wished to do, cook! Such an array of pies, cakes, pastries, puddings and trifles you never did see. There were cheeses, breads, salads, turnovers, soups, stews and pasties, enough to feed a regiment.

Furlo Stump and Foremole said they served enough drinks to float a ship, and I believe them. They had every possible ale, cordial, tea, fruitcup and fizz the cellars could produce – even one which I helped them make specially for the occasion, a mixture of rosehip, honey and strawberry that we called Tansywine.

The festivities shifted each evening from Great Hall to Cavern Hole, where the singing, dancing, reciting and music proved a delight to the eyes and ears of all. Mind you, some complained about Clecky's ballad. It was forty-seven verses long and dealt with his heroic adventures rescuing old Abbot Durral.

I am still learning the job of Recorder. My good friend Rollo is constantly guiding me, though now he spends a lot of his time with Brother Dormal. He likes to be in the orchard, gaining knowledge of fruit, plants and bees, and also he can nap whenever he pleases! Mother Abbess Tansy is like myself, still learning; she has Auma, Durral, Wullger and the elders of Redwall to help whenever she has need of them.

Oh, did I tell you? Viola bankvole has taken over from Sister Cicely in the sick bay. All of us were delighted when warm nettle broth was banished for ever, but our joy was shortlived. Viola is sometimes a bit inventive with her seagoing experiences, so now we have to suffer seaweed and cockleshell potion. Both Viola and Cicely swear by it as a cure-all.

Log a Log and his shrews and Skipper with his crew are going to stay the winter at Redwall. For the spring they have planned a Guosim otter cruise aboard the ship *Seaking*, but they will have to endure Clecky's company. He has appointed himself Redwall Hare in charge of Nautical Activities and insists on being addressed as Captain Clecky. Outrageous as ever, it is his plan to cruise in search of seals, so that he can have long conversations with them. Gerul is sailing, too, as cookowl.

Foremole and Furlo Stump have recruited Arven, Diggum and Gurrbowl as trainee cellar-keepers. Abbess Tansy remarked to me only this morning that she did not envy them their task, training those three. Auma our great badger Mother seems to grow no older; she is planning on clearing out Fermald's attic and converting it into a den where the Abbey elders can rest and relax in comfort. What a pillar of strength and security she is to us all!

Corsairs and searats have not been seen around Mossflower coast in a while now, according to Plogg, Welko and Rangapaw. Durral told me that a female corsair ferret named Romsca befriended him and saved his life when he was captured by the big lizards. Sometimes he says that he dreams of her, and the strange island beyond which the sun sets, a place of constant heat, never visited by winter. I wanted to hear more of the pine marten who ruled there, Emperor Ublaz of the Mad Eyes, but Durral says he is best forgotten. Leave it all to the long ago and far away, he says.

I am not used to writing with a quill pen, my paws get inkstained, so I am finishing writing for today. I must attend a meeting to plan the midwinter feast. Have you ever attended one? It takes place on Midwinter Eve, oh yes, midwinter has an eve just like midsummer. Any self-respecting Redwaller could tell you when it is. Here is the notice I will pin on our gate at the pathside.

'All who come in peace and friendship, stay,
On this the eve of cold midwinter's day.
Good food and drink and, best, good company,
Come share our hospitality for free.
Beneath the lanterns, sit and take your fill,
Sing and dance you may, with right goodwill,
With one condition, as Redwallers say,
If you enjoyed it, call another day,
Summer, spring, 'most any time at all,
And find a welcome waiting at Redwall!'

Craklyn squirrel, Recorder of Redwall Abbey in Mossflower country.